These Lies
That Live
Between Us

These Lies That Live Between Us

What Words Have Torn Apart:
Book One

KAI RAINE

Columbus, Ohio

This book is a work of fiction. The names, characters and events in this book are the products of the author's imagination or are used fictitiously. Any similarity to real persons living or dead is coincidental and not intended by the author.

These Lies That Live Between Us

Published by Gatekeeper Press
2167 Stringtown Rd, Suite 109
Columbus, OH 43123
www.GatekeeperPress.com

ISBN: 9781619848894
eISBN: 9781619848900

Printed in the United States of America

In memory of my mother, Beryl Nelson.
I wish you could have read this, too.

Contents

1. The Princess 1
    Ninth day of spring, 450 A.D. – Castle Dio, Ceryll

2. The Runaway 9
    Ninth day of spring, 450 A.D. — Castle Dio, Ceryll

3. The Princess 11
    End of winter, 451 A.D. – Wirrn, Ceryll

4. The Runaway 25
    Third day of spring, 451 A.D. – Peasant's Pass, the Tor

5. The Librarian's Apprentice 39
    Thirty-third day of spring, 451 A.D. – Castle Dio, Ceryll

6. The Amberrian Guard 47
    Fifth day of winter, 451 A.D. – Castle Dio, Ceryll

7. The Princess 57
    Ninth day of spring, 452 A.D. – Castle Dio, Ceryll

8. The Princess 65
    Tenth day of spring, 452 A.D. – Nirra, Ceryll

9. The Spy 79
    Fifty-first day of summer, 452 A.D. – A town on no map, Ynga

10. The Wizard.. 93
Before dawn, eleventh day of spring, 452 A.D. – Castle Dio, Ceryll

11. The Scribe.. 99
Twelfth day of spring, 452 A.D. – Nirra, Ceryll

12. The King... 115
After dawn, eleventh day of spring, 452 A.D. – Castle Dio, Ceryll

13. The Spy.. 119
Fifty-second day of summer, 452 A.D. – Unyca, Ynga

14. The Scribe.. 133
Twenty-third day of spring, 452 A.D. – Tevaë Falls, Ceryll

15. The Heir's Maid... 145
Mid-morning, eleventh day of spring, 452 A.D. – Castle Dio, Ceryll

16. The Spy.. 151
Fifty-third day of summer, 452 A.D. – Unyca, Ynga

17. The Scribe.. 161
Thirty-first day of spring, 452 A.D. – Kingsway near Farthe, Ceryll

18. The Minister's Son 173
Mid-morning, eleventh day of spring, 452 A.D. – Castle Dio, Ceryll

19. The Spy.. 179
Mid-summer, 452 A.D. – Unyca, Ynga

20. The Scribe.. 191
Thirty-third day of Spring, 452 A.D. – Farthe, Ceryll

21. The Lieutenant Ambassador 201
Mid-morning, eleventh day of spring, 452 A.D. – Castle Dio, Ceryll

22. The Spy 207
Eighty-second day of summer, 452 A.D. – Unyca, Ynga

23. The Scribe 219
Thirty-fifth day of spring, 452 A.D. – Farthe, Ceryll

24. The Falcon 231
Mid-morning, eleventh day of spring, 452 A.D. – Castle Dio, Ceryll

25. The Spy 239
End of summer, 452 A.D. – Rainforest near Unyca, Ynga

26. The Beloved 247
Thirty-sixth day of spring, 452 A.D. – Outside Farthe, Ceryll

27. The Chef's Apprentice 257
Late morning, eleventh day of spring 452 A.D. – Castle Dio, Ceryll

28. The Outcast 261
Last day of summer, 452 A.D. – Unyca, Ynga

29. The Spy 267
Last day of summer, 452 A.D. – Unyca, Ynga

30. The Lieutenant Ambassador 273
Late morning, eleventh day of spring, 452 A.D. – Castle Dio, Ceryll

31. The Beloved 279
Fiftieth day of spring, 452 A.D. – Mille, Ceryll

32. The Outcast 289
After the fray up above – Down Below

33. The Minister of the Treasury 299
Late morning, eleventh day of spring 452 A.D. – Castle Dio, Ceryll

34. The Beloved 307
     Third day of summer, 452 A.D. – Falle Harbor, Ceryll

35. The Spy 321
     First day of autumn, 452 A.D. – Rainforest near Unyca, Ynga

36. The Lieutenant's Knife 329
     Afternoon, eleventh day of spring, 452 A.D. – Castle Dio, Ceryll

37. The Beloved 335
     Eighth day of summer, 452 A.D. – Somewhere in the Dantes

38. The Outcast 345
     Twenty-first day of autumn, 452 A.D. – Mirage, Ynga

39. The Spy 369
     Forty-fifth day of autumn, 452 A.D. – Mirage, Ynga

40. The Captain of the King's Guard 371
     Night, eleventh day of spring, 452 A.D. – Castle Dio, Ceryll

Appendix 377

A Note from the Author 383

About the Artist (Cover & Maps) 384

Acknowledgements 385

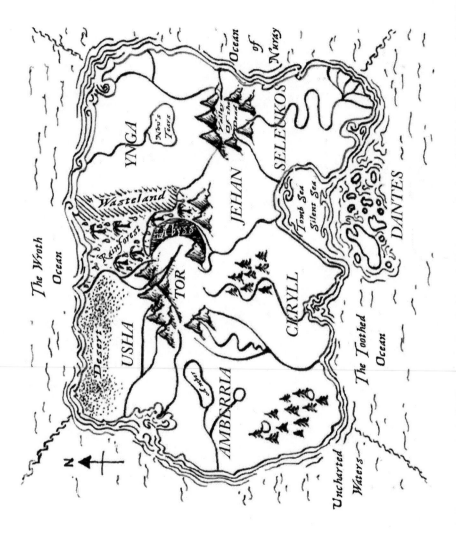

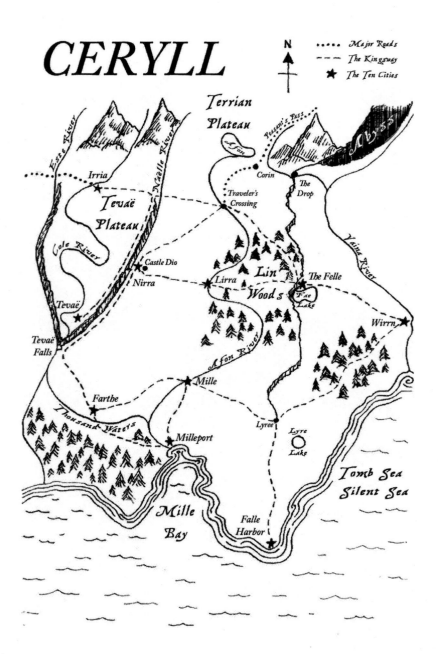

YNGA

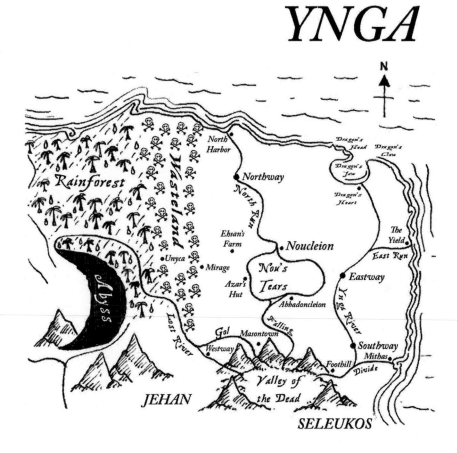

1

The Princess

Ninth day of spring, 450 A.D. – Castle Dio, Ceryll

O N THE LAST day of her childhood, Gwen woke to the sound of the wind rattling the shutters. She was warm and content—except for her feet out in the cold thanks to her twin hogging the covers. She cracked one eye open to the familiar sight of her own long golden hair lying against equally long silver hair. It was the most peaceful sight she knew. Curling closer to the warm body behind her, Gwen pulled her feet in under the blankets and groggily brought them against her companion's bare legs.

Stelle pulled away with a gasp and squawked as her hair pulled out from under Gwen's head. Then came the thud as she fell off the bed.

"*Gwen,*" she grunted.

"You were hogging the covers," Gwen mumbled, taking the opportunity to curl herself fully into the blankets, rolling around and tucking all the edges of the blanket under her body. By the time that Stelle scrambled back into the bed, teeth chattering, the edges were firmly out of reach.

"Gwen, this is my bed."

"And this is my birthday."

"Oh, charming."

"I know I am," Gwen smirked, poking her head out. Stelle yanked the exposed edge of the blanket. Gwen squealed. Trapped in her unraveling blanket cocoon, she rolled until she fell off the bed. Gwen wheezed when she hit the floor. She felt the blanket being pulled away but had no strength to do anything but breathe. The movement stopped.

"Gwen?" Stelle peered into her face. "Are you all right?"

Gwen could breathe again, so she grabbed Stelle's shin and pulled it out from under her. Stelle dropped the blanket, landed backwards on her hands and kicked Gwen in the chest. Gwen gasped more in shock than pain, unused to the tenderness of her newly swelling chest. She was preparing to return a kick to Stelle's ribcage when the door opened and they both froze. Aunt Marilene was not a forgiving woman.

But it was not their governess standing in the doorway. It was their sister.

"I came to wish you a happy birthday," said Nicki sardonically. "Must I rescue you from each other instead? Where are your maids?"

"Today is our birthday," Gwen pouted. "We sent them away."

Nicki sighed and walked across the room to rummage through the closet. She pulled out a blue gown and laid it out on the bed. It would have complemented Stelle's silvery hair beautifully. Except, of course:

"Liles if you were expecting me to wear *that* tie-all," said Stelle.

Nicki turned a frown on her. "Language. Do you have something else in mind?"

"Britches, as usual. I shall spend the day in the barracks."

Nicki's face closed off. "Stelle, I thought Father had—"

"No!" said Stelle. "He may be king, but he already forbade me from everything and everyone else I enjoy. He *cannot* take this away, too."

She pushed Nicki aside to storm to the closet. Watching Stelle's back as she rummaged, Gwen saw her grow frantic. She saw it, and it irritated her. Father had *said* that they were now ladies of court and expected to act the part. Why did Stelle think he would have allowed her to simply ignore him?

"Where are my clothes?" Stelle demanded at last.

"Stelle—" Nicki started but Stelle interrupted.

"Never mind. I know, I . . . ," Stelle swallowed heavily. Nicki placed a hand on her shoulder but Stelle shook it off. She sniffed, held her shoulders back and her head high, and said, "We can dress ourselves. We shall join you at breakfast momentarily."

Nicki nodded and left without a word, though she threw Gwen a sympathetic smile. Gwen took comfort in that sympathy.

The atmosphere did not improve after Nicki left. Stelle responded to Gwen's half-hearted attempts at conversation with monosyllables, so Gwen gave up and they dressed in silence. Breakfast was a similar affair. Only Father dared attempt to engage Stelle despite her sullen mood.

After breakfast, Gwen went as usual to join the other young ladies of court. She only realized that Stelle had followed when Adelaide said, "Is this *Estelle?* I hardly recognized her in a lady's gown."

The girls tittered. Gwen joined in out of habit.

"How ever did you manage to bring her back into civilized society?" Severine added in an exaggerated whisper that did nothing to keep Stelle from hearing. Stelle's face flushed. The ladies laughed. Gwen laughed, too.

"What wit," huffed Stelle, crossing her arms over her chest. "The Seleukoi would be better company than you imbeciles. Do you have horse dung for brains?"

The ladies gasped. Gwen choked down a laugh. But there was no sense in letting Stelle make this harder on herself for the sake of a few moments' satisfaction. Gwen grabbed her twin's arm and pulled Stelle away. She heard the ladies making comments and giggling at their backs.

"You cannot speak to them like that," Gwen hissed when they were away in a hallway. "Do you want to let them ridicule you for years to come?

"*Let them?*" Stelle retorted. "Their insults are *my* fault, now?"

"You must act like someone who understands our positions."

"Positions? As marriageable pawns, you mean? Marvelous. Watch me swoon!"

Stelle lashed out with a leg. Gwen took a step back and raised her arms and a leg in a block, but Stelle was not aiming for her. Two legs of the wooden side table cracked under her kick. The table tilted and crashed to the ground where it lay looking as miserable as Gwen felt.

"I cannot believe you," said Gwen, proud of the evenness of her voice. "Always with the violence. I shall be in the library. Stay away from me."

"And what am I supposed to do in the meantime? Roam the hallways like a ghost?"

"Or try acting *normal* for once!"

Gwen stormed off without letting Stelle get another word in. She did not often win these fights. It felt glorious.

Stelle was sullen and silent for the rest of the day, even at their birthday dinner banquet. At the party after the banquet, Stelle slinked off to sulk in a corner. Gwen at last excused herself from the flock of young noble ladies to join her.

"Finally tired of the superficiality?" Stelle drawled.

"Always," Gwen admitted quietly, though not before glancing around to make sure that no one else would hear. "But the girls are nice enough, if you give them a chance."

Stelle threw her head back. It hit the wall with a painful-sounding thump. She did not wince.

"And what would I get out of it, if they tire even you?" Stelle asked at last.

"I—" Gwen blinked at her. "Life would be more tolerable, if you made them like you."

"For you, perhaps. I prefer ridicule and solitude, myself."

"We could make fun of them," Gwen whispered with a grin. Stelle tried to hide it, but Gwen could already see her answering grin. "We could spend our evenings mocking them and laughing, just being us. You could tell me why all the things they said were nonsensical, and I could tell you what they said behind your back."

Stelle lost her fight with the grin.

"We could learn their secrets and frighten them. They would never know it was us."

"Yes," laughed Gwen. Her enthusiasm made her louder. Again she looked around to be sure that no one was listening. "See? We can make it better than tolerable. It would be fun."

But Stelle's grin was already fading. "You do it. I cannot live a lie just for a few laughs."

"But I *cannot* do it without you," Gwen protested. "If I try on my own, everyone would only be angry. There would be nothing to laugh at."

Stelle smiled softly, then shook her head. Something in her expression made Gwen afraid. "Go back to them, Gwen. I am not the court jester."

A red-hot pain shot through Gwen. "I meant—"

Stelle closed her eyes and shook her head. "Please, go. I need to be alone."

Gwen went.

She slept in her own bed that night. When she woke alone and cold, she padded across the hallway to Stelle's room and cracked open the door.

The bed was untouched. Atop the covers lay Stelle's most carefully guarded journal. It was open. Gwen glanced around the room for any sign of a trap, but there was none. She walked up to the bed and nothing happened. She picked up the journal and braced herself. Still nothing happened. She turned her eyes down and read.

It was angry, it was scathing and it was final.

Gwen ran down the tower's staircase barefooted in her nightdress, through the hallways and past the staring eyes of countless guards and nobles to Nicki's chambers. She showed Nicki the journal and sank to the floor as her sister whipped into action.

It was no use. Stelle was gone. Later, Gwen sat in silence in their father's study as he and Nicki dispatched search parties. They concocted a plan so that her disappearance would not be noticed and she could return to court life when they found her. Gwen hardly heard them. The journal entry echoed through her skull in Stelle's voice, over and over again.

For the first time in all of time and space, Gwen felt alone.

2

The Runaway

Ninth day of spring, 450 A.D. — Castle Dio, Ceryll

This place is worse than a Seleukoi dungeon. I hate waking up every morning. Sleep is the only time when I feel like I can be at peace — when I feel like a person.

I wish I had been born a man. I cannot be a cold, calculating, manipulative politician, or a well-read lady who can tolerate coyness and subtlety. And why should I? My sisters are those things, without having to pretend.

So why can I not be who I am? I say what I think. I have no patience for meandering words and foolishness. I was good at close-range combat, and I loved it. Now that even that has been taken from me, my existence in this court is entirely meaningless.

I could be a lady guard, if they would allow me. But they will not. War is a man's business. So was kingship, until Mother died without any living sons and our gracious heir became the exception. But not me. I am expected to simper and hold my tongue and be auctioned off to the highest bidder.

Is it my fault that I lack the temperament to be the princess I am expected to be? Is it my failure that I cannot live up to sisters who are naturally everything that I am not?

Fourteen years today, and I remain the most useless princess this nation has ever known. Not that I give any lies about the nation, or my usefulness. It is not my fault that the world conspires against me. I am bored. Suffocated. Exhausted.

I will try no more. I am no lady. I belong anywhere but here.

Dear sisters, who I suppose are snooping around and reading this after I am gone, I hate you both. I shall not miss you. Good-bye, and good riddance.

3

The Princess

End of winter, 451 A.D. – Wirrn, Ceryll

L IFE WENT ON around Gwen without Stelle. Barely a season went by after Stelle's disappearance before she was replaced. Oh, no one ever said so aloud. It was true all the same.

Enri had been the fourth son of the Amberrian king when he came to Ceryll to court Nicki. Within a fortnight, an arrangement was reached: Enri would become their foster brother, while Aunt Marilene would go to Amberria and marry the king's second son. It would have been one thing if the intent was for Enri to marry Nicki eventually. But it was a poorly kept secret that Nicki had begun an affair with Alderic: a tall, bastard-born guard in Enri's entourage. Gwen waited for Father to admonish Nicki for her indiscretion, but the admonition never came.

When Alderic was at last mentioned over dinner, it was only for Nicki to ask Father to make him a member of the Ceryllan king's guard. Father agreed immediately.

If Enri was not Nicki's intended, then he was the

spare heir that Stelle was supposed to have been. It both reinforced the longstanding alliance between Ceryll and Amberria and left Gwen available as a marriageable token to secure an alliance without handing her husband the incentive to assassinate Nicki to take her throne.

Gwen wanted to be angry, but she could not find the energy. She told herself that she could cope because Father had become and remained extremely lenient. What she wanted, she got. No doubt he thought that by indulging her, he could assuage his guilt about Stelle. She seized this opportunity to move her chambers, refuse to appear at court day after day, and even to resume her rock climbing lessons with Hervé, the captain of the king's guard. Rock climbing with Hervé had been a daily enjoyment for Gwen and Stelle until they turned twelve and the privilege was taken away. Surely this request, at last, Father would reject. But Father only nodded without meeting Gwen's eyes.

It was a season before it occurred to Gwen to push Father's lenience even further. By then, it was too late. Father was still malleable with sympathy, but Nicki's patience had run out. When Gwen asked to live alone in the royal residence at Milleport for a time, Father sighed and said yes, if that was what she truly wished. It was Nicki who pulled her aside; Nicki who threatened to talk Father into putting an end to the climbing lessons if she did not take back the request.

When Gwen opened her mouth to argue anyway, Nicki shut her down with gruesome details of what assassins did to princesses far from the protection of their families. Gwen's stomach was still rolling when she returned to

Father to tell him that she had changed her mind and would remain in Dio.

Nicki neither attempted to stop Gwen's climbing lessons nor did she force Gwen to attend court. But as the seasons passed, she pushed Gwen to rejoin the world in other ways. Nearly a year had passed when word came that Jehani refugees were swimming across the Vaina in droves to flee the Seleukoi speakers' raids. Nicki informed Gwen that she would be traveling to Wirrn with her, Enri and a handful of ministers and ambassadors. Gwen would have argued—but Nicki mentioned that this would not be a formal procession. Everyone would be expected to ride and pack light.

Gwen agreed to go for the adventure. After a fortnight without her climbing lessons to brighten her days, her life had gone dark again. Hervé was away dealing with a commotion up north in Traveler's Crossing. Gwen was aching for something to do.

They did not ride out through Nirra as they always had when leaving Dio. Instead, they rode out through the seldom-used gate into the fields to the east. The first day was spent riding along the kingsway through farmland until they reached a small settlement that evening. By noon on the second day, there were no houses or fields to be seen, and even the kingsway seemed increasingly overgrown with weeds and grass. That night they camped on the roadside under the stars, and the guards keeping watch did not see a single passing rider.

It was nearly noon on the third day when they began to see signs of human civilization again. They arrived in Lirra when the sun was still high in the sky, but Nicki ordered that they find lodging for the night. As Nicki went about talking to the city guard and the mayor, it occurred to Gwen that she did not have to follow her sister about like a puppy. Lirra was known for the twinkling dust-like lights that rose out of the river Afon, drifted over the city and rose up to the sky, growing brighter by night and dimmer by day. These were sights that she could now see for herself for the first time.

Gwen's attempt to slip away did not go unnoticed. Nicki stopped her at the door.

"Take a guard," she said. "At least one."

Gwen took Alderic to be contrary, but Nicki did not object or even seem affected. As exploring became routine, Gwen asked Alderic to join her each time afterwards because he was better company than any of the other guards. For the first time, she was glad Hervé was away; if he had come along, she would have chosen him to accompany her. Alderic turned out to be good company — more friend than guardian — and rarely objected to places Gwen wanted to explore. With him came Verity, his young goshawk, who took an immediate liking to Gwen.

Every member of the king's guard was given a goshawk chick upon initiation, the offspring of the alpha breeding pair in the king's aviary. Each chick was raised by its guard's own hand, eating and sleeping with him until it reached maturity. Once it was a year or two old, the guard could go out on missions with his goshawk left at Dio. When a message needed to be delivered to a guard whose whereabouts were unknown, his goshawk would be released and if he could be found, it would find him.

At less than a year in the king's guard, Verity went anywhere that Alderic went.

So Gwen explored Lirra with its twinkling lights, another city carved into the side of a cliff known as the Felle, and a handful of small, nameless hamlets in between. When they camped in the wilderness between Lirra and the Felle, she explored the Lin Woods without straying too far from their campsites. Alderic and Verity were always with her, listening to Gwen ramble (she so rarely had the chance to speak carelessly anymore) or accompanying her in shared silence.

Gwen could not understand why Enri had come along. Donatien was with them too, after all, as the Amberrian ambassador. Enri was the slowest and clumsiest rider. On the first day he managed to keep up, but it was clearly a struggle. On the second day and every day since, he and his Amberrian guards had to catch up during midday break and again in the evening. Bringing both of them seemed excessive, which was how Gwen felt about Amberrian representation at the Ceryllan court in general. Why, now that Enri had been adopted, could they not send Donatien home?

Stelle would have asked Father. Without her, Gwen did not dare.

The tone of the trip changed dramatically when they reached Wirrn in early spring.

Gwen knew that there were Seleukoi raids of villages on the Yngan and Jehani borders, and had been for years. There had been terrified Jehani folk escaping into Ceryll for just as long. She had an abstract understanding of what that meant before reaching Wirrn, but reality was nothing like what she had imagined.

In the refugee camp just outside Wirrn, Gwen saw tears, terror and silence. The uninjured Jehani refugees were huddled together, jumping and backing away from threats that Gwen could not see. Many would not go inside, but would not explain why. They only shook their heads and held their hands to their ears.

Mostly there were stories. Not told by the refugees, who refused to speak as though they were all mute. Gwen thought they were, at first. But sometimes they whispered to each other when they thought no one was looking, as if to be caught speaking was shameful. Nurses, herbalists and volunteers talked of the terror in their eyes and some of the worst of their injuries. They speculated about the horrors the refugees had survived. Gwen did not know what to make of any of it. Her uncertainty frightened her, so she said nothing.

Nicki and Enri walked among the refugees accompanied by a handful of guards, handing out blankets and trying to persuade people to accept bowls of stew. The ministers hung back and whispered amongst themselves. The ambassadors milled about, trying to get details from anyone who would speak to them. Carwyn, the Jehani ambassador, was particularly frantic. How far had the army gotten? Was the capital conquered? Baraz, the stoic Yngan ambassador, took him by the arm and led him into the tent of the camp organizers. They did not emerge for a long time, and when they did, both men were ashen. Carwyn at last pulled himself into motion and began attempting to address some of the victims gently. When he got no response, he would offer them his hopes for their recovery and move on to another. Baraz watched this for a time before walking away.

Gwen hung back and watched. The area was crowded enough without her joining the scramble through and around the huddled people. Her mind conjured all sorts of terrors: magicians weaving spells and cackling as people burned in the flames they conjured, some of them digging into the charred human remains with their teeth. Gwen trembled at her own imagination and looked away from the huddled masses.

She felt a hand on her shoulder and looked up, expecting to see Alderic. But it was Lieutenant Dara, the Ushani ambassador.

"Best not to imagine what they've been through. It wouldn't help to know."

Gwen blinked up at the dark-skinned, large-boned warrior. Somehow she looked taller and darker today than ever—or perhaps Gwen had never taken the time to truly look. For the first time, Gwen noticed that there were two long scars running down Dara's neck from behind her ear to into her leather armor.

"Have you seen many battles?" Gwen asked, cringing at the timidity in her own voice.

"Many," grinned Dara.

"But—but when? Where and whom do you fight?"

"You know that we don't pass power down from parent to child like you do here. We are led by the strongest commander. Sometimes, someone thinks he or she is better suited than the current commander, and takes up arms."

"Have you ever fought the commander?"

"When you were still in swaddling clothes, I fought in the war against the last commander. Since our commander came into power, I've led the army against five rebellions, and won again."

"You led the army? Not the commander?"

"He has a country to rule. As long as I did my job right, his work never had to be interrupted to fight the rebels. And I was excellent at my job."

Something about talking to Dara emboldened Gwen. "So then why did the commander send you away to Ceryll?"

The corners of Dara's eyes crinkled in a smile that did not reach her lips. "Because fighting Seleukos is more important now than any rebellion. We need to unite our armies before any of us is conquered."

"It seems to me," Gwen shrugged, "that you have been at court long enough to offer your army to aid us and be accepted."

"I said unite, not offer."

It took a moment for Gwen to catch her meaning. "You want to lead our army? Father might agree to that if pressed, but my sister would talk him out of it. She is far too fond of being in control."

"Yes," said Dara thoughtfully. "I had the same impression. But perhaps this sight will change her mind."

"I doubt it," said Gwen with an undignified snort. A glint appeared in Dara's eyes that made Gwen realize that she had said too much.

As Dara walked away, Gwen berated herself silently. She knew better than to give away the power dynamics in her family to other members of court, much less to foreign diplomats. She could only hope that this misstep never reached Nicki's ears. Gwen's eyes caught a movement and she squinted in that direction. An infant was waddling away.

Gwen walked, then quickened her steps into a jog after the child.

"Wait," she panted, catching the child and picking her up. (She could not tell the child's gender, so Gwen thought of it as a she.) The child squirmed in Gwen's grip and began to cry. "I am trying to help you," said Gwen. "Come, help me find your mother."

"Mama," cried the child, reaching toward the buildings of Wirrn.

Gwen did not understand at first. She could not possibly be from Wirrn; she was clothed in the sack-like hemp cloth that they were giving all the refugees who did not have adequate clothing.

Then she realized: above Wirrn rose clouds of smoke from the many chimneys and forges. Gwen's heart constricted.

"Your mama is not there, child," she said gently. The child squirmed and cried harder.

Gwen braced herself and returned with the squirming, crying infant to Nicki, intending to hand her over. But Nicki and Enri were still engrossed and no one rose to claim the infant. Gwen stood, feeling helpless and foolish.

"Why don't you ask whose she is?"

Gwen jumped and turned toward Alderic, who must have been keeping an eye on her all along.

"I do not know how," she admitted.

"Here," he said, holding out his arms. "Hand her over."

Gwen did. To her annoyance, the child quieted in Alderic's arms, unbothered even by Verity when she alighted on her master's shoulder. He carried the child over to the nearest huddle and said something to them in a voice too low for Gwen to hear. When no one responded, he moved on some distance and stopped to talk again. Eventually, he handed the child over to a large, listless man with hollow eyes.

Then Alderic returned to Gwen's side.

"He will only lose her again," said Gwen.

"Maybe," shrugged Alderic. "But we can't take away his child."

"We did not take her. She left. He hardly seemed to notice."

Alderic hummed noncommittally. Gwen sighed heavily.

"I do not think that either of us is of much use standing here. Would you come with me to explore Wirrn?"

"I don't see why not."

But there was no enjoyment they could find in the streets of Wirrn and no beauty that they could see. The misery of the camp outside hung over the city, whose streets were also full of men, women and children clothed in hemp, silent, trembling and sporting burn scars.

The sun was hanging low in the sky when they decided to return to the camp to rejoin Nicki and the others. On the walk back, absently watching the refugees they passed, Gwen realized with a jolt that she had been mistaken. They did not all fear fire and sport burns as she had thought at first.

Their constant fear was not a response to anything imagined: it was in response to the wind, fire, plants, rocks, or even dirt. It had been difficult to see at first, because each of them behaved differently. Some curled up into a ball whenever the wind picked up; others sat on other people, climbing over people and things to avoid touching the ground; most of them backed away from any flame, no matter how small.

When they returned to the camp, she chanced upon a nurse and asked. The nurse looked at Gwen with something between exasperation and pity and explained that speakers commanded the elements to do their bidding. The worst was those who were attacked with water, for they could not cross any rivers or even quench their own thirst. They never made it to the border, much less to Wirrn.

The nurse bustled back to his work, leaving Gwen trembling. Alderic silently put a hand on her shoulder and she leaned into the touch.

They slept at an inn that night, which could only spare four rooms for their party of twenty. Gwen expected Nicki to protest that they deserved better treatment as royalty, but she only thanked the innkeeper for accommodating them. As the only women in the party, Nicki, Dara and Gwen had the smallest room to themselves. There were only two beds, so Dara offered to sleep on the floor. Nicki said no, opting to share a bed with Gwen. Gwen's opinion was not asked, so she held her tongue.

In the early hours before dawn, Gwen shot up in bed, suddenly wide awake. There was a voice, she thought— someone calling out to her. But the room was dark and silent, and the more awake she felt, the more she realized that if there was a voice, it was in her mind.

She slipped out of bed, pulled on her cloak and shoes,

unbolted the door and ran down the hall, down a staircase and outside into the street. There she stood for a time, breathing the chilly dawn air and watching the street ambling through the morning around her.

"You shouldn't be out here alone," Alderic said, coming up beside her. He cradled a still-sleeping Verity in one arm.

"How did you know I was here?" Gwen's voice was barely louder than a whisper, but she could not bring herself to mind. Her heart was still racing and something felt different about the world around her.

"I heard someone running. I decided to check in case something was wrong."

"I see."

"Gwen," said Alderic, taking hold of her shoulders and turning her to face him. "Is something wrong?"

"Yes," said Gwen. Something was different today. There was something in the air, or in her mind. She blinked up at Alderic, realizing he expected her to explain. But she did not know how. "No. Nothing."

He stared at her for a moment, then nodded and released her.

Gwen sighed, closed her eyes and leaned back against the wall of the inn. He knew when not to press her. She was grateful.

That day, Gwen shadowed Nicki, helping hand out the sack-clothes, blankets and food. The crowd continued to grow as people swam across the Vaina, only for their desperation to melt into silence and despondence once they reached the Ceryllan shore.

Gwen imagined the Seleukoi army reaching the Vaina and crossing, while Ceryllans desperately fled across the

Cole to Amberria. Then, when Ceryll was conquered and Amberria was invaded, perhaps people would flee north over the mountains to Usha, if it was still free. Perhaps the Ushani armies would hold out longest, but they would be as surely conquered as everywhere else. Even with the listless Jehani victims of the speakers right before her eyes, Gwen still would choose to become one of them rather than use a power that would drive her mad and cause her to kill everyone around her.

Gwen tried to focus on helping the refugees. She tried, but a part of her mind kept whispering, *Come to me or be doomed.* Come where? There was nowhere to go.

Their army would seem like children to the army of speakers. So they were all doomed.

4

The Runaway

Third day of spring,
451 A.D. – Peasant's Pass, the Tor

A YEAR AFTER SHE threw away the name Estelle, she was fleeing north with the king's guard in hot pursuit. By the time that Sterre was trekking through the Peasant's Pass towards the Ushani border, she had been on the run for half a fortnight. Her flight had begun with no real plan to speak of. Mostly she figured she had to avoid getting caught, but that was proving harder than anticipated.

The guards showed up at Traveler's Crossing as soon as the snow thawed. Rani woke Sterre before dawn to warn her. She only had time to grab her few belongings before Rani was shoving her out the door and into Pierre's arms. Pierre more or less tossed her into the back of a wagon before hopping into the driver's seat and starting up the trail that led north of the Crossing and upwards toward the plateau. They would go to Corin to stay with his family, he said.

But the guards tracked them to Corin and Sterre knew that if she were discovered, consequences for Pierre would be dire. So with nothing but the clothes on her back, the knife in her shoe and the rope coiled around her waist, she grabbed a sack of dried foods and fled again, this time to Usha.

Every day that she had lived at the Crossing sorting Rani's extensive personal library, she had accepted that she would have to go back someday. She had only told herself *not yet*. But if she could make it to Usha, she might never have to place herself under someone else's thumb again. She wondered why it had never occurred to her before. Usha was a land of warriors. No one would care that she was female once she showed them that she could fight. Traveling the Peasant's Pass was the longest and riskiest way out of Corin, but Sterre felt confident that she had the skills to make it. For the first time, she would be fleeing not only from something, but toward something better.

Sterre slowed her run to a walk and bit her upper lip as she looked around her. The snow still dusting the ground made it impossible to conceal her tracks. The pass had fallen into obscurity since alliances had made traveling to Usha through Amberria the more attractive option: longer but far easier and with no fear of the ghosts that haunted the pass. The entrance to the pass was overgrown and difficult to find. Many no longer remembered that it was there at all. The king's guard, however, would not forget to check. She could only hope that her efforts to obscure her tracks between the main road and the entrance to the pass had been enough to give her a decent head start.

They had horses. She wouldn't be able to outrun them

if she kept to the path. But in this snow, any attempt to veer off of the path would be no less obvious and easy to follow. She could force them to abandon their horses easily enough, but even then, they were faster and her trail would be no less obvious.

Along the path here were several ticker trees: evergreens with smooth trunks and thick, long branches that grew close together. The lowest branches were about the height of Sterre's head. Walking quickly in a straight line, she inspected each tree as she passed it. At last a tree met her hopes just to the right of the path, with one branch that reached a little further out over the side of the path. She walked directly under the branch and continued someway onward. A few miles up the path, long past the patch of ticker trees, she broke into the underbrush at the left side of the road and pushed some distance to a tree trunk, where she jumped a few times to disturb the snow. Then she backtracked, matching her steps to each footprint step by step. It was slower going than she had anticipated. Every step that she took back made her heart rise in her throat. She wondered if she had taken her trail too far past the tickers. Her heart pounded in her ears at the thought of being caught and dragged back to Castle Dio; at the thought of being stuffed back into a gown and the role of Estelle.

At last, she saw ticker trees over her shoulders once again. She slowed and took particular care here to keep her steps precisely on her footprints. She stopped below the overhanging branch she had identified. Sterre bent her knees and aimed. She jumped at the branch, just managing to catch it with her arms. The branch bent downwards under her weight, and when she looked down she saw her feet dangling only a small distance above the ground. She tried to pull herself up. To her dismay, her arms lacked the strength. Heart in her throat, she slid her arms along the branch, showering nettles on the path below as she drew herself closer to the tree trunk. She pushed that observation from her mind; all she could do now was hope that this bought her some time. At the tree trunk, she was able to pull herself up onto the branch with her feet pressed against the trunk. Nettles snagged lightly at her clothes as she pushed smaller branches aside and scrambled up onto the branch.

She climbed from branch to branch, making her way around the thick tree trunk. On the far side from the path, she continued away from the tree trunk along a higher branch, feeling it bend slowly under her weight as she crawled. She moved as far as she dared, and then bit her lip as she inspected the nearest branch on another ticker.

The distance would have been no trouble had she been on solid ground. From branch to branch, it felt much further. Swallowing, she drew the soles of her feet up onto the branch and braced herself with her hands. She took a deep breath, pushed off with her hands as well as her feet, and reached for the next branch with all four limbs.

She caught the branch with her right hand and managed to wrap her legs around it. The branch bounced from the momentum of her jump, showering nettles on the ground as Sterre hung on by her arms and legs with her back toward the ground. She scrambled around so that she was lying on top of the branch, and then climbed closer to the tree trunk. There she laid her palms against the bark and breathed for a few moments, willing her heart to beat steadily again. She had hoped to continue this pattern for a few more trees to place more distance between herself and her earlier tracks but it had taken too much time and energy to make it this far. The guards couldn't be far away.

After a moment, she climbed around the trunk to a branch on the opposite side and followed that some way before jumping back to the ground. She took a moment to eat some snow to quench her thirst. Sterre then oriented herself so that she was walking approximately parallel to the path somewhere to her left and ran. This section of the pass went downhill from Terrian Plateau into the Valley of the Tor. As she ran downhill, the snow on the ground beneath her feet thinned then disappeared. At the same time, the undergrowth thickened. Still she ran. It was only when she found herself beginning to stumble on numbing legs that she sat with her back against another tree and permitted herself to rest.

After a period of rest, Sterre stood and continued. Every step she took snapped branches and crushed plants. If the guards found her trail at any point, it would be far too easy to follow. Yet the path was still riskier.

Soon she was trudging uphill again. The snow returned underfoot, the undergrowth thinned and then the trees thinned too. She looked through the trees and saw movement. Her heart leapt into her throat. *The guards.* Sterre stopped to collect herself. She had not expected her pursuers to explore the pass all the way up the Tor. Her plan to return to the path now was no longer acceptable. To continue, she would have to make her way away from the path as she climbed before the trees thinned even more.

What had she expected? Sterre had never known a member of the king's guard to be superstitious. Of course they wouldn't fear the ghosts of old wives' tales. Then again, neither did she. The thought gave her courage. She ate some more snow and moved on, veering further away from the path.

At dusk, she stopped in the shadow of a boulder with a nice concave area underneath that would shield her from the wind and snow. She went some distance away from the rock, uncoiling the rope around her waist. At a small bush she set a simple loop trap for a bird or a rabbit. Then she returned to the rock where she curled up into a ball, settled herself against the stone and closed her eyes. Sleep was a long time coming, but as she listened to the whisper of the breeze and the occasional sound of an animal without ever hearing the *thump* of a human footstep, she slipped into a light sleep.

She dreamed of her brief life as Rani's bookkeeper in Traveler's Crossing; she dreamed of her friends. She dreamed that she had never come across the battered little book in Rani's basement library—the book now sewn into the hem of her skirt—or maybe that she had burnt it, as she ought to have done. In her dream, she was in the tavern with her friends, joking and playing their game of fooling travelers into believing rumors or myths that were untrue. She spoke happily of Milleport as if it really were her hometown as her friends believed. And then someone stepped up to her. He was clearly a man and vaguely familiar, but she couldn't focus her eyes on him.

"I hear your lies," he said.

The laughter and joy of the dream shattered. "You're no Milleport girl. Every story you've told since you arrived is imaginary. You don't realize how much you lose, how much of the world slips away from you with every lie that crosses your tongue."

"Don't be absurd," said Manon, who was Sterre's mortal enemy and best friend and refused to let anyone contest her for either spot. "If anyone's imagination is overstepping the bounds of reality here, it's yours. You seem to have drunk too much tonight."

"Who are you?" said Sterre in a voice ready to crack. "What do you want from me?"

"Your honesty," said the man, except now she saw that it was a woman. She was going fuzzy around the edges as though dissolving with her surroundings. "Your life."

"I can't," choked Sterre, though that wasn't what she meant to say.

The shadow faded further. "I can hear you try to lie, Estelle. Don't do it. And listen."

Sterre awoke with a jolt. It was still dark. *Listen.* The command still echoed in her mind. She pulled her cloak more tightly around her and closed her eyes again. The dream was already fading away in her memory. This time, she dreamed of childhood bliss, chasing grasshoppers with Gwen through Nicki's garden.

It was before dawn when she woke next, but the sky was already growing lighter. The second dream had left her with a lump in her throat, and she did not remember the first. Sterre walked back to check her trap. To her surprise, there was a squirrel with its hind leg caught in the loop of rope. She tried to grab it around the middle. It twisted and bit her finger. She winced and dropped it. Watching it pull in vain at the rope, she pulled out a knife and stabbed it through the throat. She clumsily skinned and gutted the squirrel, then stowed it in her sack with snow packed around it to cook later. Smoke at dawn would be too easy to spot. She would wait until nightfall. By then she would be in the crags and it would be easy enough to find a place sheltered enough for a small fire. She still had enough dried meat in her sack to make it through a few days.

Before noon, she saw distinctly human tracks that were very fresh and intersecting her own route at a perpendicular angle. *The guards again.* Sterre swallowed thickly and reassured herself. If they were exploring the area at random, her own tracks would mingle with theirs and make her that much more difficult to track. She took a breath and walked on. She continued uphill in a northeasterly direction and encountered no sign of them until she came across more tracks the next day.

In spite of the fact that Sterre's knowledge of trapping, gutting and cooking game had been purely theoretical before she had begun her journey, she had managed to apply the knowledge effectively enough to keep herself alive. She would set traps at dusk, cook the morning's hunt in a sheltered campsite in the dark of night, sleep, then awaken to skin and gut her catch in the morning to stow it in her pack with snow. While she traveled by day, she snacked on the dried foods from her pack when necessary.

Tracks in the snow informed her that guards were ahead of her and behind her, and they showed no sign of abandoning their search. To make matters worse, within four days provisions from the pack were halved. The thought that she would soon be entirely dependent on her trapping skills was a sobering one.

On the fourth day, she did not see any sign of a guard all day. Yet she was also disoriented; she could no longer tell which way the path might lie, or how far away it might be. She was lost. Navigating by the sun, she aimed her course northwest.

She started humming as she walked. It helped her to stay calm.

On the fifth night, she woke from her slumber into the pale light preceding the dawn to realize that she was hearing voices. At first, she thought it might only be a lyrebird. But it was too cold. She panicked. Why were they still searching this far into the pass? Had her crime been so dire that they would hunt for her until they found at least a body to bring home to their king?

Sterre gathered up her things before succumbing to her instincts and running. She tripped over a rock and fell. For a few moments, sparks of light danced before her eyes. She forced herself to her feet all the same. Soon enough the sparks faded and her sight returned. She began to run again. Her right ankle protested with each step, but she ignored it. There was an enormous boulder in front of her, thrice her height and equally wide. She swerved around it and had to come to a sudden halt.

The world ended here in a straight drop so far that she could see clouds of fog below. If there was another side— and, rationally, she knew that there had to be—it was concealed by the clouds in the distance.

For the first time, she saw the Abyss with her own eyes. She understood why some called it the Edge of the World. Her heart sank. She was far further east than she had ever meant to go—and she was trapped here.

No! she assured herself. *I was trapped in Traveler's Crossing too, but I made do.* But that was an entirely different kind of trap. She shook the thought from her head and eyed her surroundings.

Neither forwards into the Abyss nor back into the arms of the guards were options. The gray boulder was tall and smooth to her right, but the cliff on her left looked harder to climb and far taller. She opted for the boulder. Grabbing two fistfuls of skirt under her cloak, she hitched it up and tied a knot, holding it around her upper thighs.

Rustles, voices and footsteps let her know that she was out of time. She kicked off her shoes and tossed them up to the top of the boulder. Her throw fell short, and her shoes bounced off the side and fell into the Abyss. Sterre gritted her teeth against the tightening in her chest and deliberately did not think about the prospect of continuing her trek barefooted in the snow. She found a handhold on the boulder and began to climb. Her panic propelled her up the side of the boulder, yet she was not halfway to the top before her arms began to tremble with exertion. *Out of practice,* she cursed. A sharp bolt of pain shot through her right ankle when she tried to use that foot to push herself up; her foot slipped and she heard her stocking rip. She felt the cold rock directly against the sole of her foot and had to remind herself that pain and discomfort were not important.

She could hear voices now, so she climbed higher,

higher, higher. The surface curved forwards and she opened her eyes—when had she closed them?—to find herself almost at the top. She forgot about her exhaustion for a moment as every element of her existence sang with triumph. The song gave her strength, and a moment later she was at the top.

She breathed heavily and looked around. Her heart sank. No matter which side she climbed down, she would be in full view of the guards below. She pulled back from the edge before they thought to look up.

She didn't know what possessed her to get on her stomach and poke most of her torso out over the edge to peer down the side of the Abyss. On this side, there was a narrow ledge some way down but otherwise nothing else of note. *Fat lot of use that is.* She pulled back onto the boulder. Still on her stomach, she waited and listened.

As her heart began to quiet, their conversation became more coherent.

". . . Off the side, but more likely up the cliff or the rock."

"She went up the rock. Just look at the footprints. Doesn't Hervé climb? Where'd he get to?"

Her blood went cold. Why was the captain here? She was trapped, with nowhere to run. And of all people to send after her. . . . She closed her eyes against memories of Hervé with his jovial grin and easy manner. She remembered him teaching Gwen and her to climb. It figured that he would be the one to drag her back.

She heard him identify himself below.

She held still—her breathing and heartbeat were too loud as he drew closer, closer and closer—until she could see the head of light brown hair rising up the side of the rock. She pushed herself up into a crouch and drew back even as a brown-haired man with an aging face and a knife scar on the right cheek looked up and met her gaze with brown eyes.

They stared at each other in frozen silence for a moment. Then she straightened and took a step back, breaking the stillness.

"Estelle," said Hervé in astonishment.

"Hello," said Sterre. She couldn't help the small smile that came over her face. "I take it you weren't expecting it to be me."

"No, I—what—how? No." Understanding dawned on Hervé's face and he looked wrecked.

"Oh, yes," she said. "I assume you're wondering if it really was me at the Crossing, with the book about the Words? It was. It's sewn into the hem of my dress at this very moment."

To his credit, Hervé collected himself quickly.

"Your friends say it was only history."

"What? They didn't have the sense to say they knew nothing?"

"They tried," said Hervé with an exasperated sigh just like in the training yard at Dio. "But you were too brazen. Too many people knew that the six of you shared a secret."

"It was all me." She stood tall and met his eyes. "It was all my fault. It was—is—important history. Hervé, it isn't the Words that were forbidden. It was never the Words. It was something else entirely, a magic of nothingness."

Hervé was already shaking his head, like her discovery meant nothing to him.

"Princess, it isn't my place to make such decisions. That's the role of your father and the council. But if I may say . . . there are any number of records written by speakers to try to justify themselves. This sounds like one of them. What *is* a magic of nothingness? What has it to do with the madness that takes some speakers, and how do we find them?"

"I don't know. It was written centuries ago, and I couldn't understand all of it. What I do understand is that the Words aren't a power or a magic at all—"

"Enough, child," barked Hervé. "Take that book out and toss it into the Abyss. Tell your father that you found a speaker's defense of the Words and mistook it for history and believed it. Apologize and he'll forgive you. He misses you so."

"Does he?" said Sterre quietly. She was entertaining the possibility in her mind. She thought of home and family and comfort and security. "And how would they explain my absence and sudden reappearance?"

"They have been saying that you took ill, Highness. So that you could resume your life when you came home."

The flame of frustration that had been cold for a year ignited again. All this time, all this effort and nothing had changed. They lied and manipulated and expected her to come home and fall in line once she outgrew the urge to rebel.

She would prove them wrong.

"Why don't you tell him instead?" she said flippantly. "Go back and tell Nicki *exactly* how you found me and lost me. She can tell the king. I won't return to a life as a pawn on someone else's board."

She spun on the ball of her left foot, bent her knee, and leapt off the edge toward the Abyss. She heard Hervé begin to call out, but the rushing of the wind drowned him out before she had even heard the first syllable.

She managed not to make a sound as she caught the edge of the ledge and her arms were yanked nearly out of their sockets. She hung there, clinging for dear life for a few moments. When she could bear it no longer, she pulled herself up.

Except, to her dismay, her arms lacked the strength. Her heart beat faster and her breath quickened. Even with the rush of fear running through her veins, she no longer had the strength to pull herself up by the arms. Instead, her hands were beginning to slip.

She looked down, hoping to see some way to push with her feet. All she saw was nothingness and she lost control of her bladder. She looked side to side, searching for a way to get closer to the wall of the Abyss. It was pointless. Her feet would not reach. Her hands were already slipping.

Moments later, she lost the last of her grip and fell through the clouds.

5

The Librarian's Apprentice

Thirty-third day of spring,
451 A.D. – Castle Dio, Ceryll

RAINIER SLID DOWN from the loft in Uncle Vere's room with his tunic and britches only half on. He hadn't been able to sleep half the night, and now had overslept. Sunlight was already streaming through the narrow windows.

"No need to rush," came Uncle Vere's voice from behind him, and Rainier nearly jumped out of his skin. "We're not working today."

"What?"

"Princess Estelle passed away last night. The king declared a day of mourning and the library is to remain closed. You'll want to dress in black if you're going to leave the servants' quarters."

Rainier's first thought was for Princess Gwenaëlle. He thought of all that she must be going through and his heart broke for her. He had never known Princess Estelle, though he had heard her mock "Gwen's puppy librarian" on an occasion or two when she thought he couldn't hear. But the way Gwenaëlle used to light up beside Estelle— he had loved Estelle for that alone. The castle had been darker and quieter since she had fallen ill. It saddened him to realize that this was how it would remain.

His second thought was that despite the tragedy, this was astonishingly convenient. The tome he had found the day before was still hidden in the shelves, in plain sight, too large and heavy to conceal any other way. If it was a day of mourning, he could sneak into the library and burn it before anyone else discovered it.

He crawled back up the ladder and found some more-or-less black clothing. He threw it on and left the room, assuring Uncle Vere that he was going to the kitchens for food.

Instead, he headed straight for the library. The hallways were quiet and he found himself softening his footfalls as though he were breaking a rule by wandering the halls. Maybe he was, for all that Rainier knew about court life. He had been here six years and never once had he thought to ask what the rules were should the whole castle go into mourning.

He unlocked the library doors and slipped inside. Rainier made a beeline to the shelf where he had hidden the tome behind several other books. It was heavy enough that he had to carry it in both arms. He carried it across the library and into the reading room, where he dropped it into the cold fireplace with a sigh of relief. Grabbing the flint stones, Rainier began to strike.

"What are you doing?"

He dropped the flint stones and looked up. Princess Gwenaëlle was peering down at him, head cocked to the side.

"N—" Rainier swallowed the *nothing* at the tip of his tongue. Her gaze was already fixed on the book in the fireplace.

"That is quite a large book. I do hope you are not burning it. Father would never allow a book to be destroyed. Neither would I, for that matter."

"Your Highness, I—"

"How many times must I tell you? You should call me Gwen. Everyone else does."

Everyone else meant princes, noblemen and guards. He had never heard her correct a servant and Rainier's status was no different. Opening his mouth to say so, he looked up and snapped his mouth shut again.

Her eyes were pink and rimmed with dark circles. The smile on her face looked forced. Her long golden hair was messy, like her maids hadn't taken the time to comb it properly this morning. The sight of her was a dagger in Rainier's heart as always; today it burned too.

"I'm so sorry to hear about—"

Gwenaëlle gave him a sharp look. "Not another word."

Rainier snapped his mouth shut. There was a moment of silence.

"I come here to get away. Can I be away here, Nier?"

"Of course," he said quietly, meeting her eyes. He knew what it felt like, to want to think of anything but a gaping wound. He thought of his father's fists, stained with blood, and shook the thought away. "Lovely weather today."

Gwenaëlle's snort was entirely unladylike. "I would

rather hear why you appear to be about to burn this book."
She crouched by the fireplace and hoisted out the book.

"Please," Rainier pleaded. "Don't—"

"Why are you so—"

Setting the tome on the stone floor and opening it to a
seemingly random page, Gwenaëlle froze. Rainier chanced
a glance at the words at the top of the page and gulped.

The Phoenix, it said there. *Weapon of Words.*

His eyes were tugged down to the paragraph below.
One passage immediately caught his eye: *known to help
those who face injustice at the hands of speakers.* Then Rainier
remembered that he couldn't be reading this and pulled
his gaze away.

Gwenaëlle didn't seem to share the sentiment. Her
gaze was fixed on the page, darting left and right across
the page. A long silence fell over them as Gwenaëlle read
and Rainier searched for something to say that wouldn't
sound incriminating.

"You cannot burn this," Gwenaëlle said at last, looking
up at him.

"You know as well as I that this can't stay here."

"No," she agreed. "We can hide it. But Nier, this
Phoenix—it could save us."

Rainier blinked at her. He had not been expecting that.
"It—This is a book of legends."

To his surprise, Gwenaëlle smiled. It didn't look at
all forced this time. "Are legends not usually based in
fact? If we can figure out what this weapon is, we might
present it to the council. We could save Ceryll in the
coming war."

"The war?" Rainier blinked. He had heard of no such thing.

Gwenaëlle looked up at him incredulously. "Yes, the war. With Seleukos? The potentate reviving the Words and building an army of speakers?"

"It . . . ," Rainier swallowed. "It sounds like a story."

"It is, and a true one. They have been raiding the Jehani and Yngan borders for years, and they have grown bolder since the spring thaw. When they invade properly, Jehan will be powerless to resist. Once Jehan is conquered, they will turn to Ceryll next."

Rainier's jaw dropped. "It can't be true. How would I not have heard?"

Gwenaëlle rolled her eyes. "I wonder that too. Perhaps all your other friends are particularly poorly informed."

A lump rose in Rainier's throat. A moment later, he composed himself and brushed aside the elation. He may be her friend, but she would never be his. She was his princess. Perhaps she even knew this. He had seen her giggle and flutter her eyelashes at a young man only to sigh heavily and collapse into a book the moment he was out of sight. He had watched as she entertained noblemen and visiting princes, encouraging their attention and gifts, only to refuse them as soon as it became too serious.

Yet she had only just lost her sister. There was a carelessness to her demeanor now, like she had given up pretense and airs for a time. He wanted to believe her, so he did.

He shook his head and refocused on the more important issue.

"But this book—"

"Do you not understand?" she said, standing up straight. She grabbed him by the front of his tunic and forced him to meet her eyes. Her gaze was fierce. "I understand, perhaps better than you do, that this is illegal. Especially after . . . after everything lately. You know."

Though her words were vague, Rainier *did* know. It was impossible to avoid whispers of the commotion in Traveler's Crossing caused by a girl from Milleport with a book about the Words. The guards sent after her had returned on the previous day with five prisoners. The girl who'd been the source of the commotion—Sterre, they called her—had fled until she fell to her death in the Abyss.

"Then you see that we have to burn it."

"No, Nier. We *cannot*. We know nothing of the Words. Any information that might help us in the coming war is precious, legendary or otherwise. We cannot afford to destroy what might be the only information we have left."

Rainier was silent. He understood. Even knowing the contents, there was a part of him that felt utterly disturbed by the notion of burning a book—at the knowledge that was being destroyed forever.

"What do you suggest, then?" he asked after a time. "Show it to the council?"

"No. They would hang you, lock me away until marriage and burn the book. But they would argue for a year or so first. No, we must read this. We will research this until we find evidence."

"Research *how*? I'm at my uncle's beck and call at all

times and, forgive me, but your family tends to keep a close watch on everyone."

"Are we not standing in the second largest library on the continent?"

"I thought that was in Milleport," muttered Rainier.

Gwenaëlle gave that a moment's thought. "Third largest, then. Quite the resource at our fingertips, and so many excuses for me to be in here."

"It's a lot of books to scour," Rainier pointed out. "With only two of us? A war could begin and end before we get halfway through."

"How fortunate, then, that my partner's life's work is knowing this library inside out." She smiled at him, all sincerity and hope. He couldn't have objected if he'd tried.

6

The Amberrian Guard

Fifth day of winter, 451 A.D. – Castle Dio, Ceryll

ALDERIC LOWERED HIS sword and regarded his three pupils from Traveler's Crossing.

"Excellent progress," he announced. "Regis, your decision to take advantage of my distraction was a good one. A little more training and you might have bested me. Pierre and Eduard, good teamwork. I'll recommend you two serve together. Teamwork like yours in battle can mark the difference between victory and defeat."

"We're not *really* serving in the army," Pierre muttered. Alderic froze in his tracks.

"That's not true. The heir—"

"—was merciful enough to keep us from being executed on account of our poor taste in friends," Regis finished, his tone and eyes icy. "So we're sentenced to serve pointlessly until the war begins, when we'll be at the front lines for our execution at the enemy's hands."

"If she even trusts us not to turn traitor," Pierre

grumbled. "There's a reason we're being trained by the Amberrian outcast. We don't even get goshawks."

Eduard kicked him in the shin.

Alderic was at a loss for words. By all rights, he should reprimand them for insubordination; he was a member of the king's guard.

"You don't get goshawks because you're in the army," he said instead. "Goshawks are for members of the king's guard. You're dismissed for the day."

He was undermining his authority, but he saw no acceptable alternative. He could not in good conscience reprimand them when they were right. Alderic was all too aware that his acquired status was that of name only. Alderic had trained alone, dined alone and generally spent his time alone, scorned by the rest of the guard until the three unwitting outlaws from Traveler's Crossing had been dropped carelessly into his tutelage. It was true, too, that Alderic still had no friend in the entire castle but Enri, Gwen and Nicki. Even the prince's two other Amberrian guards looked on Alderic with scorn.

His three charges went back into the barracks. Alderic went the other way, into the castle. A glimmer of silver caught the corner of his eye and he glanced down the hallway. It was a flicker of a skirt, only visible for a moment before it disappeared out of sight. The silhouette of a man dressed in black from head to toe was, however, standing with his hands against the edge of an alcove as though trapping someone there. Alderic approached, alarmed. As he drew closer, he could hear the Seleukoi ambassador's low, threatening tone a little more clearly.

". . . you *dare* to . . . my men . . . could *do* to you—"

"Ambassador," Nicki's voice cut in sharply, just as she came into Alderic's line of sight. Her body language conveyed to Alderic that she knew he was there, though her eyes never left the ambassador. She was every bit the regal queen-to-be, as if she weren't being threatened by the most dangerous man in Dio while cornered in an alcove. "I thank you for your warnings and will take them under advisement. Now I must insist that you allow me to pass and find your guards."

Where are *his guards?* Alderic wondered. *Where are hers?*

"Perhaps you could request that they join me in the library. I'll be on my way now."

"You will *not*." The ambassador froze briefly at Nicki's command. "You will remain here while Alderic summons a few guards"—she met Alderic's eyes—"then you will proceed to your quarters and remain there for the rest of the day."

Alderic hesitated a moment. The ambassador had not even turned to acknowledge his presence. He wanted desperately to suggest that he wait with the ambassador while Nicki summoned the guards. But he didn't dare to question her judgment in front of the ambassador. With a quick nod of acknowledgment, he turned and rushed for the door.

"But Alderic will not accompany me, I see. Seizing a few secret moments with your paramour?"

Alderic gritted his teeth at the ambassador's jibe. He reached the door, tugged it open and gave a sharp shout. Two guards came jogging across the training yard.

He heard the hum of Nicki's response. Nicki was the

sort who became quieter with anger, but the ambassador regarded her with his customary condescending amusement. Nicki had stepped forward out of the alcove, standing her ground. Alderic wondered if it was his imagination, or if the ambassador's amusement seemed to flicker out for a moment to reveal marrow-deep loathing.

Nicki side-stepped her way out of his shadow just as the guards reached the door.

"The heir requires you to escort the ambassador back to his quarters and ensure that he remains there," Alderic informed them.

"One of you will stand watch once he is safely in his quarters," said Nicki when they reached her. "The other will find the guards supposedly stationed at the ambassador's quarters and send them to me. I shall be in the treasurer's office." She turned back to the ambassador and offered a respectful curtsy. "Always a pleasure, Zephyr."

"The pleasure is mine, Princess," said the ambassador with a bow that might have seemed sincere to the casual observer. Alderic met the ambassador's eyes for a moment. He felt the full force of the man's disgust and hatred in that gaze. A moment later it was gone, hidden in a mocking smile once more before he turned around.

"Come with me, Deric," said Nicki. Alderic automatically fell into step as they walked away from the ambassador. "Thank you for coming to my rescue, but you must know that I was never in any danger from him."

"He cornered you. He'd backed you into an alcove and threatened you."

"His only entertainment this season," Nicki shrugged.

"You don't have to condone it," Alderic pressed. "His behavior crossed a line."

"Whose behavior are we discussing?" asked Gwen from behind them. They turned.

"No one," said Nicki at the same time as Alderic said, "Ambassador Zephyr cornered her in a deserted hallway. I intervened in time, but—"

"Again?" Gwen interrupted. "This is getting out of hand. You have to tell Father."

"You will not breathe a word to him. Do you understand me?"

"Nicki, just think about it for a—"

"What, Deric? Should we send him back to Seleukos? Execute him for breaking the rules we impose upon him? Throw him into the dungeons? Right now, the ambassador's presence in this castle and his mercy hold at bay a war we all know we would lose."

"And what if your lenience permits him to, oh, for example, assassinate the heir to the Ceryllan throne?"

Nicki threw her head back and began to laugh. Alderic exchanged a look with Gwen; she looked as bewildered as he felt.

"Is this *funny* to you? The possibility that you might die, that the weight on your shoulders might fall to me? Have you forgotten what is at stake?"

"Gwen," Nicki's eyes softened on her sister. "Trust that I am not risking myself. Zephyr would never harm me. He would not live to see another day if he did, and he is far too self-involved for that. He enjoys the power trip. I allow him to feel like he has the upper hand in these moments, because then he is more likely to yield the upper hand in the negotiations that matter."

"How can you be sure he wouldn't harm you?" demanded Alderic. "I—"

"Enough! I know him better than either of you. Please trust that I have everyone's best interests at heart— including yours, Gwen."

Alderic held his tongue. He glanced at Gwen and saw her face go blank.

"I apologize for the intrusion. I see my presence and opinion was, as always, a nuisance." Gwen glided off, leaving Nicki to sigh.

"I am sorry, Deric. I was coming to the training yard to tell you that Father has a new assignment for you."

"Oh?" Alderic had not spoken to the king one-on-one since he had been appointed to the king's guard. On the surface, the king had wished to get to know Alderic a little before appointing him to his personal guard. Beneath the surface, he had been digging for any hint of disloyalty. It had been a markedly unpleasant experience for Alderic, who had to relate and relive everything from his fatherless childhood and his training in the Amberrian barracks to the recent death of his mother.

"How are you finding your charges?"

Alderic blinked at the change in topic. "I . . . Well. They're learning well enough. They should be ready for duty by spring."

Nicki's eyes softened. "But they are unhappy."

Alderic felt a lump in his throat. Here it was, his first assignment: failed.

"Do not misunderstand me: I do not blame you. None of you have had it easy in this. They did nothing wrong, except listen to a friend."

"Not this again," Alderic huffed. "Nicki, she had a book about the *Words*."

"They say it was only history. Do you not trust them?"

"It's not about trust. It drove the girl mad and off a cliff. That's why it's against the law to possess or read any book about the Words."

"It is true that the law states that any book *teaching* the Words is illegal. Does that mean we should execute those who only seek to understand our history?"

Alderic sighed. "I know you meant well. Those boys are harmless. But if you show leniency this time, you couldn't guarantee that next time—"

"It used to be commonplace, four and a half centuries ago. Seleukos is reviving the Words and building an army. What do we have to defend ourselves? What do we know of what we will face?"

Alderic blinked. He'd once heard a boy ask a similar question. The schoolmaster had dealt him a sound beating. To ask such questions was to invite the forbidden knowledge. He couldn't repeat this to Nicki.

"Exactly," said Nicki, misinterpreting his silence. "Right now, we are fearful and ignorant. I had hoped that these five could help shed some light for us."

Alderic understood now. "That's why you took the girls as maidservants."

Nicki smiled thinly. "Yes. Unfortunately, they know very little. I have no regrets in saving them. But I persuaded my father with the promise of information that could be of help against Seleukos. I came up empty-handed. Now he resorts to more drastic means."

"Is this my new assignment?"

"Yes. He wants you to take a spy mission in Ynga, investigating whether or not that country is reviving the Words, or has a faction of speakers. We need to know that they will truly be our ally against Seleukos."

"The Yngan king is your cousin, isn't he?" Alderic frowned. "You know that he's against the Words. Don't you trust him?"

"Yasin is my cousin," nodded Nicki. "And we would be fools to trust him. He is a young boy who despises taking advice. Uncle Yahya was a wise man and a good king. But Yasin . . . was crowned too young."

"Ynga's more set against the Words than any other country," Alderic protested. "They call them witches— they hardly require proof to burn suspects alive! They've suffered more raids by Seleukos than anyone can count. How could a country that terrified—We all know the danger of Words. The potentate is mad. You don't need a spy to tell you that no sane person supports her."

Nicki was quiet for a moment. "Ynga has a history of being as closely allied to Seleukos as Ceryll is to Amberria."

"But that's history," Alderic objected. "Now they want an alliance with Ceryll and the other countries. Isn't that why the last king married two of his three sisters into southwestern countries?"

"And even then, he married the third to the potentate's brother."

"To prevent a war!"

"Yasin's grandmother was Seleukoi. His aunt is married to a Seleukoi. His sister is betrothed to a Seleukoi. He is an arrogant child. We would be fools to trust that his allegiances lie with us just because one of his aunts was our mother. There are whispers of unnatural things and miracles performed in the Yngan court, by the taipan herself."

Alderic did not know how to reply to this, but Nicki did not seem to expect him to.

"War *is* coming, Deric. It is only a matter of when. Any information we can obtain about other countries' likely allegiances is imperative."

"The king wants me out of Dio," Alderic realized.

A shadow crossed Nicki's face.

"He trusts you. He would not send you otherwise."

"But it helps that I'd be out of the way. And if I'm caught by speakers, I can protect Ceryll with truths, because I'm Amberrian. I'm foreign, loyal and, in the grand scheme, expendable."

"I did not invite you into the king's guard for this," Nicki said softly. "But Verity is old enough, and in these uncertain times. . . ."

"I know, Nicki," said Alderic, unable to fight a smile. This woman carried the weight of a kingdom and a coming war on her shoulders, yet still found it within herself to treat him like a friend. In all his life, no one but his mother had ever offered half the affection and concern that Nicki had shown him in the past year.

He took her hand and kissed the back of it. He felt the eyes of passing servants and courtiers on them. *Let them look—let them think what they like. I'll be gone soon.* He would not fail her.

7

The Princess

Ninth day of spring, 452 A.D. – Castle Dio, Ceryll

G WEN DID NOT plan to undertake a quest to find the Phoenix on her own until dinner on her sixteenth birthday.

In the privacy of the king's quarters, her father and sister tried in vain to act for an evening as if Gwen's aging were more important than the impending war and their well-hidden grief over their ever-shrinking family. Even her aunts and uncle were gone now, sent to Usha and Amberria as ambassadors to solidify the alliances between the western nations. Grandmother had taken to bed since Stelle's death and rarely spoke to anyone anymore.

"How can you pretend that this is worth your time?" she burst out the moment that the servants bringing the main course had left the room. "What is another year on my age when the speaker army draws nearer every day?"

"We must celebrate when there is occasion to," said Father quietly. "Our family knows the devastation of the Words better than any."

"Father," said Nicki sharply.

"What do you mean by that?" asked Gwen.

"Father has some elaborate ideas with no proof to support them," said Nicki with a glare at their father.

Father slammed his palms down on the table. Gwen and Nicki both jumped, unused to such demonstrations from their soft-spoken father.

"Nevena help me! Would you rather believe she hurled herself off a cliff because she hates or fears us? I cannot accept that. Stelle was headstrong and young, but she did not despise us enough to die rather than come home. It was the madness—it was the Words. It was not her choice."

Gwen digested this. The knot that lived in Gwen's throat loosened and she could breathe for the first time in a year. Of course—everyone said that Sterre had been driven mad, and Stelle was Sterre. Yet somehow, that last piece had not clicked into place before—maybe because she spent so long trying not to think about it.

All this time, Gwen had buried anger at Stelle for her foolishness and hatred, when the blame had never been Stelle's. It was the *Words*. The magic had driven her mad. Who knew where she had found that book? It might have been one of the books hidden in Dio's library. She might have already been affected when she ran away. That hateful page in her journal—of course, that had been the madness of the Words guiding her pen.

Gwen knew better than anyone that the library hid books that had been missed in the purge three centuries ago. After that first tome, she and Nier had found several useful books, which ultimately led them to the journal of Danti cartographer Trygve.

One of Trygve's journals described a strange event on a remote island in the Dantes, where he had seen a strange flame hovering in the air. He spoke to the flame in his mother's firetongue (whatever that meant), telling it of the three men who had killed his family. The flame flickered out, only to return moments later, and Trygve sensed that his enemies were no more. Sure enough, when he returned home, he discovered that the three men had died mysteriously.

It was more confirmation of the legend of the Phoenix than Gwen had dared to hope for.

So while Nicki and Father glared at each other across the table, Gwen sipped her wine. Moments ago, she had been wishing it was ale. Now that no longer mattered. She would be leaving the palace as soon as she could.

It took her a day to prepare, and the next day, she was ready.

When Gwen had moved her chambers from the tower, there had been discussion of cutting down the ancient blue gum tree in the courtyard outside the window. Gwen had insisted that it remain out of the need to argue more than any attachment to the tree. Father had yielded, as he had in all things since Stelle. The tree had remained, its smooth branches trimmed so that they did not grow too close to her window.

Now, that tree was her ticket out of her heavily-guarded chambers. Clothed in a servant's dress with a pack on her back and a rope around her waist, Gwen gauged the distance between windowsill and branch. It would be a risk, but she knew she could make it.

Gwen took a breath and closed her eyes. Her heart was

pounding furiously. Here she was, following in Stelle's footsteps by running away with some book having to do with the Words, just as she had followed her out of the womb.

But no: Gwen would neither be overcome by madness, nor follow her to the grave. She was leaving to save her country, not for some foolish ideal of self-fulfillment. That was the greatest difference in the world.

Gwen opened her eyes and jumped. The wind jumped with her, gusts of air holding her aloft a little longer, carrying her a little further.

She missed. Her legs fell just short of the branch. She threw her arms out, catching the branch with a painful jerk that yanked the breath out her lungs through her shoulders and scraped her forearms on the rough bark. She swung herself sideways and scrambled onto the branch. Secure there, she took a moment to breathe as the wind gusted around her.

Gwen clambered along the branch to the tree trunk. Her shoes and hands scraped the bark as she slid down the tree. At the bottom, she darted into the shadows at the edge of the courtyard. The wind was still, like a warning.

"*What* are you doing?" demanded a whisper behind her.

She jumped. Her eyes darted around in the darkness for a few moments before she found him. He stood with his arms crossed, dark clothes and dark skin almost indistinguishable in the night. Only his eyes stood out, bright with accusation. Gwen had not needed him to show up. She breathed easier anyway.

"Nier," she whispered back. "What are you doing here?"

"When I went to check this evening, Trygve's journal

was gone. I came to check that you hadn't gotten some stupid idea in your head."

Gwen narrowed her eyes at him in a glare. Nier did not appear to be moved.

"Do you check every night? That seems excessive."

"Are you trying to change the subject? I was exactly right. You're trying to go searching for the Phoenix on your own!"

Gwen grabbed him by the hand.

"Hush and come with me."

Nier came, but he did not hush. "What will your father say? Or your sister? Or the prince!"

"None of them have any sway over this decision."

She started along the edge of the courtyard, keeping to the shadows. Nier followed.

"Are you—come on, at least stop and think about this. Nou only knows where this will lead you. Do you even know how to haggle? How to talk to different sorts of people? What to watch out for?"

"Probably not. So you can come with me."

Nier's footsteps stopped and she turned around to beckon him onward.

"Do you—you expect me to just drop everything and come with you?"

"You were so eager to get an expedition approved by the council a few days ago."

"An actual expedition! With the council's support and a company of guards! Not a princess and a librarian sneaking away in the dead of night with a lead or two *hoping* to find something that may or may not exist somewhere in the Dantes."

Gwen rounded on him. "We have discussed this. The Words are involved, so this cannot be common knowledge. The council would debate it for seasons until Seleukos was on our doorstep. By then, it would be too late. It must be you and me or no one. If you will not come with me, then I shall go alone."

She spun on the ball of her foot and walked on. Nier said nothing, but he followed.

They came to a solid oak door. It led to a corridor that would lead them directly to the outer castle wall. Gwen cracked open the door and peered inside. The corridor was bare save for the torches on the walls. Gwen slipped inside, Nier behind her. At the other end of the corridor, Gwen tilted her head so that her ear was at the crack in the door.

"You think you'll be able to *hear* a guard coming?" hissed Nier. "Highness, that's—"

"Hush," said Gwen. Footsteps were approaching.

Nier narrowed his eyes and began to protest. Gwen continued in a hurried whisper.

"We will wait for the next guard to pass the door, then cross behind him. Aim for the hedge at the edge of my sister's garden. Stay behind me."

She waited only a few moments after the next guard passed and cracked open the door. She peered through the crack only briefly to confirm that the guard was a few steps away. Her heart pounded. He only had to turn around to see them. She threw the door open the rest of the way and ran out with Nier at her heels. A gust of wind swept by, muffling the sound of the door opening and the sound of their footsteps as they darted across to the hedge.

From the hedge, Gwen looked back to see Nier only halfway across the space. She held her breath, knowing that the next guard would soon appear. Nier made it to the hedge at the same moment as a guard came around the corner.

"I said *swift*," Gwen hissed, heart pounding wildly.

"The door would've slammed and given us away. I had to close it quietly," Nier shot back. Gwen was momentarily taken aback.

She shook her head. She would have to be more vigilant. She turned to proceed on her way along the hedge and through the garden. Nier followed along behind.

They walked through and around rows of hedges, trees and flowers and several ponds. The paths of Nicki's garden were woven like a maze, but Gwen had grown up running these paths and jumping over sapling hedges with her sisters. She knew it like the back of her hand.

They stopped on the far side of the garden. There lay a sea of darkness between them and the light of torches along the castle wall. There was no cover at all. Gwen could see nothing of the guards patrolling the wall, only the flickering of the torches' flames dancing in the breeze. They would have to run and hope that no one spotted them.

"We can still turn back," Nier whispered. Gwen lay a hand on his arm.

"We have to do this. If we do nothing, the war is as good as lost anyway."

Nier closed his eyes. "Yes, Princess."

"From here onwards, you will *never* address me as such. I am Elle, a common girl, and you—"

"Yes. I'll be Nier—it's what you've always called me, anyway. I just wanted to—for closure, you know."

"Come, now. We shall be back soon enough and you can go back to all the titles you like."

She turned back to the dark field that lay between her and the wall. Beyond that wall lay the city of Nirra. Gwen eyed the stone staircase up the wall and fingered the rope coiled around her waist. Her heart raced. Nier would need the rope to climb down the far side either way, but if the wall was coarse enough, Gwen could drop the rope and climb down bare-handed. She hoped so—if they had to leave the rope behind, their absence would be discovered within the hour.

Gwen took a deep breath. Then she broke into a sprint with Nier close behind her.

8

The Princess

Tenth day of spring, 452 A.D. – Nirra, Ceryll

S HALL WE SLIP out of the city through the sewers? It may be filthy but surely we would find clean water to bathe soon enough along the kingsway."

"No. We're not trudging alone along the kingsway like a pair of vagabond thieves," said Nier, distracted at last from lamenting his fear at Gwen's ropeless climb down the wall. "We're joining a caravan for safety, if nothing else."

Gwen frowned—but Nier knew this side of Ceryll far better than she did.

"All right," she sighed. "You may be right. We shall try this your way."

"Thank you." After a beat of silence, he asked, "So, what's your plan?"

Gwen looked at him levelly. "We travel to the Dantes. We ask people and look for clues. We find the Phoenix. We bring it home."

Nier stared at her for a moment.

She stared back, defying him to challenge her.

"Ask people and look for clues?" he hissed. "*Ask?* Everything else aside—and I think we can agree that there was no part of that that could be called an actual *plan*— are you suggesting that you intend go to a foreign country and find a secret, forgotten weapon that can bring down kingdoms by *asking people and looking for clues*?"

Gwen refused to be cowed by his patronizing tone. "We have a general sense of where in the Dantes it is, and we know what we're looking for."

"*A general sense?* We've narrowed it down to maybe an eighth of the archipelago. How many islands are even in that area?"

"One main island. About a dozen other little ones. Probably a few more too small to be on the map. But it must be one of the smallest ones."

"Over thirteen islands and you think we can just waltz in and. . . . If it were that simple, the Danti would have conquered us all centuries ago."

"All the more reason why there is no sense in laying out a clearer plan. We have no idea what we might find; our only real source of information is Trygve's journal, and he died half a century ago."

"Do you hear how mad you sound right now?"

Gwen glared. Nier had never been this defiant before. The more he argued, the more she argued. It was all wrong, nothing like the peaceful calm she was used to between them.

She tried changing the subject. "We should find an alleyway to pass the time until morning. Tomorrow will be a long day."

But apparently this was not a safe topic either, because Nier narrowed his eyes and asked, "Why not an inn?"

"We will get our coins exchanged tomorrow. Someone might be suspicious if we paid for a room at an inn with a black."

"I'd be more worried about getting our throats slit and robbed in our sleep . . . but do you mean to say that you don't have a *single* coin that isn't a black piece?"

Gwen tried to nip the next looming argument in the bud. "Look: that alleyway looks nice enough."

Nier did not follow her lead. "No. We have to find a way to at least get a white, if not a few violets."

"At this time of night?"

"If you knew that there would be problems with carrying only blacks, one might wonder why you didn't procure coins that we could actually *use.*"

Gwen gave up. He was being insufferable. "I could hardly go around asking for whites and violets, now, could I? What use could I possibly have for them? Half the rooms in Dio have decorations of white, violet or both."

Nier shook his head slowly. "I'm almost afraid to ask why it's easier for you to get your hands on an entire bag of black coins than a few whites and violets."

"You could refrain from asking."

"Why is it easier?"

"The treasury has plenty of black coins. They are shiny."

"Your father let you have a hundred blacks because you said they were shiny?"

"Not as such. Do you remember Ottavio?"

"The son of the minister of the treasury? Only from when he—" Nier stopped, gaping.

"He never really . . . lost interest in me, you see."

"You convinced him to—You mean we're walking around with a bag of black that was *stolen* from the treasury?"

Gwen realized too late that her admission was not well timed. "No need to fuss. I only brought ones without the king's seal on them. I checked."

"That's not the worst of it," growled Nier, stopping in the middle of the road to rub his face with his palm. "You have no idea what kind of trouble you've gotten Ottavio into, do you? I can only *hope* that your father shows him mercy."

"Why would he punish him? Nicki will know it was me."

"Maybe so! But she can't very well announce that to the council!"

"Ottavio will tell them when they ask him," said Gwen, more snappishly than she intended. The look on Nier's face was one she had never seen before.

"You have *no idea* what that would mean for Ottavio," growled Nier. He was clearly trying very hard not to shout and only mostly succeeding. "Telling the council what you did would mean more trouble for him than confessing to stealing the coins for himself. If you had been there, it might have been a different story. But after you've just disappeared, he'd be considered—" He stopped, eyes wide.

"What?"

"They'll think I kidnapped you. They'll be out for my head! And they'll say that Ottavio was my accomplice and hang him! And Uncle Vere . . . !"

Gwen sighed and put a hand on his arm. "My family will not let blame fall on your uncle. When we return, I will clear your name. And Ottavio deserves whatever fate he meets, though I doubt he will face any serious consequences."

Nier did not appear to be listening.

"It wasn't even as though it would have been that difficult for you to obtain whites and violets *legally*. Just a few hours spent negotiating with the minister or the king—"

"It was a waste of time and effort. I would have to invent a reason why I needed the coins, and establish credibility for that reason. This was so much faster. In any case, what is done is done. We should try our luck finding a place that will accept a black for a night. I am sure there is an upper class inn or two in Nirra."

"No. No, we won't look for an inn, because if we start using stolen black in this city, the guards will be on us in no time and Ottavio and I will be hanged."

"Would you stop being such a dramatic? You are worse than Stelle ever was." The words slipped out unbidden. Gwen held her breath as her heart stuttered but Nier replied without missing a beat.

"It won't matter! Ottavio and I are . . . ! You could do with a sense of danger—or even compassion for a start! Do you ever think of a person's interest in you as anything other than an invitation to be used? Did you spare a single thought for Ottavio's fate?"

"Why should I?" Gwen retorted coolly to disguise how deeply those words wounded her. After all the time they had known each other, after all he had seen of how

Ottavio and his kind treated her, what they thought of her—how *dare* he? She wished fervently that she had left him behind. "He could have said no if he had chosen. But he never does, just like all those stuck-up boys at court, because they are too eager to stay in favor with me. And why? To have my father's ear, or my sister's, through me—or even for my own proximity to the crown. They use *me*, so why is it wrong of me to use them in return?"

"Making them give you gifts and favors that will leave them a little poorer and disappointed is a far cry from getting one of them *hanged!*"

"If you don't mind me cutting in?" came a low voice from above.

Gwen and Nier looked up. Sitting on the eaves of one of the houses beside the road was a short man clothed in tattered brown robes. His dark hair was greasy, unevenly cut and stuck to his brown cheeks over an equally dark and greasy beard.

"If I may say so, this isn't the place for that. Anyone could hear you and reach certain conclusions. Now imagine if the one to hear you hadn't been one as magnanimous as me."

"Who are you?" asked Nier through gritted teeth.

"What do you want?" asked Gwen, smiling and straightening her back to show that she would not be cowed.

"I understand that you have a bag of black coins you can't use. I propose a trade."

"What sort of trade?" asked Gwen.

"Give me your hundred blacks. In return, I'll give you two hundred whites."

"That bargain is far too biased in your favor," Gwen

accused. "Each black is worth a hundred whites; surely you can offer better than that."

"Ah," said the stranger with a slow smile. "But you see, you have a hundred blacks that you can't use. Even an exchange of your hundred blacks for one white would be an advantage to you. I'm offering you two hundred whites. It's very generous, don't you think?"

"Not at all."

"Then again, I'm sure I could get even more if I ransomed you. A minister's son took a shine to you, did he? I wonder how much black he could get to save you?"

"You'll stay away from her," said Nier firmly, stepping in front of Gwen and brandishing his dagger. "You'll have to go through me first."

"Not much of a shield," the man remarked, turning his mocking eyes to Gwen. "Popular one, aren't you? Put that away, boy. You're no match for me. Besides, this ransoming business is more trouble than it's worth. Your hundred blacks in exchange for two hundred whites and my silence? It's an excellent deal."

"We accept," said Nier.

"Nier!" hissed Gwen. Nier did not react.

"Smart boy," grinned the man. "We'll make the exchange in the alcove on the western side of the main square when the moons touch."

"Why wait?" asked Gwen suspiciously.

The man looked at her. "You're quite something, darling. Perhaps your ransom would be worthwhile after all."

Nier brandished his knife again and Gwen fingered the hilt of a throwing knife concealed in her armband.

The man shook his head as he regarded them. "I don't

walk about with two hundred whites on my person. Meet me at the appointed time and you'll receive the coins I've promised."

The man stood and disappeared over the rooftops.

"You accepted," Gwen remarked after a moment. "Did you mean it?"

"I don't think we have a choice," sighed Nier. "If you would just think for a moment before you start talking—"

"You are *not* blaming this on me. What were you thinking, brandishing a knife at—"

"As for the rest, so long as I'm traveling with you, it's my responsibility to see that no harm comes to you."

"By inviting him to kill both of us? If you are going to be cannon fodder after all, you may as well act like intelligent cannon fodder. This meeting for the exchange—does it not have the makings of a trap?"

Nier spread his hands.

"We have a choice. We can either go and hope that he follows through with his side of the deal, or continue running around with a hundred blacks stolen from the king's treasury. Which would you choose?"

They stared at each other for a moment.

"I suppose we are going," concluded Gwen.

"I think I should go alone," said Nier.

Gwen glanced at the scrawny apprentice and snorted. "I am stronger."

"You should stay out of sight. If it goes well, that's that. If it doesn't, then run—you meant to make this journey by yourself on foot anyway. Just remember not to let anyone see you if you decide to walk the kingsway."

"I agree that we should not both blindly stumble into

what could be a trap," said Gwen, "but I should be the one to go."

"You can't be serious. If something happened to you-"

"I at least have some combat training—I stand a chance in a fight. And you, as you have pointed out time and again, know this side of the kingdom better than I, so if one of us must continue alone, you are the better choice. Promise me that you will, because I am not going to change my mind."

Nier closed his eyes for a moment. He opened them and looked Gwen straight in the eye. "I promise that if anything happens to you, I'll find the Phoenix or die trying."

Gwen believed him—for the first time that night, this was the Nier that she was used to. Her smile felt like a grimace. Silence fell between them. They passed two drunks, who shouted incomprehensible but unmistakably rude comments at both of them. The moons drew closer, and they parted ways at the square.

As Gwen crossed the dark square to the western edge, she tried to reconcile this quiet, empty space with the bustling market that she knew. She spotted a darker spot within the dark wall that was the alcove.

"I would have thought your beloved librarian in brittle armor wouldn't let you come alone." The man's voice cut through the silence. Gwen did not jump.

"He is not—" started Gwen, then stopped and narrowed her eyes as she glared into the dark. "Do you have the two hundred pieces of white?"

"Do you have the hundred pieces of black?" said a man-shaped shadow.

"You first."

"You're in no position to make demands."

Gwen hesitated for only a moment. "Yes. I have them."

"So do I. Place your bag on the ground. I'll do the same. Then we switch places."

Gwen placed the pouch of black on the ground. The shadow set a larger pouch down. The shadow straightened and so did Gwen. He stepped to the left and Gwen mirrored him so that they made a slow circle around the two pouches. She reached the other side of the circle; the shadow reached down to her sack and she did the same—

"*Wrong*," the voice came from behind her at the same moment as a pair of cold hands closed around her neck. She gasped for air, clawed at the hands, kicked at the person behind her—but to no avail. White and red flashed before her eyes. Darkness closed in and her chest and throat felt tighter and tighter, burning, choking.

Then she was free, crumpling to the ground and gasping for air through a raw throat. She scrambled away and the stone beneath her hands gave way to something soft and crumbly. She had backed into the pile left behind by the man-like figure. The feeling beneath her hands was familiar—*dirt*, she realized. The shadowed figure had been made of dirt.

She blinked and turned and her heartbeat quickened.

"You're a speaker," she rasped. "Seleukoi!"

"You assume I'm a speaker and therefore I must be Seleukoi," said the man, a smile in his voice. "I'd have expected more from someone seeking knowledge about the Words herself. I'm neither of those things."

"How did you—"

"How, indeed?" said the man. There was a smile in his voice but when he knelt in front of Gwen and proximity let her see his face through the darkness, his expression was deadly serious. "This time, you were lucky. You won't be this lucky again."

He stood and picked up the pouch of black. Gwen blinked after him.

"What, is that all?" she snapped. He stopped.

"Don't push your luck, darling."

"*Luck*? You are a speaker. You had me in your grasp but not only are you letting me go, you are leaving me the white! You expect me to accept this as simple good *luck*?"

The man spun around and knelt close to Gwen again.

"Your doubt now is the only wisdom I've seen in you tonight," the man whispered. "So I will tell you three things. First, there is no such thing as solitude or privacy, and names have power. Decide who you are and *be* that person until you believe it yourself. Learn to talk faster like us common folk, or don't talk at all. Second, your ability to survive is tied to your coins. Never let them off your person, not even when you rest. Third, you would serve yourselves well to make friends rather than enemies of those you meet—including speakers."

Gwen sat gaping at the man as he straightened. She knew she should hold her tongue. She pushed anyway.

"What are you?"

"A wizard, if you must know."

"You are one of my—one of the heir's—spies. She keeps speaker spies?"

"Again, for all you know, anyone could be listening, even if you aren't. You've made it easy to guess who you are. But it's nothing to me. Ignore my advice and meet a terrible end, for all I care." He jingled the pouch of black.

"This will be back in the treasury by morning. Tell the boy not to worry for the minister's son."

Then he melted into the darkness as if he had been a shadow all along. Gwen crawled over to the other bag and pulled it close. She tried to stand but her whole body was trembling and she couldn't make her muscles hold her weight.

Nier came running across the square towards her.

Gwen closed her eyes and calmed herself with a few deep breaths. Then she looked up at Nier. "Did you know that my sister had speaker spies?"

"Speaker spies?" Nier repeated, brow furrowed. "I wouldn't have thought she'd ever—"

"Neither did I," said Gwen, rising unsteadily to her feet.

"Are you telling me that he was her spy? And he was a *speaker*?"

Gwen quickly told him what had happened.

"But he said he wasn't a speaker?"

"He called himself a wizard. I read about this: speakers use word games like this to lie in truths. It makes no difference what he calls himself. The power is the same."

At least this explained Nicki's reluctance to realize that Stelle's death was because of the Words. If she admitted that, she would have to give up the power of having speakers under her command. But even Nicki clearly didn't trust them enough to use them in the army. No matter—Gwen accepted the truth, and so she would act. When she returned, she would take Nicki to task about using those who illegally learned the Words.

It was not long afterwards, after they had found a small inn nearby and rented a room for the night, that Gwen caught herself running her fingers through her hair and froze.

Golden hair was uncommon in Ceryll—anywhere on the continent, in fact. There were stories about a time when there had been light-skinned, light-haired people and dark-skinned, dark-haired people that warred for centuries. Those days were long gone. Now people could be dark or light or any shade in between and it was all the same. But lighter hair was uncommon, much less hair as gold as Gwen's. She had never given it much thought, but she realized now that it might be prudent to dye it. She went downstairs and acquired a tub of blackened water and scissors.

"What are you doing?" asked Nier, eyes widening.

"I told them that I needed to dye a dress black because I can't get a bloodstain out," said Gwen, deliberately avoiding answering the question.

"Blood? I thought we were trying not to draw attention to ourselves."

Gwen rolled her eyes. "There is a perfectly unremarkable reason why a dress might come to have a bloodstain on it."

She brushed out her hair roughly with her fingers, making sure that it was as straight as possible at the top. Then, hair to the back of her head, she closed the scissors on it without an instant's hesitation. Several snips later it was done.

"Was that necessary?"

"It was. If I must become someone else, I will use the Seleukoi name my mother gave me. I could never fool a speaker, calling myself Elle," she said darkly.

"I can scarcely refer to myself as such. It sounds too much like . . . like Stelle." She did not mean to stutter. She never had before; not when it had mattered. Not in all the times she had had to speak of her dead sister.

Nier breathed out slowly and heavily. Gwen could practically hear the questions.

"What? You may as well ask."

"I don't—It's just that you never talk about her. I know you've been in pain. If you want to talk. . . ."

Gwen turned her back on him. Now that the blame was the Words' and not Stelle's, maybe she could allow herself a little cry. She toyed with the idea and immediately discarded it. There would be time to grieve once the danger was past. Now, there were more important things.

"I do not. I will use my Seleukoi name."

"You have an Yngan name, too."

"We may need speakers' help, and I must be able to believe that I do not hate them. Only speakers have ever found the Phoenix, remember? A Seleukoi name ought to help. Now, this discussion ends here."

Nier shook his head as Gwen began lowering her head back into the basin. Afterwards, he took the scissors and trimmed her hair so it was somewhat straight.

A girl calling herself Xanthe left the inn in the morning, short black hair mostly hidden under a kerchief. No one batted an eye.

9

The Spy

Fifty-first day of summer,
452 A.D. – A town on no map, Ynga

THE TOWN ROSE out of the wasteland like a giant box. Buildings were packed together without a hair's breadth in between. Deric rode around the town and saw no sign of a road leading inward, much less any cultivated land. There were doors on some of the buildings. The side that faced the rainforest, however, was one solid stone wall. This suggested that the town was built by folk who feared the rainforest as much as Yngan folklore advised. The absence of fields suggested that the town provided some commodity for trade so valuable that they could expect to trade it for all necessary food and cloth.

Drawing closer, he grimaced as the foul smell of human waste became stronger. As he walked his horse past the wall on the rainforest side, a door opened that he had not previously seen. Deric pulled his horse to a stop as a figure cloaked in white emerged.

"Hello?" Deric called to him. The figure stopped and turned a hooded face in Deric's direction. Then he turned away to close the door and began walking toward the line of trees. Once closed, the door became indistinguishable from the wall around it.

"Hello?" Deric tried again as the figure walked across the barren yellow ground and into the trees. "I'm a traveler looking for shelter and—"

"You'd do better to go back the way you came," said the figure. He had a boy's voice.

"Wha—Who are you?"

"It doesn't matter. You're not a speaker, a merchant or a Unycan, and it's dangerous enough for us. You should leave."

Deric didn't know what a *unycan* was, but the boy was turning away and asking for a definition wouldn't stop him.

"Which are you?" he asked instead.

A sharp laugh came from under the hood. "You need to ask?"

"I don't have a lot to go on," Deric pointed out.

"Then I'll leave you to your imagination." The boy turned away.

"Wait," Deric called, but the boy broke into a run and disappeared into the trees.

Thinking better of following a boy who clearly didn't want to talk, Deric turned back to the wall instead. He looked for the stone door the boy had used. But there was no door that he could find, though he felt around and pushed at the wall. Eventually, he gave up and resumed his trek around the city.

On the side opposite the rainforest, Deric found a path just wide enough to fit a cart, under an arch between two buildings. The stones that lined this passageway were noticeably newer than those on the rest of the walls, like a section of the buildings had been knocked out to create this path.

Under the arch, dirt transitioned to cobblestone, and the silence and wind turned to the hustle and bustle of people and chickens rushing to and fro. This side smelled more of bird waste than human, and Deric found that far easier to tolerate. He tried to catch someone's eye or greet someone, but his attempts went unacknowledged. Only the covert glances directed his way assured Deric that they could in fact see him.

It didn't take long to get a feel for the town. It looked like it had been built all at once with no structure ever added or removed. The outer buildings formed a square from the inside just as they had from the outside, stone walls forming a fortress with huge oak doors and few windows. There was another inner square of buildings, more elegant and inviting, made of clay and wood, with engraved doors and many windows fitted with glass. Two paths led through the inner square of buildings to the most spacious town square Deric had ever seen. On this side, the walls were made entirely of black—not stacked bricks of black, but each side one enormous, perfectly shaped slab of black. Each wall was identical, except that on two sides the arches stood open to the paths that led to the main street; on the other two sides, one arch was filled by a magnificent ebony door and the other was filled in with ordinary stone. Three sides were covered in engravings that looked like they might be words, but used letters that Deric did not recognize. The wall with the ebony door had only four lines of engravings that formed two arcs over the door:

Pray to Ela for salvation and strength
Pray to Nevena to uphold the treaty
We are the last bastion against the Void
That would be our doom.

He stared. What was Ela? And what was the Void? Nevena's name was there, so perhaps those were other names for Nou and Nuray. Still, if so, which one was the Void? Anywhere else that Deric had ever been, that would be blasphemy.

"Hello, stranger," said a voice from behind Deric in a thick accent he'd never heard before. The man had a gruff manner and a head of wild hair and a matching bushy beard and mustache that made difficult any attempt at guessing his age. His pale skin and bright red hair were striking. But, Deric realized with a jolt as he looked around, pale skin and brightly colored hair seemed to be the norm. From the man's demeanor and voice, he must have been in his late thirties or early forties.

"Hello," said Deric, dismounting to be polite.

"I've never seen you before."

"I'm a traveler."

"Hm," said the man, a furrow between his brows. "Yngan?"

"Of course," lied Deric automatically. His heart leapt out of his chest. *No lies.* The man nodded, but it did nothing to soothe the heart pounding in Deric's throat. "Though my mother's mother was Ushani, and I never knew my father."

"Irrelevant," said the man, narrowing his eyes. "I asked only about you. Unyca's only visitors are merchants we recognize. So where did you come from?"

"Noucleion," said Deric. *Speakers, merchants and Unycans*, the boy had said. Did that mean the only visitors were speakers or merchants?

"And before Noucleion?"

"I—Pardon me, but why do you care?"

The man's brows rose. "We have a problem with witches."

"We all do in these times," Deric replied. "But why beat about the bush, when you could simply ask me to tell a lie?"

The man's eyes flashed. "Why would I do that?"

Deric blinked. "The law states that any man charged with witchcraft must be offered the opportunity to tell a lie."

"A man of learning," observed the man, eyes sharper than before. "But not a man of the world."

Deric furrowed his brow when the request for a lie didn't follow. "Should I tell you a lie?"

"You can if you like, but what would be the point? Why not give me a name to call you by instead?"

Hadn't they just discussed the point of a lie? "I'm Deric," he said.

"You can call me Melech," said the man. "Do you mean to stay for long?"

"For a little while I think, yes," said Deric cautiously.

"Be more specific. How long are you intending to stay? A few hours? A few days?"

"A few days at least."

"Hm," said Melech. "Well, I suppose you must have been traveling for days, and will have to travel several more to get to another town. Allow me to invite you to be my guest."

Deric drew his brows together. "Thank you, that's very gracious but I thought I'd just find an inn."

"You'll be disappointed."

"I don't need much space, and I have enough coins—"

"I understand, but Unyca has no use for inns or coins."

Deric blinked. This was unexpected, to say the least. But he gathered that Unyca was the name of the town. *Speakers, merchants and Unycans*, the boy had said. At least that implied that Unycans weren't speakers themselves.

"In that case," he said, seeing no other option, "I accept your invitation. Thank you."

Melech led him back out of the square and onto the street, to a door on the row of inner buildings. They secured Deric's horse by the reins to a post supporting the eaves.

Inside was a small carpeted room with a stove on one side and a stone bench on the other. In the middle stood a simple wooden table and four chairs. In the corner by the door, a steep staircase led to an upper floor. As Deric was about to close the door behind him, a young boy maybe five years old pushed through without an upward glance. Deric blinked as the boy scuttled over to take a seat on the corner of the bench, where he sat and stared eerily at Deric. His features were noticeably different from those of Melech, including his darker skin and brown hair, but his eyes and mannerisms were so like the man that there was no mistaking that this was his son.

"I'm sure you would prefer to wash." Melech indicated a far corner of the room where there was a barrel of clean water, a wash basin and a chamber pot. Deric obliged, taking the opportunity to change into a slightly fresher outfit from his saddlebag. When he finished, the boy was still staring from the bench, and Melech was sitting at the table with two steaming clay mugs.

"For me?" Deric asked. Melech nodded and he took the offered seat and mug, his back to the boy. The mug held a colorless, vaguely cloudy drink. Deric took a slow sip, ignoring the scrutinizing gazes of Melech and the boy. It was sweet, but with a sharp tang.

"Delicious. Mint and honey?"

"Yes. Now, if you don't mind—who told you about this town?"

"No one. I found it on my own."

Melech's eyes narrowed. "You decided to wander out into a barren wasteland and just happened upon this town? I find that hard to believe."

Deric inclined his head. He could answer that honestly. "I've been mapping trade routes into Noucleion. I talk to traders about their wares and their routes. I visited some of the towns that are major centers of trade as well. I wanted to figure out where each resource was found and create a report on the subject for the king."

Deric's heart pounded. He had based his trade map primarily on maps made by other men with more time, but Melech had no reason to ask about that. He also had no reason to ask *which* king Deric served.

"Whatever for?"

"Any Yngan can become a member of court if he proves himself worthy."

"So you thought you'd impress the king with a pretty paper that showed you knew something about his kingdom better than anyone?"

Deric averted his eyes and didn't answer. He hoped he looked bashful. His heart almost stopped as he hoped fervently that Melech wouldn't wait for a verbal response.

"How does Unyca come into it?"

Deric met Melech's eyes. "Have you ever heard of the black?"

Melech's brow furrowed. "The black?"

"I've also heard it called shine, stone, arale—"

"Ah, of course. The lyll. Naturally."

Deric blinked. It sounded very much like *liles*, a curse common in Ceryll and Amberria. He went on, hoping he had not betrayed his surprise. "Yes. It's a remarkable thing. It can't be worked with any known tool. It's always sold in the shape of bricks, tiles, shingles, blades, arrowheads or coins. The pieces are indestructible. In olden days, there must have been people capable of engraving it, but now—"

"Yes, yes, I know all this. Isn't it common knowledge in Noucleion?"

"Of course it is. But no one questions it. No one knows where it comes from, except that it is mined in Ynga. The merchants who are known to sell it offer explanations akin to fairy stories; I couldn't get a straight answer out of any of them. But they all also deal in wares found in western Ynga. I traveled for a time among the western towns, but couldn't figure out where the lyll came from. Then

I thought about the wasteland. Of course, crops can't be grown in the wasteland so it's not a place where anyone would live—unless they have a commodity so precious that it could be traded for all necessities."

"So you guessed that there might be a town hidden in the wasteland. Why so fixated on the lyll? Surely your report would be valuable enough without it."

"What use is a trade report that doesn't account for the highest valued commodity?"

Melech sat back, gazing upwards. At last he sat up and looked Deric in the eye.

"Tell me that you don't sympathize with witches."

"I don't," Deric said emphatically. "If I knew how to fight them, I would."

"And you're not a merchant?"

"What? No."

Melech's eyes flickered away for a moment.

"Stop looking for the lyll mine. The closer you get to finding it, the less likely you'll make it back alive."

Deric raised his eyebrows. "You expect me to simply give up because you told me I was wrong? I've found a town that's on no map, that can't possibly sustain itself."

"Yes. You've found a town. No more, no less. You're free to look about, but you would do better to take my word and leave. You will not find any mine, I promise you that."

"I don't believe that. It's the only explanation. I have every reason to believe that the mine is nearby."

Melech regarded Deric. "What if I told you that I had a way for you to win your way into the king's good graces without your trade report?"

"I . . . can't say I'd believe you."

Melech sat back and folded his arms.

"You said it yourself: lyll is indestructible. How does one mine the indestructible?"

"Specialized tools?" Deric played dumb. He knew the answer. It was why he had begun the "trade report" farce.

"*Witchcraft*," said Melech.

Deric waited, heart racing. When Melech only looked at him expectantly, he nodded as if this was only just occurring to him. "But if the mine isn't here, what does it have to do with you?"

"We are middlemen."

"Trading with whom? Surely not the Ushani?"

Melech laughed. "No. We trade with the rainfolk."

"The rainfolk?" Deric only knew the phrase from folk tales to frighten children, tales of monstrous creatures that lived in the rainforest and took human-like forms when they emerged to lure children into their domain to be devoured.

He thought of the white-cloaked figure he had encountered. Then he shook the thought from his head. Surely he and Melech were both too old to believe such nonsense.

"But surely you don't believe those stories. If they were true, why would Unyca be so close to the rainforest?"

"We live here because our town is here, and always has been. As far as we are concerned, the rainfolk appear on fixed days out of the year. We trade, and they leave. We never ask where they come from or where they go. No one had ever seen them arrive or leave."

"And . . . something changed?"

"Yes. Some of us saw them returning into the rainforest after the last trade. We know now."

"Just because they were walking into the rainforest?" Deric shook his head. "But couldn't they just as well be regular folk from a mining town in the rainforest, as far as you know?"

"No. The rainforest is a place of witchcraft. If they come and go from there, then they're unnatural."

Deric decided it best not to mention that he had hunted and camped in the rainforest as he had traveled in search of Unyca. "Yet . . . you're in allegiance?"

"No. We're *dependent*."

"I don't understand what you're trying to say, or what you want me to do."

"Help me capture them. Prove to the Unycans that they are witches, put them to trial and burn them. The capture of witches will bring you into favor with the king and you needn't mention that the lyll was involved at all. You could bring one to Noucleion alive, if you need the proof. Do this, and you'll have my blessing to stay in Unyca as long as you like."

"Wouldn't that destroy Unyca?"

"Yes. Knowing that the lyll comes from witches, we will all abandon Unyca. We'll join other Yngan towns far from the rainforest. All will be as it should always have been."

Deric considered this. *Speakers, merchants and Unycans,* the boy had said. *Can't you tell?* Melech's reasoning made sense. But it was too convenient. There had to be a catch. He did not have to pretend to lack enthusiasm. "Why do you not simply leave with your own family?"

Melech glared. "I'm not a selfish man. I'm not trying

to save myself. I revile any influence witches have over Unycans. Some agree with me, but not enough. I could not live with myself if I saved myself and my son and a few friends and abandoned the rest."

"Admirable," Deric remarked. "But I'm a complete stranger. Why would you trust me with something so important to you?"

"Because you've told me nothing but the truth."

Melech said this calmly. He was certain as no ordinary man could ever be of another. Deric's pulse raced.

"How do you know?"

"Because Dov would have heard you lie," Melech said with a gesture behind Deric.

He stared blankly for a moment, then he turned to look back at the boy, who was still staring at him. Deric had forgotten about him. Then comprehension dawned.

"He's a—"

"Do *not* liken him to their kind!" Melech cut him off before Deric could utter the word *witch*. "He only hears lies; he is the anti-witch! Our witch hunter, as the taipan is to the king!"

Deric stared at Melech.

"Do not assume that just because this place is remote, I am naive. I know the world outside as well as you do. Now, do you accept or not?"

Deric wished he could share in the certainty that the other man was telling the truth. Perhaps he was still reeling from the revelation when he responded.

"If I refuse?"

Deric expected a threat. Instead Melech's whiskers shivered and his eyes crinkled in a smile.

"Why would you? Give me one good reason."

"It's dangerous. I would be making an enemy of speakers." The more familiar term slipped out, but Melech did not seem to notice.

"You rode out into the wasteland, to the border of the rainforest on nothing but a hunch. You know that witches are the enemy already. You're not one to shirk from danger."

"No," Deric admitted.

"Do you want to fight witchcraft?"

"Of course."

"Then what's stopping you?"

Deric slid his eyes back to Melech with a smile. "Very well. I will join you. But on one condition: we won't simply burn them. We'll have a trial."

Melech's eyebrows furrowed. "We'll demand that they tell a lie. If they refuse, that should be evidence enough."

"If I'm doing this, then I want more evidence than that."

There was a moment's silence. "I give you my word that I will let you do as you please until they are proven to be witches."

They had reached an accord.

Melech led Deric and his horse to the stable: one of the buildings on the outer square of stone buildings, whose door was not the large oak door-shaped segment, but rather a heavy stone door that Deric didn't see a few steps away from the door-like segment of wall. It was only his ten years of military training that alerted Deric to the man pretending not to be standing guard near the door. As they passed the man, Deric tensed, but the man made no move to stop them. Inside, there must have been thirty stalls, but only five were occupied, including the one where they put

Deric's horse. There were two mules and a donkey, and a magnificent, almost luminously white stallion with chains around its legs and neck.

"Why do you chain the horse?" asked Deric as he untacked his horse. The stallion gave a whinny that sounded indignant.

"We can't control the beast," said Melech.

"Then why not put it down?" The stallion made a sound like a growl at this. Deric shook his head. Clearly he'd been out in the sun too long.

"He's only a horse," Melech shrugged. "Its owner is the one we'll punish."

Deric wouldn't have dared to respond to that, even if he could have thought of something to say. He pitied the poor soul in this forsaken town who'd bought a horse without knowing how to train it.

"I could help you train it, if you like," Deric said. "I used to work in the stables when I was a boy."

Melech gave him a sideways look. "Maybe," he said after a long moment of silence. "Let me think about it."

That evening they had a simple dinner of chicken and potatoes, during which Melech lectured Dov (and maybe Deric; he wasn't quite sure if this was supposed to be a lesson for him too) about the greed and evil of witches and merchants. After dinner, Melech and Dov went to bed upstairs. A bed made of spare blankets draped over the stone bench had been prepared for Deric. Though he was exhausted, it took Deric a long while to sleep. When at last he slept, his dreams were filled with witches, merchants and pyres and Dov's blank, innocent stare fading into flames.

10

The Wizard

Before dawn, eleventh day of spring,
452 A.D. – Castle Dio, Ceryll

L EAVING THE FOOL princess to almost certainly get
herself killed, Theirn walked back to Castle Dio.
Both moons were behind the clouds, shrouding
the world in almost total darkness when he reached the
western castle wall. He found the grating at the base of
the wall, where the third bar from the right was left loose.
Theirn pulled out the bar, slipped through the gap, and
replaced it. His breathing sounded loud in the darkness as
he darted across the gap toward the shelter of the garden.

There was a shout, then an arrow whizzed past his
head. Thinking quickly, Theirn spun around and held up
his hands.

"I come in peace!" he shouted. "Don't shoot!"

It came as a surprise when he was grabbed from behind
in a chokehold. Despite the shock, Theirn managed to
refrain from retaliating. Right now, Theirn did not know
how many guards he would have to contend with, and he

had no interest in dying by an arrow he didn't see coming. He only offered token resistance as his wrists were bound behind him.

"Keep ahold of him, Hervé," came a woman's even voice from behind him. "And follow me."

Theirn was yanked around to the sight of a young woman in an elegant gown and flowing black hair. He had never seen her before, but he recognized her at once.

"Highness," he gasped, as the guard's—Hervé's—arm tightened around his neck.

"Hello," said the heir conversationally, standing under the arch of ivy at the entrance to a garden. As Hervé dragged Theirn closer, she whispered something to one of the half-dozen guards around her. When she turned and walked further into the garden, none of the guards followed. Even after Hervé dragged Theirn through the arch, the guards stood unmoving just outside.

Theirn's heart pounded. He knew that he had done the right thing by not revealing his abilities. Overcoming one guard and a princess would be no difficulty at all.

They turned a corner. Hedges now hid them from the other guards. Theirn knocked the heir and Hervé off their feet with a force field. He turned to run—but his arms and legs became tangled in a plant that he hadn't noticed. He fell to the ground. Trapped face-down on the ground, Theirn summoned a blade-like wind to cut through the ropes at his wrists, freeing himself. He struggled out of the vines, but they only seemed to pull tighter.

The heir and Hervé were recovering, so Theirn blasted the plant with a force field and ran. Yet he couldn't go fast or far. Everywhere he turned, he seemed to walk into tangles of branches and vines that had not been there before.

He finally emerged into a clearing with a magnificent oak.

Beneath the oak sat Ambassador Zephyr in the grass, legs crossed and eyes closed.

"You're late," said the ambassador without opening his eyes.

"I'm sorry," panted Theirn, still trying to disentangle himself from vines.

"You met Nicole, I see," the ambassador said mildly. He still wasn't opening his eyes.

"Of course he did. Did you expect to use *my* garden as you please?" The heir's voice came from behind Theirn. He stiffened, but the ambassador was smiling, eyes still closed.

"You don't even know what this garden is."

"Of course I do. Neither you nor your man will be able to leave unless I permit it."

Theirn looked down at the vines once again wrapped around his ankles. Of course it wasn't natural. "What sorcery is this?" he croaked, but neither the ambassador nor the heir reacted. There was no sign of Hervé.

"What is he?" demanded the heir. "He uses a power that I have never seen."

"You have never seen any power but mine and this garden's," said the ambassador, opening his eyes at last. "And even these you barely understand."

"You know that I will not give you what you want," snapped the heir.

"Then your ignorance will be your downfall. Theirn!"

The ambassador barked his name, and Theirn stood at attention. "Come here and touch this tree."

Theirn prepared to shake the vines from his ankles, but they were already receding. He walked past the ambassador and touched the tree.

He was overcome by a strange sensation: something was rushing through his blood, making him feel more *present* than he ever had. It filled some place inside his mind where he had never felt anything before, that he had not realized existed. Startled, Theirn jerked back.

"Try using your power now, Theirn," drawled the ambassador. Theirn's blood went cold.

He tried to summon a wind, a force field, to gather up the soil with his mind, *anything* . . . to no avail. It was gone.

"What . . . what have you done to me?" he whispered, cold sweat running down his face. But when he turned, the ambassador was fixing the heir with a hard stare. She was tense and wide-eyed.

"If you keep playing with things that you don't understand, one day you will find yourself out of your depths."

"Why did you bring him here?" she whispered.

"Show her, Theirn."

But Theirn was too busy searching for any remaining crumb of his former power to obey.

"Theirn!"

Jolted back into his surroundings, Theirn unhooked the pouch of black coins from his belt with shaking hands. He handed it to the ambassador, who tossed it to the heir.

"What is this?" she asked, looking inside.

"From the treasury."

The heir froze. "How did you—"

"Your sister might think she was being clever, but Ottavio has a big mouth and a loud voice. Not the best choice for discretion. You might want to have a few words with him."

"Ottavio . . . the minister's son? Why would . . . ?" the heir trailed off, expressions flickering across her face too rapidly to identify. "How is she?"

Theirn didn't realize that the question was directed at him until he found himself under two steely stares.

"She's—very naive, but I left her with some advice that will hopefully help her make better choices in the—I've done everything you've asked," Theirn collapsed to his knees, shaking, and broke into a plea in spite of himself. "Please, ambassador, whatever you've done—undo it. I can't . . . I can't. . . ."

"You were never going to go free, not once Nicole found you," the ambassador responded coolly. "You should have been more cautious. I can't save you now."

The heir yanked him to his feet. She was surprisingly strong.

"Have mercy," Theirn whispered. "I've helped your sister—I've done nothing to—"

"You served the Seleukoi ambassador in my castle. That is treason." Her voice was as cold as her eyes.

Theirn looked to where the ambassador had been to plead his case, but he was gone.

11

The Scribe

Twelfth day of spring, 452 A.D. – Nirra, Ceryll

X ANTHE SAT ON an empty discarded crate while Nier negotiated with another graying, portly caravan master. She looked around for any distraction. Her gaze stopped on another girl perhaps a few years younger, clothed in rags, seated on a crate on the other side of the square and looking as bored as Xanthe felt. Maybe she, too, had been banished to the edge of the square for speaking out of turn. A passerby tossed the girl something that landed on the ground in front of the crate. The girl bent down, picked it up and pocketed it before returning to her perch on the crate. Surprised, Xanthe strained for a better view across the square.

"Liles, another beggar," someone said. But the girl was only sitting there. Xanthe had always imagined that a beggar was someone who begged.

Something came flying out of the air at Xanthe. Instinctively, she ducked. The clinking sound of the object hitting the ground drew her attention. It was a violet.

She stared at the violet then at the people around her, bewildered. Then she realized—*she* had been mistaken for a beggar.

Well, a coin was a coin, she supposed. Xanthe bent to pick up the violet.

When she turned back to Nier, he was on his way back, already nearly across the square. She turned her glare back on. He raised an eyebrow.

"Did I just see you pick up a violet?"

"Someone threw it at me."

Nier's eyes flashed. "Leave it; we don't need it. It's beneath your dignity to—"

"Liles, we are—we're spending our coins so quickly. There is no harm in accepting what came freely thrown. How did negotiations go?"

"He'll take us to Farthe for a dozen whites per person; as far as Milleport for two and a half dozen. Five dozen whites total. Perfect, don't you think?"

It was. They only had to make it to the Dantes and back across the border. Once they had the Phoenix and were back in Ceryll, they did not have to travel all the way back to Dio. Xanthe could go to the royal residence in any of the Ten Cities and the staff would contact her family. Still, if they could make it to the Dantes on a hundred of their two hundred whites, they were sure not to get stranded.

"I suppose it's not anything new for me to sit in the background twiddling my thumbs."

Nier fixed her with a hard look. "You wouldn't've had to today if you could be silent."

Xanthe channeled all her ire into her eyes and narrowed

them. "I asked one question, Nier. *One question.* It was a perfectly sensible question and you know it."

"Yes, but that's not the point."

"The point is what, then? That I'm supposed to forever behave as though I have no mind and no sense? Lovely to know that wherever I go, I'm only to be a face and a dress."

"It's just not done among caravan masters," said Nier emphatically. "Your *one question* set his mind against us. Thank goodness he didn't talk more than he did, because otherwise there might not have been a single caravan willing to take us with them."

"You are dramatizing."

"No," Nier gave a frustrated huff, and the pleading in his eyes only fanned the flames all the more. But anything else he might have said was cut short.

"You there!" came a voice. They turned and saw a guard running towards them.

"Keep your head down and *don't talk*," Nier hissed out of the corner of his mouth. "How can we help you, sir?" he addressed the guard.

"A shopkeeper says his wares were stolen by a girl with short black hair. What's your name, girl?"

"Xanthe," she responded, keeping her face downturned. It felt unnatural, and it surprised her when the guard didn't immediately tell her to look up.

"A Seleukoi name," the guard growled. "I suppose you have your papers, girl?"

"Papers? I was born in Nirra." This was not an obstacle she had foreseen.

"Hmph, and your parents gave you a Seleukoi name?"

Xanthe didn't respond.

"Sir," Nier interrupted. "Her parents are dead. I was apprenticed to her father, and I can vouch for her."

"You were apprenticed to a Seleukoi?"

"No, it was her mother with Seleukoi blood. Her father was as Ceryllan as they come."

"So what did you learn from this man who married a Seleukoi? Smithing? Cobbling?" The guard snorted derisively.

"I'm a scribe, sir."

"Really," said the guard flatly.

"Yes, sir."

"Show me."

Xanthe looked sideways at Nier. He was glancing around. He stopped on a stone at the side of the road and made a beeline for it.

"Follow him, girl," said the guard, so she did. The guard followed after her.

Nier ran a finger along the edge of the stone. It came away white with dust, leaving behind a gleaming path.

He wrote out the first three lines of *The Continental History* in the dust with his littlest finger:

The history of this continent is marked by three major landmark events. Very little is known of the first two— the southern and western migrations—but the third, the northern invasion, is well documented. Because every historical event since the northern invasion has, in some way, been affected by that invasion, it is assumed that the southern and western migrations must have had a similar impact on the world that we know today.

"What's that say?" asked the guard. Nier read it out. "And how do I know you're telling the truth? How do I know you didn't just scribble nonsense in the dust there?"

"How can I prove it to you if you can't read?"

"I suppose I'll just have to arrest you for thievery."

"You can't do that," Xanthe snapped, meeting the guard's eyes at last. He blinked at her as though surprised. "You are tasked with *protecting* the people of this city. You cannot accuse one of thievery and make an arrest without a shred of evidence! Have you never heard of the judicial system?"

The guard stared at her for a moment. Then his eyes slid over to Nier.

"She talks like. . . ."

"Her father wanted to raise her into a lady."

"Must've been overprotective as anything. Raised on ideals and shut away from the real world, was she?"

"Till the day he died."

"So did he make you marry her, or what?"

"Something like that."

"My sympathies. At least she's nice to look at."

"Thank you. I promise you she hasn't stolen anything. Feel free to search us."

Xanthe's face flamed. Her blood boiled when the guard grabbed her by the arm and started feeling around her skirts as though she might be hiding something in its folds. She held back her urge to elbow him in the neck and knee him in the face.

"Aren't you even going to tell us what was stolen?" she asked instead.

"None of your business, dearie," said the guard, and his hands came up to wander around her bodice.

"That's quite enough!" snapped Xanthe, stepping out of his reach. "I can't possibly be concealing anything there."

"Just had to check to be safe," leered the guard. "You're not hiding anything. You're free to go, on account of my sympathy for your husband. He's got enough grief without having to deal with a wife in jail for public nuisance."

"Thank you," said Nier quickly, pinching Xanthe in the arm to stop her from the outburst at the tip of her tongue. *Public nuisance!* "Thank you so much."

They left. Once they were out of his sight and earshot, Nier apologized profusely. Xanthe only shook her head. Her belly burned with fury. If she spoke now, she would berate Nier.

"I think I should go by Aysel after all," Xanthe muttered, almost to herself. "I did n—didn't foresee the problems a Seleukoi name might present."

Nier shook his head. "I told the caravan master your name was Xanthe. We leave town tomorrow. It won't help to change your name every time there's trouble."

Xanthe bit her lip. There were too many thoughts, too loud. She wanted to scream.

"I don't much like people," she admitted at last. "Men especially."

Nier didn't respond.

That night, Xanthe lay on the cot in contemplation long after Nier's breathing evened out. She had always thought that status and rankings were an arbitrary system of the royal court, quaint and irrelevant to ordinary people. Instead, social strata dictated how the world operated from top to bottom. Those who served were submissive to those whom they served whether in a palace or an inn; common folk submitted without complaint to the abuse of guards. It made her question the dynamics of her friendship with Nier. Was he truly her friend, or was he just serving his princess, letting her play friend with him?

Xanthe sat up and looked down at Nier. Soft snores were coming from his form, curled up on the floor. She softly swung her legs off the cot and approached him. He did not stir as she crouched by his head. She regarded the way he curled into his cloak, trying to make it cover him as well as provide some cushioning from the floor. Every previous morning, his speech had been slurred with the chill. Xanthe had not thought twice about it. Now she wondered at her own callousness.

She took their one blanket from the cot and covered him. She curled up to fit beneath her own cloak. It was coarser than the blanket, but probably better than what Nier had been contending with the past few nights. She curled up and closed her eyes. Eventually, sleep took her.

* * *

When she woke, her teeth immediately began to chatter. Nier was bent over her, concern written across his face. Their room was dark and the inn was still and silent around them in a way that she had not yet experienced. Xanthe sat up slowly, stiff from the cold. She sneezed.

"Why did you give me the blanket?" Nier murmured, wrapping it back around her and rubbing her hands between his vigorously. "You're freezing."

Xanthe took comfort in his concern, but couldn't bear to show it.

"You were shivering too loudly." Her voice came out sounding snappish. "Should we be leaving?"

"No need to rush."

"But it would be prudent," she said, shedding the blanket.

They bundled up their packs and exited the inn. As they were on their way out, Nier slipped into the kitchen and returned with the innkeeper's wife.

"You're off, then?" she said cheerily. "Take these. First batch of bread's just out of the oven." And she handed Nier two small bread rolls. "Wish you a good journey."

"Thank you," smiled Nier as he handed Xanthe one of the rolls.

"Thank you," Xanthe added hastily after the innkeeper's wife. As they headed out into the street, she eyed him quizzically. "Did you arrange that?"

"No. Just a kind gesture," he smiled. "Restored your faith in people, did it?"

"A little," Xanthe admitted, taking a bite of the warm, soft bread. A fresh cloud of steam rose into the air.

There was a person here or there—pulling a cart or running somewhere or slumped drunkenly against a building—but for the most part the street was deserted and quiet. The light before the dawn was beginning to illuminate the city, however, and Xanthe could see with no difficulty. She looked up and saw one of the moons still high in the sky, and sighed—and watched the cloud of her breath fade against the sky.

Despite what they had considered to be an early start,

by the time that they reached the square where the caravan was settled on the outskirts of the city, they found that they were the stragglers.

"Finally," said the man Nier had spoken to the day before. "I thought you might not show up, after all."

"Apologies for making you wait," said Nier.

"No need! We were just finishing securing the merchandise. This is the lady, I take it? Fine lass. She can travel with my daughter. Dea!" A servant girl, perhaps around age twelve, came scuttling around one of the wagons. "This girl'll be traveling with us. Take her to Cecil's wagon." Dea beckoned to her.

Xanthe glanced at Nier, who gave her a tiny shrug, so she turned to follow the girl. She was led to a wagon down the line. A pretty, well-dressed, pale-skinned, brown-haired girl looked up from inside. She looked perhaps fourteen or fifteen; older than Dea, but younger than Xanthe.

The girl looked Xanthe up and down. "Who are you?"

"Xanthe. I—My companion and I are joining your caravan to Milleport. He made arrangements with the head of the caravan yesterday."

The brunette glanced at Dea, who nodded. "The master told me she'd be traveling in our wagon."

The girl was frowning. "Xanthe is a strange name. Your family's from the east?"

Xanthe gulped. *Lie in truths*, she reminded herself.

"My grandmother on my mother's side was Seleukoi."

"Unfortunate. But you've been raised Ceryllan?"

"Yes," said Xanthe helplessly.

"Lovely," she smiled. "I'm Cecil. The caravan master is

my father, but of course there's no need to treat me special. Maybe we can even be friends."

Xanthe blinked. "Yes, a friend would be nice," she admitted.

"So, who's your young man? Is he handsome?"

Xanthe stared at Cecil and wondered if this was the sort of conversation she would be enduring for the rest of the season. "I . . . cannot say as to handsome."

"Don't be modest. Dea?"

The servant girl rolled her eyes. "He was hardly deformed or disfigured. Nothing to be ashamed of."

"Handsome, then. How did you meet?"

"She called him not deformed and you understood handsome?"

"Dea considers large ears a deformity."

Xanthe turned and regarded Dea. It was true that the girl was more fortunate in the shape and symmetry of her features than most. With different parentage, she could have been the Beauty of Dio. Even so. . . . "Do you not consider that a little excessive?"

"Not at all. When they marry me off, I'll have to spend the rest of my years looking at a man who's less than perfect. I complain while I can."

"Surely you'll get some say," Xanthe protested.

Cecil laughed condescendingly. "My, you must be lucky! A handsome man *and* the right to choose! It's different for us. I'll be married off at my father's convenience. Dea too, unless she wants to find herself on the streets with no work and no prospects."

Xanthe shook her head. "I do understand that. My marriage is—was—subject to my father's choice, too. But I always had a right to say no. *Legally* we all have the right to say no! There are laws that give us that right."

"Someone ought to tell the men. They've never heard a word of it. And if they have, they've forgotten. Who'll stop them from doing with us as they please?"

Xanthe was reminded of the scornful expression on the guard's face when she mentioned the judicial system the previous day. The awkward silence was broken when the wagon jerked into motion, tossing Cecil back into conversation.

"How did you and your young man come to be together, then? Surely you didn't elope?"

"He is not my young man," Xanthe protested.

"Then how are you traveling together?"

"He and I are scribes. We were apprenticed together. Our master died, and we chose to seek work elsewhere."

"Oh," Cecil sighed, leaning back. "Is that all? But surely you intend to marry?"

"No."

"Then who will you marry? Will you seek out other scribes?"

Scribes must marry other scribes, Xanthe interpreted. Would the onslaught of nonsense never cease? If that were a commonly accepted truth, she felt certain that she would have known. Memories of unmarried scribes in Dio gave her confidence. She took a breath, smiled as best she could, and set about explaining to the bewildered girls that scribes did not have to marry; that even if they did, their spouse did not have to be another scribe.

*   *   *

The guards did not inspect the caravan at the city gates at all, and Xanthe concealed her relief. Any facial expression was an invitation for conversation to Cecil and Dea.

To Xanthe's shock, Cecil explained at lunch time that they were not expected to leave their wagon at all, except to relieve themselves. This was Cecil's norm; Dea brought their plates at mealtimes, and took them away when they were done.

"We could take a walk together at some of the more scenic points," Cecil conceded at Xanthe's distress. But she went on to say that the first point was "only" a few days away.

At the end of a day filled with inane prattle, Xanthe was overjoyed when Nier showed up at Cecil's wagon with two steaming mugs.

"Xanthe?" he called, but she was up and at his side before he had called her. She flashed an apology and a "back soon" at Cecil and Dea's gaping faces and hopped out.

"I'm just taking her for a short walk," Nier said to Cecil with a wry smile. "If I know her at all, she's half mad from staying put all day."

"Yes," Cecil squeaked, turning a comical shade of red. It occurred to Xanthe that Nier was perhaps not supposed to be speaking to her. She pulled him away by the elbow. His attention returned to her and he handed her a mug. The mug was made crudely of thick metal and she had to wrap her sleeves around her hands to hold it. She welcomed the heat anyway.

"How are you doing?"

"Bored to madness. You?" she asked with her sweetest

smile. Nier had the grace to wince. He glanced around and lowered his voice.

"Believe it or not, this is our best chance of making it safely down to the coast."

"I believe it. I will endure it. Those two girls haven't a sensible thought in their bodies. Not that I blame them, living in a wagon while the course of their lives is decided by the caravan master's whims."

Nier shrugged helplessly. "It's how things are done. It isn't like this everywhere."

Xanthe chewed on the inside of her cheek, her thoughts suddenly paralleling those from the previous night. "What was it like where you grew up?"

Nier blinked. "I . . . there's not much to say. My father was a caravan master. I used to travel with his caravan for most of the year."

Xanthe's heart dropped into the pit of her stomach. "You said—this is a thing that only caravans do. The—not allowing women to be involved in anything."

"I don't know if it's *only* caravans. I certainly know that there are plenty of townsfolk who look with pity on womenfolk in caravan families."

"Your background was . . . fortunate for us." Xanthe swallowed and attempted a smile. "Though I do hope that the situation will change once we reach Milleport."

"Oh, I have it on good authority that it will," Nier assured her. "Milleport is a town of ideals. I hear that the whole city celebrated for a week when Princess Nicole was declared heir to the throne."

Gwen had known Milleport and its ideas better than the bigotry that was apparently a staple of life in Nirra.

But Xanthe knew nothing beyond a sheltered life shielded even from the unpleasantness of Nirra, so she listened. "You spent time there as a child?"

"No," Nier's mouth twisted. "My father avoided that city—for exactly that reason, I imagine." Then he smiled again. "But if these folk travel to Milleport regularly, I suspect you'll find them far more palatable than run-of-the-mill caravan folk!"

"But you—you grew up in a caravan like this." She was stuck on this thought.

He sighed. "Yes. I must have been among the womenfolk when I was younger, but I have no memory of it. Mostly I remember tagging along after my father. I rode on his horse in front of him, or beside the driver of the main merchandise wagon. He didn't pay me much heed, but I thought that his opinion was all that mattered. I think—looking back, I think I probably had a sister, but I'm not sure."

"How can you not be sure?"

"I hardly ever saw my mother. It was how my father preferred to run things, keeping the separation as complete as possible. Less distraction that way, he thought."

"And then you came to—" Xanthe swallowed and caught herself in time. "To my father's house."

"Yes," smiled Nier. "And things were different there. I learned a great deal more than my apprenticeship was designed to teach me."

"I can only imagine."

After a moment of silence, he spoke again. "We should get back before they take offense."

Xanthe knew that he was right. Still she yearned to protest that it had hardly been any time at all.

"But are you all right? Truly?" he asked her.

No. No, she was not. She was trapped in a wagon all day and all night. Useless in her own mission.

"Of course," she smiled. A gust of wind caught her in the back and she stumbled a few steps forward.

That night, she hardly slept. Instead she listened past Cecil and Dea's breathing to the movements of the guards keeping watch outside. What sleep she did manage was shallow and uncomfortable, filled with whispers that she could not remember when she woke.

Oh, my child. You are perfect. You are mine. Soon we will never be caged again.

12

The King

After dawn, eleventh day of spring,
452 A.D. – Castle Dio, Ceryll

JUSTE CAME TO a halt before the cell that had been empty the previous day. The new occupant was curled up into a ball. Juste banged on the bars, and the man jerked to his feet, looking around wildly.

"Your—Your Majesty," he croaked.

"Tell me your name," Juste ordered.

"Theirn, Majesty."

"Tell me about my daughter."

"Wh—which one?"

"The one who is *missing*," snapped Juste. "Or do you need more information?"

"I . . . I only did as I was told. I found her, and exchanged the bag of black she had stolen from your treasury for a bag of whites."

"Who told you to do this?"

The prisoner choked, eyes wide with terror. Juste had no patience for this.

"Tell me!" he barked.

"It was . . . it was . . . I'm so sorry, Your Majesty, I didn't think-"

The prisoner's fear gave him away.

"It was Princess Nicole," Juste said quietly, knowing that it was true.

The prisoner choked and emotions flashed across his face. At last, he nodded jerkily.

"And how is Princess Gwenaëlle?"

"I . . . I think she seemed well, Your Majesty, I—"

That was all he needed to hear. Juste stormed across Dio and into his eldest daughter's chambers.

"Wake up!" he barked at the bed when she did not immediately arise.

"Father?" said Nicole groggily. "What are-"

"Apparently I am missing yet another daughter this morning."

Nicole sat up, blinking sleep out of her eyes, but did not yet have the presence of mind to even fake surprise.

"What have you done?"

"You cannot possibly hold *me* responsible for Gwen—"

"Do *not* tell me what I can and cannot do!"

"This is ridiculous," snapped Nicole, swinging her legs out of bed. "Do you hold me responsible for Stelle, too? Am I to blame for Mother's death, perhaps?"

"You cannot guilt me into oblivion," said Juste coolly. "I know my daughters. Gwen understands obedience. She would never have followed in Stelle's footsteps unless one of us urged her to do so. What did you think you were doing?"

"Father—"

"Do not *Father* me," growled Juste. "I have indulged your secrets and your whims, but this is too far."

"You cannot believe that *I*—"

"Hervé came to me this morning."

Nicole snapped her mouth shut. Juste gave her a moment to explain herself, but she did not.

"Can you explain to me why he spent last night lost in your mother's garden?"

"I could not say. Perhaps he was tired."

"Why is there a new prisoner, who Hervé tells me wields unnatural powers?"

"I arrested him."

"In the middle of the night? What were you doing in the gardens?"

"I received word that—"

"From *whom?* Why did you not come to me?"

Nicole did not answer. Nor did she waver under his stare.

"How did Gwen steal a bag of blacks from my treasury? What did you send her out to do? Are you going to explain to me any of this? Did you hand your own sister over to Seleukos?"

Nicole's eyes flashed. "Of course not! How could you believe I would do such a thing? I did not tell Gwen to do *anything!*"

"If only I could believe you. What will the prisoner tell me if I ask him about Gwen?"

"That he retrieved the bag of stolen blacks from her, I assume."

"On your orders."

Nicole's brow furrowed, then smoothed. "No. Father, I-"

"Enough!" Juste roared, kicking a footstool into the wall. "You may enjoy playing politics, and I have indulged you because I thought you had the best interests of this country at heart. But I am still your king before I am your father, and what you have done is treason."

The blood drained from Nicole's face.

"Father, no. You know I would never-"

"I wonder if I ever knew you at all. You play a clever game of politics, but even without your sisters, you are replaceable. Guards! Throw her in the tower. And while you're at it, find the people responsible for helping Gwen to steal from my treasury and throw them in with her."

The guards hesitated, exchanging confused looks. They had been with Nicole too long; her claws were sunken deeply into them.

"I am your king!" Juste roared. "You serve me first and foremost. Now do as I say or you will join her in the tower!"

He did not miss the tiny nod that Nicole gave her guards. Only then did they obey.

Juste turned his back, ignoring Nicole's pleas. He was done listening.

13

The Spy

Fifty-second day of summer,
452 A.D. – Unyca, Ynga

WAKING IN THE home of a stranger was an awkward affair. Deric woke to the sound of voices and movement, and the smell of porridge. When he opened his eyes, he saw that Melech and Dov were moving around the room, preparing breakfast.

Deric shot upright.

"Can I help?" he asked as he stood. The question came out slurred with sleep.

"No need," said Melech. "Everything's almost ready."

So Deric sat at the table as instructed and let himself be waited on. Melech brought three bowls of porridge to the table and Dov brought three mugs and a pitcher that looked too big for a child his size to carry. Unlike dinner the night before, this food was unfamiliar to Deric. The porridge smelled a little off up close, and the taste carried a sour tang of fermentation. But Melech and Dov were happily devouring their portions, so Deric tried not to let his discomfort show. When he went to wash his mouth out with the drink, he nearly choked on the strong, unfamiliar flavor. On closer inspection, the drink appeared to be an unappetizing shade of brown.

"What is this?" he asked, tone light.

"Tamarind," smiled Melech. "We don't have a lot of it, so we save it for special occasions."

"Delicious," lied Deric with a smile.

"Papa!" said Dov.

And Deric was reminded that for all intents and purposes, he was living with a speaker.

"No need to fuss, Dov; he was only trying to be polite," said Melech with a sigh. "I'm sorry, I didn't think to ask."

"No, I've just never had a tamarind drink before," said Deric. He took a large gulp of the drink and changed the subject. "So, I was thinking that I could talk to some of the townsfolk today? Get a feel for the town."

Melech frowned. "We agreed that you'd capture the rainfolk."

"Well, yes," said Deric slowly, "but . . . I have nothing to go on."

Melech stared. "Go on? They're in the rainforest. No one here knows anything else."

"After generations of trade?" Deric retorted. "You think no one's ever heard them say something useful?"

"No one's ever talked to them," said Melech sharply.

"Ever?" Deric was confused. "How can you trade with them for . . . for years, or *generations*, from what you told me, without ever speaking?"

Melech glared. "You're not here to question me," he

said as if he had summoned him to this place to do his bidding.

Deric took a deep breath. He had been a fool. It *had* been too easy, but he'd been too tired to ask for more details the day before. "I'm trying to understand. You expect me to go into the rainforest and find them knowing nothing but the folklore I already know, that may well not be true?"

"You managed to find Unyca that way."

"True, but I wasn't walking into an enemy den! I need to know more—how many of them are there? How far into the rainforest might they be? Will they welcome me or immediately attack? How might they attack? How can I counter their attacks? Can I capture them one at a time, or will I have to take on all of them at once?"

"Is that all? There can't be many. We've never seen more than three at a time."

"Why would that indicate that there can't be many?"

"Basic strategy. You wouldn't send only three people as the vanguard unless you couldn't afford more."

"Vanguard? But they come to trade, you said."

Melech narrowed his eyes. "They're our enemies and we're theirs. We may not have fought yet, but the battle's already begun. Don't worry; I didn't mean you'd attack on your own. Just case their village and I'll bring men to raid it together."

"How many men?"

"Never mind that. Leave the strategy to me."

Deric closed his eyes briefly. "All right," he said at last. "I'll go out into the rainforest today. But I'm going to keep it a day trip—I'll be back by dark." He saw Melech opening his mouth, probably to object, and continued quickly. "If I get lost, I'll be no use to you."

Melech closed his mouth and considered this.

"All right," he agreed. The tilt of his eyebrows conveyed his disappointment.

"I'll take my horse," said Deric. "I ought to be able to cover more ground that way. And I'll take my saddlebags too, just in case."

Melech led Deric to the stable but did not come inside. As he tacked up his horse, he noticed that the white stallion was lying down today, periodically lifting its head to nod and shake it uncomfortably. It was the chain around its neck—it couldn't be comfortable to lie on it.

After a moment's hesitation, Deric approached the stall. The stallion lifted its head to give him a look that, had he not known better, he would have said looked put out. He cracked open the stall and it didn't react. He opened it further and took a step in. The stallion just snorted and lay its head back down. Then it jerked its head up to shake it again.

Deric gathered up an armful of hay and knelt by the stallion's head. Warily, he put a hand on its nose. It sniffed after a moment but didn't react otherwise, so he moved that hand around to the lower side of its head and carefully pushed upward. It gave another snort, but lifted its head. Deric pushed the armful of hay as far as he could under the horse's neck, then shoved some more hay further under its head like a pillow.

The horse lay its head back down, its upper eye fixed on Deric's. Its eyes were violet, he realized with some surprise. He'd never seen violet eyes before. It lifted its head and shook it once more to turn the chain a little further, then lay back down. Its eyes closed and Deric backed out of the stall.

He went back to his own horse and tightened the saddle one more time. Back out in the street, Melech was gone. Deric hesitated, considering delaying his trip into the rainforest just a little—but no. The man standing guard wasn't the same man from the day before, but he was eyeing Deric. Even if Melech didn't have a lie detector for a son, a town the size of Unyca couldn't have many secrets. If Deric deviated from the plan, Melech would know.

He rode up the street, out of the town and back around the outer wall toward the rainforest. He grimaced at the smell again.

Today, he noticed a lone figure standing with a spear at the wall. The man didn't move or speak, but his eyes followed Deric as he rode by.

When he reached the edge of the rainforest, he rode parallel to the line where the greenery began, searching for the tracks of the boy he had met the day before. It took him three passes because the first sign of trampled underbrush was a yard into the underbrush. He turned his horse in to follow it.

In the rainforest, the underbrush was thick and the horse could only move marginally faster than Deric could have walked. The leaves above were so thick that he couldn't see the sky, much less navigate by the position of the sun. He would have to follow his own tracks back out.

He didn't know how long he had been riding, following the tracks, when he was knocked off his horse by a kick from the side. He landed on his back and his field of vision went black. He felt sharp pressure on his chest and recognized it as a knee. Something sharp was pressing into his throat.

"Where is Tlafa?" demanded the voice of the boy.

"Who?" Deric tried to respond, but it came out as a garbled moan.

"*Where. Is. Tlafa?*" The pressure on his throat increased. He felt something warm trickle down his neck and knew the skin had been nicked.

"I don't know who that is," he managed to say this time. His vision was clearing at last.

"Don't give me that," said the figure, and his mistaken guess at her gender was the lesser surprise.

Her long, loose hair formed a silvery cascade around them as she leaned over him, glaring with violet eyes. The color of her hair couldn't be from age: she looked no more than a year or two younger than Deric. She was small and skinny, and had she not just knocked him off his horse and pinned him in one movement, he would never have imagined her capable of it. Something about her felt exotic and familiar all at once, and he couldn't understand it.

She was stunning.

Deric's heart stopped, and then raced.

"Tell me," she demanded, the blade against his throat pressing ever harder.

"I really don't know what you're talking about," he said. "Could you give me some more information?"

"My companion," she snapped. "My other half. Tlafa. You met him. Where was he?"

Deric's mind ran through the many people he had seen

in passing, but there were too many faces to distinguish and no names to put to them.

"Maybe," he said. "But I don't know that name. I'm new here, even if I did meet him, I probably couldn't tell you where exactly it was."

She glared for another moment before pulling back and sitting heavily on Deric's stomach. He saw that she was using his own hunting knife, which had been tucked into his belt. When he moved to try to sit up, she snapped into action and pressed the blade back to his throat.

"Don't move. I'm trying to decide what to do now."

She sat there for another moment, a faraway look in her eyes. This time she kept the blade to his throat, so he obediently lay still. His mind worked instead, planning the quickest way to access the blade in his boot or the rock digging into his shoulder.

But after a few moments, she asked, "What are you doing in the rainforest?"

Deric considered his answer, settling on, "I'm looking for the lyll mine."

"Why?"

"I want to know how it's mined."

"Well, that's easy. It isn't."

"It isn't . . . mined? Then how . . . ?"

"None of your concern. Will you leave the rainforest and never come back if I let you go?"

Deric hesitated. "What will you do if I say yes?"

"I'll let you go."

"And if I say no?"

"I'll kill you."

"So it seems like I should just say yes."

The girl grinned. It didn't reach her eyes. "Sure. But I told you who comes to this place. And I'm neither a merchant nor a Unycan."

She was a speaker. She would hear it if he lied to her.

"Look," he said slowly, "I can't promise to go and never come back, and I also can't let you kill me."

"Not my problem," she growled.

"Wait; let me suggest a trade."

"A trade," she repeated flatly. "You have nothing I want."

"Your companion—this Tlafa. Tell me what he looks like and I'll find him for you. In exchange, let me see the place where the lyll comes from."

She stared at him for a moment.

"I'd get in a lot of trouble if I agreed to that," she said at last. His heart leapt. That meant. . . .

"But your *companion* means more to you than that," he guessed.

"If I'm risking that much for you, then I want more than that," she said. "I need food. And a few blankets."

"But . . . aren't there a whole lot of you who live in the rainforest? Can't you just go to your village for that sort of thing?"

"I'm not leaving until I have Tlafa back."

"All right. All right, can I get up and go to my saddle-bags?"

"Will you promise not to harm me?"

Liles—he'd have to promise honestly.

"I promise," he sighed.

She stepped away. As he approached his horse, he saw his sword strapped under a saddlebag. He could reach for it while pretending to reach for the saddlebag.

"Don't you dare," said the girl, pressing the point of the blade into his left side, perfectly tilted to stab directly between the ribs and into his heart.

He forewent the sword and opened the saddlebag. When he gave her a few pieces of dried meat, she immediately tossed one into her mouth, chewed and swallowed, before starting on another one. It was as if she hadn't eaten in days.

"If you haven't eaten in a while, best take it slow," Deric advised in spite of himself.

She narrowed her eyes at him, but slowed down all the same, chewing this one more thoroughly. Meanwhile, Deric loosened the saddle and pulled out the saddle blanket from underneath.

"I'll be needing that back after you have your friend back," he cautioned. "It's not a gift."

"Fine," she said. "But bring me better food tomorrow. And I'm keeping this" —she pulled out his sword—"until you help me get Tlafa back too. You can go away now."

Deric seethed at the loss of his sword, but knew better than to argue. She had the upper hand. "Wait—where do I find you tomorrow?"

"How about right here? Your horse left tracks a toddler could follow."

Deric nodded mutely and turned his horse back toward Unyca, keeping alert in case the girl decided to attack him from behind. But she didn't. He looked around and saw her run off in the opposite direction, running so lightly that her bare feet sometimes didn't even seem to touch the ground.

Leading his horse—he couldn't ride in the saddle without the blanket padding its back—he walked as slowly as he could. He didn't know Melech well, but he already felt dead certain that the man wouldn't take kindly to his cooperating with one of the rainfolk to find their village, no matter how temporary. He couldn't afford to risk losing Melech's help. But he also couldn't lie as long as Dov was around. He'd have to avoid questions as much as possible. How could he be as reticent as possible as Melech's houseguest, without offending him? How could he find and release the girl's imprisoned lover without inviting suspicion on himself?

He told himself to worry about that after he figured out where the prisoner was being kept.

When he reemerged out onto the wasteland beside Unyca, he was startled by the voice that immediately rang out.

"Are you Deric?"

Deric managed not to jump. He turned to see a short, stocky woman with a wide smile, white hair and black skin.

Deric blinked. "Yes?"

"It's only your name!" She spoke in a rush, like her mind was moving too quickly for her mouth to keep up. "I hear that you're staying with Melech. If you want, I have a house on the outer wall that I used to rent out to a family of merchants that came out here every winter. The head of the family passed away about six seasons ago, and well! The family trade comes to an end if the only heir is a *daughter*."

Deric bit his tongue and blinked away the glare, but it was too late.

The woman's eyes sharpened; she had not missed his reaction. Inexplicably, she grinned.

"How novel. Well, I suppose not. You're from Nou-cleion, right? It's just rare in these parts. Now, you'll stay at the house?"

"A whole house? I didn't expect to find this town without inns. I don't have enough coins for that."

"Nonsense," said the woman, waving her hand. "No one in this town has any use for coins, and it's empty anyway. But I don't have time to fix it up. If you find anything broken, or break anything while you're staying, you'll have to see to fixing it yourself."

"That sounds reasonable," said Deric, then winced. It sounded uncharitable to his own ears. "That is to say, it sounds better than I imagined. Thank you."

The woman introduced herself as Aine and beckoned Deric to follow.

They walked around Unyca the long way. The walked along the rainforest side, around the far side and back, to the corner that would have been straight out from where they had started. They only seemed to be taking the long way so that Aine had more than enough time to talk. She told him about her husband, once the best-respected mayor of Unyca. Aine referred to herself as the one everyone in town relied on for information and advice. She also kept a tamarind tree and tomato field on the roof of one of the outer buildings and was the best seamstress in town. She mentioned some names, but Deric had no faces to put to those names, and none of those names was Tlafa.

At the corner where they stopped, Aine reached into an indent in the wood of an enormous door shape and pulled open a smaller, ordinary-sized door within the large door. As Deric stared up at the larger door, Aine grinned at him.

"That bit's just wall. It was only built to look like a door."

"Are there a lot of smaller doors disguised as bigger ones?" Deric asked faintly.

"More than you'd expect, I think. All the entrances on the outer buildings are disguised. What look like doors are most likely solid wall, and the doors are elsewhere disguised as walls."

"Why?"

"I suppose there was a reason once, but I don't know it. Another piece of history that time turned to sand."

Aine stepped inside. They emerged into a courtyard with a well and a simple, one-stall stable. There was a door to his right that Aine said led into one of the warehouses. She led him through the door straight ahead. Deric followed her into the dark.

It took a moment for his eyes to adjust. The interior was cramped, in need of some repairs and a good cleaning, but it would serve him well. There was a small kitchen on the ground floor and two rooms with cots on the upper floor.

"If you'll take it, you can repay me by helping me out with sorting warehouses when you have the time. If you make it a regular thing, I'll throw meals into the deal."

It sounded too good to be true. Deric might have been suspicious, but he knew Aine's type: the lonely widow who just wanted someone to care for. It was an advantage he hadn't dared hope for. He accepted and Aine left through the courtyard, into the warehouse. Deric meanwhile put his horse up in the stable in the courtyard.

He spent the rest of the day cleaning the house: clearing cobwebs, airing out mattresses, noting where rot had set into the wood.

In the evening, he left the house through the front door, directly onto the main street. He went to give Melech the news. The information was met with a smile that didn't reach Melech's eyes. He only said that he hoped Deric still intended to honor their agreement.

"Of course I do," Deric replied, surprised. It would be a long time before he would realize the significance of what had transpired.

14

The Scribe

Twenty-third day of spring,
452 A.D. — Tevaë Falls, Ceryll

THE WIND RAN through Xanthe's hair and kerchief. She imagined the sensation was like the way Mother's fingers used to stroke her hair back and out of her eyes. The sight before her had been painted for her in words, paints and embroidery since as long as she could remember, but she had never seen it in person.

The sharp, rocky cliff face that towered above Xanthe marked the end of Tevaë Plateau, carved out by the rapids of the Este to the east and the Naëlle to the west. Here the two rivers met at last, forming a pool beneath the cliff. From the cliff above, the waters of the Cole tumbled down into the pool. Thusly formed, the Tevaë Falls was the only place on the continent where three rivers merged into one. The river that flowed out of the Tevaë Pool carried only the name of the Cole and flowed southwest until it met the sea, serving as the border between Ceryll and Amberria.

"I did tell you it was quite a sight," said Cecil, yelling

to be heard over the roar of the waterfall. Xanthe jumped at the voice, and realized that she had forgotten about her companion standing beside her.

"Yes, it is," said Xanthe, turning back to continue watching the pool and waterfall. "It's not as beautiful as I expected."

"They say that only those weary of life can behold the Tevaë and remain untouched," said Cecil.

"Then maybe I'm weary of life," Xanthe snorted. "This is hardly touching."

"What a liar," Cecil said with a roll of her eyes. Xanthe did not argue. Cecil was not easily dissuaded from her ideas. After a silence, Cecil spoke again. "You know, they named the princess after the Cole."

"Each of the princesses was named after one of these three rivers," Xanthe corrected, then bit her tongue a moment too late. She kept her face impassive.

"Oh, yes, the gold-and-silver twins," said Cecil with an impatient roll of the eyes. "An airhead and a corpse, right? I heard the talk in Nirra."

Xanthe had no investment in the dealings of the king's court in Dio, so she laughed. It sounded fake. "I've heard much the same," she said.

"It's such a shame there were no princes. But I suppose that when the princess weds the Amberrian, our kingdom will be in hands capable enough."

"You don't believe the heir is capable enough?" asked Xanthe. The implications of those words did not reach her until she had finished speaking; yet even then she could not bring herself to regret them.

"Oh, I would never dare," gasped Cecil, wide-eyed.

"She'll make a wonderful queen, of course. She visits the Ten Cities regularly, and speaks to the common folk. Those who speak to her have only good things to say. But she must wed a good king, after all."

"I suppose," lied Xanthe. She took refuge in the thundering of the waterfall.

Once upon a time, a girl named for the Este said to a girl named for the Naëlle, "We are only tributaries. We feed the Cole, and that is all." They had laughed. It was a joke at the time. Now one tributary was dead; the other might not be far behind. The river they supposedly fed thrived alone, and would continue to thrive without them. It was no longer amusing. It felt uncomfortably true.

"I asked Dea to sneak us some bread." Cecil reached into her cloak and pulled out two cloth bundles, one of which she handed to Xanthe. She took the bundle and unfolded the cloth to find two slices of buttered bread, still warm from the fire.

"Thank you."

As they ate, Cecil asked, "Do you really plan to find work before a husband?"

"Of course," said Xanthe.

Cecil shook her head. "I knew that things were different for scribes, but I didn't think it would be so . . . I mean, you don't even seem to know what it's like for women in more conventional positions. Didn't you have any friends when you were in Nirra?"

"No," said Xanthe carefully. "There was too much training."

"Amazing. I didn't know they worked scribes so hard — but then again, I suppose they'd have to. Reading and writing must have taken you *years* to learn. I can't even imagine what it must be like, memorizing all those little squiggles, and then *putting them together* . . . oh, I could never dream of it!"

"It's not so much as that. Mostly it just takes time to learn to form the words perfectly in ink, and some of the longer words are difficult to memorize, I suppose, but reading and writing themselves aren't that difficult. I could teach you to spell some simple words, if you like."

Cecil leaped to her feet so quickly that Xanthe found herself looking around to see if something in the area had startled her.

"Oh no," said Cecil, suddenly wide-eyed with fear. "I . . . I know how dangerous mistakes can be. If I accidentally used the powers of the . . . the Words . . . without meaning to, I mean, the sorts of stories people tell about. . . . No, I'm happy leaving the reading and writing to you scribes. I . . . I think I should return to camp, now."

Cecil spun on her heel and began walking back to camp so quickly that it seemed to Xanthe that she was restraining herself from breaking into a run. That was odd. Xanthe had thought that Cecil wouldn't dare go anywhere alone, not even with the camp just over the hill. Xanthe stared after her as she swallowed the last bite of the first slice of bread and sighed to herself. The second slice she wrapped back up in the cloth and put in the inside pocket of her own cloak, just in case she felt peckish later.

The pocket was empty. Xanthe's blood ran cold: Trygve's journal should have been there.

Xanthe rushed back to camp and was still pawing

through the contents of the wagon for Trygve's journal, trying to appear calm, when the wagon jerked into motion. But it wasn't there. She checked her pack for the fourth time; no, it was definitely missing.

"Are you looking for something?" Dea asked at last.

"I had a book. I can't find it now."

"Oh, that," said Cecil airily. "Dea burned it. No need to thank me."

Xanthe's mind came to a halt for a moment.

"What?"

"I made sure it burned completely, and no one saw it," Dea added. The anger that came over Xanthe was so strong that the world around Dea seemed to shiver.

"Why?" she demanded quietly.

"You of all people should know the danger of leaving Words around for long," said Cecil.

"I'm a scribe! I *write* those words!"

"Yes, for messages to be written, read and then burned."

"What are you even talking about?"

"You must know the Words," said Dea. "Forbidden, dangerous?"

"Of course I know the Words. They're a *power*, a sort of magic, nothing to do with writing."

"That's not what I've heard."

"So you *burned* my *journal*?"

"I was doing you a favor," snapped Cecil. "Your ignorance could have doomed us all. You owe me your life! Some scribe you are!"

"No, I don't, because that journal was harmless! I needed it!"

"I know—you made your intentions clear when you

tried to . . . to indoctrinate me! But you won't drag us down with you."

"What are you even—" She cut herself off, squeezed her eyes shut and balled her fists. It was too late. No amount of yelling would bring Trygve's journal back. Xanthe's anger drained into terror as she realized that without it, they had even less hope of finding the Phoenix. And without the Phoenix, they would become shells like the Jehani refugees. Or, Xanthe supposed, they might be dead instead. She wondered which was the better option.

* * *

Though Xanthe's rage cooled and Cecil apologized for not explaining the dangers of the written Words first, Xanthe could not bear the sight of her. But she also could not bear Nier's company, because she knew that she would eventually have to tell him that she had lost their only lead. Xanthe spent her days silently sitting put, fantasizing about leaping from the wagon and outrunning the caravan. She took evening walks by herself because she thought she would lose her mind if she did not, and a guard would always appear to escort her, no doubt sent by Nier or the caravan master.

She endured a full five days of disquiet. On the fifth day, her fantasies progressed from running away to throwing herself under a wagon to end her misery—and moments later, she realized what she had thought and was frantically swallowing against the bile that welled up her throat. Hervé's words came back to her: *She jumped, Highness. I tried—I'm so sorry. I tried to stop her. But she jumped.* Of course, she hadn't known then that it had been the madness. Still, she never wanted to even consider making the same choice.

That evening, Xanthe threw caution to the wind. If the guards were the only company she could stand, then she would make the most of it. She carried her bowl of stew out of the wagon and over to the circle of guards at suppertime. When she seated herself between two whose names she couldn't remember, she could hear the silence as half the camp turned to stare. The guards' conversation had paused as well. Even the expressionless Grosvenor, the leader, raised a brow at her. Xanthe pointedly raised a brow back at him. Eudon, who was by far the friendliest if somewhat flirtatious, hid a smile by taking a bite of his stew. Roul, who wore a perpetual scowl when she was near, narrowed his eyes at her.

"We were discussing the merits of that rock over there for lookout tonight. The conversation would not be to your taste."

Xanthe swallowed carefully and met Roul's eyes squarely before she slid her gaze over to the rock that Roul had indicated. The boulders that sprinkled the grassy terrain were particularly numerous here, providing shelter from the wind as they made camp for the night. Xanthe narrowed her eyes at the rock in question and turned back to Roul.

"You would choose the rock with the least height as your lookout?"

"Accessibility is more important than height," explained the man to her left, probably Degare. "The others may be taller, but what purpose would it serve to keep lookout there if it were difficult to descend at a moment's notice to alert the camp?"

"And if a group of bandits realizes that the lookout is so easily avoidable, they could sneak up on the camp effortlessly by simply hiding in the shadows of the other rocks. Are a few extra moments really so important if you have better visibility?"

"At any height, there are some blind spots. The difference in time it would take to climb up and down would be more than a few moments."

Xanthe glanced at the taller boulders beside which the carts stood, her gaze settling on the dents and crevices that she knew were there. After a moment, she turned back to the men and raised a brow at them.

"Am I to understand that you never learned to climb rocks properly?"

"Are you suggesting that *you* could climb the highest of those and come back down at all, much less *quickly*?" asked Roul. There was a smirk in his voice, and Xanthe knew a challenge when she heard one.

"What will you wager?" she asked.

"Oh, no wager, milady," said Roul. "I'd hate to deprive you of any of your few possessions."

"Likewise," Xanthe said. "How about food? Whoever loses this wager must give the winner half their portion of stew."

Roul shrugged. "If you insist."

Xanthe smiled and set her bowl down at her seat. "Perfect. I was just thinking that this was a little too hot."

"Don't be foolish, Xanthe," said a guard with graying

hair whose name she did not remember. "Roul, hold your tongue."

"This isn't so foolish," said Xanthe with more confidence than she felt. "I think you all need me to prove myself, and he's the only one with the sense to be honest."

"Stop," said Grosvenor. "If you fall and break your neck, it will be our heads."

"Nonsense," said Xanthe lightly. "If I fall, tell Nier that I wouldn't listen to reason. He tries enough to know it's true."

With that, she jogged off, beelining for the tallest of the boulders. She had been looking at them since the wagons had stopped. The quickening beat of her heart was familiar in a way that made her stomach ache with nostalgia. Xanthe unlaced and kicked off her boots before she tied her skirt at her side so that it hung no lower than her knees. She chose her starting point and began to climb.

The climb made her heart pound in her chest. The wind climbed with her. She pulled herself to the top. She took a moment to breathe, standing there above everything, looking across the still darkness as though she could see the horizon beyond. She indulged in the sight for mere moments before she took a breath and clambered back down the rock, her hands and feet finding the holds with ease now that she knew this face of the rock.

At the bottom, she untied the knot in her skirt and pulled her boots back on. She made her way back to the guards' circle, aware that Cecil's father, Nier and everyone else in the camp had conspicuously averted their eyes. No one said a word as she sat back down and retrieved her bowl. It was still warm, she noted with pleasure on the first bite. The guards said nothing. When Xanthe raised her eyes to look at Roul, he was studiously digging away at his bowl.

"Still too slow for a guard alerting the camp of an attack," said Grosvenor, breaking the silence. "The other one is good enough for a lookout."

"But I was faster than you thought possible, I'd wager."

"No more wagers. You've already won half of Roul's supper."

"Here," Roul said moments later, holding out the half-finished portion.

"Thank you," said Xanthe. She placed it by the fire to keep it warm while she finished her own portion. Roul stood and left the circle. Nothing more was said for a time.

"Where did you learn to climb like that?" Eudon asked at last, looking at her like he was seeing her for the first time. The heat in his gaze made Xanthe avert her eyes.

"I knew a man who was good at climbing when I was a girl," she shrugged. Her cheeks felt warm. Why? She never blushed. "He offered to teach me and I enjoyed it."

"And here I was, thinking you scribes were weak and slow." The twinkle in his eye softened his words. Xanthe grinned at him.

"That was in bad taste," Nier said later, catching her on her way to Cecil's wagon.

"Don't tell me," she said, taking care to keep her voice low, "You think that I should be keeping company with Cecil like a *proper* maiden."

Nier pursed his lips. "I realize that you enjoy being

boyish for all to see," he said. "I realize that Cecil is not precisely a friend to you. But a young woman spending her time among guards? You have no idea what people will say—"

"That I'm a whore?" asked Xanthe brazenly. Her voice rose.

"Be *quiet*," hissed Nier in vain. Xanthe was already launching into an outburst.

"This may be difficult for you to comprehend, but I'm a *scribe*. I'm not a noblewoman with a reputation to be carefully protected."

"You don't need to be a noblewoman to be worth protecting. I know that . . . I understand that you feel confined; I promise that I do, but this isn't safe. No scribe girl ought to be able to climb the way you did. No scribe girl would ever attempt to befriend guards."

"But it can be dismissed as a quirk of personality," Xanthe replied confidently. Nier drew a short breath and opened his mouth. Xanthe was quicker. "Do not try to command me."

She turned and headed for bed. She did not turn when Nier called her name.

In the morning, she joined the guards for breakfast, holding her spine straight, her shoulders back, her chin up, and her sweetest smile on her face. When she sat herself amongst them, there was only a moment's hesitation before they either nodded or smiled at her in turn and carried on with their discussion of preferred weapons.

When Xanthe eventually interjected that her preference was for the longbow, there was not so much as a raised eyebrow. Eudon chuckled and winked at her.

"Of course you would," snorted Roul. "A coward's weapon for those who can't stomach a real battle."

"Or for those who prefer strategy, speed and tact over blind bloodlust and brute force," said Xanthe. A lively debate commenced, in which only Grosvenor remained silent.

Xanthe found herself chancing a glance in Nier's direction. His eyes met hers. She held his gaze, expecting him to avert his eyes. Instead, he held her eyes with as much determination as she felt. Not one muscle moved in his face to betray what he was thinking.

At last, Xanthe was the one who looked away. She turned back to the still-raging debate and threw herself into it with relish.

15

The Heir's Maid

Mid-morning, eleventh day of spring,
452 A.D. – Castle Dio, Ceryll

IT WAS NOT uncommon for Princess Nicole to be up early, so when Manon realized that the chambers were deserted, she set about making the bed. Then she noticed the footstool splintered into three pieces against the wall and knew that there was trouble.

Sterre had become the last friend Manon had ever trusted or loved. Manon was grateful for her life and what remained of her freedom. Folk said that the Words had driven Sterre mad and off the cliff, but Manon knew better. There had been no madness, just stubbornness and unwillingness to accept the consequences of her own choices. *It's only history*, Sterre had said, then at the first sign of trouble she ran in the night with Pierre without a thought for the rest of them. When that didn't work, she abandoned Pierre too and when all else failed, she threw herself off a cliff. Now Sterre was dead and the rest of them were prisoners.

Manon neither trusted nor loved Nicole. But without her, Manon would lose what little life she had left.

She abandoned the bed—there were other maids to take care of that—and stopped the first servant she saw in the corridor.

"Where is the princess?"

"Which . . . it doesn't matter, don't know either way," shrugged the servant. "Apparently both went missing last night."

Manon stumbled back, pulse racing. No. It couldn't be. She went straight to the barracks.

"No one talks to me any more than they talk to you," protested Regis when she asked him what was going on.

"You live every moment in such close quarters with other soldiers and guards," Manon insisted. "You must have heard something."

"I don't even know what you want to know," Regis said testily. "You could ask Eduard or Pierre, but—"

"The princesses are missing."

"So? You have a day off."

"Regis," Manon hissed. "There was a broken footstool by her bed."

"Maybe she tripped. Maybe she got a little rough with a midnight visitor. So what?"

"She doesn't *have* midnight visitors, and I've never seen her break anything she didn't intend to! Something's wrong, and without her. . . . Oh, never mind, you're worse than useless these days. I don't know why I still bother."

Manon turned her back on him and started to leave.

"Don't say that," Regis protested, catching her arm.

"Wait. I think . . . I heard something about more guards being stationed at the tower this morning."

"Which tower?"

"The prison tower, obviously."

"Why would that—" Manon broke off, her mouth going dry. "You don't think—"

Regis narrowed his eyes at her. "Do I think the princesses got thrown into the tower? Don't be ridiculous."

"You're right, of course," Manon lied absently. "I'll go ask elsewhere."

"Why not enjoy the time off?" said Regis. "Forget about trying to find her; she's probably off somewhere doing royal . . . things."

He sounded sincere and serious, but Manon gave no weight to his opinions anymore. They had been close once, before Sterre. Everyone at the Crossing thought they would get married. Now they were worlds apart. Regis didn't understand the intrigues and secrets that were pivotal to court life, and didn't care to. As a soldier, he could afford not to care. As the maid of the heir who was also the shadow, Manon would be a fool to do the same.

Nicole too-frequently manipulated everyone around her, including the king; when she could not, she went behind his back and did as she pleased anyway. From the start, it had chilled Manon to watch Nicole treat her father and sovereign like a pawn. But it had also worked in Manon's favor, because Nicole's efforts had granted her a pardon.

If Juste had turned against his daughter, Manon's pardon might also be revoked. So she gathered up a basket, a cloth, some paper, ink and a pen from her room.

She placed the cloth in the basket, and then slipped the paper, ink and pen beneath it in a corner. She then went to the kitchens to fill the basket with muffins. She proceeded to the tower.

She was stopped at the entrance.

"I'm lady's maid to Princess Nicole," said Manon, heart in her throat. "I'm bringing food."

She pulled back the cloth covering the basket, keeping the corner with the stationery in shadow. The guards exchanged a look and conferred in whispers. They did not ask Manon which prisoner the heir had concerned herself with. It was as good as confirmation.

"After I've brought this through, I'm sure I could bring another basket for you hardworking men," Manon said with her most charming smile.

It worked.

Manon did not have to go far. Clothed in her nightdress, Nicole was in a large prison cell at the base of the winding staircase, along with a short, glaring man who looked like he had not bathed this year. Several more guards stood watch alongside this cell. There was no sign of the younger princess, but that was not Manon's concern.

Nicole noticed her at once. "Manon." The astonishment in her voice was so faint that anyone else might have missed it. But Manon was not fooled.

"May I go in?" Manon asked a guard, showing him the contents of her basket again. "I've only brought her breakfast."

"Fine," said a guard. "But no whispering—anything you say, we hear, or you're not coming back out again."

Manon's heart beat wildly in her throat as the door was unlocked and she stepped through.

"I brought you this, milady," she said loudly, holding out the basket. As she offered it, she turned it so that the side with the stationery was closest to Nicole.

"Thank you, Manon," said Nicole, accepting it. She looked casually through its contents, her face giving nothing away. "How is your morning so far?"

"Very good, milady." Manon understood the meaning of the question: *keep talking*. "If you please, why are you in here?"

The heir smiled faintly, still rifling around in the basket. "Oh, nothing at all, really. My sister seems to have done something to put our father in a foul temper this morning. It is only a misunderstanding. It will be resolved soon enough. Muffin, Theirn?" she addressed the man sitting against the far wall.

"I'm not your poison taster," he scowled. "I hope you choke and die."

A chill ran down Manon's spine. She wondered if he knew he was playing with fire.

"Suit yourself," said Nicole, taking a bite herself. "Manon?"

"If it pleases Your Highness."

Nicole handed Manon a muffin—and hidden beneath it, a folded piece of paper.

"Now, perhaps you could eat your breakfast on the way to Prince Enri's chambers? I was supposed to confer with him over lunch. Do tell him that I am unavailable."

"Yes, milady. Thank you, milady." She slipped the note

up her sleeve before she left. When the guards peered suspiciously at the muffin, there was nothing there to see.

Manon made for Enri's chambers. On the way, she pulled the paper out of her sleeve, unfolded it and looked. But Sterre's lessons had not been enough to teach her to read these hasty scribbles, so she folded it up again.

Enri habitually slept until midday, so it did not surprise her when the guard at the door stopped her and said that the prince was unavailable.

"Never mind that," said Manon. "I *must* speak with him now. I have a note from the heir."

The guard stared at her and Manon wished fervently that Alderic were still around. For all his fickle loyalties, he at least would have understood the urgency.

"Please, my job depends on this," she begged, looking as helpless and feminine as she could.

The guard sighed and went in to rouse the prince.

"What's this about Nicki?" Enri asked when he appeared, bleary-eyed and bedheaded.

"She regrets to inform you that she is detained and can't see you as planned today," Manon said as she handed him the paper.

"What plan?" he asked absently as he opened the paper.

Manon may not have been able to read the scribbles, but she could certainly read the ashen expression on his face.

"Where is she, exactly?" he asked quietly.

Manon told him.

16

The Spy

Fifty-third day of summer, 452 A.D. – Unyca, Ynga

SINCE MELECH HAD not instructed him to do anything
specific that day during their brief conversation the
previous evening, Deric spent the morning helping
Aine sort crates in one of her warehouses. While they
worked, she shared the town gossip with him, though
there were still too many names for Deric to follow. He did
recognize the name Mor, which frequently emerged as the
voice of reason. But no one ever mentioned the name Tlafa.

Aine invited Deric to her home for lunch. When he
accepted, she led him not to a building in the inner wall,
as he had expected, but into another warehouse and up a
ladder into a loft. The space was just tall enough for Aine,
but Deric had to crouch. There was another ladder leading
up into a skylight—to her rooftop garden, he guessed. The
stove directly beneath the skylight informed him that it
doubled as a chimney.

Something about the space—its smallness or barrenness,
perhaps—made Deric's heart constrict for Aine.

After some time rummaging around in the far corner behind the stove, she brought two plates of bread with sliced tomatoes and a strong-smelling cheese. Though it was food that might have been considered peasants' food in Amberria, Deric thanked her profusely. He hadn't seen any cows, so he knew that the cheese must be traded. The tomatoes were no doubt from Aine's rooftop garden. Like the tamarind drink, this was a meal of precious commodities to Unycans.

He wanted to tell Aine that she didn't have to go to such trouble for him—he would be happy to eat whatever she usually ate. But he didn't want to sound ungrateful either.

After the meal, he took his leave of her—but not before she gave him a small basket containing a dozen potatoes, what must have been several pounds of flour, and a dozen eggs.

"This should last you half a fortnight at least," she said. "But let me know when you need more. If you want to make bread, come to me for the yeast."

"Thank you," said Deric, deciding not to mention that he had no idea how to go about making yeasted bread. He knew it only took flour and water to make flatbread, so he would stick with that. He could make three quarters of these provisions last half a fortnight; a quarter of each ingredient would have to be enough for the rainfolk girl.

That afternoon, he rode back into the forest, using a spare blanket from the house as a saddle blanket, with the food concealed in his saddlebags.

Holding a spear, a new man stood outside the wall today. He looked vaguely familiar. Staring at the man (who stared right back) as he rode past, it dawned on Deric that this was the same man whom he'd seen standing guard on the street in front of the stables.

He realized at once that this must be the outside of the stables. There must be another hidden door in the wall that the man was guarding.

But why were there guards around the stables? What were they guarding, and from whom?

The rainfolk girl was very put out with Deric.

"What am I supposed to do with these?" she demanded. "I can't eat these."

"You cook them," Deric explained. "Make a fire and put them on the embers. Or I could bring you a pot so you could boil them."

"I know you can eat them cooked," she snapped. "I'm telling you that I *can't* cook them. Bring me something I can eat."

"It's easy to learn," Deric said, exasperated. "Just let me show you—"

"You can show me all you like; I still won't be able to. Just bring me food I can eat or the deal is off."

Deric gave her more of his dried meat instead.

"What've you learned about Tlafa?" she asked through a mouthful of food.

"Nothing," said Deric. "I haven't even heard his name."

"Of course not," she snorted. "No one in Unyca would know it."

Deric furrowed his brows. "Well, I've heard no mention of a prisoner either."

The girl sighed. "Of course not," she muttered. "They wouldn't think of him as a *prisoner*."

Deric crossed his arms, irritated. "Then maybe you could help me by telling me what I'm looking for."

"Why?" she asked. Her nonchalant attitude infuriated Deric.

"Because you asked me to help you! You were adamant that you needed my help to get your Tlafa back. But you're not even pretending to act like a person whose lover is being held captive."

The girl didn't look at all chastised. If anything, she looked amused. "Who said anything about a lover?"

"You did! Yesterday!"

"Clearly you misunderstood something. But I don't understand what my relationship with Tlafa has anything to do with anything."

Deric didn't realize quite how frustrated he was until a growl escaped his throat.

"Your lot really think I'm a fool, don't you?"

"My lot?" She looked genuinely puzzled, and even more amused.

"Your lot! With your vague plans and bribes and secrecy and extraordinary hospitality in a place that's clearly extremely wary of outsiders! I might let you use me as a pawn, but I'm not as oblivious as you seem to think!"

There was a moment of silence.

"I'll give you a vague plan and secrecy," said the girl. "But I wasn't aware I'd bribed you or been hospitable. If anything, I threatened you."

She was right. Deric acknowledged it, and apologized for the outburst. She snorted.

"Don't be ridiculous. Thanks for that. So some of the

Unycans are trying to bribe and host you into helping them, are they? What are you supposed to do?"

Deric scowled at her. He'd almost forgotten that she was a speaker. He didn't understand it—he wasn't the sort of person who trusted easily, and this girl was the enemy—she was a speaker. But it was like a part of him was determined to relax in her presence.

Of course—it was the Words. She had cast a spell to make him let down his guard.

"I see through your witchcraft, speaker," he said. "And you won't be getting anything else out of me."

The girl's eyes sharpened. "Yngans—even Unycans— don't use that word. Where are you from?"

"What, witchcraft?"

"Speaker."

Deric panicked. "My mother was Amberrian, and I . . . I guess I have a few holdover habits."

"Hm," she said.

Silence fell over them. It struck Deric that he might have talked himself into a corner. He needed her to at least trust him enough to bring him to her town.

So he took a chance. "I've told you something about me. Now tell me something about you."

"Why?"

"You want my help, don't you? Help me see you as more than the rainfolk girl who took my sword."

"You need my help too," she retorted. "You'll never find where the lyll comes from without me."

"True," he conceded, "But I wager I care about that less than you care about getting Tlafa back. And I can get another sword and hunting knife."

"Not in Unyca." But she sounded a little less certain now.

"Just one little thing," he said. "How about your name? So I can tell Tlafa who sent me when I meet him."

"You won't have to. He'll know."

"Fine, then just so I can put a name to your face."

"Esther," she said.

"Esther," he repeated.

"Tell me your name too and I'll tell you something else."

"Deric," he replied. "What else will you tell me?"

"If you want our agreement to stand, bring me food I can eat without using fire."

"That wasn't the deal," Deric objected.

"What deal? You made up the rules. I never agreed to follow them."

"Just give me a hint—anything, a *crumb*—so I can try to find Tlafa."

Esther considered this. "You've seen him already."

"Yes, but I'm telling you, I don't *remember*. How does this mysteriousness help? Do you want me to find him or not? Just hair color, or eye color, or something!"

"White hair and violet eyes," she said.

"So something like you?"

"Whiter than my hair. And violet eyes, I said."

Deric let his confusion show. "So . . . brighter violet than your eyes?"

"My eyes aren't violet," she said in exasperation. "Are you blind?"

"I thought you couldn't lie."

Esther stared at him. "My eyes are violet? Truly?"

Deric raised his eyebrows. "You didn't know your own eye color?"

"I suppose you think it's foolish that I don't look myself in the eye when I talk?"

"Even if you've never seen a mirror, you must have seen your reflection!"

"I make a point of not looking at my reflection."

"Why?"

"No reason you would understand. I'm far too tired for this. Come back tomorrow when you have food I can actually eat."

With that, Esther turned and ran back into the trees. She was slower than she had been the day before, seemingly encumbered by her boots fashioned out of large leaves and bound with vines—boots she had definitely not been wearing the day before.

He rode back to Unyca, considering his own outburst.

Esther's agenda was easiest to figure out: her friend or whatever had been taken captive and she wanted him set free.

But Melech and Aine . . . ? From the tamarind drink to the tomatoes and cheese, they were being far too hospitable. Every other Unycan treated him like a sprite, avoiding and ignoring him. But these two—one with a grand plan to orchestrate a mass exodus, the other the wife of the late mayor—treated him like a personal guest.

He felt like a fool for not seeing it immediately. Melech's plan couldn't be a complete secret—all the more if he'd already taken one of the rainfolk prisoner and was keeping him captive in that tiny town. He'd said himself that he needed to convince the other Unycans that the rainfolk were a threat. There must be a group that opposed Melech's ideas.

And along came a convenient outsider who could be sent into the rainforest to investigate the rainfolk without upsetting the status quo for anyone, Unycan or rainfolk. Deric's help could tilt the carefully balanced scales in Melech's favor. The opposing group would want to stop that from happening, either by getting Deric out of the way or wooing him to their own side. Deric hadn't noticed anyone trying to attack him, but Aine was certainly not being subtle about trying to get into his good graces.

The guards. Standing at both doors into the stables. Why would a town in the middle of nowhere need guards to stand at doors so well-disguised? They could only be standing guard against other Unycans. And if the trade with the rainfolk was truly the center of the conflict, then there was only one thing that they could be guarding. Aine had even walked him all the way the long way around Unyca—to have more time to talk, he had thought, but it had been to avoid the guard seeing her with him and telling Melech before he'd accepted the house.

Deric felt like a fool. Thirty stalls, mostly empty. He'd been inside the stables twice, and had never thought to look for a figure smaller than a horse. And obviously, he'd been close enough that Tlafa had seen him.

Another realization occurred to him, also belated.

How had Esther known that Tlafa had seen him?

To that question he had no answer.

Deric rode the long way around Unyca again. He didn't go out into the streets. He was in a nest of taipans and he hadn't even noticed.

At least there was Melech, he thought. Melech's

motivations were as true and straightforward as Deric's own: self-defense against the speakers. Even if he couldn't trust the man with his secrets, he could ally himself with his cause.

He knew what he had to do.

The next morning, he worked for Aine again until lunch. He carefully tried to remember everything she told him.

In the afternoon, he brought Esther a boiled potato, boiled egg and some flatbread, with his apologies.

"Would you like to spar?" he asked her.

"What makes you think I know how?"

Deric hesitated a moment. Had he misread her? No. She was testing him.

"You knocked me out of my saddle by swinging from a tree. That's not something you just figure out how to do. You must've been trained. I thought you might enjoy it."

"You're right, there. I would. No weapons of any kind, and no dealing serious damage?"

"No headshots?"

"Why not? As long as they're not hard . . . ?"

With that, she leaped into the air to deliver what might have been a roundhouse kick to his head. He crossed his arms instinctively, blocking her. As she landed, he swiped her feet out from under her. She landed on her hands and kicked straight out, catching Deric in the chest.

Her aim was off-center, so Deric turned with the impact, throwing her off balance.

Battle commenced.

"Where did you learn to fight like that?" Deric panted a little while after, pinning her to the forest floor. He hadn't expected it to be easy, but he also hadn't expected her to be such a challenge.

"That would be telling," she smiled. "But I haven't trained in a long time. We should make this a daily thing. You're out of practice too—that punch to my ribs was weak."

"I was taking it easy on you," Deric lied.

She smirked. "I can hear you lie, remember?"

The reminder that she was a speaker jolted him back to reality, dispelling the comfortable atmosphere and the warm, fuzzy feeling that had been filling his chest. But as he left Esther that evening, he realized that the comfort and warm feeling had come right back, stronger than before.

This isn't real friendship, he tried to tell himself. It was only a trick. He ignored the part of his mind that said that he was lying to himself.

When he returned to Unyca, he went to Melech and pledged his loyalty. Anything Aine told him he would share, he promised, and proved it by sharing everything he could remember so far. Melech's response was a grin so wide that it was visible through his beard.

"Welcome to the witch hunters, Deric."

Then he gave Deric a katar.

17

The Scribe

Thirty-first day of spring,
452 A.D. – Kingsway near Farthe, Ceryll

NOT THAT WE don't enjoy your company," said Eudon on the day that Xanthe decided to walk alongside the caravan rather than suffer another day with Cecil and Dea in awkward silence. "But if bandits strike, you're defenseless out here."

"We've been on the road for over a fortnight without any sign of bandits. What is the chance that they will appear now?"

"Dangerous words, Miss Xanthe," said Eudon gravely. After a pause, he lowered his voice. "What happened between you and Miss Cecil?"

"Oh, just some dramatics," said Xanthe airily. "She got it into her head that the written word is somehow related to the forbidden Words."

He frowned. "Isn't it?"

"No!"

Eudon inclined his head to her. "You're the scribe, so you would know."

"Do *you* believe it?" Xanthe demanded. "Would *you* turn me down if I offered to teach you to read and write?"

Eudon smiled with a twinkle in his eye. "Of course not. I'd never turn down any offer from you."

Xanthe could not resist returning his smile, her heart fluttering in her stomach. Her eyes followed the way his dark red hair swept across his clean-shaven cheeks and her pulse raced.

"Any offer at all?" she teased, feeling strangely warm.

"Any offer at all," Eudon repeated. His eyes darkened.

Xanthe found her heart pounding, the atmosphere suddenly heavier.

"Ride with me?" he said, gesturing to his horse. "It's not right that you should walk alone."

"Surely that would interfere with your duties." Her heart raced at the thought.

"Hardly. It will make it easier to protect you, if it comes to that."

He stopped and she half climbed as he helped lift her onto his horse, setting her in front of him. As they rode, she was aware that she had never been this close to a man before. Every part of her that touched Eudon felt alight. Most distracting of all was his breath against her ear as he murmured, "Comfortable, Miss Xanthe?"

"Very," she smiled, though she was not quite sure if it was true. It was not unpleasant, but it wasn't precisely what she would have called *comfortable*.

They rode in silence, Xanthe trying and failing to ignore the way Eudon's arms and hands brushed or rested against her waist and arms. She wanted to lean back and rest against him, so she did—and he released the reins with one hand for a moment to wrap an arm around her and pull her more firmly against him, no doubt adjusting her for his own comfort.

Her heart raced, wildly, and Xanthe had to concede that this was probably attraction. It was an unfamiliar sensation. It occurred to Xanthe that Eudon was keeping his horse in the shadow between two wagons. The only one who could see them was the driver of the wagon behind them. She wondered if this was deliberate. She lay her arm over his that was around her, marveling at the way his brown hand made hers look pale beside it.

She thought of the life behind her, and the life that lay ahead. She thought of how she might get stranded in the Dantes, or die on the way there or back; she thought of what life had been for Gwen and of how she would be Gwen again, bound to rules and decorum and a loveless marriage made to ally her kingdom for the coming war.

So she turned around and kissed Eudon on the mouth. He started for a moment before kissing back enthusiastically. His hand came to the side of her throat and his lips caught hers, drawing away only to dive back in.

Xanthe had allowed some suitors the occasional kiss but had never felt anything like what she felt now. Her body felt both numb and aflame. She felt lost when Eudon's tongue came against her lips and then slipped between them, but she never wanted it to end. His hand ran down her back and around so that his arm wrapped around her waist, holding tight. She knew that he wanted her closer, because she wanted that too. She lifted one leg to rest in a comfortable bend against the horse's neck so that she could turn more fully to face him, wrap her arms around his neck—

"Xanthe," came a familiar voice from above that stopped her heart.

They broke apart and looked up. Xanthe was already rearing to fight him tooth and nail—but she stopped short with one look at him. Nier stood beside the driver looking neither angry nor admonishing. He didn't even look shocked or hurt. He simply looked tired, like he had been woken from sleep he desperately needed.

She looked back at Eudon but the flame was out and cold. She felt childish and shaky.

"I should return to my wagon," Xanthe murmured with a weak smile to Eudon. She moved to jump down from the horse.

She was stopped by a whistling sound, followed by a thud. Eudon picked her up by the waist and all but threw her at Nier and the wagon driver. Xanthe felt arms pulling her to safety as she fought for a foothold amid the sudden clamor. She was manhandled down on her belly, a body falling on top of hers. There were shouts around her, but she was too dazed to make out any words. As her wits returned, she realized that the sounds outside were an attack.

"Bandits," she murmured.

"Yes, Xanthe," said Nier's voice immediately above her. "Bandits. You have Eudon and an archer with very bad aim to thank for your life."

Xanthe had no retort. The shaking of the wagon suggested that they were still moving.

"We're running?"

"We're only a day outside of Farthe," snapped Nier, sharper than she had ever heard. "The closer we get to the city, the more likely that they'll give up. Weren't you listening?"

"But what about the guards?"

"This is their job. They risk their lives for people like us. That's why they get their own horses."

"But there are only four horses between the six of them," Xanthe pointed out, feeling childish even as she spoke. "Eudon—what if he gets killed?"

The pressure on her back let up. She was rolled over roughly so that she was on her back instead, looking directly at Nier. He was still holding her down by the shoulders, and his eyes were more glaringly serious than she had ever seen them.

"Xanthe," he hissed. His voice was barely above a whisper. "You knew that it wouldn't be easy. This was *your* decision."

"Don't *lecture* me," snapped Xanthe. A drop of warm liquid dripped onto Xanthe's cheek. She wiped it away. "I know the stakes better than you. And stop *holding me down*. Get off of me right. . . . Are you bleeding?"

She noticed that her fingers were red where she had wiped her cheek. Then she saw the red spot spreading across his shoulder.

"Nier, you've been shot."

"Yes," he said through gritted teeth, "I can feel that. Thank you for noticing."

There was a blunt thud inside the wagon. She looked to see a quivering arrow in the wagon floor some distance away. The three other passengers in the wagon were cowering behind some crates that they had piled up like a barricade. They were either unconcerned or oblivious to Nier's predicament.

Xanthe opened her mouth to beg them for help and snapped it shut half a moment later. She glared at the cowering men as she pulled herself out from under Nier and inspected the wound.

"Get *down!*" hissed Nier. His hand grasped her wrist and tugged, but he didn't have the strength to pull her down.

"While you bleed out?" asked Xanthe, and was surprised to find that her voice remained as level as ever.

"At least you'll be safe," said Nier.

Xanthe saw red. "Don't you dare," she hissed at him, conscious of the passengers behind her. "*I* was going to do this alone. You . . . If you hadn't spotted me that night. . . ."

"You had no plan. You wouldn't have made it out of Dio."

There was another thud as an arrow embedded itself in the floor.

"That may or may not be true," conceded Xanthe without batting an eye as she adjusted Nier's body to lie prone so that she could better see his wound. An arrow shaft was sticking out of his tunic in the back of his shoulder, blood oozing into the cloth around it. "But you're here now. You don't get to die like this."

"I'm all right," said Nier. "Just a scratch. Now get down before *you* get shot!"

"Yes, of course. When I see a man lying in a pool of his own blood, I think how *all right* he is."

"There is no pool," protested Nier. Xanthe ignored him.

"Are there any bandages or herbs in this wagon?" The question she directed at the men, but they did not respond, too busy cowering behind their wall of crates. Xanthe grabbed the nearest crate and started digging through it.

A roar behind the wagon distracted her enough to spare a glance. There was a large man on horseback, riding after their wagon with his sword brandished over his head. His face was contorted in a parody of rage, and Xanthe felt a hysteric urge to laugh. Then he froze, crumpled and fell from his horse. Xanthe caught a glimpse of Roul behind the bandit's toppling body. She turned back to the box.

It was a box of food, full of precious smoked beef, cheese, and foreign herbs and spices. A suspicion struck her and she began eagerly digging through the spices. She soon found a box with an Yngan seal. On opening it, she found a dry, reddish powder. She touched it to her tongue: cayenne.

Xanthe silently thanked Nevena for Nicki's old habit of monologuing about plants. She gritted her teeth and braced herself. In one swift, firm move, she pulled the arrow free of Nier. Ignoring his surprised cry, she pulled the hole in his tunic a little further apart and inspected the relatively clean wound. She could only look for a moment before it was obscured by blood welling up and flowing across his shoulder. A glance at the bloody arrowhead of black (black, used as an arrowhead—she fumed at the wastefulness) assured her that she needn't worry about broken pieces of arrowhead in the wound. She took a handful of the cayenne and sprinkled it over the wound with one hand. With the other, she ripped a strip from the hem of her skirt.

She heard a low moan from the vicinity of the men. She ignored them. Last she had looked, no one had been harmed. She suspected that they were looking in horror at Nier's wound. She wondered absently if they were more horrified by the blood or by her wasteful use of the cayenne.

She pressed down on the wound with the scrap from her skirt. Nier groaned. When she chanced a glance at his face, she saw that his eyes had rolled back.

"Nier?" she called. He didn't answer. *Passed out*, she decided and buried her worry beneath comfortable exasperation. She turned her attention back to the wound. The flow of blood was beginning to slow. Then, for the first time, she realized that she hadn't heard any arrows or commotion outside for some time.

"Are we safe now?" she asked the men, only a moment later realizing how juvenile the question sounded.

"As safe as anyone can be on the kingsway without any guards," said the driver. "We'll be safe if we can reach Farthe before dark."

Without any guards. The words echoed in Xanthe's ears. A lump rose in her throat.

Her heart ached with homesickness. She missed familiar sights and sounds. She missed Hervé and Alderic and even Enri. She missed her father and her sister. She missed *Stelle*.

She curled her hands in Nier's hair and dropped her forehead to his. Her tears rolled down her cheeks and fell onto his. Let the men in the caravan think this romantic. Let them think she was as weak as they thought their womenfolk.

She cried at the thought that she might lose Nier. But more than that, she thought of the sister she had already lost and cried over her for the first time. Nier's forehead was warm against her own. She drew comfort from the contact and allowed herself to cry until she had to release Nier to vomit out the back of the wagon. Then, with the violence of her grief past, she curled next to Nier on the wagon floor. Tears continued streaming down her face. She buried her face in Nier's uninjured shoulder and let the tears fall for once.

She pressed against Nier's side and took comfort in his warmth. She laid a hand lightly on his chest and felt his heartbeat strong and unfaltering. Despite herself, she turned her head further into Nier's shoulder and felt the grief drain from her. Drowsiness took her.

You would do better to abandon him here, my babe, said the voice in her dreams. *But then again, you won't listen to me, will you? No matter. As long as you come south.*

* * *

The caravan members had no sympathy. Before the wagon had even come into view of Farthe, the men were accusing Xanthe of theft and unseemly conduct. Their accusations were echoed by the caravan master when he was brought up to speed while they were stopped to water the horses. Xanthe threw caution to the wind and argued fiercely, much to the men's discomfort. But they did not care that the cayenne had been necessary to save Nier.

When they rolled into Farthe that night, she paid the caravan master nine whites: three more whites than originally promised, and three whites fewer than the caravan master insisted were necessary to cover the cayenne powder Xanthe had used. Though there seemed little danger of being turned over to the city guard by the grumbling merchants, Xanthe wouldn't risk giving them time to think. She asked to be let off at the first inn they came across in the outskirts of Farthe.

No one objected. Nier had developed a fever and his wound was still oozing, so Xanthe found herself on the side of the road supporting Nier with one arm and holding both their packs in the other. She stumbled into the inn only to be greeted with apathy.

"I don't talk business with shrews," the innkeeper said so dismissively that Xanthe could only imagine it was a joke in horribly poor taste. When he made no move to say anything else, the rage took her.

"You will talk business with me."

The innkeeper's eyes snapped up to meet hers. Xanthe scarcely recognized her own voice; it sounded eerily like Nicki's. "I will pay you three whites for a room with your best bed for a fortnight. For another two whites, you will provide two meals each day, and a bowl of clean water and a clean cloth and any herbs I ask for whenever I require them."

"A lot of demands," remarked the innkeeper, straightening his back. "And for three whites? Might as well offer me bread crumbs. Go away; I don't rent to beggars."

"I am offering you considerably more than these

services are worth," Xanthe guessed. "Now show us to our room."

"Three whites'll get you a night, but that's all. It'll be thirty whites for both of you for a fortnight. You don't like the price, go find another inn. Or better yet, sleep in the dust where you belong."

Xanthe glared. He knew that she had no choice. "Thirty whites for a fortnight in your best room, with two meals a day for each of us and fresh water and herbs and any other supplies as needed."

"Thirty whites for all that, as long as I deem the herbs and supplies reasonable."

"Fine. But I do expect your *best* room, with a very comfortable bed."

"The best room is two floors up."

"We can climb."

The going was slow, but they managed to make it up the stairs and settle Nier into the bed. The innkeeper provided warm water, cloths and herbs, grumbling all the while. Xanthe focused on tending to Nier and tried very hard not to think about what was to come.

18

The Minister's Son

Mid-morning, eleventh day of spring,
452 A.D. – Castle Dio, Ceryll

THE GUARDS CAME for Ottavio in the morning, dragged him into the tower and tossed him into a cell as if he were some common criminal. There had obviously been some terrible mistake. His father would soon get him out, and the guards would be punished.

Ottavio let the guards know this loudly.

"Liles, will you shut up?" snapped another occupant of the cell. He was lounging against the wall, filthy and careless. Ottavio saw at a glance that he was a thug.

"Let him get it out of his system," said a calm, familiar voice. "The louder he is now, the sooner he will tire."

Ottavio spun around to stare at Nicole, clad in only a nightdress. Slowly, a grin stretched across his face.

"Well, well, well," he remarked. "How the mighty have fallen."

Nicole raised an eyebrow, arrogant as ever. She glanced up briefly, looking straight through him and then back down again, as if the basket of food she was fiddling with was more worth her time. It made Ottavio's blood boil.

"What, nothing to say for yourself? I might offer to protect you from that thug over there, if you treat me nicely."

"How generous." She spoke absently, like she did not really care.

"*Thug?*" squawked the thug. "I'll have you know, I'm a completely respectable—"

"*Respectable?*" scoffed Ottavio. "You are in *prison*."

"As are you," the thug sneered.

"*I* am a minister's son, and clearly here as the result of a misunderstanding," Ottavio sniffed, straightening his shoulders. "When I am released, the king will owe my father a great many favors to make up for besmirching our honor."

"*You're* the idiot who stole from the king's treasury," sighed the thug, suddenly dismissive. It was not even a question, as if the absurd accusation was already proven.

"I would *never*," said Ottavio. "Let me speak to the king and I can tell him—"

He broke off because peals of laughter were suddenly ringing through the cell. He turned to stare at Nicole. He had never even seen her crack a genuine smile before. Her laughter was so hearty—so unlike the cold, power-hungry shrew he knew her to be—that he felt thoroughly wrong-footed.

"What do you suppose she finds so funny?" Ottavio addressed the guards outside the cell. They ignored him.

"Your obliviousness, I'd say," drawled the thug.

Ottavio flushed. "How *dare* you—"

"So you *didn't* give the younger princess a bag full of blacks?"

That he had done. "But she's the princess," Ottavio pointed out, speaking slowly because clearly the thug did not understand how things worked.

"And the coins belong to the king," said the thug.

"Who is her father."

"So?"

"So . . . she only wanted to see them and touch them. It was harmless. I always intended to return them to the treasury today."

"Then you should thank your lucky stars I got them back before she left Nirra."

Ottavio, who took great pride in his scholastic excellence, reminded himself that the thug had likely not had the luxury of an education.

"These things may be difficult to understand to one such as yourself, but Dio is not technically part of Nirra. And the princesses are not leaving Dio in the near future."

Nicole was laughing again, looking at Ottavio for the first time like she truly saw him. It felt like ridicule. Even the thug looked amused.

Before he could demand an explanation, all three of them were distracted by a commotion at the tower doors. After some fuss, the Amberrian prince came marching through, his face thunderous and his guards behind him.

"Let me in; I need to talk to her," said Enri.

The guards hesitated a moment and then let him pass.

"Talk so we can hear you, or you don't come back out," one told him.

He entered the cell. Nicole had abandoned the basket

at last and backed into the far corner, forcing the prince
to walk all the way through the cell. Ottavio edged closer.

"NICKI," Enri said loudly (unnecessarily so), his voice
echoing off the walls, "HOW ARE YOU FARING IN THIS
UNCOUTH PLACE?" Quietly and rapidly beneath the
echoes, his lips barely moving, he hissed, "What's wrong
with you?" Ottavio would have missed it if he had not
been carried closer to the pair as he edged further away
from the thug's unsettling grin.

"IT IS NOT IDEAL," Nicole responded in the same res-
onating volume. "I'm sorry," she whispered quietly and
quickly. "BUT I AM SURE IT IS ONLY A MISUNDER-
STANDING. Didn't mean it, needed you here. ALL WILL
BE WELL SOON."

"NICKI! You can't threaten me," hissed the prince. "I
AM SO GLAD TO HEAR THAT YOU ARE OPTIMISTIC.
Then expect me to dance for you. I KNEW IT HAD TO BE
A MISTAKE. I've a mind to let you rot here."

"I AM SO GRATEFUL FOR YOUR LOYALTY, ENRI,"
said Nicole with a glint in her eyes, placing her hands on
his neck so she could kiss the prince on the cheek. Ottavio
was only standing a step away now, and still he barely
made out the whisper: "Your choice, but remember what
I did for you. The company in here has already made me
very cross."

That was insulting. Ottavio glared openly.

"Clearly one of your cell mates wants to get to know
you better," said Enri loudly, though not as exaggerated as
before. "I think he may be jealous of me."

Ottavio bit his tongue against the denial that rose in his

throat. Even though she was imprisoned, he knew better than to insult Nicole outright.

"Never mind him. He knows better than to cross me." Nicole slid her hands down Enri's neck and shoulders, and then stepped back.

There was a moment of silence.

"If that's all you came to say, get out," snapped a Ceryllan guard.

Enri turned and left the cell. He walked toward the tower door, but halfway there, he hesitated and looked back.

"Has she cried? Begged? Yelled? Shown any emotion at all?"

"She laughed."

"But nothing . . . vulnerable? Not even when her father ordered her arrested?"

"None of us were there. Her personal guards brought her in."

"Shame. They are as tight-lipped as any."

The guard did not reply, but the prince was already leaving. He seemed to be scratching at his neck under his collar as he walked out of the tower.

"What was that?" Ottavio hissed at Nicole, but she ignored him. His stomach growled and he turned to the basket, but the thug was already pawing through it. The thought of eating food touched by the unwashed slob made Ottavio's stomach turn. He turned to the guards instead. "Has my father been informed of my arrest? When will he be speaking to the king?"

The guards ignored him once again.

"If he speaks to the king about you at all, he'll be apologizing for his son's idiocy," the thug said.

Ottavio gritted his teeth. He was above conversing with this man. He dedicated himself to memorizing the faces of the guards outside the cell. When he was free, he would make sure they paid.

19

The Spy

Mid-summer, 452 A.D. – Unyca, Ynga

B Y THE TIME that he'd been in Unyca for half a fortnight, Deric had fallen into step with his game. He helped Aine and remembered her gossip, went to the rainforest to talk with Esther, and reported to Melech in the evenings. But he never told him about Esther. He only said that he hadn't found where the rainfolk lived yet, but was making progress—and was grateful that Melech was too determined to maintain plausible deniability to ask for more details.

He didn't just spar with Esther. He told her deceptive truths about himself, and she occasionally responded with a crumb about herself. The crumbs weren't enough to learn much of anything about her, but they showed Deric that she was beginning to thaw.

Not telling Melech about Esther was strategic, he told himself. When a corner of his mind whispered that he was lying to himself, he pushed that away. If his afternoons in the rainforest with Esther made up the only part of his day he looked forward to, he never acknowledged it—not even to himself.

Deric sometimes woke from dreams that featured her smiling eyes and deep laugh and wondered if he wasn't lulling himself into complacency instead. A little longer, just a little longer, he kept telling himself.

Two fortnights passed this way. At last, he was forced to either take action or admit that there was a deeper reason why he didn't want to.

So he went to Melech in the night and told him to arm his men the following day. He believed he had a way to find the town, he said, but the rainfolk might come to attack Unyca when that happened.

He intended to tell Esther that he knew where Tlafa was, but that they needed more people to rescue him. He would go with her to the rainfolk town, and when they returned with reinforcements, Melech and his men would be ready. Esther he would keep safe—Melech had promised him a prisoner to take back to Noucleion, and Deric would make sure he kept that promise.

He tried not to think about what Esther would think of him after that. It wasn't important, he told himself. She was a speaker. But that night, he dreamed of Esther's violet eyes anyway, wide and horrified at his betrayal.

The morning he planned on putting things into action, he descended the staircase feeling as if he hadn't slept at all. He set about starting a fire in the stone hearth to make food for himself and to take to Esther. When he had fanned the fire into flames, he looked up—to a pair of violet eyes staring back at him. He would later consider himself fortunate that he leapt backwards into the mantlepiece, and not into the fire.

"You."

"Me," agreed Esther.

"Why are you here?" he gasped at last.

"Did you think you could play me for the fool?"

"What?"

"Stop playing this game of yours!"

Deric felt a gust of wind rush through his hair. She must have left a door or a window open, he realized. He would have to close it. Unyca was a town of thin walls already. If Melech got wind that she was here. . . .

"Give me a moment, I have to go—" He knew his mistake a moment later, when Esther's eyes narrowed and her hands shot out to wrap around his neck, pinning him to the wall as her thumbs dug into his windpipe.

"If you think I'll let you call your friends, you're madder than your leader," she whispered.

Deric coughed, fighting to push words up through his throat. He couldn't manage more than a croak. Panic gripped him—she was different from the way she was when they sparred, as if she genuinely meant to kill him. He struck the inside of each of her elbows with the side of a hand. When her grip loosened, he took hold of her wrists and was about to pin her arms behind her back. She made a sound that he thought was anger and a gust of wind pushed both of them a step back. In his shock, he loosened his hold and she spun around and pinned him again, this time with her forearm against his neck. This time, however, she let the pressure be a simple threat, leaving him his voice.

"Why are you doing this?"

"I—" Deric took a breath and exhaled slowly. "Give me a moment."

"I'd prefer an immediate answer."

Deric ignored her and breathed in and out slowly a few times. As the air cleared his mind, the earlier shock drained from his mind as well.

"I . . . I think there's been a misunderstanding. Doing what? I was just making food to bring you—"

"You told that leader of yours to arm himself today. Did you plan on luring me here to be burned alive?"

"No!" said Deric emphatically. "I wouldn't let them lay a finger on you."

"Oh, drop the act," she snapped. "It's tedious. We both know that you despise speakers and have only been trying to butter me up for some sort of plan."

"If you believed that, why did you go along with it?" Deric asked.

"I wanted to know what you were planning."

"Then why not wait for me to do whatever you thought I was going to do?"

A look flashed through her eyes—something frightened and vulnerable. She moved her arm from across his throat to grab his shoulders and pull him close. Their eyes were locked, faces close, and Deric knew that she was going to kiss him. His pulse raced.

Instead she punched him in the gut. Her punch was powerful, but it was the accompanying wind that immobilized him, pinning him firmly to the wall.

Realization dawned at last.

"You control the *wind*."

She rolled her eyes. "No, I really don't. But well-spotted, at last, that we're connected. Snails move faster than your mind. I've no use for you."

"Esther," he said. She froze and looked back at him. He hadn't said her name aloud since the day that she told him what it was. Emotions danced across her face before it went blank once more. "I like you, as a person—very much. But you're a speaker, and that's not something I can just overlook. We all face a threat from Seleukos that we cannot comprehend. I promise that I bear you and the rainfolk no ill will. I only want to understand."

"But you do fear us."

Deric swallowed and cast his eyes downward, unable to tell the truth and afraid to lie.

Esther sighed. "You speak as if you're aware of how little you know, but you're willing to judge anyway. If not for this threat from Seleukos, I'd wager you wouldn't even acknowledge that you don't understand what you fear."

"That's the nature of the threat," Deric tried to explain. "We know that we know nothing of our enemy's methods, but if we try to learn, we risk the madness that would make us destroy ourselves and those we love."

"The enemy's methods? The potentate killed one sister and imprisoned another to seize the throne. That tells you all you need to know about her."

"That's not what I mean. I mean we can't defend ourselves from the Words, and we can't learn about them without risking the madness, so—"

"The only thing that's wrong with regards to the Words is your laws," snapped Esther.

"What would you know of *our* laws?"

"Too much! Do you think I started out with the rainfolk? I tried to study history, just to learn—and I was nearly arrested for it! And worse still, I learned later, I *had* to learn to speak, or else. . . ." She swallowed. "The point is: Words aren't dangerous. But I can see whatever I say you're going to believe whatever you please. If I had any kind of choice, I'd leave and probably kick you in the gut for good measure. I've never had any patience for men like you."

"Don't act like you know what's happening in my mind," snapped Deric. "You haven't even tried to explain yet. Why not say your part and then let *me* decide what I think of it?"

They stood for a moment, gazes locked. It was in that moment that it dawned on him that her story—not originally of the rainfolk, trying to learn the history of the Words—sounded oddly familiar. Could it be that this was Sterre, presumed dead after she jumped into the Abyss? He tried to hide the revelation from his face. After a moment, she turned away.

"All right. I'll explain the basics. But promise me that you'll stop to think about it—and remember that I can't tell you anything but the truth."

Deric agreed. Esther poked around the kitchen and quickly found two mugs, the barrel of water, a lemon and a knife. She filled the mugs with water, cut the lemon and squeezed it in. She handed him a mug and took a seat at the table as if it were her own kitchen. He took the seat across from her. She took a sip of her drink. Deric held his mug and didn't follow her example. He met her eyes, daring her to tell him to drink. She didn't.

"Let's go back to the beginning," she said instead. "Tell me everything you know about why the Words were outlawed."

Deric opened and closed his mouth a few times. He'd expected her to start talking—not to ask what he knew. "Everyone knows that tale." He was stalling. *It's history*, he assured himself, but he wasn't so sure anymore. Esther raised her eyebrows expectantly.

Deric cleared his throat. "Nearly five hundred years ago, this continent was ruled by one king, who had seven sons."

"Four sons and four daughters," Esther corrected. "But an unimportant detail. Go on."

"It was seven sons. I've *always* heard seven sons."

"I believe you. Please continue."

"This king was wise and kind. When all his sons were nearly of age, he decided to choose the most worthy among them to rule after him. On the first day of his youngest son's eighteenth winter, he made his intentions known to his sons. He gave them two years to prove which was most worthy to be the next king. The eldest journeyed southeast and learned the ways of war. The second journeyed south and learned the ways of peace. The third journeyed southwest and learned the ways of wisdom. The fourth—"

"Oh," said Esther, staring at him as if seeing him for the first time. "Oh, by the stars. You don't just have an Amberrian mother. *You're* Amberrian."

Deric felt the blood drain from his face. "What gave you that idea?"

Esther scoffed. "The whole story you've been telling me is nonsense, of course. Seven sons? Journeys in different directions that teach each son only one thing? This isn't history; it's a fairy story. And the pivotal third son finds wisdom in the southwest, where Amberria lies. Probably not a story more than a century old, either, if Seleukos is where a son learns *war*."

"This is history," Deric protested. "Not a fairy story."

"Why don't I tell you the version that I know?"

"Do I have a choice?"

She started her tale without bothering to answer. "Four hundred and fifty years ago, this continent was ruled by a king and queen who had four sons and four daughters. All but one of their children were beloveds, each by a different element. It was customary that, if a royal child was a beloved, that child became heir to the throne. Yet, blessed with seven children who were all beloveds, the king and queen had to choose a successor. When they all came of age, they decided to hold a series of tests to see which of them was most suited to rule."

"I don't think I understand you," Deric interrupted. "Beloved by their subjects, you mean?"

Esther glared. "You see, this is why history was watered down into a fairy story. You can't even comprehend what happened anymore."

Deric shook his head. "I'm not sure I understand why you're giving me a history lesson at all."

Esther slammed her fists down onto the table in a crash that made Deric jump out of his skin. The wind kicked up around her, swirling her silver hair about. Then the wind died down as abruptly as it had begun.

"No," she agreed. "You're right. This is pointless."

"I don't understand. What are you trying to tell me?"

Esther pursed her lips for a moment. She sighed and shook her head, rising to her feet. "This was a mistake. I've never been good at explaining. This is a waste of our time."

"No," Deric protested, panicking. If she left now, she wouldn't let him find her again. He wouldn't be able to help Melech and would have to return knowing nothing more than that some of the rainfolk were speakers who mined black. "Please. I'm sorry I keep interrupting. Maybe . . . maybe we should start with something more. . . ." He searched his mind frantically and remembered. "Your companion. What happened to him?"

Esther narrowed her eyes at him. She hesitated a long moment. "Yes," she said at last. "I think that might be the place to begin, after all. It happened after spring's trade. . . ."

She described how she and three of her companions (Tlafa, Lialli, and one she called "my Aial") had arrived in Unyca to trade. All had gone as usual until they took a few steps into the rainforest. Her Aial sensed something and told them to stop; but before they could do anything, twelve men jumped out of the trees with ropes and nets. All three of them were captured, but Lialli burned her net away and Aial sank beneath the ground and dug away from his. Tlafa swept his captors off their feet and could have escaped, though the net was still tangled in one of his wings.

Wings? Deric wondered, but didn't interrupt.

Esther alone had been unable to escape. The wind was too distracted by Tlafa's gusts to hear her. (Deric desperately wanted to ask why the others seemed to be able to control elements, but Esther had to be heard. He bit his tongue.) Aial and Lialli escaped, moving faster than the men could follow and Tlafa went with them—but in moments he realized that Esther had been captured and turned back.

The men, satisfied that they had at least caught one of the rainfolk, were dragging Esther back out of the rainforest. But Tlafa caught up and created gusts to sweep them all off their feet. Tlafa ran among them, creating winds to distract them while Esther scrambled out of her bonds and escaped back into the rainforest. The humans couldn't see Tlafa's wings or the net caught in them.

Neither Tlafa nor Esther had seen the child. The child caught the edge of the net that no one else ought to have been able to see, and pulled with a strength that no ordinary human ought to have had. The child stood firm while Tlafa was sent sprawling.

By the time Esther realized that Tlafa had been captured, he was already being dragged into Unyca, and warning her to stay away.

"I've been biding my time nearby ever since," Esther finished. "I'd scour Unyca for him if I thought it would help, but if I get captured, no one else is coming for us."

Silence fell.

"May I ask some questions?" Deric asked. Esther shrugged noncommittally. "Why could the others control the elements, but you couldn't?"

"Because they're elementals and I'm not."

"But you do control the wind."

"I told you, I don't control it. I'm its beloved."

"What does that mean?"

"It means it likes me. If I make a request, it usually heeds me."

"So a beloved is like an elemental in training?"

Esther made a sound half way between a groan and a laugh. "Of course not! Elementals are what they are. They're created that way as much as you and I were born human. Any species can be a beloved if they have a strong connection to an element."

Deric processed this. "So all of you can communicate . . . through the wind?"

"No."

"But you can communicate without being near each other."

"Just me and Tlafa."

"Because you're both . . . connected to wind, somehow?"

"Yes."

"Esther . . . ," Deric took a breath. "What about the madness? You must know the dangers. This will only lead to destruction. Couldn't you . . . stop being a speaker?"

"You don't understand *anything!*" Esther leapt to her feet. She was out the back door before Deric could stop her. He sighed heavily. He bit down on the urge to follow; he wouldn't be able to catch her anyway.

Something heavy had settled in the pit of his stomach. He wasn't sure if it was because he'd messed up his mission, or because he likely wouldn't ever see Esther again.

20

The Scribe

Thirty-third day of Spring, 452 A.D. – Farthe, Ceryll

XANTHE SPENT TWO nights and a day tending to Nier alone. Nier remained unconscious or delirious and the wound did not seem to be healing. She would have gone for an herbalist, but the innkeeper cautioned that any herbalist who would come to an inn in the outskirts for a pair of nameless scribes was either a fraud or a speaker.

At dawn on the third day, the innkeeper came knocking and told her she had a visitor downstairs. She followed him down, worried that the caravan master had come to collect his dues. The moment she saw the head of dark red hair, she knew it was Eudon. Overcome with relief, Xanthe ran over to embrace him. He embraced her in return. They exchanged a mumbled chorus about wondering if each other were dead, and she gathered that he had been furious to learn that she and Nier had been left on the roadside despite Nier's injury.

"I asked to be left there," she explained, pulling away.

"I was worried they might decide to make us pay more if we stayed longer. You heard that I used some of their cayenne powder to treat Nier's wound?"

"In passing," shrugged Eudon. "Though I still don't even know what that is."

"It's a spice. It's common in Ynga, I think? Anyway, how did you find us?"

"I just rode along the main roads near the kingsway on the northern outskirts and inquired at the inns I found."

"That sounds tedious."

"It wasn't, really. I had to be sure you were all right. And this was only the second inn I tried."

Xanthe furrowed her brow. "Do you think the caravan master will come after us?"

"I doubt it. Chasing a few scribes over a few pinches of a spice isn't their style." His eyes grew serious. "How's Nier? It was only a metal arrow, right?"

Xanthe hesitated. "Why do you ask?"

"They had some weapons made of black. Not many, but enough to be concerning."

"I know," Xanthe snorted. "What a waste. The most precious material in the kingdom, used as a weapon."

Eudon looked at her seriously. "Black makes the worst kind of weapon. A smith who knows how to work it can make a weapon that won't leave anyone alive. Get so much as scratched by a black weapon and all hope is lost."

Xanthe felt the blood drain from her face. She turned away to dart back up to Nier, but Eudon caught her by the arm.

"Xanthe," he said. "Tell me Nier wasn't hit by black."

She said nothing. He released her and she ran back up

the stairs. She peeled the bandages from Nier's wound and swallowed the bile that rose in her mouth. The wound was oozing blood again, but now the blood was mingled with a white pus. The skin around the edges of the wound had gone gray. Despite her best efforts, it was festering.

"You can't do anything for him," said Eudon from over her shoulder. She hadn't realized that he had followed her. "You can slow the bleeding, but it will never completely scab over. You can clean the wound, but it will fester all the same."

Xanthe swallowed around a lump in her throat.

"I won't give up till he's dead," she said tonelessly. "I can find an herbalist. Someone can help him."

Eudon sighed.

"I know it's hard," he said gently, putting a hand on her shoulder. She stiffened and turned to glare up at him. But Eudon's cockiness was gone, and his face was solemn. Then he said, "Tell me what I can do to help you," and some of Xanthe's walls melted.

"Will you help me find an herbalist to help him?"

"Of course," he said, and he did.

He came with her to walk around the streets of Farthe, asking after herbalists.

They found three over the course of the day. But the moment they heard that the patient had been wounded by black, they shook their heads and said there was nothing to be done. Xanthe begged them to just come and see Nier, to only try, and when that failed Eudon insulted their integrity as healers. But none would be swayed.

At dusk, Eudon led a disheartened Xanthe back to her inn.

"I'll come back tomorrow and we can look some more," Eudon said.

"You don't have to," said Xanthe, but she was smiling.

"I know," he said softly, enfolding her hands in his. "But I can't leave you to go through this alone."

Xanthe leaned up, kissed him chastely once, and entered the inn without looking back at him, lest he see her flaming cheeks.

Night was difficult. She slept in short bursts, waking every time Nier moved or whimpered. She continued to clean his wound and considered cutting away the graying skin; but she worried that that would only make it worse.

In her sleep, she heard the disembodied voice.

Leave him, child. You can't save him, and you must reach me soon or all will be lost.

Who are you? she replied. *Can't you save him?*

I am bound by the ancient treaties to be powerless on the continent. You must set me free.

If you were free, she asked, *could you save Nier?*

If I were free, scoffed the voice, *then* you *could save him.*

What does that mean? she demanded, but her eyelids were fluttering and the voice was fading. *Can I save him now?*

Xanthe opened her eyes and blinked the sleep away. She had a feeling she was expecting something, but did not know what. She looked at Nier's prone body. He was still breathing. She checked under the bandages to find more pus and the gray shade spreading on his skin. She went down to the kitchen to ask for a bowl of broth that she tried to feed to Nier. She got him to swallow three mouthfuls and considered that a victory.

Shortly after dawn, Xanthe was outside the inn. Eudon was already waiting.

"You could have come inside," she said.

"If I had, the innkeeper would have gone to fetch you. If you were sleeping, I didn't want to disturb you. I imagine you don't find it easy to sleep."

She was touched at his concern and smiled helplessly.

That day, they went further than the day before, straight into the center of Farthe. She absently noticed that even the common folk seemed to be dressed in colorful, flashy clothes, and that people traded insults as a matter of routine. In other circumstances, she might have found it fascinating. Now it was only background noise.

They found three herbalists who said the same sorts of things as the three the day before. But the third was less forthcoming. When he heard Xanthe's name, he narrowed his eyes and looked her up and down.

"You might try Paraskevas," he said quietly. It was, like Xanthe, a Seleukoi name, and that did not escape Eudon.

"Are you sending us to a speaker?" he growled.

"Of course not," the herbalist intoned, looking straight at Xanthe. Somehow, the air around him pulsed. "I'm a law-abiding man."

He gave them directions to Paraskevas's residence all the same.

"I don't trust him," said Eudon when they had left. "He didn't mention this Paraskevas person til he heard your name."

Xanthe was inclined to agree. They did not go to Paraskevas, and continued to call on other herbalists. No one else mentioned any Paraskevas, but they also all declared Nier a dead man. Eudon walked Xanthe back to the inn at dusk.

"We'll try again tomorrow," he said. "It'll be all right." The air around him pulsed, unsettling Xanthe. Eudon kissed her, longer than the previous night. She responded, but perhaps because she was feeling unsettled, she felt no spark today.

They said their goodnights and Xanthe returned to Nier's side. He was wheezing. She cleaned his wound and tried to feed him broth, but couldn't get him to swallow.

It was completely dark outside when she made up her mind.

Pulling her cloak around her to hide her gender, she ran out into the street and sprinted down the streets to the city center. Fortunately, both moons were out, making it a bright night. In the city center, the streets were illuminated by lanterns, making it even easier to find her way. Xanthe found the house of the third herbalist they had visited that day, and followed his directions to Paraskevas's home.

She had been told it was a house with a green door. But the street was a narrow alleyway away from the lanterns, and the moons did not provide enough light to properly discern color. She walked from one end of the alley to the other, inspecting each door. She didn't want to knock on the wrong door in the middle of the night.

At last, she made her best guess and knocked. There was no response, so she knocked again with more force. When no response came again, she pounded her fist against the door, calling, "Paraskevas? I'm looking for Paraskevas!"

The door opened and a middle-aged woman of Xanthe's height and build appeared.

"Do you know what time it is?" she grumbled.

"My friend got hit by a black arrow," said Xanthe. "His wound is festering. I was told someone called Paraskevas could help."

"Even if there were such a person here, you couldn't afford such a thing," said the woman rudely. "But there isn't, so best look elsewhere. Better yet, say your prayers and keep him company til he meets Nuvay."

She tried to close the door, but Xanthe shoved her foot in the way and slipped inside.

"How dare you?" Xanthe hissed. But the woman didn't back down.

"No," the woman hissed back. "How dare *you*. You come into our house in the middle of the night, making accusations and demands."

"What accusations?" demanded Xanthe.

"You *know* what accusations!"

"No I *don't*! I only want you to save my friend!"

"Take your lies somewhere else, you filthy—"

"Laine," a man's voice cut in, "leave her alone. Look what's happening."

Xanthe blinked and realized that a light whirlwind had started—*a whirlwind inside a room*. The front door had been closed and there were no windows, yet there was a wind.

"What . . . what are you doing?" she asked quietly. She began to tremble. The wind grew faster. "Are you speakers?"

The man came up to her.

"Breathe, child. Don't mind the wind. Just breathe."

"But you—why are you doing this? What are you going to do to me?"

"Nothing. We're doing nothing. This is you."

"*I'm not a speaker,*" said Xanthe. The wind picked up even more. Two of the chairs fell over.

"I know," the man sighed. "Breathe. Don't think; just breathe with me. Think about your breath, and match it to mine."

He breathed slowly and deeply. Xanthe breathed with him. The wind slowed, then stopped. Xanthe stood.

"I'm sorry to have bothered you," she said. "Clearly I was mistaken. I'll go now."

"Not at all," said the man. "I am Paraskevas and I do have a reputation for treating those who can't afford herbalists. But I've never healed a wound from black. It's said that only speakers can do that. So you can understand why your request upset my wife."

"I'm sorry," said Xanthe. "But that wind just now—you are speakers, aren't you?"

"The wind wasn't us," Paraskevas said gently. "It was you."

"But . . . but I didn't do anything."

"No," he agreed. "You didn't. Strictly speaking, it wasn't you, but the wind itself. It's attuned to you, you see."

"You shouldn't tell her such things," said the wife, who was visibly agitated.

Xanthe didn't understand, and said so.

"You are what was called a beloved in the old days," said Paraskevas. "An element is attuned to you, and loves you. It will care for you until your last day, if you learn to speak to it."

"Speak to . . . the wind?" Xanthe understood now. The

man was clearly mad. Perhaps this was what the madness of speakers looked like.

Paraskevas looked at her like he saw through her and shook his head. "I'm afraid I've frightened you. That wasn't my intention. Maybe we can set this conversation aside and you can show me to your friend?"

Xanthe warred with herself.

"No thank you," she said at last. "I'm sorry to have bothered you. I'll be on my way now."

Paraskevas's eyes seemed sad as he opened the front door and let her out. Xanthe walked out and away without a backward glance.

21

The Lieutenant
Ambassador

Mid-morning, eleventh day of spring,
452 A.D. – Castle Dio, Ceryll

DESPITE HER POSITION as ambassador and the alliance between the countries, Dara wasn't afforded much respect in Ceryll's court. The kingdom's antiquated patriarchy and birthright laws meant that most only saw her as a lowborn girl trying and failing to fill a man's shoes. The king and heir were respectful enough, but they refused time and time again to cede control of their army, or even a portion of it, to Usha.

Every Ushani ambassador was trying to get control of their host country's military, but there was a reason why Dara had been demoted to be ambassador to Ceryll. Amberria and Ceryll were the two most pivotal countries, because if one folded willingly, the other would too. Once they had three nations' armies working as one, it would be easy to convince the remaining three to join. United under the Ushani commander, Seleukos wouldn't stand a chance.

Dara and her Ushani retinue were the only ones in the Ceryllan court who knew war. The king and heir thought their diplomacy could hold it off but Jehan was all but conquered already. The army was advancing and time was running out. The more land and people conquered, the fewer soldiers they would have to join them.

But even in Wirrn, with victims of the Seleukoi army before her eyes, the heir had refused to plead her case to the king. Dara knew then that straightforward requests were off the table. If she wanted to gain control of the Ceryllan army before most of the guards and soldiers were lost to the invaders, she needed to beat the heir at her own game. She needed to find a way into the king's ear without the heir's interference.

Despite the urgency, Dara knew well that haste would only ruin her. So she settled in to wait. Conveniently, shortly after their return to Castle Dio from that trip, three disgruntled young men from the north had been unceremoniously deposited into the barracks. Dara struck while the iron was hot and had three spies in the king's army.

But the trio weren't liked or trusted by the other soldiers and guards, and rarely ever heard anything useful. Dara waited half a year while the Seleukoi army advanced— slowly, so slowly, what were they waiting for?—trying and failing to find someone else at court that she could bribe or blackmail.

It was in mid-autumn of the year that they visited Wirrn that Dara made up her mind to assassinate the heir. With the heir and shadow gone, Gwen or Enri—both so very weak and malleable—would become the new heir; some hapless noble without Nicole's knowledge or influence would become the new shadow. Dara would have a far better chance of convincing the king. And if he still refused, she could always kill him, too.

But another half a year later, the heir was proving impossible to kill. A dozen assassins were dead and a dozen more missing.

In early spring, Dara at last dispatched Chan in the night to kill the heir in her sleep. Chan was her most trusted companion masquerading as her servant.

Chan returned in the dead of night reporting that the heir had not been in her bed.

"Why didn't you wait?" snapped Dara.

"Her guards always sweep a room before she enters. I have to enter the room after she's already there."

In the two seasons that he'd been urging Dara to let him do the deed, Chan had made a point of learning every detail of Castle Dio and its secrets, and the heir and her guards' habits. He periodically made suggestions for the next attempt to emphasize that he would know what to do.

"I wish you'd just let me kill the king," sighed Chan. "That would be easy enough. I swear the heir acts like there's an assassin around every corner."

"It's kept her alive," Dara snapped. "We have to find somewhere she'd never expect to be attacked. Do *not* lay a finger on the king while the heir lives. She's enough trouble as heir; I don't want to find out what a nightmare she'd be as queen."

Chan returned to try the heir's bedchambers again in

the early hours of the morning—but he returned saying that while the bed looked slept in and there were signs of a struggle, the heir was, once again, missing.

"You promised me you could do this," said Dara.

"And I can," said Chan. "Two attempts and I haven't been captured or killed yet."

"You've also gotten nowhere near her. Figure out where she is and *do it*."

So Chan left to investigate. But when Dara got information, it wasn't from Chan, after all. It was from the boys from the Crossing, whom she'd nearly forgotten as wasted investments. Regis came knocking that morning. When she opened her door, he was looking up and down the deserted hall like the embodiment of someone up to no good. He wouldn't be useful for any sort of subterfuge—but then she'd already known that.

"The king might have arrested the princesses last night," he told her. Dara snorted and went back to her morning training routine, flipping into a handstand.

"You brought me a 'might have'?"

"Manon—one of the heir's maids—is looking for the heir and seems worried. I tried to dissuade her, but she didn't listen. If she helps them escape—"

Dara stopped in the middle of a handstand pushup and lowered her feet to the ground. She stood upright and turned to face Regis.

"Tell me what you know."

He told her.

"And is anyone investigating whether there's any truth to this speculation, or are we operating on pure imagination?"

"Of course," said Regis. "Pierre will come report to you soon as—"

On cue, Pierre entered the room. His eyes were wild.

"It's true," he gasped. "The heir—she's in the tower. In the center cell on the ground floor with some other fellow named Theirn, who's accused of treason. Some sort of operative for the heir behind the king's back, apparently. He's bitter about where his efforts landed him."

"They let you in to see her?" asked Dara absently.

"No. Well, yes. I made up some nonsense that one of the guards inside had lost his dagger—I showed them mine—but when I hung around asking Theirn questions, they threw me out quickly enough. It's fine; they just think I'm being my nosy self. But I won't be able to get back in."

"Not a problem," lied Dara. "And what about the other one?"

Pierre shrugged, spreading his hands. "I don't know. She wasn't in the cell where the heir and Theirn are."

"Well done, boys," smiled Dara. "Now go back to the barracks and go about your day."

"How will we know if—"

"If there's news, I'll keep you informed. Now go!"

They left and Dara swept into action. A disgruntled former operative of the heir, imprisoned in the same cell as she? It was too perfect to be true. All she had to do was put a knife in his hand—even better if he believed it was the king ordering the heir's execution.

In other circumstances, she would have tried to engineer the situation in reverse: making it look like the operative was mistakenly given the knife that the heir was to use to kill him to gain her pardon. Most in that situation would turn around and kill who they thought was their would-be murderer, and in the instance of discovery, that would turn suspicion on those who wanted the operative dead. But without even knowing who the operative was, that wasn't a strategy that Dara could risk.

She sat at the desk and began to write a note. Two lines in, she froze. There was no guarantee that the man in the cell with the heir could read. Because Usha took such care keeping its population literate and educated, she tended to forget that this was not the case in Ceryll, where literacy was a privilege of the upper classes and scribes. It was so uncivilized.

She bit her lip and leaned back in her chair, twirling the pen in her fingers as she thought. After a few moments, she straightened, grabbed a fresh sheet of paper, and began to draw instructions.

22

The Spy

Eighty-second day of summer,
452 A.D. – Unyca, Ynga

D ERIC WAS PREOCCUPIED when he went to Aine's
warehouse to help her that morning. He would
have to find a way to explain to Melech that his
plan had failed before it had begun, without letting on that
he'd known Esther all along.

He didn't stay preoccupied for long. Aine was in an
agitated state when he arrived. For the first time since
he'd arrived, they worked in complete silence but for
instructions she barked at him, as if she was angry.

Deric's heart dropped into his stomach. Had someone
told her that he'd been betraying her confidences? At last,
he decided it was better to ask what was wrong than to
leave it to his imagination.

"Didn't I tell you I knew everything that happens in
this town? I know about your agreement with Melech.
I know you've been telling him everything I told you.

I know you've been stringing that poor girl along, and judging by the way Melech's witch hunters are sharpening their spears today, I know you're about to betray her."

"That *poor girl*?" Deric demanded. "If you know everything, you know she's a sp—a witch!"

"Don't treat me like the ignorant folk in this backward, forsaken town," Aine snapped right back. "I've noticed the way you speak. You'd call the lyll black; you'd call witches speakers and witchcraft Words. Most folk in Unyca have never been out of this town. I'm different—I was a Jehani merchant's daughter before I was a wife, and if I know anything at all, *you* are not Yngan. I'd guess Ceryll, but it could just as well be Amberria or Usha."

Deric's heart stopped.

"I'll tell you one more thing," Aine went on. "You don't understand the first thing about what you're looking for. You paint the witchcraft as *wrong* and are satisfied. You haven't stopped to consider that perhaps it is not the power, but the wielder."

"Witchcraft is outlawed everywhere!"

"Not in Seleukos."

Deric felt vaguely ill. "Sympathizer! I could turn you in to Melech. You would burn." He said the words with more conviction than he felt. How many sympathizers were there in Unyca and how many witch hunters? If Aine's faction wasn't significantly smaller than Melech's, he wouldn't be able to touch her without risking the wrath of those who followed her.

Aine only looked weary. "Go on. Do it, if you believe it will give you peace. But know that you and he are the same: children terrified of what you don't understand."

Rage and betrayal flared in Deric. "What *I* don't understand? Are you claiming you know about the Words? That's forbidden for a reason. I'm prepared to burn you myself and take my chances explaining to Melech later."

"You don't know a thing!" roared Aine, standing to her full height. Though she was shorter than Deric, he felt dwarfed. "Have you ever seen a village, houses and people alike, burned to ashes by a witch? I have. Have you ever met a young child, taken by a witch and forced into the worst kind of slavery for season after season, biding her time in misery and horror until she at last found a moment to slit his throat? *I have.* Do you think that these laws, these burnings, do anything to keep us safe? No. Witches *control* fire! Fire won't harm them!"

"Fire—" Deric choked, mind in a jumble, staring at Aine. "But . . . if you've seen all that, then how could you sympathize with the rainfolk girl?"

"If she had wished us ill, Unyca would be ashes."

"But it isn't so simple. The madness—the law—"

"I know nothing of the madness. I don't know why the law is the way it is."

"Why haven't you told the town?" Deric asked, seizing on this question like a lifeline to sanity. "Why haven't you told Melech?"

Aine shook her head. "It didn't used to be this crazed, before. By the time I realized that the fear and hatred were growing in Unyca, it was too widespread and I was afraid to speak. Melech never liked me. He would have me burned without listening."

"If you explained—"

"Why? No one would change their minds. Hatred is like that. No sense in reasoning with it."

"Then why are you telling me?"

"I hoped that you might be different," said Aine, her eyes softening. "You fed the girl and didn't tell Melech about her. She couldn't have lived on a potato, an egg and a flatbread a day, but you did try."

"You were feeding her too," he realized.

"And I warned her that you were about to start something this morning. I told her to go back to her people—you won't find her again."

Aine had warned her to leave—but Esther had come into Unyca to confront Deric instead. It made him want to run to find her and embrace her and try to start again.

But it was too late for that.

"You've seen the devastation speakers can bring with your own eyes and still you defend them?"

"I don't defend them all. But the girl's done nothing to hurt us. She's trusted you and me. She only wants her horse back."

"Horse?" Deric repeated, wrong-footed.

Slowly, all the pieces slotted together. Tlafa controlled the wind, with wings that ordinary people couldn't see. He'd never heard of invisible wings, but winged horses were as common in legend as firefoxes, dweorgs and water sprites. If the legendary creatures were the rainfolk . . . and the rainfolk were elementals. . . . He thought of Esther's story. One member of her group had sank into the ground—a dweorg. Another had burned away her bonds—a firefox.

The white stallion in chains. That had been Tlafa, his wings still invisible.

Deric had to leave. He had to find Esther if he could. He didn't know what he would do when he found her, but he knew that he had to try. There was nothing left for him in Unyca—nothing but Tlafa.

He didn't know what he said to Aine, but whatever it was, she let him leave without a fuss. He ran up the street and through his house to the courtyard. He didn't bother tacking up, just slipped the reins over the horse's head and mounted it bareback.

He rode through the rainforest to the place where he and Esther used to meet, but of course, she was nowhere to be seen. He called her name and searched for tracks leading further into the rainforest, but to no avail.

So he picked a direction at random and rode, calling out Esther's name now and then.

He came to a river and stopped. It was visibly deep, and the current was too rapid to ford. He turned to follow it upstream.

He hadn't gone too far when he followed the river around a corner into a clearing and was met with an unexpected sight. Esther was emerging from the river and hastily pulling her long white cloak on.

"What are you doing here?" she squawked.

But he was speechless, staring at her bare legs.

They were pink. It was not the pink of flushed pale skin. There was no skin at all. He could see the pulsing red flow of blood through transparent vessels. He could see the pink of what he suspected were muscles beneath.

It all seemed to be held in by something transparent that made up not only skin, but also blood vessels and part of her muscles.

He only saw it for a few moments before the cloak hid everything. But that sight was enough to chill him to the bones. He tried to remember why he had assumed that Esther was human. Deric's hand crept toward the katar concealed at his waist that had been a gift from Melech.

He chanced a glance up at her face again and met her familiar violet eyes. She looked only frightened. He dropped his hand.

"What are you?" Deric asked quietly.

"Human."

"How do I know you aren't lying?"

"For crying out loud," snapped Esther. She lifted the cloak up to her knees. He could see the blood flowing in networks of transparent vessels in, out and over pink muscle all the way down to her feet. It seemed to him that he could see some of the white of bone and cartilage in her feet and ankles. "Look your fill. I'm a human; make no mistake. I'm a human who was fortunate enough to be near the Elayil when I learned how fire despised me."

"Elayil?"

"Water elementals," she snapped. "They take it upon themselves to heal and give aid wherever they can. When I tried to speak to fire, it reached out and licked what it could reach of me. Lialli—a fire elemental—took me to them and they eased my wounds and restored my legs to me the only way they could: in water."

"The transparent parts are water?"

"Yes. Now, have you looked your fill?"

"Fire despises you?" he whispered, looking up at her eyes again.

"It does," she answered quietly, dropping the cloak once more. "It's why I needed you to bring me food that I didn't have to cook."

"Aine told me speakers controlled fire."

"No speaker controls anything, but there are some whose wishes fire would be inclined to heed, like the wind heeds me. What else did Aine tell you?"

"That she was helping you. And she told me her story."

"What does that have to do with anything?"

"It made me think—if she can see a girl tortured by a speaker and still believe that not all speakers are all bad, maybe—Esther, if you hadn't been a speaker, I'd have been on your side from the first day I arrived."

But Esther looked confused. "Her daughter was tortured by a speaker?"

"What? Her daughter? No, it was some child she came across when she was traveling with her father. Or . . . did she adopt the girl?"

"No. . . . A different story, maybe," Esther said.

"Why? What did she tell you?"

"She told me you were selling her out to the man who calls himself the leader of the witch hunters." She answered with a challenging look that let him know that she was deliberately misunderstanding the question.

"I was," Deric admitted.

"Why shouldn't I turn and run?"

"I came to find you to tell you—I know now. Tlafa was

the—what I thought was a white stallion in the stable. I was. . . . You've talked about elementals of rocks and fire and water, and Tlafa's invisible wings. These elementals are dweorgs, firefoxes, water sprites and winged horses, right?"

"What difference does that make?"

"Yngans fear the rainfolk like they're some mysterious monsters. But all the stories of creatures by those other names—they're always benevolent. If the stories are true . . . !"

"You're changing your mind about trusting me because of a few stories?" Esther snorted and turned away. Deric reached out and caught her wrist.

"Wait, I meant to say—it's all stories to me. I've never seen a speaker in action. I've only been taught to fear them. Before I came here, the only thing I knew of speakers was the horrors I saw in victims of the Seleukoi army. But now I've met you and Aine—and Tlafa, even if I didn't know him at the time. I was drawn to Tlafa and to you. Every instinct in my body wants to trust you. So—let me trust my instincts this time."

"And do what?" demanded Esther, though her face was darkening with a flush.

"I told Melech and his men to stand guard today. Let me stay here with you until they let their guard down— then we'll break into the stable and escape with Tlafa."

"You've had two fortnights to come up with a plan, and that's the best you could do?"

"I wasn't spending those days trying to come up with a plan. I was trying to figure out how to play you, Melech and Aine in a way that suited me."

"But now you've changed your mind," she said, raising

her eyebrow. "Why should I trust someone who planned to betray me until this morning?"

"Because even while I was trying to figure out how to play you and Melech against each other, I was always trying to work out how to keep you safe."

"I don't need you to protect me," she said coldly. "It doesn't change that you intended to betray me."

"I didn't know you! All I knew was that you were a speaker and that speakers are a threat."

"You barely know more than that now!" she retorted.

"I know that Aine told you to run away," he said quietly. "Instead you came straight to me."

Esther looked away.

"You can hear lies?" he asked.

"I can."

"I care about you. I've been telling myself I didn't, because I thought—I didn't know anything but fear of speakers. I'd been taught that they were evil, the enemy. But I liked you so much that I've been struggling all along to think of you that way."

"I hope you don't think you're being flattering," said Esther. "It's common sense to not view someone as an enemy if they've done nothing to you."

"But not for me," Deric stressed. "Not for someone trained in the military to view the enemy as no more than that."

Esther raised an eyebrow. "I thought you were uncommonly good at melee. So you're an Amberrian soldier. What brings you all the way out here?"

The words caught in Deric's throat. Esther's eyes narrowed.

"You can't trust me with the true reason you're out here—is that it?"

"No, I. . . ." Deric closed his eyes. His stomach roiled, but the decision was already made. "I was sent here by the king."

"Sent to *Unyca*? What for?"

"No—to Ynga. To make sure that the country is as against the Words as it seems to be on the surface."

Esther started to laugh. "And you've been wasting your time playing small town politics in Unyca?"

He felt his face heat. "I couldn't find any evidence of speakers in Noucleion, but I realized that the black might not be something that could be mined without magic. I followed the clues and found Unyca—and then I thought if I could find where the rainfolk lived, I'd have my answer."

"And you do. You know exactly what the rainfolk are, and you have my word that they're not linked to Seleukos in any way. They'll never fight in a human war. So you can go back to your king and make your report."

"I can't do that," Deric confessed. "I can't leave you here, caught in the middle of another war."

"That's a dramatic word."

"It's the word that Melech—the leader of the witch hunters—uses."

Esther shook her head. "You were a witch hunter just this morning."

"I thought it was in alignment with what I was supposed to do! I thought that—"

"You thought what?"

Deric shook his head. "What matters is that I know now. I want to help you."

"Even though I'm not as quite human as you thought?" she challenged. "Even though you know nothing about me?"

"I know enough," said Deric.

And somehow, she agreed to let him stay.

23

The Scribe

Thirty-fifth day of spring,
452 A.D. – Farthe, Ceryll

THE FOLLOWING MORNING, Xanthe did not wake until long after dawn. When she woke, she tried again to get Nier to swallow some of the broth left over from the night before. She managed to coax two swallows and sighed in relief. Then she realized that he had swallowed five mouthfuls in two days, and wondered how long before he died of thirst. His lips were already cracked and white with dead skin that stood out against his graying black skin.

It was near noon before she remembered that Eudon might be waiting for her. She checked outside and sighed with relief to find that no one was there. She also peered into the tavern, just in case—and there he was, nursing a tankard of ale.

"I wish you wouldn't waste your time on me," Xanthe said, sitting down across from him. "Everyone around here seems to have decided that Nier is a lost cause."

"Then you shouldn't have to face it alone," he said gently, reaching across to squeeze her hand.

"I didn't think you were like this," she admitted off-handedly. "You seemed more. . . ."

"More what?"

"Arrogant? Self-involved?"

"Would you have preferred that?" he gave her an exaggerated cocky smile, and Xanthe laughed in spite of herself.

"No," she smiled. "You have a rough exterior that hides selflessness and compassion. That's . . . rare. I adore it."

His face sobered.

"Xanthe—Miss Xanthe. I have to admit, I haven't been that selfless in this. I know—I know it isn't the time for this, but once Nier gets better, I'm going to ask you to be my bride. I'll provide for you, and we can settle down in whatever town you like. You won't have to work anymore—"

"What if I want to work?" Xanthe interjected, surprising herself.

Eudon quirked a smile. "Then far be it from me to stop you. I've never met a woman like you, and I want to be near you."

Xanthe was speechless. Her mouth was dry and her heart pounded. She told herself that it was ridiculous. As Gwen, she had received more marriage proposals than she could count. But then again, Gwen's proposals had always had political undertones and had never truly been about her. Perhaps that was why Gwen had never felt for anyone what Xanthe felt for Eudon.

"I . . . I have to think about it," she stammered. "Excuse me."

She returned to Nier's bedside in a daze. *Marriage, to Eudon.* She hadn't even realized that she'd been dreaming of such a thing until he suggested it. Xanthe automatically cleaned Nier's wound again and fed him broth. She managed to make him swallow three more spoonfuls.

It was the stray thought, *What would Nier say?* that shattered her bliss. And then came the shame, because she should have known better. She had always known better. She had always been the one *telling* Nier that she knew better whenever he worried that she was leading her suitors on too much. She had not meant to lead Eudon on. She had simply forgotten who she was for a time. Her secrets were too big and too important to share.

She had been behaving like she had the authority to make choices about her life, but she didn't. She never had, but now all she did had to serve the mission. From her carelessness with Trygve's journal to her relationship with Eudon, she had forgotten her cause. Nier had tried to tell her and she had dismissed him.

Xanthe looked up in time to see a clean cloth fluttering off the pile and into her lap.

Her blood went cold and she looked around. There was no one there but Nier and her. Yet the cloth had moved of its own volition.

She thought back to the night before and wondered if her judgment of Paraskevas had been sensible, or only in service of her own feelings. She couldn't be sure—and that was answer enough.

Xanthe shoved the cloth out of her lap and left the inn to walk straight to Paraskevas's house. This time, the door opened after her first knock and Paraskevas's wife stood there again, glaring at her.

"A cloth moved itself into my lap," Xanthe said without preamble. "What's happening?"

"You had better come in," sighed the woman, stepping aside. Paraskevas was sitting at the table on one of the chairs that the wind had knocked over the night before.

"Sit down," said Paraskevas.

Xanthe obeyed. The wife pushed a steaming mug in front of her, which Xanthe eyed suspiciously.

"It's only rooibos tea," Paraskevas smiled. "From Usha. Would you tell me your name?"

"Xanthe," she said.

"Seleukoi," he noted. "Do you come from there?"

"So is yours," she retorted. "Do *you* come from Seleukos?"

"I do," he said. "My parents had certain ideas about how my life was supposed to go. I disagreed. Then I met Laine here and decided to run away with her."

Xanthe looked up at Laine. "So you're from around here?"

"In a way."

A brief silence fell.

"So are you from Seleukos?" Paraskevas asked again.

"Is it important?" asked Xanthe.

"No," he smiled. "But I would like to get to know you a little. It's hard to trust a stranger; I'm sure it's the same for you. I'll answer your questions, but I'd like you to answer mine too."

Xanthe hesitated. If he was a speaker, he would hear lies.

"I'm not Seleukoi," she said. "My mother's mother was. I'm born and raised Ceryllan."

"And you were given a Seleukoi name as what, a joke?" interjected Laine. "Or did your parents wish you ill?"

Xanthe scowled, liking her less every moment. She was not thinking when she responded, "They gave me a Ceryllan name."

"Then why don't you use it?"

Xanthe opened her mouth and closed it.

"Stop hounding her," said Paraskevas.

"She's hiding something," said Laine. "Who would choose to go by a Seleukoi name in Ceryll in these times? What if she's a spy?"

"I'm not a spy," Xanthe said honestly.

"Then tell us your Ceryllan name," said Laine.

"Why should I?"

"What have you to hide?"

Xanthe scowled. What, indeed? If she had learned anything, it was that no one knew or cared about the gold-and-silver twins. Certainly not enough to know their names. So she said, "It's Gwenaëlle."

Laine's eyes went wide. She plopped into the chair beside Xanthe, staring at her.

"*Paraskevas*," she said breathlessly, not taking her eyes off of Xanthe.

Heart in her throat, Xanthe stood and started edging for the door.

"I'm sorry, I think I—"

"You misunderstand," said Paraskevas, who was looking at her with fascination. "It's the first time that

Ghyslaine here has had the chance to meet one of her nieces. She never thought she would see any of you."

Xanthe furrowed her brow. "Ghyslaine?" That had been her grandmother's name on her father's side, but she had died in childbirth decades before Xanthe was born.

Laine reached out to clasp Xanthe's hand. Xanthe wanted to pull away, but something compelled her to stay.

"I was named for my mother," Laine said. "She died to give me life, so my father gave me her name."

Xanthe wanted to object. Aunt Inas, Aunt Marilene and Father rarely spoke of their dead younger sister, and Grandfather never said a word about her—but she was *dead*. Then again, when Stelle ran away, Father and Nicki had debated whether to say that she was ill or dead. She ought to have wondered then. How many other "dead" family members had run away? How much of the world at court was illusion, and how much of it was real?

She could see the family resemblance in Laine now: Aunt Marilene was in her lithe build and no-nonsense body language, Aunt Inas in her cheekbones and eyebrows, and Father in the deep blue of her eyes. She looked especially like Stelle—and probably Gwen herself too, though her skin was far lighter, her face was lined and creased with age, and her hair was as black as Nicki's.

"What . . . what does your family call you?" Laine asked—or should that be Aunt Ghyslaine?

"Gwen," she said.

"Gwen," Laine repeated with a smile.

To hear her name after all these days sent a warmth coursing through her veins. She hadn't realized quite how much she missed her family until this moment. She had never been away from all of them for even a day until this trip, and now it had been more than a fortnight. Even this member of her family that she had never met gave her a small taste of home that she hadn't realized she'd been craving.

"What are you doing in Farthe using a Seleukoi name?" asked Laine, like she wanted to be scolding but couldn't quite manage it through her smile.

Gwen hesitated. Emotions danced across Laine's face and she dropped Gwen's hand and pulled away.

"Of course," she shook her head. "You don't trust me. That's wise. No need to tell me anything. Let *me* tell *you*— we're leaving Farthe tonight."

"We?" Gwen asked sharply. Her hackles rose—she had not come away from court only to fall under the thumb of some long-lost relative.

"We," Laine nodded, "Paraskevas, Roch and I."

"Roch?" Gwen repeated.

"Our—your cousin."

Gwen's heart raced. Had Paraskevas been of noble blood, had Laine remained at court, he might have been next in line before Nicki. It would have hinged on the ruling of a council that resented being of less importance than the female heir. They surely would have ruled in a male's favor. Gwen wondered absently if Roch knew how close he had come to being king.

But that was neither here nor there. She pulled her mind back to the present, where Laine and Paraskevas were leaving—and Nier was dying.

"Why?" she asked. "Why are you leaving so suddenly?"

"You told us yourself last night," said Paraskevas

quietly. "An herbalist sent you here for a task only possible to a speaker. We're not safe here. You're welcome to come with us."

"Of course," Laine nodded. "In fact, you must. I won't take no for an answer."

Gwen might have reacted negatively if Paraskevas had not immediately turned a hard look on his wife.

"It's her choice," he said. "Don't push her." He turned back to Gwen, where an idea was forming in her mind.

"Can my friend come too?" Gwen blurted.

Laine and Paraskevas exchanged a look.

"Your friend wounded with black?" he asked.

"The same," Gwen confirmed.

"He's dying. I already told you. We can't care for a dying man while we travel."

"But you also said that a speaker can cure him," she pointed out.

"I said that only a speaker could cure him."

"And you're a speaker. Can't you at least try?"

"I'm not a speaker," he said, meeting her eyes. The air stirred around him. Gwen opened her mouth to object before realizing that speakers couldn't lie. Her brow furrowed.

"Then why are you running? Some random man tells people you can do something only speakers are supposed to be able to do—so what? What difference does it make to you? Clearly you would pass the test of lies."

Paraskevas crossed his arms lightly, creases in his brow deepening as he looked at her. Gwen felt like he was looking straight through her, but she met his gaze and did not shirk.

"We were running from him," he said slowly, "and also from you."

"From me?" Gwen blinked. "But you just invited me to come with you."

"Yes. If you were a stranger, there was nothing we could do but run. But you are family, so if you will trust us and let us trust you in return, we can help you."

"You *just told me* that you wouldn't help Nier," Gwen said impatiently.

"Not with your friend. With the wind."

Gwen almost asked what he meant—then she remembered the whirlwind last night and the cloth this morning.

"Are you saying—the madness? I learned too much about the Words and now I—" She felt sick.

"No," said Paraskevas. "No, or else this would not be a problem. You are a beloved."

Gwen stared at him, then at Laine, who was nodding solemnly.

"You don't even know me," she said. "Just because we share blood doesn't—"

"*A* beloved," said Paraskevas. "There are speakers, then there are beloveds."

When Gwen stared at him uncomprehendingly, he explained that Words were only a language. Language—a word Gwen only knew from a book, for there was only one on the continent. People spoke differently in some parts, but it was only in their pronunciation and choice of words. Scholars called those differences *dialects*. History books said that there were once many languages spoken a millennium or two ago. Perhaps the Words were among those languages. The Words, Paraskevas said, were not to communicate with other creatures, but with the elements themselves.

"What does any of this have to do with me?" Gwen interrupted after a time.

"The difference between speakers and beloveds is that speakers choose to learn. They can choose not to learn and all is well. Beloveds *must* learn."

"I don't understand. What about the madness? The madness that caused the Destruction! It was why the Words were banned!"

"I don't know about what happened at the Destruction, but the madness is what comes over beloveds who don't learn to speak to their element. It usually takes hold in adolescence or early adulthood."

Gwen stood up with such force that her chair fell behind her. She ignored it.

"You don't know what you're talking about. The madness claimed my—someone close to me. She was reading about the history of the Words. She jumped off a cliff."

"Then she was not reading the right things—and even if she were, it is a hard thing, learning to speak to the elements out of a book. It was not what she learned, but what she did not. She was lucky that the madness only took her. You're headed down the same path, and you might take all of Farthe with you."

Anything Gwen might have said was swept away by that last comment. She had sworn to herself that the one thing she wouldn't do was follow in Stelle's footsteps.

"Then what can you do? Take me away from the city to some abandoned field and abandon me to go mad and die alone?"

"I can teach you to speak. You would never go mad."

"You *just said*—"

"I lied."

"But speakers can't lie."

"They can hear lies, and they can also lie. There is too much that you don't know for me to explain it all now. We're leaving tonight when the second moon rises. You're welcome to come with us, but if you do, you must let me teach you."

"And if I say no?"

"Then you die here," Laine interjected sharply. "Along with any number of innocent people."

Paraskevas said nothing, only looked at her.

Gwen gritted her teeth and clenched her fists. The Words took Stelle away. The Words were what the Seleukoi speakers used against the Jehani. Yet even now she was conscious of the wind brushing her cheeks. It was comforting. How long had it been doing that?

"When did the elements pick me?"

"Not all the elements, just wind," Paraskevas said. "At birth. It's always at birth. In the old days, people would give birth in rivers or oceans or near rockslides or volcanos in the hope that the child might be born a beloved. It's been forgotten, but the purpose of birthing rooms is to keep elements as still as possible to try to prevent beloveds from being born."

"But I was born in a birthing room!"

"Is there not air in a birthing room? In the end, the elements do as they please."

Gwen bit her lip. She knew that he was telling the truth. She thought of the way she had been watching air pulse or stir around people lately. Those were lies, she realized, and Paraskevas hadn't lied since he said he wasn't a speaker.

There was a part of her that wanted to scream, to storm out and tell them to get out of her life and never show their traitorous faces again.

But Gwen had been well-trained for court. She knew better than to react on emotional impulse. She had set out to save her country. They said that one had to know the enemy to fight. What better way to know speakers than to learn the Words? It had been nagging at her that the Phoenix might be a weapon that could only be used by speakers. She had been planning to bring it back to Dio before worrying about using it. Here before her was a far more elegant solution.

"I'll come with you," said Gwen, "on one condition."

Once the war was won and her part was played, then she could sentence herself to death for the terrible crime she was about to commit. But she would not see Nier die alone—or die at all, if she had any say in the matter. And soon, Nevena help her, she might get that say.

Just hold on a little longer, she thought at him.

24

The Falcon

Mid-morning, eleventh day of spring,
452 A.D. – Castle Dio, Ceryll

ON THE MORNING when Juste came storming in,
railing about Nicki's deceptions and Gwen's
disappearance and implying that he had *jailed
his heir and shadow,* Odilon's blood ran cold.

Nicki didn't tell him the secrets she kept—hadn't for
years. As far as he knew, no one knew exactly how much
she knew. But she wielded her knowledge well, using it
against what had to be half the residents of Castle Dio to
keep them under control. With Nicki out of the picture,
that half of Dio would very likely decide to act out. Most
of those would not be a problem. But in these trying times,
there were several factions in the castle that had reason to
want the king or the heir or both deposed. Odilon thought
first of the ambassadors, then of the ministers, then of the
guards—and then had to stop, because his stomach was
turning.

Odilon didn't stop Juste's rant. He was practiced

at nodding and making periodic noises of agreement. Meanwhile he worked out how he could justify getting Nicki out of the tower before the worst befell her. It was pointless to reason with Juste when he was in a mood like this one, especially as the truth was not one he would appreciate. But if he waited until Juste's temper cooled, it might be too late.

The shadow politics had been left to Nicki for too many years. Odilon was out of practice, and even after Juste was done ranting, even after they parted ways to go about their day, he could find no excuse to defy the king and release the heir. He sat in his office, helpless and chilled to the bone.

Nicki, on the other hand, was more resourceful than he had imagined. From her cell in the tower, she sent Enri to his door. It was such an unexpected move that Odilon at first did not understand Enri's presence in the castle's west wing.

"Yes?" he asked blankly. "Are you lost?"

"Nicki said to say—it will be Ynga or the treasury first."

Odilon dropped his pen and stood from his desk. "You talked to her today? In the tower?"

Enri nodded jerkily. "She said to say that there are too many guards inside and that two pawns are with her. One of them is a minister's son. She said to say he is your ticket."

Odilon clicked his tongue. "Noted. Anything else?"

Enri hesitated. "Not for you. . . ." The hesitation on his face suggested that he wanted to tell Odilon anyway. It was the face of a man who had just realized that he was a pawn in someone else's game. That would not do—if

Odilon let him go and he talked to the next person, the result could be disastrous.

Getting to Nicki before any assassins did was imperative. It was even more imperative to keep her web from unraveling. It was her own careless treatment of Enri that had caused this crisis. She could wait a few extra moments.

"Listen," said Odilon. "I have served Juste as his man for twenty-five years. And I was his closest friend for twenty-five years before that. I am his most loyal subject."

Enri tensed and began to back away. Odilon stepped forward and yanked him close by the arm.

"No, *listen*. He would run this kingdom on idealism and the word of the law, which is admirable and inspiring. But no court can operate that way. The laws contain loopholes that can be exploited. Every day, rebellions brew beneath the surface, and if we let them brew until they were in breach of the law, it would be too late to stop them. I have spent most of my life protecting Juste from the shadows so that he can run his kingdom on his ideals. Because I trust him, do you understand?"

"Yes, I—"

"No, I don't think you do," he said, slipping into the faster, common speech of his childhood. He and Queen Consort Esther had begun the work together, and he would have floundered after her death if Nicki had not come to his door asking him to teach her what to do. "I'm old, as you can see. Nicki does what I can't do anymore. She crushes the seeds of defiance, so that Juste can rule his kingdom the way he believes is right."

Enri was very still.

"I trust her as much as I trust Juste. You can trust her, too. She believes in Juste's ideals as much as I do—but we also are not able to ignore harsh reality. She'll use you, but be faithful and she'll also be fair, and even kind."

Less kind than she had been before Stelle's death—but Enri hadn't known her then.

"She. . . ." Enri swallowed thickly. "She told me that once I was her foster brother, she would never use my secrets against me. But she did."

Odilon suppressed a sigh.

"I'd put that down to a bad morning," he said wryly. Under normal circumstances, Enri was never aware when he was being manipulated. Nicki's careless treatment of him said volumes about her state of panic. "Now, can you wait here, or do you have other places to go?"

"She told me to. . . ." he swallowed.

Odilon nodded. "Then do as you're told. I have my own work to do."

Enri looked like he had more questions, but he held them back. Odilon didn't let his relief show. He was too old and too cynical for this.

Odilon walked into the tower with a nobleman's attire under his arm. Sure enough, Nicole was in a cell with Ottavio, son of the minister of the treasury, and some man he didn't recognize.

He knew Ottavio well. The boy was a fool, and had never made any secret of his plans to seduce Gwen so that she would persuade Juste to let her wed him. He had even bragged to his circle of friends of his plan to arrange an "accident" for Nicki afterwards, so of course she and Odilon were well aware of the plan. Fortunately for Ottavio, Gwen had always been too clever to be seduced.

"I've come to release the minister's son," he said. "Why are there so many guards in here? There're plenty keeping watch at the doors outside. Surely you all have something better to do?"

"The king ordered—" one guard began, but Odilon waved him off.

"Very well, then you can all stand watch outside."

The guards exchanged looks.

"Give me the key to this cell, and go on!" Odilon barked, and they obeyed.

When Odilon unlocked the door, the minister's son tried to step through it as if he thought *he* was really the one Odilon had come for. Odilon stopped him with a hand to his chest. The boy stopped, looking confused.

Understanding dawned on him when Odilon passed the clothes to Nicki. He tried to push past Odilon as Nicki shed her nightdress shamelessly and quickly put on the clothes. Odilon struck the boy in the neck with the side of his open palm, watching without sympathy as he crumpled to the ground, gasping for air.

Nicki stepped over him without a glance.

She didn't say a word as Odilon led her away, hair hidden beneath the hat, face downturned. They walked quickly and silently out of the tower, down the hall to the west wing and into his office.

When the door closed behind them, Odilon burst out, "What is *wrong* with you?"

"Sorry," said Nicki, sounding not at all like she meant it. "I was caught off guard by a lot of things at once."

"You cannot let yourself get *jailed* like that—and the way you treated Enri? You had him ready to tell me more than was intended for me."

"Thus I sent him to you first," she replied smoothly. "I knew you would offer him reassurance."

"Do not play that game with me, child," said Odilon, reminding her that he had known her all her life. "I know carelessness when I see it."

"Sorry," she said again, only slightly more sincere. "I was caught off guard. Manon surprised me with a breakfast basket, with a few treasures inside. I had to think fast."

"I have never known you to have trouble with that," said Odilon.

"I do better when I have a little bit of time to plan," she admitted. "I had to decide who to summon in an instant, and I could not risk him not coming immediately."

"If you had just summoned me—"

"And how would that look? My maid goes straight to the falcon who sets me free? No. Besides, any note I sent through Manon had to be carefully worded."

Odilon raised an eyebrow, remembering Enri's cryptic wording.

"I had to take *more* care with Manon," Nicki amended.

"But perhaps you can trust her more than you thought," Odilon murmured.

"Perhaps," hummed Nicki. "But we will have more important matters at hand today."

"What do you expect to happen today?"

Nicki told him about Minister Septimo and Ambassador Baraz. Then she told him her plan, which ended with her back in the cell for Juste to release her, leaving

Odilon to take the credit for thwarting the assassination attempts.

"Should we not intervene immediately?" Odilon asked.

"I think it would be best to let these plots play out," shrugged Nicki. "Since we know what they intend to do, we have the advantage. Do you disagree?"

"Do not play me," scowled Odilon. "By taking the credit if this succeeds, I also risk the blame if it fails. Ask for my help if you want it."

"I would never play you, dear Odi," smiled Nicki, using her childhood name for him. "That was me asking."

Odilon couldn't help meeting her smile with his own. He went to a side table and poured two small glasses of liquor. He handed one to Nicki.

"Long live the king," he said. "May no one die today."

"Long live the king," Nicki echoed. "May no innocents die today."

They drank.

25

The Spy

End of summer,
452 A.D. – Rainforest near Unyca, Ynga

AMPING IN THE rainforest with Esther began awkwardly. She seemed determined to keep Deric at arm's length, an ally and nothing more. He was willing enough to go along with this, as she clouded his judgment enough as it was.

That was easier said than done. Esther had constructed a lean-to where she slept, but it was just big enough for one. With the two of them occupying the tight space, they had to sleep close together. Deric was plagued by insomnia, too aware of Esther's body right beside his own to sleep for most of the night.

The first day was the most trying. Esther was put out when she realized that Deric hadn't brought any food with him, reminding him that Aine believed that she had fled and wouldn't be bringing them anything. An argument ensued, only to be awkwardly resolved when they both realized that as Deric could use fire and both of them could hunt, this was not a problem. That matter had scarcely been resolved when another tiff began after Deric requested the return of his hunting knife.

On the evening of the second day they spent in the rainforest, they approached Unyca. Esther assured him that she would keep requesting the wind to keep her informed of their surroundings, which would allow them to detect any Unycans well before they were detected. They hadn't even come into view of the wasteland when Esther stopped him and whispered that there were twenty men hiding in the trees up ahead. They turned back, returning every evening afterwards to see if the men had retreated. But every day, there were still twenty men lying in wait.

Esther had gone back to wearing the leaf boots immediately.

It was the third day before Deric commented.

"You weren't wearing those boots the first few times I met you," he observed.

"No," Esther agreed.

"But your legs looked . . . normal."

Esther's face broke into a smile. "One of the benefits of being *Qyul*—of air. The air can bend light differently, so people can't see Tlafa's wings, or to make my legs look like a normal color."

"Why the boots, then?"

"I'm only a beloved. If the wind became distracted, I'd be left undisguised."

"But I know what your legs look like now."

Esther scoffed. "Yes. And I saw the look in your eyes when you saw them."

Deric rolled his eyes. "It's my first time seeing human flesh replaced by water. Is it any surprise I stared?"

"I'm not a spectacle to be gawked at," she said sharply.

"No," said Deric quietly. "So will you show me again?"

Esther stared. "Why?"

"I want to be your friend. I want us to trust each other."

"Trust?" Esther scoffed. "After you tried to spring a trap on me?"

"I understand," said Deric. "But . . . just know that when you're ready, I'd like it if you could be yourself. At least here, where there's no one else to see."

He felt Esther staring after him as he walked away to gather firewood.

But the next morning, she didn't put on the boots. Deric couldn't help smiling. Esther saw his smile and scowled back.

"They weren't comfortable," she explained.

"Then I'm glad you're not wearing them anymore," he replied.

Their day went about as usual until evening, when Esther rounded on him abruptly.

"Do you know that you're projecting your attraction to me so strongly that the air can *feel* it? So the air is telling me that you want me, constantly."

Deric wished the ground would open up and swallow him whole. A strangely calm corner of his mind wondered idly if he could get the land to do so if he were a speaker.

"I'm sorry," he muttered. "I can't—I mean, you're very. . . ."

"I don't understand," Esther said. "You were horrified last time you saw my legs."

"Your legs don't come into it. It's . . . you're very much at ease, now. I told you—I like you. You're clever and you make me laugh."

Esther stared at him.

"How can my legs not come into it? They're part of me."

A frustrated groan leaked from Deric's throat. "Enough about your legs. It's—I have no idea—maybe it isn't an unusual thing among speakers, but I'd never seen anything like that before. It caught me off guard. I didn't mean to make you so self-conscious."

"So you find them unremarkable?"

"Of course not." The truth came out with ease. "They're fascinating. They draw my eyes, and I keep wondering what they would be like to touch. But I understand that you want to be treated as if they were unremarkable, so I'll treat you as such!"

"So your interest is because of my legs."

"No! I thought you said the air could . . . I was interested even before I saw—"

Esther stepped up to him.

"Touch them, then."

Deric stared at her. "I didn't mean. . . ." But he trailed off, uncertain how to end that sentence.

"Go on, feel them."

He knelt before her. He reached out and spread a hand over one of her feet. The texture was more like glass, though it was as supple as skin. He laid two fingers over the largest artery on the arch of her foot, feeling her pulse beneath his fingers. It was ordinarily difficult to feel the pulse here, but in Esther it was unmistakable. The transparent skin seemed to transmit the sensation directly to his fingers.

"Is your curiosity sated?" asked Esther.

Deric looked up at her and met her eyes. The light that shone there, combined with the beginning of a smile curling at the corner of her mouth, drew Deric in.

"May I?" he asked quietly.

"May you what?" Her eyes were challenging.

He flattened his palm over her foot, enjoying the feel of her warm, glassy skin. He spread the other hand over her other foot similarly. Holding her gaze, he slid his hands up her ankles and to her calves beneath her skirt.

"How far up does it go?" Deric dared to ask.

In response, Esther hiked her skirt up to her thighs. Deric was caught between the awareness that he ought to cover his eyes and his fascination at the way the blood vessels and veins faded into dark scar tissue above her knees, which in turn faded into regular, unmarked skin at mid-thigh.

"It must have hurt."

"Like death itself," she agreed. She didn't lower her skirt, nor did she avert her eyes from his.

He slid his hands up to her thighs, holding her eyes and searching for any sign of discomfort. He felt rather than saw the smooth glassy skin transition abruptly into rough scar tissue. He slid his hands further up still and felt her regular, human skin. He was acutely aware of the heat beneath his palms.

Esther was beginning to look distinctly flushed.

"Would you like me to stop?" Deric asked, proud that his voice remained level.

"I was going to say, why stop here?" she said instead, pushing his hands away from her legs. She bent down to kiss his mouth. It was dry and clumsy, and Deric was caught between the sensation of her mouth, awareness that he had no idea where to put his hands, and fear that she was about to lose her balance and send them him toppling backwards.

"That doesn't work," she muttered. She dropped to her knees beside him and pulled his head to hers, bringing their lips together again. On level ground, the angle was far more comfortable. This time the contact was electric. Deric wrapped his arms around her back and pulled her closer.

*   *   *

"Just to be clear," said Esther later, "we're not courting."

"I didn't think we were," said Deric, ignoring the bitter barbs that her words became in his chest.

"There won't be any talk of love or any such nonsense."

Deric wanted to argue that love was not nonsense. He refrained, sensing that Esther would dislike that response. "What are we, then?" he asked instead.

"We're friends," she said.

Deric decided that that might be enough. A moment later, a chilling thought made him sit bolt upright.

"Tlafa!" he exclaimed.

"What about him?"

"Was he . . . watching? The whole time?"

"He can't actually *see* anything unless I send him a picture. If you must know, Tlafa would find involvement in this just as distasteful as you seem to. Elementals don't do silly things like love and romance."

"Don't they?" Deric asked absently, too busy being relieved to pay much attention.

"No. Elementals are created, not born. Can I have my pillow back now?"

Deric lay back and Esther curled up to him, appropriating his shoulder as a pillow. Soon enough, he heard her breathing grow slow and deep with sleep. Deric reminded himself that soon enough they would be freeing Tlafa and parting ways. He reminded himself of Nicki's struggle against Seleukos and the trust she'd placed in him.

Their rainforest life became comfortable after that.

Until one morning when the night rains continued into the daylight. Summer was over. Esther turned to him with wide eyes.

"It's trade day."

26

The Beloved

Thirty-sixth day of spring,
452 A.D. – Outside Farthe, Ceryll

GWEN AND ROCH went to buy provisions while Paraskevas and Laine packed up their essential belongings and prepared a wagon hidden in a small stable at the edge of town. Part of their challenge had been to buy provisions in small enough quantities to avoid suspicion. But Gwen was a stranger who could make those purchases without arousing any suspicion. So she used Roch's coins to buy crates full of dried meat, potatoes and other foods, as well as two barrels of water. Everything else was already in the wagon, ready to go. Go they did that night, smuggling Nier carefully out of the dark and quiet inn.

They didn't travel on the kingsway, nor did they head for Milleport. The kingsway was too dangerous without any guards and Milleport had too many people, said Paraskevas. They couldn't risk being seen before Gwen knew how to appease the wind, at least. It would take Gwen at least a season to learn what he had to teach her, so there was plenty of time to make it to Falle Harbor on the back roads. Gwen couldn't think of a way to object without explaining about the Phoenix, so she didn't.

Laine was better than Gwen at getting Nier to swallow broth. She got three spoonfuls down his throat as soon as he was settled in the wagon. While they were on the road, she coaxed down a spoonful here and there, explaining to Gwen that they couldn't put too much in his stomach at once after it had been empty for days. But meanwhile, under the bandage, the wound continued to fester. There was a stench of rot rising from the wound and Gwen didn't know what to do.

The first day was dedicated to getting as far from Farthe as possible. Gwen's lessons would begin on the second day, she was told. But Nier didn't have that much time. After considerable argument from Gwen, Paraskevas handed the reins to Roch and bent over Nier muttering sounds. Gwen sat back, squeezing Laine's hand so hard it must have hurt, though she didn't complain.

But after a time, Paraskevas looked up and shook his head.

"I'm sorry. There's nothing I can do."

That night, Gwen couldn't sleep so she crawled over to Nier and lay alongside him, feeling his heart beat under her hand. His pulse was still there, strong and even. It didn't feel like the pulse of someone already as good as dead.

She lay there, drifting in and out of a light doze. And she remembered the voice in her dreams—she *remembered*.

You said I could heal him, she thought as hard as she could. *You said you could teach me.*

No answer came.

I know you're there, she thought furiously. *I know you're the wind!*

Oh, babe, came an amused laugh. *You learn you're a beloved and you think you understand. But perhaps you're not that wrong. Perhaps I am the wind, in a way.*

Help me help him, Gwen demanded.

What for?

Because I have to find the Phoenix! Or else all is lost!

That it is. But you don't need him.

That's not for you to decide!

No, sighed the voice. *No, I suppose it isn't.*

Gwen was woken by the sound of her own voice muttering syllables that meant nothing to her. She fought to keep herself in a dream state as long as she could, but wakefulness came and she no longer knew what to say.

When she opened her eyes, she met the wide, startled eyes of Paraskevas.

"What was that?" he asked.

Gwen did not answer. She pulled back the bandages that covered Nier's shoulder. The wound had scabbed over harmlessly; the skin around it was black and healthy. Paraskevas watched in silence as Gwen wrapped the shoulder in fresh cloths.

"You didn't tell me you already knew how to speak," he said when she had finished.

"I don't. The wind taught me."

"The *wind?*"

"Yes."

"Those were not Words of wind."

"What do you mean? Are there different Words?"

"For every element. Some use similar Words, as the elements themselves are related—fire and lava, lava and rock, rock and soil—but they are different."

"So if I wasn't speaking Words of wind, what was I speaking?"

"I don't know."

Silence fell as this washed over Gwen. Then Nier coughed—a dry, painful sound—and Gwen was distracted trickling water into his mouth. He grabbed onto the dish and gulped it down eagerly, and she had to hold him back lest he make himself sick.

"Maybe I ought to start teaching you now," said Paraskevas when Nier settled down.

"In the middle of the night?"

"As soon as possible seems wise. There are two rules you must learn and remember, whatever else may happen: do not command and do not lie."

"What? You told me speakers can lie."

"Speakers, yes. Beloveds too, but you must learn it. For now, while you are only just learning to speak, you must avoid lying."

Gwen's throat closed. Paraskevas smiled kindly.

"Don't be afraid. We'll try not to ask you too many questions, and if you don't want to answer, then say so. But don't say good morning if you don't think it's a good morning; don't thank anyone if you don't mean it. Don't worry about politeness—I won't hold it against you, and when they wake, Laine and Roch will assure you that they won't either. Do you understand?"

Gwen opened her mouth to say yes and closed it again. "Not really," she said a moment later. "But I'll try. No lies and no . . . commands?" That seemed odd. She was not in any position of authority.

But Paraskevas was nodding seriously.

"This is more important once you start speaking in the Words. You won't do any harm by speaking a command in our language. But one command in the Words can anger the elements. We are specks of dust compared to them. And while they might acknowledge us and even love some among us, their love can be easily extinguished. If you accidentally speak a command to the wind, you could lose its love and your life, or worse, your mind."

"No commands," Gwen repeated. "All right."

"When you speak to the wind, you will phrase everything as a request or a question. There will be no room for semantics or debating your meaning. If the wind hears a command, your justifications won't matter."

"I understand."

"I hope you do," said Paraskevas. "Now, during our lessons, please call me Aiar. It means one who teaches in the Words of soil."

"Why the Words of soil? I thought you were teaching me the Words of wind."

Paraskevas smiled. "Yes. But I am not a beloved so, like most humans, my closest relationship is with soil. Whatever Words I teach you, you would call me Aiar because that is nearest to the element that has claimed me."

"Why would humans have an affinity for soil?"

Paraskevas gave this some thought. "No one knows for sure. There are those who say that we were shaped from soil, or that we are soil's children. But what is for certain is that every creature has an element that it is closest to, unless born a beloved."

"Could a human be a beloved of soil?" Gwen asked, curious.

"I imagine so," said Paraskevas. "Though I've never heard of such a person. You have an affinity to soil as much as I do. It simply will be insignificant to you next to the love that wind has for you."

"Oh," said Gwen.

"*Yiu* is the word for agreement and acknowledgement in the Words of wind."

"*Yiu*," Gwen repeated obediently.

The lesson continued until the sun rose. It was as Gwen was drifting into sleep that she realized that she had not once thought of Eudon in all the commotion. She thought of him alone in Farthe, waiting for her to give an answer only to find her gone. Her heart clenched, but it was a dull feeling and sleep soon took her.

*   *   *

When Gwen woke the following day, the wagon was still and deserted. She sat up with a start when she realized that even Nier was missing. Alarm wiped all traces of sleep away and she crawled out of her bedroll and jumped out the back of the wagon. She was in a field of grass as tall as she was, though the area around the wagon was flattened. The sun was high in the sky. She couldn't see the others, but the wind carried to her the smell of smoke and cooking meat. They must have stopped to hunt and cook lunch, she realized.

She was just turning to follow the smell when Nier came barreling around the corner of the wagon, clutching his shoulder and panting.

"Xanthe!" he gasped. "We've got to run—these people are Seleukoi speakers."

Gwen opened her mouth and closed it again, wondering how best to calm him down without lying.

"They're not Seleukoi," she settled on. "Don't worry; they're helping us."

"What do you *mean* they're not Seleukoi?" he hissed. "The man called himself *Paraskevas*. Do you think that's a common name anywhere?"

"I was using a Seleukoi name too," Gwen pointed out.

"Don't you recognize . . . what do you mean, was?"

"They know who I am. They're taking us to Falle Harbor."

Nier laughed hysterically. "And I suppose it's a coincidence that they're taking us to the easternmost harbor, closest to Seleukos?"

Gwen shook her head. "Calm down and let me explain it all from the beginning."

"We don't have *time* for that," Nier hissed. "What in the *world* possessed you to trust the potentate's *cousin*?"

"I promise it's all right—" Gwen cut herself off when his words sank in. "Cousin?"

"*Yes.*"

"Wha— That can't be right. The potentate doesn't have any cousins that old. I'm certain there were only three—"

"Not her *first* cousin! Second cousin."

Gwen tried to recall, but drew a blank. Instead she clung to what she knew.

"You didn't even know Seleukos was invading Jehan until I told you. You can't know—"

"That was a year ago," Nier retorted. "A year we've spent hunting for a weapon of the Words. The only known speakers are in the Seleukoi court. It made sense to learn as much about it as I could."

"Still," said Gwen, shaking her head. "You clearly don't understand. Laine—his wife, Ghyslaine—is *my* aunt. My father's sister."

This gave Nier pause.

"Are you sure?" he asked at last.

"N—" *No, I just made this up,* Gwen almost retorted before remembering that she was supposed to not lie. And not command. She had a feeling that she hadn't been doing well so far. "Yes, I'm sure," she said instead, as scathingly as she could.

"But they—well, the man at least, Paraskevas, is a speaker. He muttered at the ground and a fire pit appeared!"

"Don't you remember Nicki's spy in Nirra? He told us to make friends of speakers. That's exactly what I'm doing. And I'm learning the Words, to boot."

"What . . . but *why*?" Nier demanded. "You're betraying the very country that you set out to save!"

"You clearly already made up your mind, so I don't see why I should waste my time trying to explain myself."

"If you can't explain yourself to *me*, how are you ever going to explain to your father? I mean, your sister may have given us her blessing to *research*, but this . . . !"

"*Blessing*? What do you mean my sister gave her blessing? When did you ever—" Realization dawned on Gwen. Dio was Nicki's oyster and everyone in it her puppets. She had been a fool to believe that Nier was an exception. "You were her spy all along."

"*What?* How could you think that? But don't change the subject! You're learning the *Words*. Your father—"

"My father trusts me and knows me," said Gwen coldly. "He will understand that I was doing my part to help him."

"*Gwen!*" came Paraskevas's voice as he appeared around the wagon. "*Stop lying*. And get ahold of yourself!"

Gwen realized that they had begun to shout (at least in part) because they had to in order to be heard over the roaring wind.

"*Nia qiulai*," Gwen muttered, breathing deeply as she had learned just last night. "*Nia qiulai*."

Eventually, the wind calmed.

"It is best not to agitate her right now," Paraskevas said to Nier.

"You're a Seleukoi speaker and the potentate's cousin," Nier retorted coolly. "Why should I trust you?"

Paraskevas paused. Emotions danced across his face, settling on a wry smile. "I am Seleukoi," he said. "And I am a speaker. Aglaia is my cousin. But I am as dead to my family as Laine is to hers, and I have not seen Seleukos in twenty years. I would help Ceryll fight Aglaia's armies if they ever let me."

"You could be lying," Nier pointed out.

"To you I could," Paraskevas nodded. "But Gwen would hear it."

"He's telling the truth," Gwen said quietly, challenging Nier with her eyes to question her judgment. He lowered his eyes.

"I will explain all of this to you, Nier. But I suggest you two keep apart for a time until you, Gwen, learn to manage your emotions."

There was no way to warn Nier not to mention the Phoenix without arousing suspicion or a windstorm. So Gwen spent the rest of the day learning to close her eyes and focus on her breath and the air. Whenever she grew irritated, the wind picked up subtly.

"How long do I have to do this?" she asked Paraskevas at last, when the sun was going down.

"As long as is necessary," said Paraskevas. "But perhaps this is enough meditation for today. Let us do another lesson."

Gwen swallowed a sigh.

27

The Chef's Apprentice

Late morning, eleventh day of spring
452 A.D. – Castle Dio, Ceryll

BRICE'S EARLIEST MEMORIES were hazy. The only thing he remembered knowing was that he was an orphan on the cliffside streets of the Felle. He remembered begging and stealing with no plan or goal beyond surviving to see the morrow. He remembered that part of begging and stealing meant paying a portion of his earnings to the thief lord, leaving him with barely enough to get by day to day.

His first clear memory, the beacon of light that split the fog of his childhood, was the day he'd met the scarred old man.

He'd stolen a loaf of bread from a cart, not knowing whose cart it was, or even why that might matter. As he'd run away, he was caught by the arm and looked back into the eyes of a graying old man with deep lines on his face and five parallel scars down the left side of his face.

To a young Brice, the man had looked terrifying.

"What do you think you're doing, boy?" asked the man.

Brice had tried to drop the bread and run.

"You won't be running from me," the man had said calmly. "Now, answer my question."

"Stealing," Brice said quietly.

"You were stealing," the man had agreed. "Do you know whose bread that is?"

Brice had shaken his head.

"It's the king's."

Brice hadn't known what that meant, so he stared blankly at the man.

"Is he important?" he'd asked.

The man first stared at him a moment, then began to laugh.

"The most important man in the country," he'd said when he'd finished laughing.

"I'm in trouble," Brice had realized.

"You are," the man had said, and then asked after Brice's parents. When Brice said he didn't have any, the man asked who looked after him.

That was how Brice unwittingly aided in the arrest of the thief lord of the Felle. The scarred old man fed him a meal and asked him if he wanted to be able to eat his fill every day without stealing. Brice said he did.

The man, who Brice would later learn was the falcon, let him ride with him on his warhorse. When they had arrived at Castle Dio, he was installed in the kitchens, where the servants were warned to keep an eye on him lest he decide to steal anything.

But Brice got to eat his fill every day, and so had no

inclination to steal. Soon enough, the chef herself took a liking to him and made him one of her apprentices.

He ought to have known that it was too good to be true when he met Roshan. He'd met her in the courtyard early one morning when he was carrying out the old ashes from the kitchen. She was beautiful, funny and charming, and he'd fallen in love with her on the spot. Somehow, she loved him too.

It wasn't ideal, of course—she'd come to Ceryll as Ambassador Baraz's concubine. But she loved Brice, and Ceryllan law didn't recognize Yngan harems. He felt certain that when the time was right, they could appeal to the king to grant them the right to wed.

So when Prince Enri arrived and told him what Roshan was about to do, Brice didn't believe it was possible. He said so at length, telling off the prince as he hadn't dared to speak to royalty since he'd understood what the word *royalty* meant. Enri shrugged and left and Brice went on with his chores believing the matter was settled.

But then Roshan showed up, talking her way into the kitchens with an invitation Brice definitely hadn't extended. She sauntered up to Brice and kissed him, and he desperately, desperately wanted to believe that this was a coincidence—that she'd only been as desperate to see him as he was to see her every moment of every day.

He kept his eyes cracked open as she kissed him and saw her sprinkle something over the tureen of soup meant for the king's lunch.

Brice couldn't help identifying the blue crystals before they dissolved, and his heart sank even further. He hadn't wanted to believe. But in the years he'd been apprenticed to the chef in the king's kitchens, he'd become well-versed in the appearance of various poisons. If used correctly, *vitreus caeruleus* was the perfect poison to kill a king: in small quantities, it had no effect, and so the dish would sail past the poison taster. But one bite too many, and it could stop the heart in a death too-frequently mistaken for a heart attack.

Brice closed his eyes and tried to enjoy this last touch of Roshan's lips, but he felt no joy in it now. Her lips felt wet and slimy. It had all been a lie. She served Ynga and Ambassador Baraz, after all. She'd used Brice.

Of course, she wanted to hang around the kitchens after that.

"I won't get in your way," she assured the chef.

"I'm more worried about you distracting Brice," huffed the chef.

"I'll just stand here in the corner and watch him," said Roshan with her most disarming smile. It worked, and she sat with an eye on the tureen of soup until the very moment when it left the kitchens to be served at the king's table.

Then she took her leave, kissing Brice goodbye.

Now that he was rearing to leave, he felt how she, too, was not quite fully *there* in the kiss. Couldn't wait to return to her master's embrace, no doubt.

Brice waited for her to leave and then raced out of the kitchen, ignoring the chef's bewildered calls after him. He raced after the servers. He had to get to the king before that soup was served, or it would be his life.

28

The Outcast

Last day of summer, 452 A.D. – Unyca, Ynga

THE WIND CARRIED to Esther's ears the sound of her Aial and Lialli walking through the rainforest with the cart of black. She told Deric to wait at their campsite and ran with the wind to join them.

He won't stay put, said Tlafa.

Hush, said Esther. *He's learning.*

"You're alone," Lialli observed, still in fox form, in the Words of fire. "You've had all season and still you and Tlafa haven't been able to get him out?"

"Be calm, Lialli," said Aial in the Words of rock. "Esther has the wind's love, but that isn't enough to go up against all of Unyca. Recall that she couldn't escape them last season, which was how Tlafa ended up captive in the first place."

Deric, never one to follow her instructions, showed up behind her.

"It's another human," hissed Lialli, lashing out with a kick to his chest too fast for human eyes to follow. Deric crashed into a tree trunk behind him and crumpled, unconscious.

"Stop!" cried Esther in the Words of wind. "He's my friend!"

Aial and Lialli stared at her.

Friend? said Tlafa. Is that still what you're calling it?
Captivity's made you more insufferable than usual.

There's nothing else to do here, Tlafa replied, projecting deep, mind-numbing ennui. *I have to live vicariously through you.*

"You declared yourself separate from the world of men when you came to us," said Aial. "Have you changed your mind?"

"It wasn't about changing my mind," said Esther, checking Deric for serious injuries. He was breathing; his pulse was strong, and she found no sign of bleeding. "I had to eat. I couldn't cook. I had to make friends of humans to get food."

"You ought to have come back down," said Lialli. "You didn't do Tlafa any good up here."

What does she know? demanded Tlafa. *She's never been bonded. You stayed as near me as you could.*

Esther scowled at Lialli and echoed Tlafa's thoughts. "What would you know? You've never been bonded. I wanted to be as near him as I could be."

"Never mind," said Lialli tightly. "We're returning home."

"What?" cried Esther. "What about trade day? You came up here with all that lyll stone and now you're leaving? You said the trade always had to be done!"

"The trade was part of"—Lialli used a phrase that

Esther didn't recognize in the Words of fire—"but that's finally ended. Nevena is dead and"—another word she didn't know—"is broken. Can't you feel it?"

Esther had no idea what she was supposed to feel. In her year among them, she'd never heard them speak of Nevena as though she were a reality.

What does this mean? she asked Tlafa, but the thoughts that he sent back were a jumble of *fire-wind-time-agreement* and confused her even more.

"What do you mean Nevena's dead?" she asked. "How can—"

But she couldn't finish the question because she didn't know the word for *goddess* in the Words of wind, rock, fire or water, and when she asked Tlafa, he kept sending her the air Word for *water*.

Be quiet, she thought at Tlafa in irritation. *You're no help.*

She addressed Lialli and Aial in the language of men instead. "How can a goddess die?"

Lialli looked confused, but Aial turned to her and translated.

Lialli began to laugh, bursting into sparks in the air that danced about and rejoined in her tall and lanky human-like form. "She thinks Nevena's a god!" In the Words of fire, the word for *god* literally meant *immortal hero.* "Are we gods, too?"

"Her reign was long," said Aial. "It lasted many human lifetimes. And Nevena served them as we never have. Perhaps god isn't a bad description." In Aial's Words of rock, *god* literally meant *biggest of all stones.*

"I want to be a god," said Lialli. "If I go about granting humans' wishes for vengeance, will they worship me too?"

"Be careful," said Aial. "The new Phoenix may be young, but it could still extinguish your flame if you anger it."

"But it'll be Nevena's pick," Lialli pointed out. "Everyone knows what a soft heart she had. She'll have picked another like that to follow."

Why does everyone keep talking about Nevena? Esther demanded of Tlafa.

This time, his explanation was more straightforward, and she understood at least that Nevena had been a powerful elemental.

"Four and a half centuries is a long time," cautioned Aial. "Even for the Phoenix. And beloveds are few and far between now. We don't know what she was like at the end. Best to keep to the agreement until it comes to speak to us."

"You're such a bore," scowled Lialli, but she didn't object when Aial continued toward Unyca.

Is it safe? asked Tlafa. *What about the ambush?*

"Let me come with you," Esther said. "There might be an ambush at the edge of the rainforest."

Neither objected. But there was no ambush today. They walked up to the wall where Aial coaxed the rock open as usual, and they walked into the empty trading space.

Then they waited for the first Unycan to show up. Shortly after, they began to arrive, one by one, trading bundles of useless trinkets for black. It was as though nothing had changed.

Something felt off. Esther kept her guard up, but couldn't put her finger on what it was. The wind was restless, certainly, but there was also a strange feeling coming from the stones of the building, as though they were restless too.

Do you feel this? she asked Tlafa.

Feel what? he replied.

Is this . . . restlessness because Nevena died? she asked.

Tlafa projected annoyance. *They might not have felt it Down Below, but you've been up here the whole time. She died a season ago, a few days after they captured me. If you didn't feel it then, I don't know why you'd feel it now.*

Esther looked to Aial, who was acting as if this were any other trade day. She tried to dismiss the feeling as imagination. If something were wrong with the stones, she assured herself, Aial would be the one to register it first.

The Unycans treated trade day like some sort of religious ritual, entering the trade room one by one, always in the same order. Every man, woman and child over three years of age came to trade. One person would leave the room, and a moment later the next one would enter.

So when the procession broke and no one came in for several moments, the restless feeling reignited and Esther turned to Aial.

Before she could open her mouth, the ceiling came tumbling down.

Esther!

Tlafa's cry in her mind was the last thing she knew before the world went dark.

29

The Spy

Last day of summer, 452 A.D. – Unyca, Ynga

DERIC CAME TO on the rainforest floor to birdcalls and a splitting headache. It took him a moment to recall what had happened. His memory conjured up the small, brown dweorg and large orange firefox that had kicked him in the chest. The dweorg had been pulling a cart full of black, he realized.

It was trade day.

He pulled himself to his feet and stumbled in the direction of camp. He made it there, untethered his horse and scrambled up onto its back. Deric turned its head in the direction of Unyca and nudged it with his heels, hoping it would carry him back to the town. His vision was blurry with exertion and he couldn't guide the horse.

He would realize in retrospect that he had been extremely fortunate, as he'd forgotten about the witch hunters' ambush.

But that thought would be a long time coming, because just as he came to the tree line and saw Unyca's wall, the outer building at the center on the rainforest side collapsed in a cloud of dust.

Deric stood, staring. How was that possible? One building couldn't possibly collapse so neatly that way, not when the entire row of buildings had been built sharing their continuous walls. Then he realized—this must be the dweorg's doing.

The rush of concern sharpened his mind and vision and he nudged his horse left, toward the side of the wall with the stable.

No one stood guard outside today, but Deric had become intimately familiar with the position where he usually stood. He dismounted and felt around the stone wall until he found a loose stone. When he pulled it out, there was a groove on the inside, like a handle. He took hold and pulled. A section of what had appeared to be stone wall opened into the stable.

No one was there. Even the mules and donkey were gone. There was only Tlafa, tugging frantically on his chains.

Deric leapt off his horse and rushed to Tlafa. After some yanking, he realized that the chains weren't going to give. But they were bolted into the wood on the side of the stall, so he drew his katar from his belt and began hacking away at the wood around the bolt.

Between Tlafa's yanking and Deric's hacking, they got the bolt free soon enough. The moment he was free, Tlafa leapt over Deric, the dangling bolt barely missing his head. Tlafa knocked the door into the street down with his front hooves. He leapt out and was gone.

Deric panicked for a moment—why had he gone *into*

Unyca? They would be discovered—before he realized that the noises coming from the street were chaotic and panicked. There were screams and running footsteps, and when he approached the now-empty doorframe, he saw flames, flying rocks and men brandishing spears while many others inched or ran along the side of the street to avoid the violence.

He hesitated. He wasn't properly armed for this—Esther had never returned his sword—and he'd be a fool to go up against spearmen or elementals with nothing but a katar. For all he knew, Esther wasn't even in there. She'd reunited with the rainfolk and left him unconscious on the rainforest floor, and now Tlafa was free. Deric could ride south, back to Ceryll without reservation. Whatever this fight was about, joining it would be nothing short of foolish.

But Tlafa had leapt *into* Unyca. Esther had stayed near Unyca for Tlafa, and if he was diving straight back into the town, then it must be because that was where Esther was.

Muttering a curse, Deric mounted his horse and nudged it into the street. He rode past at least a dozen spearmen fighting the firefox, whose form he barely glimpsed before it grew into a ball of flame that had the spearmen running in the opposite direction.

He rode past the dweorg, tossing boulders at Melech and Dov, while Dov caught and tossed boulders several times his size back at the dweorg. After a few of these exchanges, the dweorg dove into the ground and a moment later, the ground opened up beneath Dov and pulled him under, sealing up above him.

Deric paused at Melech's anguished cry, as the man dug into the ground for his son.

There was nothing he could do, he told himself, and he rode on towards the cloud of dust that was still rising on the rainforest side.

Deric reached the wreckage just in time to see Tlafa fly out the top towards the rainforest, an unconscious white-and-silver form on his back.

That appeared to be that. Deric turned and saw that there was a row of men armed with spears behind him.

"You pledged yourself to our cause," said one. "But you've turned traitor."

"Now, just a moment—"

"None of your excuses." That came from Melech himself. "Get these witches to give me my son back."

"I can't," said Deric. "I'm not—"

"You went to try to lure the witches here and they captured you and converted you instead. Don't think you can fool me—you're not the first!"

Melech lunged at Deric with a katar in each hand. He wasn't a trained soldier and his movements were slow and easy to dodge. More concerning were the seven spearmen around him, who took the move as their cue to attack.

Deric managed to slip sideways between two spears, grabbing hold of the shafts and pulling, then shoving their blunt handles into the stomachs of the men wielding them.

But the remaining five took that move as a cue to reorganize in a better formation, surrounding Deric and leaving him with no way to attack any among them without being stabbed in the back.

He dropped and rolled, knowing that he would be

stabbed or kicked, but hopefully not before he managed to trip one of the spearmen and create an opening to escape—

The ground opened up beneath him and the dweorg pulled him into a tunnel at the same moment as the spear aimed for Deric caught the dweorg in the shoulder instead.

"Go!" gasped the dweorg as he was pulled up and more blades appeared aimed at him. The tunnel entrance closed behind Deric, leaving him in darkness.

Deric swallowed and began feeling his way through the tunnel. He could hear Melech and the spearmen shouting, but he didn't hear the dweorg make another sound.

30

The Lieutenant Ambassador

Late morning, eleventh day of spring,
452 A.D. – Castle Dio, Ceryll

WHAT DO YOU mean she's not there?" Dara demanded.

"I mean exactly what I said," shrugged Chan. "She's not there."

"Are you sure you had the right cell?"

"Do you think there are many cells on the ground floor at the center of the tower?"

"How should I know? I've never been in there." Dara's eyes narrowed. "Do you suppose she's escaped?"

Chan shrugged. "You're the strategist. I'm only your blade."

Dara clucked her tongue. "That doesn't mean you can't have an opinion."

"I'd think it was a bad idea to escape the tower after the king himself ordered your arrest. But the heir doesn't seem to operate under normal rules, so what would that matter?"

"Hm. Where are the knife and the note, then?"

"I don't have them."

"What?"

"I'd already dropped them into the cell before I realized that the heir wasn't in there."

"How could you miss that? You must have had to make sure you delivered the note and knife to the right person!"

"There were two people in the cell. I couldn't see either of their faces. One was dressed in fancy, flowery clothes. I assumed it was the princess's nightclothes. But as I was leaving he turned, and it wasn't her."

Dara closed her eyes. "Maybe Pierre made the same mistake. Do we at least know whose murder we ordered?"

"There's talk that Minister Septimo's son was arrested."

"Oh, wonderful. Next thing I need is an angry *minister*. You do realize that I can't actually massacre the entire Ceryllan court?"

"It would be so much easier if you could," grumbled Chan. "But the note was cryptic. It won't be traced back to you. Especially since you've got no grudge against the minister's son."

"No. Time's running out, and with the politics of this court in this state . . . ! For all we know, Regis and Pierre set us up, and those assassination orders will be used to make a case against us. We have to get rid of her today."

"I've tried three times and each time she wasn't where we thought she would be. Either she's spying on us or she's as lucky as lucky gets."

Dara closed her eyes. "There's only one person in the

castle who wants the heir out of the way as desperately as we do."

Chan looked confused. "Baraz? But you said you couldn't trust him."

"I can't. He's related to the Yngan king, so he's probably related to the Ceryllan lot too. These people are all about blood loyalty."

"Then who . . . ?" He trailed off and expressions danced across his face.

"You can't mean Zephyr."

"The enemy of my enemy is my ally."

"Why would he help you? He has to know that you only want the heir dead so you can amass a bigger army to fight his country."

"Leave that part to me. Go arrange a meeting with him, as soon as possible."

"Aye, Lieutenant."

Chan left the room through the window, and Dara sat down to wait. It wasn't long before Chan returned through the door, the Seleukoi ambassador behind him.

"Ambassador Zephyr," greeted Dara, offering him a chair and wine.

"Lieutenant Dara," smiled Zephyr, accepting the chair but not the wine. "To what do I owe this pleasure?"

There was no time to waste on pleasantries. "Do the Ceryllan guards know you're here?"

Zephyr snorted. "Please. I can elude them whenever I want."

"A straight answer, if you don't mind."

An amused light entered Zephyr's eyes. "No. They don't know I'm here."

"We have a problem, you and I."

"Do we? Last I checked, you were allowed to go where you liked without having to sneak away from guards like a disobedient child."

"I'm talking about the heir."

"Nicole? *She's* our biggest problem? She's not even queen yet. She has no power."

"Don't insult me. You know as well as I that she's the puppet master here. She has the king's ear and spies around every corner."

Zephyr leaned back and smiled. "I'm listening."

"I'm suggesting that we team up to remove her from the picture."

"And how would we do that?"

"Any number of ways. First I need your word that you'll cooperate."

Zephyr laughed. "Why would I do that? For all I know, your plan will lay the blame at my feet."

"It won't. All I need is for you to help me create an opportunity. My knife will do the work, and our agreement will never be known."

"What if I go straight to the king and tell him after you've done the deed?"

"Then it'll be your word against mine. Which do you think he'll believe?"

"Ah," said Zephyr, leaning forward. "And there, you see, we have a problem. If I help you and afterwards you go to the king and blame me, I'll be executed. If you want my cooperation, you need to give me something to prove we have an accord."

Dara narrowed her eyes at him. "In that case, we'll

exchange tokens. I'll leave my ceremonial katar in your possession, and you'll give me something of yours."

Zephyr regarded her for a moment. He hummed, reaching absently for the gold chain around his neck, revealing a pendant that had been hidden beneath his tunic. It was a small sphere made of elaborately interwoven strands of gold, silver and black.

"And what sort of token did you have in mind?" he asked as he fiddled with the pendant.

Dara narrowed her eyes. Toying with the pendant may have seemed an absent gesture in another sort of person, but not in Zephyr. He was trying to lead her.

"Don't try to fool me. The black in that pendant is fake. Even if it weren't, I've no use for a pretty trinket. Give me your signet ring."

Zephyr smiled, replaced the pendant into his tunic and lowered his right hand. He pulled the ring from his left thumb and handed it to Dara. She inspected the bronze flame set inside three spheres of gold. It was genuine.

Alliance established, she began the discussion of strategy. Zephyr didn't share Dara's urgency, and seemed surprised to learn that the heir was seemingly imprisoned. When she told him the details, he was all the more skeptical.

At last Dara managed to convince him to create a diversion near the heir's bedchambers or cell that night, depending on the information they had about her location.

Only after Zephyr left did Chan remark on the wrinkle in his brow that had been present all the way through the conversation.

"I've never seen him so tense," he said.

"Tense?" snorted Dara. "He was as flippant as usual. I only hope he knows how to create a diversion."

"He was playing flippant, but it was less convincing than usual. Maybe this was a bad idea," said Chan. "I should steal back your katar. We'll take our time, try again. We shouldn't trust him."

"A little late for that, don't you think?" Dara couldn't disguise her annoyance. It wasn't like Chan to flip-flop like this.

"I know, but I have a bad feeling about this."

"We can't change our minds now," she said.

"Let me try one more time," begged Chan. "Without Zephyr. If it works, I'll steal your katar back tonight."

"If you insist," sighed Dara. "But don't get yourself caught or killed."

Chan nodded stiffly and climbed out the window.

31

The Beloved

Fiftieth day of spring, 452 A.D. – Mille, Ceryll

THE AFON WAS too deep and fast this spring to attempt fording. When they reached the river and realized this, they had to choose to follow it north to Lirra or south to Mille. Lirra would have been too far off course, so Mille it was.

"When we see the town, you'll start meditating," Paraskevas told Gwen. "Keep meditating until I draw you out of it. Just like any other day. We'll take the northernmost bridge and head back out of town as soon as we can."

"How long will that be, Aiar?" asked Gwen.

"I couldn't honestly give you a timeframe."

So when Paraskevas told her to start meditating, she did.

Gwen had grown to like meditating. In a meditative state, she didn't feel any different from the wind. It was as though she could forget that she had a mortal body of flesh and blood and be one with each piece of wind around her: this breeze singing of freedom, that air sighing with ennui, a gust cutting through both of them with glee.

Here, in the silence of her mind, she could release all her worries and fears and simply *be*. It was not a sensation she had ever known and it was comforting. Her guilt over Eudon was immaterial there, a situation that could not be helped. Even the grief of Mother's death fell away and, as long as she was meditating, she could feel as whole as she had as a child before she had ever known the death of a loved one.

But the more she meditated, the deeper she sank; she became aware that there was a place where she got stuck. She knew that place intimately. It was the place that had loved Stelle; that place had been locked shut two years ago, then barricaded further with her death last year. She tried to unlock that place, but her mind resisted, too practiced at keeping her out.

When Paraskevas whispered to the wind around her, drawing its awareness to him and hers with it, Gwen blinked her eyes open to find her sight fuzzy and her limbs so stiff they were painful to move.

The lighting looked suspiciously like dawn.

"How long has it been?"

"A day and a night," said Laine. "Take it easy; it won't be easy to move again."

As Gwen stretched her limbs—a surprisingly slow, painful process as she unfolded herself—Paraskevas and Laine explained that Jehan was conquered, and many Ceryllans living in the east were flocking to Mille to cross the Afon. Mille's city guard could scarcely control the chaos, and it had taken them a full day to push through the flow of carriages, wagons and people coming from the opposite direction across the bridge.

Gwen considered this. Time was running out. At the same time, something else nagged at her consciousness. Nier was not in the wagon. As usual, she supposed, he was riding out front with Roch. She had barely seen him in a fortnight, since the day he had regained consciousness. Gwen had heard Paraskevas explain her situation to him; had heard him request that Nier try to keep away from Gwen as much as possible because he seemed to make her emotionally unstable, which made the wind a danger to them all; had heard Nier agree and grow friendlier with Roch as they drove the wagon together day after day. She had not seen the need to intervene because it all seemed to be working out for the best.

But now she missed him. She heard him and Roch laughing quietly together and telling each other stories of their lives that Gwen didn't know. It hadn't bothered her at first, but day by day, she found herself wishing she could be a part of that friendship rather than the vulnerable subject of her aunt and uncle's tutelage and care.

When she forgot not to think about it, she wondered if Nier truly thought of her as friend, or only as a princess to look after at the heir's order. She felt no anger at the thought—only sorrow.

"Is there any convenient place we can make camp this afternoon?" she asked. "I want to talk to Nier."

Paraskevas furrowed his brow and Laine's expression froze. They exchanged looks.

"If that's what you want," he said at last. "If you think you're ready."

"I am," she said. Paraskevas nodded.

When they stopped that afternoon, Gwen poked her head out the front before Nier and Roch could go off on their own as they usually did.

"Nier," she said quietly. "Can we talk?"

Nier stared at her, wide-eyed. Roch narrowed his eyes suspiciously.

"Your Aiar agreed to this?" Roch asked.

"He did," said Gwen. "Can we, Nier?"

"If you like," said Nier, and a smile tugged at his mouth, softening his cautious choice of words.

They walked together into the tree grove that lined the northern edge of the road. Gwen felt Roch's suspicious glare on the back of her neck until they were out of sight. Then she led Nier further still, until she was certain that none of them would be able to hear.

They came to a halt in a clearing, and Gwen turned to Nier. Their eyes met. She found that she didn't know what to say. After a moment, he spoke.

"You didn't tell them about the Phoenix?" he asked.

"No."

"You could have warned me. I almost mentioned it to Roch before I realized I'd never heard a word of it. Where did you hide Trygve's journal?"

Gwen's heart clenched. Of course. She'd never told him.

"It's gone," she said.

Nier stared at her for a beat, then took a deep breath, rubbing his forehead tiredly. "How did that happen?"

"Cecil burned it."

"And when was this?"

"I don't know—she told me the day we were at the Tevaë Falls."

Nier heaved a sigh. "That long. Why didn't you tell me?"

Gwen thought about it. "I suppose I didn't want you to scold me. I thought it might prove to you that I couldn't do this."

"You must have known that that's neither here nor there. It's gone. That's done. Now we have nothing to help us but what we can remember of Trygve's writings. I wouldn't have scolded you; there's nothing we could have done about it."

"Just because you believe it now doesn't make it so," said Gwen mildly, softening her words with a smile.

"But you're a speaker now."

"Better—a beloved."

"Yes. So maybe we can find it the same way Trygve did. He described calling to the fire for Nou, Nuray and Nevena?"

Gwen snorted. "Speakers don't pray to Nou, Nuray and Nevena. Speakers know that there are only the elements, and we are but specks to them. Nou, Nuray and Nevena are gods of those who don't know the Words and can't hear the elements."

"All the same," said Nier. "There was a passage about *Mother's firetongue*. Surely that means—"

"I agree. He probably spoke the Words of fire. But Aiar doesn't know the Words of fire." Gwen knew that he knew what Aiar meant. She had overheard Roch explaining to him about humans and soil a few days ago.

"Maybe it doesn't have to be fire. Maybe soil or wind will do just as well. The point is we still might be able to find it."

"Hopefully wind. I'm not learning the Words of soil beyond the basics. But what do I even say? Trygve didn't say what he said."

"Did you bring me out here just to tell me about that?"

"No," she said. "Nier, I'm sorry for how I treated you. You've been . . . kind, if not a true friend to me and I've been ungrateful in return."

"Wait," Nier narrowed his eyes. "What was that? What do you mean, *not a true friend?*"

"You were my sister's spy," Gwen said, smothering irritation. "You told me yourself."

"I didn't, because I wasn't!" Nier argued. "The only interaction I ever had with your sister was when she came asking about that book we found the first time. I assumed you'd told her, so I said we were doing our best to find something that would help the country fight an army of speakers, and she thanked me and left. That was it."

Gwen pursed her lips. He was telling the truth.

"When was this?" she asked.

"I don't know . . . last summer?"

That long ago. In light of that, Gwen realized she had been foolish. Nicki's arms extended only across Dio, and perhaps Nirra. They were out of her domain now.

"I'm sorry," she said honestly. "I should have trusted you."

"No," sighed Nier. "You grew up in court. You told me yourself, it's safer to mistrust wrongly than to trust wrongly."

"But you've earned better than that from me," Gwen said quietly. Nier didn't respond. "It wasn't really about you. You must know that. After Stelle—I haven't been the same."

"I understand—" Nier started, but Gwen cut him off.

"No. No, you don't, because everything you know was a lie. She didn't have the plague, and she certainly didn't die of any illness."

Gwen told him Stelle's story. Nier listened without comment until she finished.

"So," said Nier when the wind had calmed. "Sterre was your sister all along."

"She was," said Gwen. "And you know the worst part? I thought she'd been driven mad. Father believes it. I blamed the Words. I thought, if she found that book in the library like you did, then went mad . . . except the book isn't what made her go mad, so that wasn't right. And the more I learn, I realize . . . once the madness sets in, beloveds curl up into a ball and try to shut out the world, or run about screaming incoherently. They're dead within half a season, Aiar says. Sterre ran away a year before she jumped."

"Still, the jumping itself might have been the beginnings of madness."

Gwen hesitated a moment. "Hervé described it to us, me and Nicki and Father. It didn't sound anything like what Aiar describes. It sounded like Stelle being obstinate and stupid."

"She meant the world to you." There was no question in Nier's tone and that unleashed the fury that had built as Gwen relived Stelle's selfish choices.

"Yes, she meant the world to me! I thought we were in the same boat. I had dreams, too! I thought I might be a magistrate or sit at the royal council! Dreams I had to abandon because those were not the roles I was born to play. At least I would always have Stelle, right? Except

I didn't, because the brainless mouse threw herself off a *cliff!* And the last words she ever left for me were *'good riddance'!*"

Nier looked alarmed. He knelt in front of her and gripped her by the shoulders.

"I understand that you're angry and I will listen, but Gwen, *the wind!*"

Gwen blinked and noticed that the wind was gusting around them with enough force that tree trunks were cracking. Nier's eyes were tightly closed against the flying debris. She breathed deeply, stilling the turmoil in her mind.

"*Nia qiulai,*" Gwen murmured out loud. "*Nia qiulai.*"

"Look at me," Nier told her firmly when the wind had settled. "She loved you. You should never doubt that."

"You can't know that," Gwen scoffed. "You didn't even know her."

"No. But I know you and I know that you loved her. I know that she was angry. And I am certain that she loved you as certainly as I know that you love me."

Gwen stiffened. "A bold assumption. And a mistaken one at that."

"Not the kind of love where we run away to get married and live on a farm. The kind where we run away to save the kingdom and share our secrets."

Gwen's breath hitched. "But I don't know any of your secrets," she said.

"I'd like to tell you one, if you would like to listen," Nier said.

"I would like to hear it."

Nier told of a lonely boyhood in a trader's caravan.

He could scarcely remember his mother. His father was strict and beat him often, but young Rainier hadn't known enough to feel anything but adoration for the man. When he was told at the age of nine that his mother had died, he had been away from her for so long that he couldn't even remember her face. But he did notice the flecks of dried blood on his father's hands, and the fog of his upbringing gave way to the first pangs of confused terror. At the funeral, his mother's brother took him aside and offered him an education and a future in Castle Dio. When Rainier's only hesitation was his father's reaction, Uncle Vere assured him that he needn't worry. Rainier spent the day by his mother's grave, away from everyone. Uncle Vere found him there at dusk, bringing a sack of Rainier's few belongings and the assurance that his father had agreed.

Rainier never saw his father again. He had never found the courage to ask Uncle Vere what became of him. The longer he spent at the royal library with Uncle Vere, the more he looked back on his father's violent outbursts and sharp words with horror. He still dreamed about those flecks of blood on his hands sometimes, and wondered if they had been his mother's. He still got caught in pensive moments where all he could do was wonder what sort of woman his mother had been.

"And yet you wanted us to join a caravan?"

"I don't—" Nier broke off and shook his head. "It was that or travel the kingsway alone. We wouldn't have stood a chance if bandits found us."

Gwen thought back to the turbulence of their friendship while they were in the caravan. She leaned her head against Nier's shoulder.

"We were in the same boat. We were both so miserable, and I—I assumed it was my burden alone. I did to you what Stelle did to me."

"But you cared for me when I was shot. You wouldn't abandon me when everyone told you it was hopeless. You healed me."

"It was luck," Gwen confessed. "Aiar and I still don't know how I did it."

"But I'm still here, and that's what matters to me."

There was a silence.

"Thank you for telling me your story," said Gwen. "Thank you for trusting me."

Though she was not looking at Nier, the wind conveyed his nod to her. Gwen remained with her head resting against his shoulder. They simply sat for a time.

32

The Outcast

After the fray up above – Down Below

WHEN ESTHER CAME to, it was to the familiar dark lights from the lyll stone that made up the Abyss wall. She was also curled up against the familiar warmth of Tlafa's body.

I missed you, she thought at him, curling closer.

Don't be ridiculous, Tlafa replied. *You were about to miss me a lot more. If your Aial hadn't made a hole for you, you wouldn't've survived that building falling on you.*

How about the others? she asked.

You think a falling building could hurt a Tyal or a Koelu?

It might have sounded reassuring once. But it wasn't an answer. Esther had lived among elementals long enough to know a lie packaged in a truth when she heard one.

What happened?

You hit your head, Tlafa replied. *Maybe you should rest before you start worrying about—*

What happened, *Tlafa?*

He showed her: Deric hacking away the wood to release

Tlafa, Tlafa pulling Esther from the rubble, and what he'd seen of the fray before carrying Esther straight back into the Abyss. Lialli returning and asking Tlafa to go up to retrieve two prisoners: Deric and a young boy who looked suspiciously like the Koelu. Deric explaining that Aial had been injured to save him.

They took Aial?

It's too late. There's nothing we can do.

But he's head of the Koelu. What are they going to do?

They're holding a war council.

Who's *holding a war council?* Esther demanded, irritated with Tlafa's obliqueness.

Everyone. The Tyal, the Koelu, the Qyul, even the Elayil.

Didn't every one of you tell me that the People would never involve themselves in a human war?

But this isn't a human war, Tlafa explained patiently. *It's ours. They've used us for four of your centuries, and now they tried to kill some of ours on trade day. Even if Nevena were still alive, they broke the terms of the treaty.*

They don't remember, Esther said. *Haven't you explained to them? Human lifetimes are so short compared to yours. If you go and attack them now, it'll only make the humans fear you more.*

You don't understand, he replied solemnly. *Aial tried to make us keep the treaty and they drew his blood. Not even Nevena would've condoned this. They're not going to leave anyone alive—and they expect Nevena's successor to show up to help us kill them all.*

Us? Esther scrambled up. *Tlafa, you're not going with them.*

They tried to kill you too, he said. *They kept me captive for a season and never fed me once—if I'd been mortal, I'd be dead.*

But you're not, and I'm not, Esther pleaded.

I'm not the one you have to convince.

Esther scrambled to her feet and Tlafa rose with her. At his urging, she mounted him and he flew her to the war council. It was being held in the moss-covered clearing that was the remains of the area of the Black Forest where Esther had once tried to speak Words of fire. Each group sat perfectly occupying a quarter of the space in the clearing. There were the Koelu dweorgs, still and motionless like brown boulders against the gray moss; the Tyal firefoxes, constantly in movement, shifting and changing like the flames that they were; the Qyul winged horses, shimmering white and swaying with the wind; and even the Elayil water sprites, blueish glassy spots on the moss that she might have missed if she didn't know what to look for.

At the center stood the trembling Koelu-looking boy.

"What are you doing here?" demanded the head of the Qyul in wind.

"I've come to join the war council," Esther replied, also in wind.

"You're not one of the People," hissed Jiggae in rock, who sat in the place of head of the Koelu.

"So eager to replace Aial, were you?" asked Esther.

"How dare you," he responded. "*You* led him into this; this is because of *you*—"

Both Lialli and Tlafa hissed at Jiggae.

"You've always been against hosting humans," Jiggae said to Lialli. "Why do you defend it now?"

"I was there and you were not," Lialli said coolly. "This wasn't Esther's doing. If anything, she was the only one who their foolish attack might have extinguished."

"We're not here to argue," said Ela quietly, in water. The ancient leader of the Elayil, Ela was quiet, small, soft-spoken and nearly transparent. But when she spoke, the whole clearing went still and turned to her. "We're not even here because of the broken treaty. They collapsed only the trade hall. They could not have done so without speaking the lyll as we do."

"Yes," said Lialli, lowering her head in respect. "And Qalau identified this as the one that did it." It took a moment for Esther to remember that Qalau was her Aial's given name. Lialli shoved the small boy in Ela's direction. Ela walked closer to him and peered up into his face. The boy trembled.

"What's your name?" she asked him in the Words of rock. He didn't respond—only stood there trembling. She turned to Lialli. "Can you be sure? He doesn't speak the Koelu Words."

"I can explain," said Esther, stepping forward. All heads turned toward her, wearing varying degrees of incredulity. "I mean, I can't explain everything. But I know his story."

"Then tell us, child," said Ela.

So Esther told Aine's story as best she could in the Words of wind. A merchant's daughter, Aine had fallen in love with a Unycan man as they visited the town year after year. When she came of age, they pushed through all who objected and married anyway, beginning a life in Unyca together. Though their marriage caused a great deal of anger among Unycans who firmly believed that marriage with outsiders was forbidden, they paid those people no heed. They had been blessed with one child who lived past infancy: a daughter.

That daughter fell in love with a visiting merchant. This time, the Unycans were determined not to permit the marriage, and when it seemed like the merchant might try to spirit the girl away, a dozen Unycan men visited him in the night with katars and warned him to go and never come back.

He left, but Aine's daughter was already pregnant. When the Unycans learned this, many wanted her to kill the child or give it to a visiting merchant before marrying the Unycan they had chosen for her. The girl appeared to agree. But when the time came for her to give birth, she disappeared and was never seen again.

A year later, at the trade, the rainfolk came to Unyca with an infant child. Aine wanted to take in the child, certain that he was her grandson; but the Unycans agreed that she had already done enough damage by corrupting her daughter's mind with her foreign ways. The child was handed instead to the man who had been intended as Aine's daughter's husband: Melech. Rather than kill or abandon the child, he had raised Dov as his own, though Aine had never been permitted to speak to him.

When Esther fell silent, the clearing was still.

"This would be about five years ago?" asked Ela.

"Yes."

"Qalau went to trades alone in those days, and he hadn't yet been named leader of the Koelu. Perhaps he helped the daughter."

"He was always morbidly fascinated with mortal creatures," said Jiggae with disgust.

"He might have hidden her by the Lyll Circle," said Lialli. "No one ever goes there except to create. If her child was born there—and if Qalau was there, trying to help her create. . . ."

"It's a *human*," spat Jiggae. "Humans don't create in Lyll Circles!"

"But they do create," Ela insisted.

Esther interrupted with a brief explanation human reproduction. The elementals—who were created through chants at the Lyll Circle in a ceremony that took less than a day—seemed to take the news with varying degrees of interest and horror.

"So . . . it would have come out of another human?" Ela asked. "After being in there for three seasons?"

"Yes," said Esther.

"But then how could Qalau have had anything to do with it?"

"Birth—when the baby comes out of the adult—is not easy," said Lialli. "Esther told me, many humans die this way. Since this child's mother was never seen after his birth, perhaps she died then. Qalau is kind. He would have tried to help her. But all he knew was creation. If he was trying to create as the Koelu do while the human child was being born. . . ."

"Are you suggesting that the child could have become Koelu?" snapped Jiggae. "It's human!"

"No—he's less than Koelu. But more than beloved. Perhaps he was made part Koelu and part human."

They all looked at the child. He was trembling.

"I want my papa," he whimpered. Hearing the human language jolted Esther into action.

"I'm sorry," she said to him gently. "Your papa isn't here right now. These people are trying to figure out why you can do what you can do. Could you understand anything they said?"

The child shook his head.

"Can you tell me your name?"

"Dov," he replied softly.

"Dov," Esther repeated. "Did you make the building fall down?"

Dov trembled. "Papa said it was the right thing to do," he said. "Papa said it would make the bad witches go away."

"Can you explain how you did it?"

"I told the building to fall down. And it did."

"You *told* it?" she asked, her voice sharper than she had intended. The boy began to cry. Esther sighed and looked up to blank faces.

"You'll have to translate, I'm afraid," said Ela. "None of us has command of the words of men like Qalau."

So Esther told them what Dov had said. There was an uproar.

"We have to extinguish it!" said Jiggae. "If it commands, we can't know what destruction it might bring."

"He is a *child*," said Ela. "We do not blindly extinguish any creatures."

"They took Qalau," countered Lialli. "A light for a light."

"From what Esther tells us, he is dear to the man who leads the attacks against us. We'll bring him back up above and trade him for Qalau. Esther will come with us to translate and explain to them that the child must learn. If they refuse to heed us, then the destruction they bring upon themselves will be none of our concern."

"But what if they attack again?" asked Jiggae. "What if they've already extinguished Aial?"

Esther almost spoke up to point out that Lialli herself had suggested that Dov was as good as Qalau's son—but Tlafa held her back. Elementals didn't as a rule have any special attachment to those they had a part in creating, he explained silently. Dov had been raised as a human to fight the People.

A loud argument ensued, but the final outcome was already clear as day to Esther. They would trade Dov for Aial—but they would also be ready for war. Many of them were chorusing that the Phoenix would not stand for this—the Phoenix would come and help them to destroy Unyca. There was too much certainty in their voices and too many of them to talk out of it.

Deric wants to talk to you, Tlafa nudged her.

She turned to see Deric on the edge of the clearing, looking confused. She walked over to him.

"What's going on?" he asked quietly.

Esther explained the gist of things.

"But that's terrible. Esther, we have to go and warn the Unycans to run."

"They brought this on themselves," she said coolly.

"Some of them, yes," said Deric. "Melech and his . . . witch hunters, yes. But what about Aine? What about her people, who were fighting him?"

Esther hesitated. He was right. She wished she'd thought to make that case before. She turned back to the elementals, but there was too much anger there now— even Ela's words were increasingly falling on deaf ears, and voices rose with declarations of war.

"I'll go," she said. "I'll warn them. You stay here with

Tlafa and Dov—the child. Make sure they don't hurt the child, and Tlafa will make sure they don't hurt you."

Then Esther whispered, *"Fiasqite evaz, qya?"*

The wind heeded her request and lifted her up, carrying her higher, higher and higher into the clouds.

33

The Minister of the Treasury

Late morning, eleventh day of spring
452 A.D. – Castle Dio, Ceryll

MINISTER SEPTIMO WAS interrupted for the fifth time that morning by a servant. He fired the girl immediately, as he had the last four. He was irritable, panicked and in haste.

Ever since Queen Consort Esther had died without providing the king with a son, the nation had begun to fall apart. The violet mines had all run dry; Seleukos began amassing an army of speakers, and the Ceryllan people were divided between the meek who were content to be ruled by a woman and the rightful Kingsmen who would fight to see a king on the throne. Septimo had joined the cause at the start and assumed the leadership of the Kingsmen faction after the two leaders before him had been executed for treason. Septimo prided himself on his patience, which he knew would win him the fight. It was simple: Ottavio would woo and win Gwenaëlle, and if the king would not consent to that marriage, they would simply elope. Once that was done, it would be simple to hire an assassin to kill Nicole. Things had been looking up.

But now, thanks to Ottavio's idiocy, it was all up in flames. Septimo had to move fast. If Juste or Odilon began to investigate his family and found any hint of his carefully laid plans . . . ! He would not see the gallows like the two before him.

The time for patience was over. He had to move immediately. He extracted monkshood poison from the plant carefully and methodically. Panic would not be the death of this plan. Then he took a scroll that had required Juste's perusal that morning and carefully detached the upper edge of the paper from the wooden handles. It took a good chunk of the morning to manage this without damaging the document, but at last the paper came free. He pulled out the wooden roll that he had specially prepared, with a fine needle embedded in the upper left handle, where Juste habitually held the scrolls as he read. Septimo worked out the placement and carefully glued the paper back to this handle.

Then, realizing that the upper and lower handles were visibly mismatched, he spent even more time time detaching the lower one as well. When a matching handle was attached to the lower edge, he rolled it back up and bound it in a strip of paper that he sealed with wax. He then carefully dipped the entire handle with the needle into the vile of poison. While it dried, he emptied the vile into his chamber pot, tossed the empty container out the window into the pond below, and left his office for the throne room.

A nobleman he didn't recognize barreled into him, and he dropped the scroll.

"Apologies, minister," said the nobleman, or nobleboy, thought Septimo snidely, for his voice clearly hadn't cracked yet, though he was trying to make it sound deeper. Though he didn't recognize the boy, he recognized the clothes as Odilon's. So the falcon had bastards running around the castle like they deserved to be treated as nobility, did he? Septimo would be having a word with him. Then again, there would be no need after Juste had been deposed.

"Watch where you're going," said Septimo as the boy reached down to pick up the scroll. He nearly stopped him, but there was no need: he was holding it by the center, over the wax seal.

"Apologies again," said the boy.

Septimo took the scroll carefully, turned his nose up at the boy and proceeded on to the throne room. There was more commotion than usual, but as a minister of the council, Septimo could push ahead of the line of people waiting to have their trivial problems heard by the king.

He arrived just as Juste was standing from the throne and calling a recess for lunch—lunch? Was it already so late in the day?—and hastily placed himself in Juste's path.

"Apologies, Your Majesty, I just need you to look over this one document. It will not take you more than a moment, if you please . . . ?"

Juste narrowed his eyes at Septimo in anger. Septimo stood his ground, though cold sweat ran down his back. Then Juste shook his head and ran a hand over his face.

"My apologies as well, minister. I apologize for being ungracious this morning. We both seem to be cursed with wayward children."

Septimo swallowed his objection that at least *he* only had one son who was easily beguiled, not three daughters overeager to rise above positions befitting their gender. Juste was too blinded by affection to see reason in this respect. But he would soon be of no more trouble.

"What is this document now?"

Septimo handed it over. His heart was in his throat.

Juste broke the seal and opened it, holding it by the top left handle as he always did. He did not wince when the needle must have pierced him, but as he unfurled the scroll, his brow furrowed.

He looked back up at Septimo.

"What is the meaning of this?"

He tilted the scroll so Septimo could read it. It was not the scroll that Septimo had prepared. It contained only a few words.

Your Majesty, the scroll read, *the bringer of this scroll wishes you harm. I suggest you arrest him immediately. I will bring proof momentarily. Your faithful servant.*

Septimo recognized the script. It was Odilon's hand. His blood boiled: *the boy.*

"Your Majesty," Septimo pleaded, "the falcon is lying to protect himself. He brought his bastard-born son into Dio, and he knows that I was going to tell you."

"I am not going to arrest you without proof," frowned Juste, "but the man I have known all my life would not stoop to such lows."

That was when there was a resounding crash and commotion from beyond the inner doors, where Juste would eat. At Juste's signal, guards rushed to open the door.

A tureen of soup had been overturned, and a well-dressed servant had a ragged boy with an apron by the front of his shirt, and was hitting him.

"Stop," commanded Juste in his cool, dangerous way. The servant froze, going ashen. "What is the meaning of this?"

"He . . . he tried to tell me that the soup was poisoned, milord. He wouldn't tell me why, and—"

"Release him," ordered Juste, and the servant dropped the boy. "Come here, boy," he ordered the boy.

"Y— Your Majesty," stuttered the boy. "I—"

"What makes you think my meal was poisoned?"

"I . . . I saw someone put poison into it."

"Where?"

"In the kitchens."

"What were you doing there?"

"I . . . I'm your chef's apprentice, milord."

"And who are you accusing of putting poison in my food?"

"Roshan, milord."

"Ah—I am not familiar with that name."

"She's Ambassador Baraz's concubine, milord."

Juste looked taken aback. Septimo stole a look at Baraz. The Yngan fool had gone gray. But Septimo may owe him a debt of gratitude—perhaps in this fuss, the scroll would be forgotten for a time. He only had to find the original scroll and destroy it before Juste saw it.

He slipped away from the fray toward the doors of the throne room.

"Where do you think you're going?" said the voice of the falcon, and a hand caught his arm. Septimo turned, ready to fight—but Odilon was flanked by two captains of the king's guard.

"To find you," said Septimo with assumed brashness. "Perhaps you could explain to me your nonsensical accusation."

"No," said Odilon. "I think we'll be doing this where Juste can hear. Bring him," he ordered the captains. As Odilon began making his way into the crowd around Juste, one of the guards grabbed Septimo by the wrists and held them behind his back as he pushed Septimo after Odilon and the other guard.

When they returned to the other side of the crowd where Juste stood, they saw the crowd watching a dog that was lapping up the spilled soup. Suddenly, the dog began to wretch and crumpled to the floor. The crowd began to buzz. Juste raised a hand to silence them.

"Baraz!" he called. "What is the—"

There was a sudden movement in the crowd, and Odilon's other guard leapt forward to meet it. The guard tussled with a servant in Yngan garb, and when he stood, he held a dagger.

"Your Majesty," said the guard, holding it out to Juste. Juste accepted it and looked at it expressionlessly. Even from a distance, Septimo could see that it was Yngan: a curved and engraved handle set with precious gems, with a blade of black.

"I wasn't . . . !" stuttered the Yngan servant, wide-eyed. "I never—"

"Hold your tongue," snapped Juste. The servant's mouth snapped shut. "Baraz," he addressed the ambassador, "your concubine is accused of attempting to poison me, and your servant just tried to attack me with a black dagger. Both of them will be arrested, though I will guarantee them a fair trial."

"Thank you, Majesty," croaked Baraz.

"Were you part of this, Baraz?"

"Of course not! I had no idea—I am so sorry, Your Majesty; had I known . . . !"

"Very well," nodded Juste. "Then I would like to offer you and your entourage the protection of my guards. No doubt there will be some . . . hard feelings in this castle for a while."

It was a masterful move, Septimo had to admit. If Baraz accepted, he was in the same predicament as the Seleukoi ambassador, a prisoner in all but name. But to refuse was to practically admit involvement in not one, but *two* attempts to assassinate the Ceryllan king.

The Yngan servant gave a cry of horror and made to push past the guards. There was a tussle, and the servant slumped to the floor. The sword of the guard who had first stopped him came away bloody.

"Now," said Juste, turning back to Odilon and Septimo. "Odilon, do you have something for me?"

"I do," said Odilon, producing the scroll. "I suggest you avoid touching the handles."

Septimo closed his eyes. He was no different from the last two, after all.

34

The Beloved

Third day of summer,
452 A.D. – Falle Harbor, Ceryll

IT WAS SUMMER by the time that they rolled into Falle Harbor. They had slowed down ever since passing Lyree. Paraskevas, Laine and Roch had started to attempt to convince Gwen and Nier to come with them on their plan to sail to the southern mainland.

"The Words aren't outlawed there," said Paraskevas.

"We could live as we please, away from all this fear and chaos," Laine cajoled.

But Gwen said no, and Nier insisted that he would go where Gwen went. At last, they had to accept that Gwen's mind would not be changed. Sometimes she wondered if she ought to tell them about the Phoenix, if only to provide a better explanation of her reasons. But she didn't dare risk it.

Gwen had been taught about the designation of the Ten Cities in 399 A.D. by her great-grandfather. Each of the Ten Cities was guaranteed a city hall, a library and its own city guard, as well as access to the then-new kingsway. Nine of them were designated because they were the biggest cities, but Falle Harbor alone was the exception. The king had been hoping to see increased trade with Jehan and Seleukos, and so designated the easternmost harbor town as one of the Ten in the hope that it would grow.

The availability of a Ceryllan harbor city did not spur isolationist Seleukos into trade, and the Jehani, whose only coastal towns were on Tomb Sea, would not set up any sea routes. Traders from the Dantes continued to favor Milleport, and rather than grow, Falle Harbor remained as small a town as the day it had been designated one of the Ten.

Even knowing that, its smallness defied Gwen's imagination. Falle Harbor comprised one dock and two buildings, the city hall and the tavern. The hall was a crudely renovated boathouse, and the library a small room within the hall that seemed to have only the crudest sense of organization. The Falle Harbor guard was made up of one captain and two guards. The captain was also the mayor, and the tavern keeper was also the librarian. The two guards, for lack of anything else to do, spent their days at the tavern or fishing. The tavern keeper and the captain and two guards lived together above the tavern, with the two guards' wives and children.

The residents of Falle Harbor were less like inhabitants of a city, and more like several autonomous, large families along the coast that happened to live within a day's journey of the harbor. Some were simply fishermen and some were fishermen who called their homes inns whenever travelers needed a place to stay; but every family farmed or fished to obtain the food they required. The tavern keeper often sent the guards fishing to feed the household, and sometimes his customers.

The tavern was the hub of the town's modest activity, frequented by fishermen and presumably travelers when there were any. It was situated against the edge of the cliff next to the wooden staircase that led down to the wooden dock against which all vessels larger than a fisherman's rowboat were anchored or tied off. Gwen and Nier were welcomed with the hunger of a small community eager for any new meat.

To enthusiastic urging, they politely told the stories of their lives as scribes, and shared stories of Farthe and Nirra. In return, they were given more information about life in Falle Harbor than either had ever cared to know.

At last, Gwen found an opening to tell the captain that they were looking for passage to the Dantes.

"Difficult time for that journey," he said thoughtfully.

"Why, are the currents seasonal?" asked Gwen. But the captain and tavern keeper laughed and shook their heads.

"Nah, nothing like that. Just that there isn't any reason for anyone to be crossing in summer, see? People tend to cross in the spring or autumn, not so much in the summer. Trade's best just after or just before winter. And folk looking for work head out in the spring, so that they're there once summer comes round. A few Danti came through this way in the spring, but they'll still be in the bigger cities, trading until later in the summer. Few enough people come through here as it is. No one's going to be turning back yet."

Gwen and Nier exchanged a dark look. This was not a development they had anticipated. From the beginning, Gwen had intended to cross from Milleport where ships could be found going to and from the Dantes in every season but winter. If they had to wait an entire season, they might as well travel back to Milleport.

"You're sure?" asked Gwen. "There's not a single person who might cross to the Dantes before autumn?"

"Who wants to know?" asked a voice from behind her, making her jump and spin around.

The speaker was a tall woman whose waist-length braided hair suggested that she was Danti. She was, however, attired in the Ceryllan style in a simple ankle-length dress of brownish, natural colors. Yet something about her was strange. Gwen took in her large forehead and narrow eyes and tall stature, trying to figure out what made her look just a little different from anyone Gwen had ever seen.

"I do," Gwen replied, studying her. "Did you *dye* your hair green?"

"No, it's natural," said the woman, rolling her eyes. There was no lie. "Want to put that stare away?"

Gwen gulped and tried not to look guilty. "I'm from the north. I guess I'm not used to. . . . Sorry. So, you're Danti, then?"

"Yes and no. We spent a lot of time there, but we're from Vandya originally."

"We?"

"My brother and I."

"Wait," said Nier. "Vandya as in . . . somewhere on the

southern mainland? Are you going back there? Because we know three people who want to go there."

"But they're not here. Do you want to go to the Dantes or not?"

"We do," said Gwen quickly.

"Why the hurry?"

"Why don't you tell me your name first?" Gwen retorted.

"How about you tell me yours?"

"Gwen," said Gwen.

"Gwen," the woman repeated, raising a brow. "Nice name." Lie. "I'm Nimua. My brother and I were planning on starting on our way back within a fortnight, if we could find any passengers willing to pay a few whites or silvers."

"Thank you," said Gwen, meaning it more than she ever had.

"Not so fast," said Nimua. "What do you and your husband want in the Dantes this time of year?"

"He's not my husband," said Gwen.

"Ah," said Nimua with a slow smile. "Like that, is it?"

Gwen experienced a single, horrifying moment in which she realized that she had no way to respond honestly without inviting more questions.

"Yes," said Nier, putting an arm around Gwen's shoulders. "We're eloping. She comes from money, and I'm from a humble background. We wanted to go to the Dantes and start a life there, but her family found out and now we need to get there as soon as possible."

Gwen offered a smile that felt stiff. Nimua, however, only glanced briefly at Gwen, giving Nier a long, hard look instead. Gwen swallowed, a sound that rang guilty to her ears.

Nimua smiled. "Fine, then. Come with me—you'll have to meet my brother before we make any deal."

The captain, tavern keeper and the guards' families raised their tankards of ale to them as they followed Nimua out of the tavern. She led them down the stairs to the docks. There was no railing on either side, and Nier held Gwen's hand on the way down. Under other circumstances, she would have pulled her hand away in spite of the dizziness that crept up on her whenever she looked down. In truth, the delighted gasps of the wind as it bounced off the cliff face in powerful gusts were more reassuring than Nier's hand, which felt feeble by comparison. But Nimua was glancing back at them now and again as though expecting them to trip, so Gwen closed her fingers around Nier's hand.

She did reclaim her hand at the bottom of the stairs, as she and Nier raised their brows to see Nimua hopping into the first vessel to their right. It was such a small thing that Gwen wouldn't have spared a glance if they had walked past it. It was a sailboat with a hatch at the center of the deck that presumably led to a tiny storage space below. There was certainly enough deck space for four people to sit comfortably on the prow, but she suspected it would not hold up well in a storm. Gwen found herself wondering if this would be a good idea after all.

"Dagda!" called Nimua down the stairs. "Dagda, I found some passengers!"

"Hm?" came a muffled voice, and then a head appeared. His green hair was the exact shade of Nimua's and he was also a head taller than Gwen, but there the similarities ended. His hair stuck up in all directions unchecked, and his beard looked more like he'd forgotten to shave this season than like he'd meant to grow a beard. "And what do you two want in the Dantes this time of year?" he asked.

Gwen sensed something off about him and snatched Nier's hand back in her own. She didn't dare impart a more overt warning, but Nier seemed to understand. *He might be a speaker; no lies.*

"We've already told Nimua all there is to say," he said.

"The girl's a noble," said Nimua lightly. "Families objected, ran away, and so on. They want to cross to the Dantes before her family comes after them."

"That true?" snorted Dagda. He aimed his question directly at Gwen. His mouth curled in a sardonic smile, but his eyes were dark. Gwen thought she could feel them piercing through her mask, and she swallowed. "You're a noble?"

Gwen took a moment so that her reply would not seem hasty, and tried not to let her relief show.

"Yes," she said. "It's all true."

"Really, now?" said Dagda, lowering his eyebrows. "You must have a pretty black coin to pay for your passage then, yes?"

"No," said Gwen. "We can spare a few dozen whites, but that's all."

"Not very rich for a noble," Dagda remarked.

"Well," said Nier, "it's not as though we left in the most ideal of circumstances."

"And before we talk of price," added Gwen, "is this boat even safe?"

Dagda huffed and narrowed his eyes. "Best boat you'll ever see in these parts of Ceryll, girly. Those big ships see more of a risk in a storm than we ever do. The *Sea Skipper* and I, we've been making this journey together for the better part of a decade. She won't be the one to fail us."

At the very least, Gwen noted, he believed it.

"Now," said Dagda, "we're back to the issue of your passage."

"Nimua said a few whites," Nier said.

"Nimua has no head for business."

"We could work," Gwen suggested.

Dagda laughed out loud. "Is that so? Have you ever sailed? Do you know anything about boats?"

Gwen looked down and swallowed.

"We can help out with any chores," said Gwen.

"And if that's not enough," added Nier, "we can pay off our debt by working for you in the islands."

Gwen looked at him sideways: could they spare that time? But then again, they could always find a way to leave if the siblings wanted them to work for longer than they could afford. The important thing now was to cross the sea.

"So you say now," snorted Dagda. "But will you feel the same after we've arrived?"

Gwen leveled him with a look that said, "I am very insulted that you would think that of me" without her ever having to utter a word. Dagda's confident grin wavered for a split second.

"Hush, Dagda," said Nimua. "It's not as though we're ferrying them somewhere special. They just want to get to the Dantes; they don't care where. Two whites apiece is plenty."

Dagda grunted in what Gwen could only assume was agreement. Just like that, the matter was settled. Nimua informed them that they would depart at dawn on the fifth, in two nights' time. With that, she climbed into the boat after Dagda without another word or even a glance.

"I guess that's that," said Gwen blankly.

"Is he a speaker?" Nier asked Gwen about Dagda later that night, as they were settling in to sleep around the fire with Aial's family.

"I don't know," Gwen whispered back. "Something feels odd about him, but I couldn't say what. But whatever it is, we'll be all right. I'm a beloved of wind, and the boat's a sailboat. It'll help us to reach the Dantes safely, at least."

"I suppose," said Nier.

In time, Gwen would look back on this conversation and wonder why she had been so confident. Perhaps she had been addled by that voice in her head that she had come to accept was a part of the wind, whispering assurances and excitement that she was finally setting sail.

I'm waiting, my babe. We'll be together soon—oh, so soon.

*   *   *

When they realized that Gwen and Nier had found passage with Vandyans, Paraskevas and Laine wanted know if they could hire the twins to sail them to the southern mainland. But Nimua would not hear of it.

"We can take you to Dante Bianca," she said. "You can try to find passage in the harbor there. But no further south than that."

Paraskevas and Laine agreed; but they wanted another few fortnights to sell their wagon and all the possessions they couldn't take with them. Nimua seemed willing enough to do this, much to Gwen's displeasure.

So Gwen offered a solution. "Could you take me and Nier up to an island, then come back for them? We only want to go to one of the northern islands, so you'd have plenty of time. And you'd be paid twice."

Nimua frowned. "I don't like that. If we come back here and you've changed your minds. . . ."

"Roch can go ahead with you," said Laine. "He can help Gwen and Nier settle down, and you know we wouldn't abandon our own son."

Nimua seemed dubious, but at last she and Dagda agreed to this plan.

The day that they departed, the sun was hidden behind the clouds. Paraskevas and Laine came down to the docks to see them off.

They parted with smiles, certain they would soon be reunited. Gwen turned her back and did not look back as Dagda and Nimua untied the boat from the dock. Beside her, she saw Nier following her example out of the corner of her eye.

The first day at sea was the worst. Gwen and Roch's stomachs roiled from the moment they left the harbor. They spent the entire first day in shared misery, unable to stomach anything long enough to make a difference. Nier, in contrast, found his sea legs with ease. He certainly looked a little grayer than usual, but wasn't confined to lying on the deck in misery. Gwen remembered very little about that day except the discomfort.

The second day was more tolerable. She woke feeling better than she remembered feeling the day before. The wind's song soothed her as it danced across the deck and over the course of the day, she found herself better able to move about. By evening, she was joining in the others' conversations and paying attention while Dagda explained to Nier how to catch the wind in the sail.

Roch was still as seasick as he had been at the start.

"So," said Nimua, sitting down beside Gwen at the prow. "What do you think of sea travel?"

"It's . . . new," Gwen said.

Nimua laughed. "I know what you mean. I'd never have taken to boats if Dagda weren't so keen. Did you have any siblings?"

"I had a sister. She's dead." To her bewilderment, the wind stuttered around her. *It wasn't a lie,* she thought at it pointlessly; love did not enable the wind to read her mind. Perhaps she couldn't phrase it that way because she also had a living sister.

"I'm sorry," lied Nimua. Gwen had to fight a sudden flash of red. How dare this woman offer such simple words if she couldn't even have the decency to mean them? "No, I know you can hear I'm not sincere—I'm genuinely sorry that you had to lose your only sister."

That was true, and Gwen wasn't about to correct her misconception. Except. . . .

"Hear what?"

Nimua threw back her head and laughed. Her hair caught the wind behind her, and for a moment Gwen thought that she looked like a painting. Nimua looked Gwen in the eye and smiled.

"You just have this jumpy air about you, like you're worried what we might ask you. Seleukos isn't the only place in the world where the Words are legal."

"The Dantes?" gasped Gwen. The implications—the *secrets!*

"Of course not," said Nimua, cutting off Gwen's horrified imaginings. "We're from Vandya. Words aren't outlawed anywhere in the mainland. It's something else that's illegal there. Dagda is that something else. That's why we left, to be honest."

Gwen glanced back at the stout man who was happily explaining to Nier how to read the waves when operating the helm.

"Usually we just pretend that we've caught an exceptionally good wind when we arrive after four days' sailing," confessed Nimua. "But no point with you. You'd hear the lie. Besides, you have your own secret to hide. Dagda can push us faster than the wind can. He's carrying us now: wind alone would never carry us this fast."

Gwen looked up at the sail. The wind was laughing and singing in delight, as it had been since the boat had first left the harbor. When she listened closely, she realized that the wind was dancing across another force that was carrying it faster than it would have gone by itself. The wind saw it as a game, and gusted even more strongly across that force, propelling the *Sea Skipper* forward even faster.

"When will we be arriving, then?" she asked. "Do you think?"

"Afternoon tomorrow," grinned Nimua. "Assuming I sail

us for the night. We can only speed up as long as Dagda's up and about. And it exhausts him to do it too long."

Gwen silently apologized to Dagda for thinking him lazy. Though, she admitted to herself, his apparent inability to use a hairbrush or a razor didn't do a lot to recommend him.

"We should be crossing into Danti water anytime now, though," said Nimua, standing. "Come with me: you'll be laughed out of any inn in the Dantes if you can't find your sea legs. Help me prepare dinner."

Gwen smiled and got to her feet. She was no longer stumbling as though she might fall overboard at any second, but she nevertheless clasped the wooden railing around the outer edge of the deck for stability. She followed Nimua to the hatch and unpacked a meal's worth of dried meat and flatbread while Nimua filled four flasks with water.

"The best thing about having Dagda at the sail is that you know that we'll sail steady," said Nimua.

"I wouldn't call this steady, precisely," said Gwen as the *Sea Skipper* tipped and slid down the slope of a swell before rising over the next. She wondered what normal sailing in a boat this small felt like, if this was what it felt like "steadied" by Dagda's magic.

The boat shook violently. The two flasks that Nimua had placed on the deck tipped and rolled overboard. The meat and flatbread in Gwen's arms followed shortly as the boat tipped sideways.

"Dagda!" snapped Nimua. "What are you *doing?*"

"It's not me," said Dagda. His voice sounded hoarse.

"It's not . . . it's not even really the waves. I'd say it's the wind, but . . . it wasn't doing this before."

It *wasn't* the wind, Gwen wanted to say. It wouldn't have mattered. The boat was shaking more violently and Gwen clung to the opening of the hatch desperately. Her gaze swam until it latched on Nier, clinging to the railings on the other side of the deck, looking as though he'd caught hold of them only after sliding halfway off the deck beneath them.

Please help him, Gwen asked the wind. For the first time since she had learned its Words, the wind ignored her. It laughed in delight; swirled nonsensically and incomprehensibly. Aiar had told Gwen that she was insignificant, only a speck in time to the elements. This was the first time that she felt it. The wind was so loud, so *present,* and yet it refused to heed her. The boat shook again, and began to tilt sideways. Nier began to slip. She understood, now, why Aiar had spent so much time impressing upon her the danger of issuing a command: the urge to do so now, when she stood to lose much and the wind would not listen to her, was powerful.

But she did not command.

Gwen let go of the hatch to slide down the deck toward Nier. Her best hope was that if she and Nier fell together, the wind might save them both. She would slide straight under the railing at this rate. She reached out her hand to Nier. He reached back.

A moment before their hands touched, the world around Gwen disappeared into a column of flames.

35

The Spy

First day of autumn,
452 A.D. – Rainforest near Unyca, Ynga

LEAVING DERIC ALONE with Tlafa, whose enormous wings had long since become visible, and Dov amidst a mob of angry dweorgs, firefoxes, water sprites and winged horses had been the worst choice Esther could have made. He was painfully aware that if a couple of elementals decided to kill the humans in their midst, there was little Tlafa could do to stop them.

But when the group in the clearing dispersed, it wasn't in Deric's direction. The winged horses took flight, and the firefoxes dispersed into sparks and flames that flickered up and up and up. The dweorgs latched onto the wall and began crawling upwards like insects.

Deric didn't realize that the water sprites were headed in his direction until they were already upon him. He braced himself, but they weren't coming for him. They moved around and between Deric and Tlafa to dive into the dark river behind them.

"Why aren't they going up?" Deric asked Tlafa, who made an irritated sort of noise that he understood all too well. "No, even if you explained I wouldn't understand," he agreed. He did understand the way Tlafa angled his body and shook his head, though. Deric stepped up to pick Dov up. But the child squirmed and screamed.

"We're going back to your papa," Deric explained to him. But the child would not be soothed. "See the pretty horse with the wings?" he tried instead.

Dov quietened.

"We're going to get on its back, and it'll take us back up to your papa. We're going to fly!"

"We flew down here," sniffled Dov. "It was scary."

"Well," said Deric, thinking quickly, "I'll hold on to you this time. I promise you won't fall."

That at least got Dov to let Deric pick him up. They climbed onto Tlafa's back—an awkward business, because there were wings where Deric would usually put his legs when riding a horse. He had to sit much further forward than he normally would have so that his legs came out in front of the wings. He was painfully aware of how unstable he was, unable to grip with his knees as he usually would.

But he held on to Dov firmly, determined to help the boy feel safe.

Tlafa flew them straight up, through the clouds, out of the Abyss and over the rainforest. The view from the sky was more magnificent than any Deric had ever seen, he reflected as he looked down at the thick canopy of the rainforest, broken by the river meandering through the middle before ending in a cascade into the Abyss. He wondered if Tlafa would let him fly with him again at a time when he could enjoy it.

Unyca from above looked just as Deric had imagined: two squares of buildings with a square street between them and an open square at the center—and now a gaping opening on the side of the outermost square that faced the rainforest. The winged horses, firefoxes and dweorgs were standing or hovering by the tree line as if waiting for something.

Humans were flooding out of Unyca from doors on every side. But in the square at the center stood several dozen people with Melech before them, holding a katar to a brown blob before him.

Esther's Aial, Deric realized. He was still alive.

And before them stood Esther, alone, arms crossed and holding her ground as though she thought she was a match for the at least fifty people she was facing.

Tlafa landed beside her.

"As promised," said Esther coolly, "your son is unharmed. Now return your prisoner to us, and we will return ours."

"You can't do it," said one of the Unycans. "You know as well as we do that Dov is one of them. There's no pretending anymore."

"Don't you *dare* say that about my son!" growled Melech. "Dov is one of ours, and I won't stand for such talk." He turned back to Esther. "Send him across the square to us, and we'll release this . . . creature."

"You first," said Esther. "You're the ones who've shown time and time again that you can't be trusted."

Melech gritted his teeth and hauled Aial to his feet, and

gave him a shove. Several voices spoke out in protest from behind him, but a glare from Melech silenced them. When Aial was halfway across the space, Esther took Dov from Deric's arms and set him down.

"You can go to your papa now," she told him, and Dov ran across the square.

He was scarcely half way there when Aial collapsed face down, a katar sticking out of the back of his neck.

There was silence for a moment, then Esther let out a cry and ran to him. He was bleeding as red as any human, and his eyes looked as vacant as those of any human corpse. As he watched, the skin began to crumble into dirt and the vacant eyes began to take on a brighter violet hue.

There was a flicker, and then the firefox that had kicked Deric in the chest leapt past him, taking human form and diving into the mob behind Melech to embrace one of the men. All of the men looked as confused as Deric for a moment—and then they smelled burning at the same time as the man in her embrace began to scream. Lialli didn't relinquish her victim until he was a blackened char. The men around her tried to strike at her with spears or katars, but she flickered away from every attack without releasing the man she was holding onto.

When the men realized that they couldn't attack Lialli, they turned to Deric and Esther and the army of elementals flooding into the square behind them. Though Deric had only a katar and Esther was unarmed, each of them was better trained than all their attackers combined. It was easy to dodge their clumsy attacks.

The result of the battle had always been a foregone conclusion. The Unycans didn't stand a chance against the furious elementals. Maybe this was why they were caught unaware—too overconfident that they could handle themselves. Deric didn't see Melech talking to Dov; he didn't see where the axe came from.

Deric didn't notice anything until Esther screamed Tlafa's name. He turned just in time to see the axe come down on Tlafa's neck. The majestic creature collapsed to the ground in a pool of white fur, white feathers and red, red blood. Behind that body stood Dov, holding an axe twice his size, trembling and wide-eyed.

Esther leapt at Dov and Melech aimed his spear at Esther. Deric moved instinctively, throwing himself to collide sideways with Esther, knocking her out of the spear's trajectory. He twisted to catch Melech's spear and jammed his fist holding the katar into Melech's throat.

Dov's screams and sobs fell on deaf ears. Two other men were already making for Esther, who was lying on the ground beside Tlafa's head staring into his vacant eyes. Deric moved to deflect their attacks.

The battle didn't last long and Deric couldn't have said how many people he'd killed by the end. Perhaps only Melech, perhaps ten or twenty. It was hard to tell, because even if he only injured an attacker, that attacker was not given the chance to escape before destruction rained down upon him.

The elementals flattened Unyca. Every stone collapsed to dust and every crate and beam burned to ash. When the dust cleared, all that remained of Unyca was the wall of black around the inner square, a bizarre room with an arch on each side and no roof, rising out of the wasteland.

The only non-elementals left in that square were Dov,

Esther and Deric, standing or lying in an arc around Tlafa's body. Inexplicably, there were a few violets scattered among the rubble.

Deric wondered numbly if the fleeing Unycans had been allowed to flee, or if they had been slaughtered too. He braced himself for the elementals to exact their vengeance on him, too, but they turned and disappeared into the rainforest.

Dov was shaking and crying. Esther lay there, expression vacant and hollow like she was dead too. Deric reached forward to check, but his fingers were shaking so badly that he couldn't tell if she still had a pulse. He put his katar under her nose and it fogged. She was alive.

He tried to rouse her, to make her see they had to go, but she didn't respond.

So he picked her up, draping her over his back, and drew Dov by the hand. The boy followed him numbly into the rainforest.

Deric took Dov and Esther to the campsite, where he showed Dov how to weave the fibers from leaves into bags.

"We're going to have to travel across the wasteland," he explained to the boy. "And we'll need a lot of food and water to do that."

"What about Papa?" asked Dov.

"He's gone," Deric tried to explain. "We have to keep going."

"But I want my papa," Dov cried.

In the end, most of the preparations were made by Deric alone. He found his horse not far from the campsite, and found his hunting knife and sword. He hunted a large tapir with his sword—not an experience he wanted to ever have to repeat—fashioned a waterskin out of its bladder, and smoked what parts of its flesh looked edible. All the while, Dov went between sleep and meals in sullen silences or body-wracking sobs, and Esther sat or lay like a statue wherever Deric put her, only drinking when water was poured into her mouth. He could not make her eat.

It took him a day and two nights and then they were ready to go.

He put the blanket he had given Esther over his horse's back, and placed over that a pair of makeshift saddlebags that he'd managed to make out of leaves and vines, one on either side of the horse, held together by several vines. Esther and Dov sat atop the blanket and the vines.

Deric led the horse with the precious waterskin tied to his belt.

It took them a good three days to make it to a town. Their water ran out in the middle of the second day. Though they drank it sparingly, it was not enough to sustain three people and a horse. By the time that they arrived in Mirage, Deric felt like he was only kept upright by the terror that his horse might collapse before they found water.

The innkeeper they came upon was a decent fellow who gave them plenty of water and allowed them to sleep in the stables without question. It wasn't until the following morning, when he felt more like himself again, that Deric realized that the stables were looking awfully full—and not with livestock.

Many of the Unycans who had fled had ended up in Mirage, he learned from the innkeeper. No one had any coins, and no one could explain where they had come from. For the first time in a season, Deric realized that the pouch of gold pieces in his belt would be useful.

He made a deal with the innkeeper and exchanged most of his coins for free lodging and food for the Unycans for the rest of the season—and a room for Esther and Dov and himself. He carried Esther up to the room and tucked her into bed. She was still catatonic, and still only drinking what he poured down her throat. He was about to go downstairs to ask where he might find an herbalist when he saw movement on the windowsill out the corner of his eye.

It was a goshawk. Not any goshawk—it was Verity.

Verity stared back, then gave a small, gentle call. Deric stared a moment more before noticing that something was wrapped around Verity's leg.

Hesitantly, he reached forward. When Deric began untying the twine from her leg, Verity nuzzled his hand with the top of her head. A small piece of parchment came loose. He read the note. It was only a single unsigned line telling him to head directly for Noucleion, but Deric knew its sender.

His mission was over. Yet Esther needed him now. He couldn't go, but nor could he bring her back with him. Nicki would offer no safe haven for a proven speaker. He could bring her partway and then leave her somewhere along the way that seemed safe. That would require an explanation that he could not give without being either dishonest or disloyal.

Deric sat beside Esther with his head in his hands for the rest of the morning.

36

The Lieutenant's Knife

Afternoon, eleventh day of spring,
452 A.D. – Castle Dio, Ceryll

C HAN HID IN the shadows of the throne room, watching the chaos unfold that ended with Baraz under Ceryllan guard and Minister Septimo arrested. *Fools,* he seethed. What a waste of assassination attempts. Did they think that the imprisoned heir was effectively out of the picture? Or did they not realize that the king wasn't the true power?

But none of this was important to Chan. He just needed to know where the heir was.

He didn't know what drew him to the nobleman slipping out of the throne room as the falcon presented the king evidence of Septimo's clumsy attempt at an assassination. (What did Septimo think would happen if that had worked? The cause of death would be crystal clear, and so would the orchestrater.) But Chan had lived as long as he had by trusting his instincts, so he followed.

He watched the figure walk towards the tower—

but then it stopped at the entrance to the courtyard and doubled back. Chan scrambled to hide in an alcove. He wasn't well hidden, but as long as he remained still, most people wouldn't notice him. As the figure approached, however, it became clear that she was very aware of Chan.

The clothing might have given anyone else pause, but Chan had spent seasons studying the heir. He knew her as soon as she turned to face him. His pulse picked up.

"Chan, is it not?" she said conversationally, coming to a halt several steps away. "Ambassador Dara's servant."

"I . . . Your Highness?" Chan tried to sound confused. "Why are you dressed like that?"

Her face broke into a terrible smile. Chan's heart was hammering like it wanted to escape his chest. Though he knew that a princess without her guards was harmless, his instincts were screaming at him to run.

It was foolish. This was a golden opportunity. His fingers twitched, ready to pull a blade out of his sleeve. Three steps and he could slit her throat. He just had to get a little closer.

"Your Highness," he started, putting his hands up and taking a step forward.

"Stop," she said sharply. "And step back."

Chan froze.

"Step back, I said. You will step back, or you will regret it."

Chan could have laughed. What did she think she had to bargain with? "I'll regret it? What do you think you'll do?"

He took another step forward. But the heir didn't even look frightened. He would have thought her foolish—but he already knew that she was anything but. She'd lost Dara two dozen assassins in two seasons. He flicked the knife handle into his hand and was about to move to close the remaining step and slice her throat when—

"Kill me and Dara's katar gets delivered to the king. Both of you will be executed."

Chan froze. He felt the blood drain from his face.

"How did you . . . ?"

"Drop the knife, Chan."

Chan thought quickly. It was a risk, but she was more likely to be bluffing than not.

He went in for the kill.

And suddenly he couldn't move. His arms were securely bound by the vines of five separate potted plants in the corridor that he'd never paid any particular notice before.

"What magic is this?" he hissed.

"Drop the knife, Chan," Nicole repeated.

Numbly, he complied. She told him to take three steps back and he did. She bent down to pick it up.

"How did you know?" Chan asked quietly.

Nicole was still smiling when she straightened. "I thought you knew that I had spies everywhere."

"But . . . but no one was there," he protested.

She raised an eyebrow at him. "I have eyes in many rooms."

"No," said Chan, who knew Dara's room and its surroundings well enough to know what she meant. "I know where those *eyes* are—all three peepholes. There was no one there, then."

"Are you so certain?"

"I am."

"Then you are a fool."

Perhaps he was. He had made tiny holes beneath the peepholes and placed some soft feather fibers over those holes. If anyone was at the peephole, their breath created a breeze that made the fibers move, alerting Chan and Dara without either ever having to say anything that might give away that they knew they were being watched. Perhaps the heir's spies had realized this and learned to turn their heads or hold their breaths.

But there was nothing he could do now. If the price of removing the heir was Dara's head, then he refused to pay it.

"I suppose you'll take me to the tower now."

"The tower?" asked Nicole with a chuckle. The vines released Chan and receded innocently into their pots. "Now, why would I do that? No. I think that would be excessive. After all, you have seen the error of your ways."

Dread rose in Chan's chest. "I'm not going to be your lapdog," he spat. Ignoring his protesting instincts, he lunged for her with another knife hidden in his sleeve.

The heir stepped aside and parried his strike with the knife he'd tried to use earlier.

"Who said anything about a lapdog?" she asked casually as she parried a second strike. She moved coolly and confidently. It wasn't like anything Chan had ever experienced. It didn't feel like he was fighting a well-trained warrior so much as it felt like she could anticipate his every move.

Instead of parrying the third strike, she caught his wrist and twisted around so that his arm was locked, and struck.

Chan screamed as he felt his elbow break. Nicole released him and stepped back, picking up the second knife that he'd dropped.

"All I need you to do is not breathe a word of this to Dara. Do not let her know that I know about your feather trick. Go on plotting my assassination with her and Zephyr."

"And what, make sure the assassination attempts fail?"

"Not at all. You have my blessing to be as earnest as you like in your planning, as long as you do not actively attack me."

Chan narrowed his eyes at her. "I'll be loyal to Dara until my dying breath," he said.

"Of course you will. That is why you must not tell her anything. If I even get a whiff that she knows about our conversation here, that katar will be brought before the king along with tokens from the last twenty-four assassins she dispatched at me. If you attack me again, I'll put you in chains and make you watch while I tell her how you failed today."

"How can you expect me to go on plotting your assassination without being able to actually carry it out? Dara would know within a day that something was wrong."

"So tell her the truth," she shrugged. "That you could not kill me. Advise her to send other assassins. My only conditions are that *you* not try to kill me, and keep this conversation a secret."

"Why?" asked Chan. "Why not just kill me?"

"Why kill you when you pose no threat to me?"

With that, she turned her back on him and walked away. He thought of pulling the knife out of his shoe, or the one in his belt, and throwing it into her back. It would be so easy. But if it didn't work and Dara was executed, it would all be for nothing.

Chan closed his eyes and prayed for death. When death didn't answer, he turned and walked slowly back up the hallway. He returned to Dara a powerless pawn.

37

The Beloved

Eighth day of summer,
452 A.D. – Somewhere in the Dantes

GWEN OPENED HER eyes and looked around. She was in a cave with no obvious exit, or perhaps the inside of a bubble. The walls of the bubble looked something like contained flames. As she watched, the flames moved as if licking an invisible barrier. She sat up slowly, and only then became aware of the woman who stood watching her.

"I apologize, that wasn't very graceful. I'm out of practice at this. I haven't sought out a guest in . . . oh, it must be a hundred years. So many people pray to me these days, but none of them know what they are asking for. I've taken to ignoring them all."

Gwen stared. The woman had brown skin and black hair—or so Gwen would think, and then she would shift to orange skin and white hair, or yellow skin and red hair. She, like their surroundings, was in a constant state of flux. Yet some features of her face remained constant: big, bright, violet eyes and a wide, expressive mouth. She was smiling, but it didn't reach her eyes.

"Where's Nier?"

"Not here. I've been dying to meet you." The woman chuckled, as if this was a joke.

"To meet . . . me?" And at once Gwen realized why the woman's voice sounded so familiar. "You're the voice. The whispers in my head."

The woman reached out as if she had not heard. "Tell me who you are."

Gwen pursed her lips and said nothing.

"Gwenaëlle Xanthe Aysel de Ceryll," whispered the woman, and her mouth twitched. "Such a stuffy name. But your mind . . . ! It's even more brilliant up close. I should have seen it sooner. You were the quiet, proper one, while your sisters always stole the people's attention away. You've lived in their shadows, taking pride in your knowledge and your mask, for they were your shield. Now the tides have turned. You'll be more than they'll ever be."

Gwen stared. She couldn't breathe. The woman didn't seem to notice.

"You still have such love for your Stelle. We have that in common, you know. I wanted her, but she wouldn't come to me. I clung to her until she fell, and her mind led me to you. I found you in that town you call Wirrn. I wondered if you'd be like her, at first—but then your librarian found that book and you were as drawn to me as I was to you. Your desire to escape and your resentment of your sisters have served us well. Your attitude about the Words, on the other hand. . . . That's not ideal.

"But it doesn't matter. I'm out of time, and you're better than I dared to hope."

The woman released Gwen and she could breathe again. She stood and looked unblinkingly into Gwen's eyes. Gwen's heart and mind were laid bare before this stranger, but she wasn't afraid.

"How?" Gwen whispered. "The Words don't work that way. You can't read my mind."

"Oh, child," said the woman, and her eyes softened. "You are but a babe. Your Words ring fresh, untouched by time. How can you think you could possibly know what Words are, when even creatures who dedicate their lives to them barely scratch the surface?"

"You know everything about me. Can't you tell me something about you?"

"Something?" the woman asked. "What would you like to know?"

"How about—do you have a name?"

"A name," she said, almost wistfully. "Nevena. I was Nevena."

"Nevena . . . like the goddess?" Gwen gasped. Nevena cocked her head, but didn't answer. "You aren't—" Gwen swallowed around her dry throat. "It was you that healed Rainier. Wasn't it?"

"I only told you how."

"What? How?"

"I told you to ask the water and fire in him to calm."

"You couldn't do it yourself?"

Nevena's eyes flashed with something that seemed akin to amusement. "I could have tried. But the elements on the continent do not often heed my wishes from so far away. They resent the treaty we've all had to keep while the mortals spiraled out of control."

"But . . . but what are you? Why can you read me?"

"I am air and I am fire. I am here and now, and I am everywhere and forever. I am an elemental created to see the world simultaneously as mortals do and as the timeless do. I am what is and what must always be. I am the Phoenix of the Continent. I, child, am what you will be when I am no more."

"The . . . the Phoenix! But I thought. . . ."

"You thought I was a weapon. Many do, in the world of petty little men."

Gwen suddenly became aware that they were speaking in the Words of the wind. *"Why speak in the Words?"* she asked in her own language. It felt strange, like cool flames on her tongue.

"I'm afraid I've forgotten those words of mankind," said Nevena. "I've forgotten much of humanity. I used to respond to prayers—no more than one per season, as the treaty dictated. Yet for the longest time, I haven't been able to remember why. They are so . . . *quaint.* I know I'm done. It's your turn to make things right."

"No. I'm only one girl. I can't do anything." Gwen did not hear the Words leave her mouth, but her ears heard them as clearly as if they had. Nevena smiled genuinely for the first time since Gwen had laid eyes on her.

"I could not remember what it was to not know," she said. "You have reminded me. I must end, now. I am weary and the Phoenix may be anything but weary. When the Phoenix is old and weary or young and ignorant—these are the times when the continent tears itself apart with strife. Your work will not be easy. I waited too long—but the world had turned against the Words, and so finding an heir has not been easy for me, either.

"You thought that you came to this place to save your kingdom. Now you will find the entire continent's fate in your hands. It will be difficult, but know this: *I chose you.*"

"You said you chose Stelle," Gwen spat. "I was your—" *consolation prize,* she realized she didn't know how to say in the Words of wind.

Nevena smiled brilliantly, sparking at the eyes and mouth. "Yes, and I have never been more grateful to have been mistaken. She had the potential to sacrifice for the many, but never did. You, on the other hand—you've proven your willingness to give anything. You've sacrificed everything to find me for a mere possibility of hope. You are perfect. Your gift is less than fate and more than blood. You will succeed."

"What do you—"

The bubble that had contained the flames burst, and the flames consumed them both. Nevena was smiling as she was consumed and vanished, like she was being burned away. It was fire and wind, Gwen realized, trying to scream or struggle away. It was futile. She was already consumed, and would die in moments like Nevena.

But she didn't feel like she was dying. The flames were warm and comforting, like a familiar embrace. Gwen relaxed, falling into a meditative state. It felt better than being home. Gwen closed her eyes and felt the part of her mind that was her *self* drifting away.

Then she could feel the world. She had more than sight, touch and hearing: she *was* the world. If she chose,

she could look out across the sea to the furthest corners of
Ynga. She could see straight into the Seleukoi palace, and
feel the potentate's anger as if it had once been her own.
She could see any person she chose to see, into their minds
and hearts—

But she couldn't, she realized. Only a handful of people
were so open to her mind as the Seleukoi potentate. Most
people were blurs to her senses, and she couldn't quite
focus on them in any way. Then she became aware of
the wind, and the flames, that danced all throughout the
world.

"Oh, wind . . . why did you fail me?" she whispered,
knowing that it would not ignore her.

The wind stopped, and slowly *looked* at her.

"Ah . . . Phoenix. Welcome. Do remember to have
some fun this time. Your entrapment in that thing that the
man-creatures do was so very tiresome. You must have
freedom!"

Her shock reverberated through her body in a flaming
shudder. Never had the wind stopped to address her this
way. That gust was already gone, however.

"Won't you carry me?" she asked another gust.

"Why?" it chortled. "Carry yourself."

She could. She could blow across the sea in a wave-
breaking gust, so she did. She could burn forests, so she
did. She could dance and swirl and go back to find . . . what
had she been looking for? Oh, yes! The man-creatures!
Why had they seemed important? They were slow and
oblivious to the elements around them.

It was only after she had twirled around the wooden
debris floating in a section of unnaturally still sea a few

times that it occurred to her that this wasn't quite what she was looking for. There was a flock of birds taking flight, flames rising from a nearby piece of land, a gust of wind beginning to twirl into a tornado too, and a man-creature on a piece of wood. . . . It was all so very distracting.

She heard something and had to concentrate to stop moving in order to hear it better. Still she could not quite hear it. Then, at last, she remembered: this was the water.

"You poor thing," the sea was saying. "You must take care not to be like her."

"Why?" she asked, clumsy Words of water that she found in a memory of a former life both her own and not. "This is wonderful: I am wind! I am fire!"

"Do you remember what it felt like to love?" whispered the sea. "Do you remember your precious ones? What of those for whom you grieved?"

Stelle. The name was an arrow of clarity that pierced an elation like she had never known. Stelle, who had been a half of her, and then gone, leaving in her wake nothing but hollow, pointless hatred. Stelle, everything and nothing. How had she forgotten?

But there was more than Stelle. There was something else. She reached into the memories, fighting a part of her that didn't want to know. And then —

"Rainier. What happened to Nier?"

"What do you think happens to helpless little man-creatures when a being of wind and fire swoops down to collect one of them on a flimsy little tree-thing?"

"No," said Gwenaëlle, and she *felt* the word sing through her. Suddenly, it was far easier to focus. She was still wind, hovering over the sea, but she was also Gwenaëlle.

Gwenaëlle thought of her fading, paper-thin memories of a dark, imperious sister. She thought of the librarian who had looked at her and was at her side when no one else would be; who berated her when she was too far out of line. She reached out with her mind and her self for someone, anyone she had cared for who was still alive and well.

She found Eudon. She tried to go to him, settle down beside him and let him see her. But he did not notice. He was in a tavern, drinking. She brushed his hair out of his eyes.

"You've got a draft in here," grumbled Eudon to the barkeeper.

"You're drunk," admonished the barkeeper. "There're no drafts in my inn."

"I know a draft when I feel one!"

Other patrons were whispering to each other, but of course Gwenaëlle could hear them if she chose to.

"He's been here every night for a fortnight."

"Longer than that. Folk say he got his heart broke by some girl that was staying here in the spring. He's waiting for her to come back."

"Poor bloke. Good-looking, too; he'd hook another fish in no time if he pulled himself together."

Gwenaëlle tried to speak to Eudon, to get him to hear her, but all she succeeded in doing was setting fire to his tankard of ale. This resulted in a fistfight breaking out between Eudon and a large man beside him. Gwenaëlle left as she heard Eudon's arm crack as he fell into the bar. In her alarm, she didn't realize that she had set fire to the wooden floor and barstools until it was too late. People began screaming and rushing about. She left, feeling ashamed and like a helpless, unwitting poltergeist.

She swooped across the sea to the continent: over the Tor and the desert beyond, and back over rivers and through trees. No one noticed her. She swooped and danced and stood briefly atop the highest peak of the Tor as no man had ever done. She tried to split the trees growing on the mountainside, but she could only rustle the branches. She tried to set a fire in the rain-soaked hearth of a starving family in a cottage in the foothills of the Tor. She could only light a corner of the soggy firewood, and she couldn't keep the flame going for long before it hissed out.

She closed her eyes and drifted up and up, to the snow atop the highest peak of the Tor. Her mind still picked up desires, hates, anger, loves, delights and sorrows from every side. She could remember thinking how difficult it had once been to shut out the wind; now it was easy to ignore the cries. It was easy to sink into the snow and think of how she had lost Stelle, killed Nier and broken Eudon's heart. It would be easy to sit up, become the wind once again and cease to care. But why should she? She may have been a mere pawn in court, but she had enjoyed it. She had loved, and had been loved.

She thought of the mission she had set out to accomplish. She was the Phoenix. She was wind and fire. She could return to Ceryll and try to win them the war. But as long as she remained Gwenaëlle, all she could do was set small fires and make little gusts of wind. What could she do in a war? If she relinquished her identity, the war would be too trivial to concern herself with. It already felt trivial. The continent was full of countries struggling to survive, full of fear, and she could not muster the will or the strength to take on the mess.

Gwenaëlle lay in the snow and rolled over. She looked at the mark that looked distinctly human. She wondered if feeling strongly enough could make her human again, leaving her to freeze to death in the snow here. The first drop of flame onto the snow beside her took her by surprise. It was followed by another, and another and another. She was crying flames.

Atop the Tor, Gwenaëlle the Phoenix grieved in fire.

38

The Outcast

Twenty-first day of autumn,
452 A.D. – Mirage, Ynga

ESTHER WOKE IN the dark to the sound of silence in her mind. It hurt no less than it had all the other times she had woken. She closed her eyes and attempted to sink back into oblivion.

Her body could sleep no longer, however. She guessed that she had been sleeping for several days and nights and was not surprised. She fought to pull the drowsiness back even as it slipped away.

It slowly dawned on her that she was not alone. There was a warm body beside her and a warm arm around her. She knew that it was Deric.

So sentimental, she thought with disgust.

You're that, too, Tlafa would have said. The silence in her head was deafening and made her want to scream.

Esther pushed his arm away and rolled out of bed. She noticed bits of dirt speckling the bed. Of course, she hadn't bathed or changed in . . . how long had it been?

A bath was in order, Esther decided.

Wandering through the unfamiliar hallways of what appeared to be some sort of inn, she found a large basin, a bucket and a well in the courtyard. She carried buckets of water from the well to the basin, taking her time in filling it. There was no hurry. There would never be any need to hurry again.

When she stripped and got into the basin, the water was cold but she barely felt it. She methodically washed the dirt from her hair and the grime from her skin.

When she stepped out of her bath, she reached for her cloak—and then paused. This cloak had been woven out of hair from the manes of Tlafa and his people. It had symbolized her place among them.

Tlafa was dead. She was no longer one of the Qyul.

Suddenly furious and nauseous, she kicked the dress into the cold kitchen hearth. Dripping and naked, she walked back down silent hallways and up the staircase to the room where she had awoken.

There was a cot in the room that she hadn't noticed before, where two eyes were staring balefully at her. She ignored the eyes and found a cupboard, from which she took a thin spare blanket. She wrapped it around herself twice under her arms and tied two corners together behind her neck to secure it. Satisfied that she was at least somewhat clothed, she returned to bed and curled herself up in a ball at the edge on top of the blankets, out of Deric's reach.

She did not know how long she lay there, neither sleeping nor thinking. She heard Deric getting up and beginning to move about, quiet as though he thought she was asleep and was trying not to wake her. She heard whispers—he was probably speaking with the occupant of the cot. Eventually, they left the room. Esther relaxed and continued to lie motionlessly.

She may have heard knocks, or voices. She paid them no heed. Footsteps came up the stairs.

"Esther?"

She ignored Deric.

"Esther, I brought some soup. You should eat."

Food. How trivial. The smell reached her and made her stomach turn. The footsteps receded but the smell remained.

At last Esther moved. She saw the bowl sitting by the door. Calmly, slowly, she stood up and walked to the door. She picked up the bowl. She carried it to the window, opened the shutters and tossed it outside, bowl and all.

Then she went back to bed and assumed her earlier position.

Deric did not come back.

She must have drifted off to sleep, for when she opened her eyes, it was dawn once more. Deric was wrapped around her again. When she pushed his arm away and sat up, she noticed that the speckles of dirt were gone from the bedclothes.

Esther lay back down and pulled Deric's arm back across her body. He was warm, she told herself. Warm was nice.

When she woke up next, she was alone. She felt Deric's absence like a needle, inflaming the gaping wound that was the absence of Tlafa. She sat up and was momentarily confused at the pull at the back of her head before she realized that she was still clothed in the makeshift dress of a tied blanket. She felt behind her neck and found that the knot not only still held, but contained some of her hair. It was too much trouble to undo and retie the knot without her hair in it.

Esther slowly rolled out of bed and ambled downstairs instead. She would stop at times for no particular reason, simply unable to find a reason to move. She was vaguely aware of people she didn't know walking around her, sometimes addressing her. She paid them no attention. Deric appeared when she was standing stationary on the bottom step.

"Esther," he smiled.

Tlafa would have told her to smile back, she thought. At once she wanted to be anywhere else. She turned and slowly made her way back up the stairs.

"Won't you eat something?" Deric called after her. She ignored him and crawled back into bed. She distantly heard him saying something but she closed her eyes and listened to the wind's hum until he was gone. She heard him leave a bowl by the door again. This time, she could not bring herself to do anything about it. Closing her eyes, Esther waited for sleep until it claimed her at last.

To her horror, in her sleep, she saw Gwen. *Gwen* with sad, dead eyes that made Esther feel like a pinnacle of happiness by comparison. It wasn't right—she had always been the one who felt things more strongly. Gwen was the emotionally stable one.

"What's wrong with you?" Esther demanded.

"You're dead," said Gwen. "Go away."

"I would if I could, but I seem to be stuck here."

"Of course. Even in my hallucinations you don't want anything to do with me. Go away and let me try to die."

Panic took hold of a part of her heart that Esther hadn't realized she'd missed.

"You can't die," she said—no, begged.

"I am aware. I can try all the same."

Esther swallowed. "What's this about? I've been gone for years, for you."

"Oh, and that makes it all better, does it?" snapped Gwen, sitting up at last. "My twin left me with a 'good-bye and good riddance' and threw herself off a cliff. But it's been a year or so; I should be all better now. Is that what you think?"

Esther swallowed. Lead set in her chest and she felt the blood drain from her face. She remembered considering leaving an angry, hurtful note. She'd been so sure she'd decided against it. She couldn't remember the last time she'd thought about it.

But if she had—in all her angry imaginings, had she ever truly thought about how Gwen would feel, how things might look to her?

"I didn't mean it like—" Esther had to stop there. She couldn't even remember leaving the note. Perhaps she had meant it that way.

She swallowed.

"It's not all that bad. You have Nicki. You have all the court fawning over you. You have Father. You have that . . . who was that ridiculous boy in the library we used to laugh about? He adored you so. Watched you when he thought you weren't looking. Like a puppy, remember?"

To her shock, Gwen let out a sob that became a howling

wind. Tears of flames streamed down her cheeks and melted the snow beneath them. Esther stared.

"I wish you would stop that. This is excessively dramatic, even for a dream, and it's not like you at all. I feel like you're about to catch fire. I'm very bad with fire, you should know."

"Shut your *selfish, lying mouth!*" Gwen shrieked and burst into a flame. Esther leaped several steps back. She found herself stumbling uphill. She looked around to realize that Gwen was slowly melting a crater in the snow. It was objectively magnificent and subjectively terrifying. She had never been frightened of Gwen before. "This is *not* about *you*, you pig!"

"I'd like to remind you that if you kill me now, you'll probably regret it," Esther remarked conversationally. It was only a dream. The flames weren't a real threat.

"How can I kill you when you're *ALREADY DEAD?*"

Esther swallowed around the lump in her throat. "Much as I admit that this is somewhat eye-opening, I'm grieving, too. You don't see me burning holes in mountains."

Gwen glared sullenly at Esther. The flames seemed ever so slightly tamer. "Are you? Who are you grieving?"

"My other half."

Gwen glared some more. "Not funny."

"Not you. I had a. . . ." Esther's breath hitched. She tried to remind herself that it was only a dream. It didn't help. "I was bound to someone. We shared our minds ever since . . . well, ever since I jumped off that cliff."

Gwen sighed and closed her eyes. The flames died around her. "I suppose it shouldn't surprise me. Of course you'd just up and find someone who. . . ." She swallowed and shook her head. "Of course I was replaceable to you. You left, you abandoned me. I never meant to you what you meant to me."

"How dare you?" Esther felt her face flush and her breath caught in her throat. She heaved an exhale and something snapped. "How *dare* you? I needed you. *Needed*, Gwen! I was *miserable*. You were the only one I could stand, the only one I cared about. All I had were you and the barracks, and then it was only you. But *you* never needed *me*. You would giggle with your crowd of ladies at how *unladylike* I was. You would sit in the library reading for entire afternoons and joke about how you preferred the puppy librarian over me, since he didn't *nag* you. You would ignore me when I would beg you to come with me to *do* something. I needed you so much, and you would neither fight Father nor give me more of your time. You had no regard for my needs. I had no choice: I had to leave."

"You—" Gwen shook her head emphatically. "Stop talking about him like that."

Esther was so genuinely confused that she forgot to be angry. "Who? Father? I have—"

"Nier."

It took a few moments for Esther to place the name. "Rainier. Your pup—"

"*STOP!*"

Esther blinked. It took a few moments, but the pieces came together and clicked. "Ah. I'm sorry for your loss, truly." And she was. But all the same. . . . "But you can be thankful that you never shared a mind with him. It's . . . the worst kind of torture."

Gwen stilled. She stood slowly and walked toward

Esther with cold, sharp eyes. Esther found herself fighting the urge to retreat.

"Don't you *dare* tell me I can be thankful," Gwen hissed. "You always think you know best. You don't, do you understand? You don't get to make this about you! *You can't understand how I feel!* If you could, you'd never have gone and died!"

Esther swallowed.

"Don't say that, please," she said instead. "I'm not dead."

"Yes, you are," Gwen sobbed. "Why are you doing this to me? You jumped off a cliff!"

"I jumped. The wind caught me—the wind and Tl—Tlafa."

Gwen's sobs stopped abruptly. She met Esther's eyes. "Tlafa. That name . . . a Qyul?"

Esther nodded. "We were bound by the wind during that fall. He was . . . he was to me what you were back in Dio, I suppose. Except more. He would make me laugh when I was annoyed, and I would make him happy when he was upset. We would think of ways to lie in truths together when Aial was cross. We heeded each other when no one else could reach us."

Gwen snorted. "Then he was more than I was. We were never half so close."

Esther's heart constricted. "I think we were, once. We fell out of balance. But I always loved you. I still do."

She stepped up and embraced her twin. The flames of Gwen's body licked Esther but did no harm. They felt comfortably warm instead. After a moment, Gwen's arms wrapped around Esther in return. Their embrace lasted a long while.

"I wish this were real," sighed Esther. "I never want to wake up. I want to stay here. With you."

"Real," Gwen whispered at last, arms tightening around Esther. "Is it really you? Are you alive? Somewhere in the world down there?"

"Hm," Esther hummed. Gwen was warm. She wanted to fall asleep in her embrace and never wake up.

"But you're not really here," Gwen murmured, as if to herself. Esther hummed in confirmation anyway. "If you stay here, you will die."

"How do you know?" Esther asked blearily, tightening her arms around Gwen. "This is a dream."

"No, it isn't. I don't understand it and your body isn't flesh. But you're *here*. I feel it. I know it." Gwen breathed deeply in and out once and then pushed Esther away. "I am the Phoenix, and I will not let you die again."

The world went dark.

Esther woke in bed in the unfamiliar inn. A man she did not recognize was trickling water into her mouth. She did not have the energy to protest or struggle, so she simply swallowed. Her stomach turned, but she craved more. She reached for the cup only for the man to catch her hands and push them away.

"Slowly, now," he said. "You'll be sick if you drink too quickly."

When the cup was empty, he carefully laid her back on the bed. Esther suspected that she should care that a stranger had to hold her up and feed her water. She could not remember why. Her eyes drifted shut, though the voices in the room still reached her.

"Make sure she drinks," the stranger was saying. "Several times a day. You can also feed her broth this way, but make sure she gets enough water. If she grows hungry, start with soup. Make sure she eats slowly."

"Thank you, Hed," replied a familiar voice.

Deric. A tension disappeared that Esther had not even noticed. The air whispered around her as sleep embraced her once again.

She woke several times to find herself being fed broth or water. After that first time, however, it was always Deric; and every time, she felt a little more lucid. She didn't dream of Gwen again.

"Can I eat now?" she asked at last.

"Of course," said Deric, a smile spreading across his face. Esther noticed that the smile was pinched at his eyes and around the corner of his mouth. She dismissed the observation, her mind too foggy to do anything else. He lay her back down and disappeared, reappearing shortly with a bowl.

Eating was awkward, to say the least. Esther's hand would not hold steady enough for her to feed herself, so Deric fed her bite by bite. She didn't think about it; perhaps she couldn't. After a while, she felt her eyelids droop and her stomach begin to protest. Too tired to speak, she simply closed her eyes and refused to open her mouth for the next bite. Deric needed no more than that. He helped her lie back down and took the bowl away.

Days and nights blurred together. Sometimes Esther was alone. Sometimes Deric fed her. Sometimes Esther still woke to find Deric's arm wrapped around her waist as he snored softly somewhere beside her. Gradually, color and sound returned—how odd, she hadn't even realized they were missing—and her awareness of the world around her expanded. Slowly, she felt her mind returning to her. She began to listen for the wind again.

One morning, she opened her eyes to the sight of Deric's face in the faint morning light. He was still sleeping, breathing slowly and deeply. Esther realized that they were not touching this morning. His arm lay folded between them, perhaps having pulled away in the night. Esther contemplated this for a moment without thinking anything coherent. At last, she gave in to the compulsion and reached out to take his hand, intending to pull his arm over her.

As she began to draw his arm toward her, his eyelids fluttered and opened.

Their gazes met. Esther froze.

"You're awake," he said.

Esther gave a non-committal grunt. Deric smiled. The walls around her heart gave way just a little.

"Where do you eat?"

"In the tavern downstairs."

"Then I'll eat there today. And I'll feed myself."

"I think that's a wonderful idea," said Deric. His words rang sincere.

*   *   *

Esther began to improve rapidly after that. She began to do more every day in small steps. Deric had procured clothes for Esther to wear, including dark stockings she could wear in order to walk about outside. Though Esther did not feel safe wandering about through a town full of people who ostensibly hated speakers, the stockings made her feel far more at ease. Hed came by from time to time, asking after Esther's condition. It was only after she was certain that he had not seen her legs—"You were under the blankets the whole time! He couldn't have seen anything."—that she consented to speak to him. To her own shock, she warmed to the kind, soft-spoken healer quickly.

But the cot had gone ever since Esther had become more lucid. She knew exactly why. Even if she hadn't registered it at the time, she now knew who those baleful eyes had belonged to.

"I want to talk to Dov," Esther announced to Deric at last. Deric froze, then turned to face her.

"I'm not sure that would be wise."

"Dov needs to learn the Words."

"And you plan to teach him? After . . . after what happened?"

Though she had anticipated resistance, Esther narrowed her eyes at him. "I don't know. If he doesn't anger me too much, I'll teach him to save his life. So send for him. And make yourself scarce until he leaves."

To her surprise, Deric obeyed with no further protest. She pulled out Deric's katar from under the mattress, where he didn't know she knew it was hidden. She pushed it blade first up her left sleeve. Then she sat at the small table in the corner to wait.

Waiting was easy. She neither anticipated nor dreaded Dov's arrival. She merely waited.

When he arrived, Dov did not knock. He opened the door. Their eyes met.

"Welcome," she said.

"Your eyes used to be purple," said the boy.

"Aren't they anymore?" asked Esther.

"They're brown."

"Interesting."

"Are you going to kill me?" asked the child. His voice shook.

"That depends," smiled Esther. "Do you think I should?"

Dov blinked at her. "Deric talked about you."

It was strange, hearing a name she loved from the mouth of someone who had taken another love from her. "Did he now?"

"He said if I talked to you, I'd understand."

"Do you?"

"Not really."

Esther sighed and leaned back. "You still haven't answered my question. Do you think I should kill you?"

Dov hesitated a moment, looking up at her with wide eyes. "No."

"Why not?"

"Killing is wrong?"

"You don't sound too sure. Why is that?"

"Well, Papa said . . . and I—"

Esther slammed her hands down on the table with such a crash that Dov jumped.

"If you have something to say, then say it. Stop beating around the bush."

"I killed . . . I killed Tlafa."

"Yes, you did."

"Papa said it was the right thing to do."

"He was wrong."

Dov shook his head. Esther sighed.

"I don't have to kill you, you know," she said conversationally. "If you don't learn to speak, you'll most probably die. But you'd also most likely take half the town with you. What do you think of that?"

"Papa said Tlafa was lying."

"Tlafa came from a place where Words—witchcraft—was an essential part of life. Your father only knew to fear it. You listen to the rocks and draw strength from it, but then you shun it in return by refusing to speak to respond. How does that make sense?"

"But Papa said—"

"I don't care what he said," Esther interrupted. "Tell me: will you learn to speak or not?"

Dov stared at her, wide-eyed. Esther waited, meeting his gaze unwaveringly.

His eyes flickered away. "I don't—"

"It's a simple question. Will you learn? Yes or no."

Dov choked and tears began to fall from his eyes. Esther watched, expressionless.

"Y . . . yes."

Esther breathed out slowly.

"Good. I don't know if you've ever heard them, so I'm going to tell you the rules. While I am your teacher, never break these rules or I will be extremely angry. And you don't want to find out what I'm like when I'm angry."

The lesson went more smoothly than Esther might have expected. Though the tears running down Dov's face continued to flow for a long while at the start of the lesson, he paid attention and learned quickly. Knowing that he was part-Koelu, she had expected him to take to the Words of rock naturally; even so, the ease with which he learned and retained the language astonished her. Esther watched him closely for any sign that he might change his mind.

Eventually, she realized that Dov was slowing down from exhaustion.

"Go and rest," Esther told him. "Come back tomorrow."

Dov nodded and slipped out quietly.

Esther waited until he was a good distance away before she stood, slipped the katar out of her sleeve and put it back in place.

She was in bed and the light was fading by the time Deric returned. Esther listened to the air whisper about him moving through the room. She surmised that he was inspecting it for signs of an altercation.

"No blood or wreckage?" Esther asked when Deric's weight hit the mattress.

"None whatsoever," Deric replied without missing a beat.

He began to undress and Esther averted her eyes. A moment later, she realized the absurdity of acting as though there was any modesty to preserve between them. Yet it felt strange. So she turned to fully face Deric and stared openly at him.

It took Deric a moment to realize that she was watching. When he did, he stumbled over his trousers and his face flushed. He couldn't hold her gaze, though the way his eyes kept darting to meet hers and then away again suggested that he wanted to. Esther's heart warmed and she reached her arms out to him.

At last, Deric met her gaze and held it. However, he did not move towards her. Esther's heart skipped a beat and she wondered what she would do if he rejected her. A moment later, Deric sat down and slid over to link their hands together.

"Can I ask how things went with Dov?"

Esther huffed. "He was willing to learn. I started teaching him."

"He can lie, you know."

Esther rolled her eyes. "The Words don't make anyone incapable of lying. It's inadvisable, especially for beloveds. But I could lie, if I had a mind to."

"So the test of lies is just as ineffective as the execution in flames."

Esther raised an eyebrow at him. "Maybe for the man from Aine's story. Not for me. Flames would be incredibly effective."

Emotions flickered across Deric's face and he gathered her into his arms. Esther felt a little indignant at the gesture. Nevertheless, it warmed something in her chest, so she allowed it. She twisted around to tilt her head so that their mouths could meet. He responded enthusiastically.

*　*　*

Esther's lessons with Dov became a daily fixture, though he still stayed in a different room, where Deric joined him whenever Esther needed her space.

It took nearly a fortnight for Esther to look Deric in the eye and say what she knew she had to say.

"Thank you so much."

"For what?" asked Deric, seeming honestly confused. Esther couldn't help but smile.

"For everything. Looking after me when I couldn't. Helping me to recover. For being with me this whole time. If not for you, I. . . . Thank you."

"I—" Deric seemed to be at a loss for what to say. Esther rolled her eyes.

"You don't need to respond. I just wanted to thank you."

"My mother died," Deric blurted.

Esther blinked.

"Some time ago, my mother died. I never knew my father, and being bastard-born, I didn't have many friends. I was at a loss for how to go on, when I met two young women who had just lost a sister. We grieved together, the three of us. They told me about their sister and I told them about my mother. We laughed and cried and somehow, we managed to make it through the worst of it. When I think about what might have happened to me without them—"

Something in Esther's chest was constricting. Against all reason, she wildly envied the two women who had been given the chance to share their grief with Deric. She felt suddenly small and childish and wished that she had not slipped so far into helplessness. She compared herself to these faceless, nameless sisters who had struggled through their grief side by side with Deric and felt weak and useless.

She wanted to ask what they were like. She wanted to

ask whether he thought of them while he was with her. She wanted to ask if he was going to go home to them when he left Ynga.

"Do you miss them?" she asked instead.

"From time to time," Deric sighed. Esther felt like she couldn't breathe. She breathed in and out deeply a few times and calmed her mind.

"I'm glad that you had them to support you," she said.

"I'm glad that I could be here to support you," Deric replied.

She thought of his mother. Should she express sympathy for his loss? There was nothing she could say that she would accept if it were said about Tlafa, so she said nothing.

She embraced him instead. He returned the embrace. They stood with their faces buried in each other's necks for a very long time.

*   *   *

As autumn drew on, Esther began to allow herself to relax not only in Deric's presence, but also in Dov's. She let him see her legs and explained her tempestuous relationship with fire. She saw Deric teaching Dov how to fight hand-to-hand in the inn's courtyard through the window one morning, and wondered if they had perhaps become something akin to a family.

Later, she would curse herself for becoming so complacent; for not seeing what was forthcoming. Deric grew more open around Dov. Esther saw only the growing familiarity and affection. Some nights, Deric looked at her as if he desperately wanted to say something. Esther thought that she knew what it was. Esther believed that she knew Deric.

"What is it?" she asked gently one night. "You give me that look sometimes, like you want to say something."

Deric was silent for a long moment.

"I wish there didn't have to be any secrets between us," he said at last.

"Are there?" asked Esther, heart suddenly pounding in her ears.

"We've never talked about our pasts."

"Does it matter?" It came out more snappish than she might have wished.

"Maybe," he sighed. "I know that you're Sterre."

Esther froze. "Sterre."

"Yes. You—you talked about how you had tried to read a book about the history of the Words, and it backfired. I know that story. It ends with a girl named Sterre jumping into the Abyss to escape the king's guard."

Esther's heart started beating again, and then it raced. Sterre felt like lifetimes ago, a chapter out of someone else's tale. Esther tried to remember Manon, Gigi, Regis, Eduard and Pierre and the affection she had once held for them. She could scarcely remember.

"I'm not Sterre," she said honestly.

Deric snorted. "Of course you're not. You told some hogwash of a story about finding the book in Milleport Library."

She couldn't help herself. "Why would that story be hogwash?"

"Because you said you saw the librarian's daughter's beau smuggling it in."

"And?"

"The librarian's daughter doesn't have a beau."

"How would you know?"

Deric looked at her with amusement. "Because his eldest daughter was barely seven years old."

"Ah," said Esther. "I see how that might make that story less credible."

"No one working in the library in Milleport had ever heard of a Sterre."

"They might have been lying."

"*Sterre*," said Deric.

"Don't call me that." Esther's voice was low and dark. "I'm not Sterre."

"See? Secrets."

"Hush, Deric, give me a moment!" Esther snapped. "I need a moment."

He obliged.

Esther's mind whirled.

"So . . . this is common knowledge everywhere, now?"

"No—just in certain circles."

"And what circles might those be?"

There was a long silence. "Among Amberrian and Ceryllan guards."

"I can understand Ceryllan guards, but how would Amberrian guards know?"

"Some time back the Ceryllan king took the youngest Amberrian prince as a ward, and the Ceryllan king's sister married the second Amberrian prince. There's been a close relationship between the kingdoms ever since."

Esther blinked. "King . . . Juste? Adopted Enri? And Marilene married Achille?"

"That is the gist, yes." Deric gave her an odd look.

Esther chewed on her lip and tried not to think about the implications. Another life, she told herself. But unlike Sterre, Estelle didn't feel so far away. It felt like she could trip and fall into being Stelle again.

"Esther," said Deric. "Please."

She closed her eyes. "You aren't my beau, Deric," she muttered through gritted teeth. "What good would it do to tell you? I'm not the person I was before I lived with the rainfolk."

"I see," said Deric after a moment. He sounded defeated. "Just . . . just one question, then. You . . . you spoke knowingly of Seleukos and the potentate once. How did you come to know so much?"

"I talked to a Seleukoi man," said Esther. "Why?"

"That sort of information. . . ." Deric trailed off and licked his lips.

"Oh, I see. You wondered if I was Seleukoi myself?" Esther smiled thinly. "I'm not."

She did not elaborate further and Deric did not ask. Esther believed that she had ample time to begin breaking her story to him.

When she woke the next morning to an empty bed, she didn't think anything of it. She rolled over and went back to sleep, enjoying the full space of the bed. She woke again when the sun was high in the sky.

The room was still completely silent.

"Deric?" she called. There was no answer.

She climbed out of bed, clamping down on the rising concern. No doubt he was out and about in town. She wrapped herself in a blanket, planning to go downstairs to find something warm to eat.

She stopped when she saw the small sack and a letter on the table. Esther's heart went cold. She reached out for the letter anyway, and read it.

Esther crumpled up the letter and threw it across the room where it landed in the chamber pot. Rage burned in her belly. How dare he leave?

"Goodbye, I suppose," she said to the room. *Good riddance*, she nearly said, and held her tongue. The memory of those words drove the anger out of her and left her cold, helpless and alone. She shivered. Then she steeled herself.

Esther changed into a dress and stockings. For the first time, she stepped out of the inn onto the street alone. She spotted Dov helping the innkeeper carry crates. It would have been a comical sight, for the crates were several times Dov's size.

She should never have left things to Deric for so long. It was only a matter of time before people began asking questions—especially in a town as small as Mirage. What had he been thinking?

She knew what they had to do. Until Dov learned to speak, they either had to be in a place so remote that no one would come across them or in a city so big that no one would take note of them.

The latter was far easier, especially with Noucleion only a fortnight's journey away.

She pulled Dov aside that night and told him to quietly pack up anything he wanted to keep.

"We're leaving Mirage?" asked Dov quietly.

"I think it's for the best," Esther said gently.

Dov nodded.

39

The Spy

Forty-fifth day of autumn,
452 A.D. – Mirage, Ynga

Dear Esther,

I'm so sorry that I couldn't tell you this face to face. I have to leave. I still have a duty to my king to fulfill, and I know that you wouldn't come with me, and even if you would, I couldn't guarantee your safety. I know that you and Dov will be all right here. I'm leaving you my horse and all the coins I had left. I hope that it's enough for you to make a life for yourselves.

I will come back to Mirage to find you, if I ever have the chance.

I leave with you my deepest affections.

Deric

40

The Captain of
the King's Guard

Night, eleventh day of spring,
452 A.D. – Castle Dio, Ceryll

THERE WAS NO such thing as a good day that began
with betraying the most dangerous person in the
kingdom to the most powerful, but Hervé hadn't
seen any choice in the matter. He'd seen even less choice
when Nicole came to him when she was supposed to be
in the tower, dressed in a nobleman's attire and pressing
a dagger into his hand with instructions and a warning.

Hervé had killed an innocent man today. But the man
had resisted—tried to push past the guards to get to the
king. Nicole had promised him that the man he framed
with the dagger would be set free, but there was no way to
reassure him in that crowd. If he'd spoken up, the assassins
after good King Juste would have gone free—unacceptable.
But letting a man through after he'd just announced that he
had a dagger—it would have been unthinkable.

He wished he could have believed it was an instinctive kill. But no—there had been a moment of cold clarity that the only way to save the king was to kill this man. And so he had moved, and the man had died.

Worse than the murder was the remainder of the day, stuck at Juste's side wearing a mask of indifference. He was trapped now. He couldn't confide in Juste this time; his own transgression was too horrible. He ought never to have listened to Nicole.

Hervé was still on duty that night when Juste was drinking by the fire in his office and a knock sounded on the door. Juste ordered the visitor to enter. In stepped Nicole, wearing a stately gown for the first time that day. Hervé stiffened, but her eyes slid over him.

"You summoned me, Father?"

"Nicki," said Juste heavily from his seat by the fire. "Come. Have a drink with me."

"Thank you, Father." She took the seat across from him as he poured her a glass of his prized mint liquor. They didn't raise their glasses to one another. They immediately took gulps of the liquor.

"So," said Juste after a long silence. "We are down to two."

"Not for lack of assassination attempts."

"True," chuckled Juste darkly. "Three in one morning. A record, I think. I owe my life to Odilon, Hervé and that boy from the kitchens."

"We are very lucky," Nicole murmured, her eyes fixed on the fire. She was fiddling with a pendant at her throat. "To be surrounded by those so loyal to us."

"About Gwen."

"Father, I—"

"No, let me speak, Nicole. I will not apologize for my reaction. But I also see . . . this is no life, the way we live."

"I would not agree."

"Oh? Would you wish this life on anyone you love?"

Nicole didn't respond. She released the pendant and Hervé saw that it was a sphere made up of intricately woven pieces of gold, silver and black. She seldom wore the pendant, but he knew its significance: its colors were those of her and her sisters.

"The librarian told the guards his apprentice is missing."

"Is that so?"

"Was he the one Gwen was so fond of?"

"I believe so."

Juste sighed and looked away. "Well. I suppose that explains it. I hope that they find happiness."

Nicole's brows rose. A smile tugged at her lips that she quickly smothered. Hervé wondered dully if she had talked her sister into leaving because Gwen was better-loved. How he wished that Gwen had been the heir instead.

"What shall we do about Baraz and Septimo?"

"I defer to your wisdom, Father."

"Perhaps Septimo has been punished enough. Ottavio's death was my error. I should never have put the three of you in the same prison cell."

"It was not your fault, Father."

There was a moment of silence, and Hervé reflected on the tragedy, too. Ottavio's body had been found not long after Nicole's release. The cell doors were open and the few guards remaining at the tower had seen nothing. The other prisoner was gone. He did not know how, but he had no doubt Nicole was somehow responsible for that death as well.

"Regardless of what our investigations turn up," said Juste, "I will send a company of our own to Ynga before the year is out. A gesture of goodwill."

"Very well. Then I shall accompany them."

Juste raised his eyebrows. "To reclaim that guard of yours? Have you changed your mind about that mission of his?"

Nicole shook her head. "No, though I will take his goshawk with me, if you permit. I wish to meet the taipan. I believe that she could aid us in the coming war."

Juste and Nicole's eyes bored into each other.

At last, Juste shook his head. "I would not send you if it were up to me. I would remind you that you are the only heir, and you are invaluable to the council as the shadow. But no walls hold you when you do not wish to be held. So I warn you instead: it will be a long trip. It is far too dangerous to travel through Jehan right now, so you will have to travel through Amberria and take a ship from Mouth Bay."

Nicole raised an eyebrow at him. "With an official procession, it could be a year before I return."

"Exactly."

A silence followed in which Nicole sat back and Juste sipped his drink. Hervé's heart pounded.

"All the same," Nicole said at last, "I must insist. If Jehan is conquered, this is our last chance to forge a strong alliance with Ynga."

"Then you shall go," nodded Juste.

Hervé's heart leapt and he had to fight to keep his expression blank.

"Septimo was talking about a boy wearing Odilon's clothes. Yet Odilon seemed to know nothing of such a person."

"How odd."

"*Nicole.* There is only one person in Dio for whom Odilon would lie to me."

Nicole averted her eyes. "I go where I am needed."

"That you do. And I owe you my life for it. So if you are adamant, then to Ynga you shall go."

They poured fresh glasses and gave a silent toast. Then they each downed their second glass in a single gulp.

Nicole was leaving. It was the best news in the world.

Appendix

A Glossary of Terms

aial — "one who teaches" in the Words of rock.

aiar — "one who teaches" in the Words of soil.

Elayil — People of water living Down Below. Known Up Above as water sprites.

Koelu — People of rock living Down Below. Known Up Above as dweorgs.

liles — a curse word.

lyll — of or relating to pure elemental power.

Nevena — the goddess of perseverance, mercy and vengeance.

nia qiulai — "please be calm, wind" in the Words of wind.

Nou — the goddess of birth and creation.

Nuray — the goddess of death and destruction.

Qyul — People of wind living Down Below. Known Up Above as winged horses.

speaker — a western term referring to one who practices the forbidden magic; *OR* one who speaks one or more language of the elements.

tie-all — a curse word.

Tyal — People of fire living Down Below. Known Up Above as firefoxes.

witch — an eastern term referring to one who practices the forbidden magic.

witchcraft — an eastern term referring to a magic power that has long been forbidden on the continent.

Words — a western term referring to a magic power that has long been forbidden on the continent; *OR* languages of the elements.

yiu — "yes" or "I agree" in most Words, including the Words of wind.

People of Import at Castle Dio

The Royal Family

King Juste V OR Juste Séraphin de Ceryll — current king of Ceryll. Third-born and only son to former King Séraphin and Queen Consort Ghislaine.

Nicole Eunike Sotiria de Ceryll — first-born to King Juste V and Queen Consort Esther. Heir to the throne. Sits on the council as the shadow.

Lady Sovanna — wife to late king Séraphin and stepmother to Juste V.

Toussaint Benoit de Ceryll — second-born to late King Juste IV and Queen Consort Genevieve and brother to late King Séraphin. Uncle to Juste V.

Nicoletta d'Amberria — wife to Toussaint and youngest daughter of late King Angelino d'Amberria and his wife Queen Inas d'Ceryll.

Inas Genevieve de Ceryll — first-born to former King Séraphin and Queen Consort Ghislaine. Sister to Juste V and Marilene. Sent to Usha as Lady Ambassador in 451 A.D.

Maylis — husband to Inas and former corporal in the king's guard. The son of a captain in the king's guard under King Juste IV. Accompanied Inas on ambassadorial mission to Usha as Corporal Ambassador in 451 A.D.

Marilene Leanne de Ceryll — second-born to former King Séraphin and Queen Consort Ghislaine. Sister to Inas and Juste V. Acted as governess to her nieces Gwenaëlle and Estelle until Estelle until 450 A.D. Shortly thereafter, she was sent to Amberria to wed

Achille, the king's second son, to cement an alliance between the two nations.

Estelle Astraea Esther de Ceryll — second-born to King Juste V and Queen Consort Esther. Took ill in 450 A.D. and died in 451 A.D.

Gwenaëlle Xanthe Aysel de Ceryll — third-born to King Juste V and Queen Consort Esther. Darling of the court.

Enri d'Amberria — sixth-born child and fourth son of Amberrian King Sylvain. Adopted by Juste as part of the alliance also cemented by Marilene's marriage to Prince Achille d'Amberria.

The Ceryllan Council

King Juste V — Sovereign. See above.

Nicole de Ceryll — Shadow. See above.

Odilon — Falcon. Childhood friend of Juste. Appointed to the council on the day of Juste's coronation.

Winoc — Master Minister. The oldest of the ministers.

Septimo — Minister of the Treasury.

Kylian — Minister of Cities.

Onésime — Minister of Rivers and Roads.

Lamont — Minister of Law.

Yves — Minister of Crops and Farmlands.

Ansaldo — Minister of Alliances and War.

Cosme — Minister of Royal Affairs. Former steward to Lamont.

Thierry — Minister for the People. Former mayor of Milleport.

Raymon — Minister of Libraries and Learning.

Ambassadors and Foreign Parties

Ambassador Donatien — Amberrian ambassador and married to Martina.

Lady Martina — second-born and oldest surviving child of former King Achille. First cousin once-removed to current King Sylvain.

Lieutenant Ambassador Dara — Ushani ambassador and former right hand to Commander Phirun.

Chan — Dara's Knife and right hand.

Ambassador Baraz — Yngan ambassador and second cousin to King Yasin.

Roshan — Baraz's concubine.

Yasmin — Baraz's concubine.

Parisa — Baraz's concubine.

Ambassador Zephyr — Seleukoi ambassador and second cousin to Potentate Aglaia.

Ambassador Carwyn — Jehani ambassador appointed by People's Lord Flann.

Ambassador Njall — Danti ambassador appointed by the Council of Elders.

Alderic — bastard-born Amberrian guard once in the employ of Prince Enri. Appointed by Juste V to the king's guard after Enri's adoption.

Manuel — Amberrian guard in Prince Enri's employ.

Pedru — Amberrian guard in Prince Enri's employ.

Other

Hervé — a captain of the king's guard. A member of the king's guard under former King Séraphin and a sparring partner of Juste V's when he was a prince.

Ottavio — son to Septimo, Minister of the Treasury.
Vere — royal librarian.
Rainier — apprentice and nephew to royal librarian Vere.
Manon — lady's maid to Nicole.
Gigi — lady's maid to Nicole.
Regis — a young soldier in training.
Eduard — a young soldier in training.
Pierre — a young soldier in training.
Brice — apprentice to the royal chef.

A Note from the Author

Dear Reader,

This is my first novel, and it's been a long time coming.

Stories are my lifelong love. I can't remember the first time I made up a story, I was age 11 when I wrote my first "official" work: a screenplay for my school. It was a fun little sci-fi adventure that we filmed and I later expanded into an unpublished novel.

This particular story began when I was 12 as a series of songs: a simple tale of three sister princesses. The protagonist was a young Nicole, who loved her little sisters but didn't like the pressure of court life. She ran away to have daring adventures and discover romance.

I was about 16 when I realized that there was a dissonance between the personalities of my characters and the actions they took to serve the plot. My entire story was *wrong*.

I scrapped everything and started over, focusing on all of the sisters rather than isolating one in the spotlight. Estelle and Gwenaëlle each got their own stories, of which they were the protagonist; some elements of the original story survive in their stories. Nicole, of course, never ran away: politics are her craft.

After that, everything fell into place. Nevertheless it's taken me the better part of a decade to work out how to tell this story. I don't know how many times I've "completed" the first novel in this series only to scrap it and start over. Now it's ready; I relinquish it into your hands.

Thank you for reading this story (unless you just flipped to the back, in which case welcome!), and I hope to see you back for the next book in the series.

—Kai Raine

P.S. If you'd like to learn more about me or my stories, come visit me at *www.kairaine.com* !

About the Artist (Cover & Maps)

Equipped with a calligraphy pen and a pot of ink, Kelly Tinker can illustrate anything imaginable.

She grew up as a dedicated reader and loved illustrating the vivid descriptions that stood out. Drawing scenes, bookmarks, and covers became second nature for her as she sought to visually interpret the written worlds described.

In her free time, armed with a strong sense of humor, Kelly amuses herself with the creation of her own imaginative creatures and graphic novels.

With a degree in art from the University of Alaska Fairbanks, Kelly is a self-proclaimed jack-of-all-trades dabbling in sculpture, metalsmithing, painting, and graphic design.

You can check out her metals and sculpture portfolio at: https://klowrymetals.carbonmade.com/

Acknowledgements

Thank you to everyone I met at the San Francisco Writers' Conference 2017, who helped me polish my pitch, enlightened me on the world of indie publishing, and generally helped me see how to truly take a step toward making writing my life. Thank you to everyone at Gatekeeper Press for helping to make this book a reality.

Thank you to all my beta readers and editors. To Karin Odegard, for reading two and a half drafts and giving me lots of helpful and encouraging feedback. To Simon Schnyder, for unwavering support, for spending hour after tedious hour going over chapters with me time and again, draft after draft for three years, and for this last year of shoving me kicking and screaming toward publication. To Ryan Courdy, for the frankest, most helpfully cutting criticisms I've ever received. Also to Kristina, Byron, Neha, Isabel, Estelle, Amanda, Libby, Thomas and Frederick.

A huge thank you to my family, who support me and sometimes share in my excitement and stories. Special thank yous go to my aunt on the East Coast, who never for a moment let me doubt her support of my aspirations; to my aunt on the West Coast, whose enthusiasm for my progress gave me the courage to take huge steps forward and invest in my career; to my uncle in NY, who held up the mirror and psychoanalyzed me through my prose; to my uncle in CA, who gave me advice on the business angle of writing and publishing; and to my fairy godmother, who supported me and contemplated the complexity of people with me through difficult times, which inevitably bled into the telling of this story. And to my mother, who taught me her love of books and fantasy, whose thoughts on this story I will forever wish I could hear.

Last and farthest from least, thank you to Kelly Tinker: for inking my maps, for the feedback on my prose, and whose wonderful cover art I'm honored to have for this book.